THE TALE OF
FINDO GASK

A first novel by Huw Thomas, Undiscovered
Authors National Fiction Winner.

THE TALE OF
FINDO GASK

By
Huw Thomas

ISBN13 978-105108-21-3

Printed in the UK by BookForce

BookForce UK's policy is to use papers that are natural, renewable and
recyclable products and made from wood grown in sustainable forests
where ever possible

BookForce UK Ltd.
50 Albemarle Street
London W1S 4BD
www.bookforce.co.uk
www.discoveredauthors.co.uk

DEDICATION

To:
Eileen Betteridge – for encouragement that finally paid off
Cheryl Atkins – for being a loyal reader and critic
Carolyn – for everything

1. Smoke

The man on the ladder was feet from safety when he slipped. He swayed for a moment, already half unconscious. Two workmen reached out to pull him onto the scaffolding and a cry went up from one of the firefighters on the ground below. But the hands grasped only at air and the man tumbled sideways.

Down on the other side of the road, the photographer who had been snapping pictures of the rescue rattled off another half-dozen shots, capturing the moment of tragedy.

The falling body vanished briefly into a billow of smoke. It reappeared a few feet lower, brushing the scaffolding as it fell. Clipping a projecting pole, it span further out into the gap between the two buildings. Seconds later, the body crashed onto the top of a wire fence separating the blocks of flats, bounced once and crumpled limply.

Three firefighters, closely followed by two onlookers and the photographer, dashed forward. The heat from the burning building was intense and showers of embers drifted around them.

They were nearly at the body when one of the firefighters became aware of the civilians. He stopped and held out his arms.

"Get back!"

The other two turned but the photographer hesitated.

The firefighter glared. "You can't do anything here. You want to help, go and tell the paramedics to get a stretcher." He stabbed a gloved finger at the camera. "Just don't get that thing in our way."

The other two firefighters were already by the fallen figure, protecting it from drifting sparks with their own bodies and holding an oxygen mask over the man's face.

Up on the scaffolding, one of the workmen reached out cautiously. The man had fallen from a ladder slung horizontally between the building on fire and a neighbouring five-storey block still undergoing renovation. One end was jammed through a broken window on the top floor of the burning building, the other rested on the scaffolding. There was another man still on the ladder. He was young, little more than a teenager, and lay across the rungs unmoving.

The ambulance was just pulling away when the police arrived. The unmarked car stopped fifty yards off and the two men inside sat looking at the scene for a minute before getting out.

The younger of the policemen was in his mid-thirties and looked tired. He led the way as they skirted the back of one fire engine and headed towards the white-helmeted man directing operations. The detective waved a hand to get the other's attention.

"DS Andrews," he said. "You in charge here?"

The station officer blinked. "CID? Quick off the mark aren't you? I was expecting uniform, not you lot. Hope you don't expect me to tell you how this started." He scowled. "But if you're looking for a crime, find the bastard who rented out those flats with no fire escape."

Andrews shook his head. "I was on my way anyway, nothing to do with the fire. Had a tip-off Findo Gask was here."

The firefighter looked surprised. "The thief?"

"Yeah." The policeman nodded towards the burning building. "That's Lydon House isn't it?"

The station officer snorted. "Was. Won't be much left by the time this is out." He frowned at the policemen. "Findo Gask was supposed to be in there?"

"That's what we were told."

"Who by?"

"Anonymous caller."

The firefighter shrugged. "Aren't they always." He nodded at the building. Clouds of steam were mixing with the smoke as jets of water were directed up over the roof and through the windows at the flames still raging inside. "You're welcome to go and look for him."

The first pictures were already at the paper's newsroom by the time the man in the ambulance reached hospital. Their arrival pushed the newsroom's usual late-morning hubbub to critical level.

"We can't pull the front page now." The chief-sub looked furious. "The presses are already lined up."

"Well, fuck 'em. They'll just have to wait." The news editor shook his head. "This is a cracking story and we've got it first. No one else will have pictures to touch us. I want this splashed big across the front and on two and three."

The chief-sub looked resigned. "What're we going to pull?"

The news editor shrugged. "I don't give a shit. Spike what you like. Just make the space; this is a real story." He spun on his heel. "Rosie! How those words coming? You finished yet?"

The police headquarters at Alexander Cross was three miles from the fire but Ross Kirkbride could see the thick plume of rising smoke. The fire had been burning for some hours now and the chief superintendent stared at the smoke for a moment before turning back to his young DI.

"So, any news?"

Charlotte Brown laughed. "Progress? Of sorts; yes. Anything useful? No." She shook her head. "We did finally manage to persuade the Frenchwoman to give us a description. Talk about vague. She's the one witness that's actually seen Gask face-to-face and she's about as useful as a fish on a bicycle."

Kirkbride pulled a face. "That good?"

Brown shook her head. "Worse. And she kept changing her mind. I wouldn't waste time on her description. I don't know what her problem is – whether she just doesn't like the police, thinks she's too high and mighty or if it's just a French thing – but interviewing her was a waste of time."

Kirkbride nodded. "So, no closer to a reliable description?"

The DI shrugged. "Nope. But I've got one possible lead."

"What's that?"

"We've traced the angle grinder used when Colin Speed was sprung from East Allonby nick. They never took off the serial number. We've managed to go through the manufacturers in Germany and track down where it was sold. The shop was in the city and they've only sold two of this model in the last six months. A local builder bought one and still has his. The other was a cash sale three days before the prison break."

"And?"

"The shop always asks for customers' addresses for its invoices. It's probably false, but the address given was in Corporation Road – just around the corner from where that car was found."

Kirkbride smiled. "Good. Well done." He glanced out of the window again. "What's the story with the fire? I heard there had been a possible sighting."

The DI shrugged. "Bit odd really. We had a tip-off. Usual thing: anonymous caller claiming to have seen Findo Gask. Control passed it to me. I sent Andrews to have a look. Ten minutes later we got a report of a fire at the same address."

Kirkbride pulled a face. "I hope our Mr Gask hasn't decided to start up a new line in arson." He scratched his nose. "What do you think?"

"I'm not sure," said the DI. "The caller was male, sounded young. Wouldn't give details. Just said Findo Gask was in flat three. No suggestion anything was going to happen. No threats."

Kirkbride pulled a face. "Bit of a coincidence though. Anyone at the scene fit the bill?"

"Well, sounds like there were at least four people inside when the place went up: two women, a child and a young man. We're still checking on the man but apparently he's not from round these parts, so he doesn't sound likely."

Kirkbride nodded. "Could be our caller."

"Yeah."

"So, was it arson?"

"Don't know. Place had just been done up – lot of new wood and paint. Looks like the fire started on the ground floor but that's about all the fire officers at the scene will commit themselves to so far. Quite a twist though."

"What's that?"

"Some passer-by managed to rescue everyone before the fire brigade got there. Used a ladder to get across from some scaffolding on the neighbouring building, climbed in through a top-floor window and got them out."

Kirkbride raised his eyebrows. "Brave."

"Yeah, but the poor sod slipped at the last minute and fell off the ladder. Five floors."

"Ouch."

"Yeah. They got him up to the hospital. Should pull through but sounds like he was pretty smacked up."

Kirkbride frowned. "Any ID on him?"

Brown grinned. "You cynical bugger."

The chief superintendent smiled. "Years of experience. Besides – even if he did slip – it still sounds a remarkable feat of agility for someone who just happened to be passing."

The DI nodded. "Well, I'm not sure anyone's got a name yet but if you want to know what he looks like, check out today's daily rag."

"Why's that?"

"A snapper got there same time as the first fire crew, got pictures of the whole thing. Apparently this guy's face is front page news."

2. Uncertain beginnings

Findo Gask was a thief. Born in a ditch, raised in slums and educated by the underworld, his life was forged by mischance. An unwanted brat from a pointless alliance, he was the youngest of seven children by various fathers. He entered the world as a runt: small and scrawny but slippy with it. Given the circumstances, his likely prospects were poverty or petty lawlessness – obscurity either way.

But Findo Gask surpassed expectations, choosing neither expected path. Rather than obscurity, he found notoriety. Not from any conscious choice, just a logical reaction to the world around him. From childhood onwards – unfettered by instruction – he made his own choices and fixed his own rules. Only the reach of his imagination defined his limits and Findo Gask was never a dull boy.

And so by the time he reached adulthood Findo Gask was famous – even if the stories about him were increasingly clouded by rumour and myth. It is true he was a thief. But he was no common felon and his talent was of no normal order. He was a larcenist of the highest calibre – an artist. He was a stealer, purloiner, cat burglar and, perhaps, robber too – but never a mugger, thug, or bag-snatcher. His attitude to property was simple: if he could take something, it was his. His law of person was equally clear: he never knowingly did harm to another unless they harmed him first.

Whether Findo Gask was a criminal is a matter of debate. He broke laws, but only those protecting a system to which he had no allegiance. He had his own moral code – and mostly kept to it. But it was his code. Findo Gask was never asked to be part of society and considered that he owed no debts where he had taken no benefits. In his lifetime, Findo Gask became a legend. And like all legends, his life spawned more lies than an ocean of lawyers.

The tale of Findo Gask began on a tenth-hand mattress on the floor of a squalid room in a derelict housing project. There, beneath a window overlooking a car park littered with broken glass and two burnt-out cars, his mother-to-be grappled loosely with a man who had paid her a drunken compliment half an hour earlier. Minutes later, genes mingled.

Findo Gask's mother was known as Bosnia, an epithet that suited her history. Once, rival factions had fought over and for her. She had been a prize, claimed by the chiefs of the toughest crews. And later – too raddled and ravaged to appeal to more picky suitors – she had played regular host to contingents of the British army.

By the time Findo was conceived, Bosnia's name had changed so often it was uncertain whether even she could remember what it had been originally. In earlier careers – as part-time model, dole-cheat and street girl – she had used all kind of monikers. Eventually, however, she became known to all as Bosnia and accepted the name, wearing it as a badge of warped pride.

Just over eight months after the sweaty tangle that produced Findo, Bosnia was on her way home after a hard night out in a nearby town. It was while part way through performing another function – the driver of the car having stopped in a lay-by so that she could pay for her lift – that Bosnia went into labour. The driver, a married man, shoved her out of the car. Bawling obscenities at being abandoned, she staggered onto the verge. The car pulled away, leaving Bosnia by the roadside. Peristaltic waves overcoming her, she stumbled off her high heels and into a wide and damp ditch. There, after just over half an hour, her seventh child came slithering reluctantly into daylight.

A while later, breath back and clothing more or less rearranged, Bosnia picked the baby up and pulled herself out of the ditch. She had cut the umbilical cord with the knife she always carried and tied it herself. Having produced only one child in hospital, Bosnia was used to dealing with her own births.

On the walk back to town, still befuddled from the combination of the previous night's entertainment and having just given birth, it occurred to Bosnia she should give her new child a name, even though she had yet to check its sex. A little further on, she passed a side road with a signpost indicating some obscure hamlet. Bosnia mulled the name over. For some reason the words appealed.

And so, Findo Gask was given his name. (Bosnia unable to pass on her own surname because she had forgotten it.)

A few hours later, the tiny child was deposited on another grimy mattress. His mother left, in need of a drink or something stronger.

With Bosnia gone, the boy's eldest sibling picked him up. A bloated girl of almost eleven, she wiped him roughly clean and wrapped him in newspaper. Placing him in a couple of carrier bags, she carried Findo to a flat three floors below. There, a tall man in a long coat handed over four grubby ten-pound notes and dumped the baby into a travel cot, stolen a few days earlier.

The man, who had pockmarks all over his face and track marks up and down his limbs, took Findo across town by bus. At the door of a woman living in another, slightly cleaner block of flats, he was exchanged again – this time for five crisp, new twenty-pound notes. Findo's new owner carried the cot inside, placed it on a table, gingerly pulled back the newspapers and peeked inside.

"Jeez, but you're ugly," she said.

The start was inauspicious but the next few weeks of Findo Gask's life were the most comfortable of his childhood. He was washed, dressed in clean clothes and changed and fed at regular intervals. He slept in the warm and dry, lying on sheets in a proper bed – an experience he did not have again for seven years. And when she was not busy with clients, his surrogate mother would pick him up and sit with him, cuddling and rocking him as she talked about her day.

A few days after being sold, Findo Gask took part in his first criminal activity. It began at the local housing office, where his 'mother' laid out her tale of woe: living with four children, crammed into a one bedroom flat at the top of a high-rise.

A hard-faced officer who heard similar pleas every day was told of the impossible strain faced by the close-knit family, how the new baby did not sleep and kept the older children awake, leading to them falling asleep at school and getting into trouble. The woman explained how difficult it was to get three children and a pram to a fifteenth floor flat with no lift, carrying bags up stinking flights of stairs, past junkies and winos. The children had to sleep in the one bed, while she – who should be getting her strength back after a difficult pregnancy – slept on the couch.

There was no father to turn to. He had gone to Aberdeen to look for work but been killed in a road accident eight months ago. The couple had been together since school and, although never married, had been in a close and loving relationship. Now, here she was, effectively a widow, with a young family to look after and no one to help her.

Findo's 'mother' laid it on well. She was passive but firm. She appealed to reason rather than haranguing the officer. She shed a few tears at the right moment and then dried up before anyone got embarrassed.

Next came a quick visit to the benefits office to claim welfare for the baby. A second visit to the housing office followed a week later, this time with three older children, borrowed for the part and taken out of school to prove the point. Findo's new 'brother' and 'sisters' looked tired and sad, yawning occasionally and sitting sullen and taciturn. This time, Findo's 'mother' turned up the histrionics, sobbing as she said she would have to consider having the new baby – or even all the children – taken into care. Then she broke down, weeping openly as she said it would be kinder to break up the family than live this way.

She capped the performance by drawing her family into a tight embrace, telling the officers she did not blame them personally – she knew they were only doing their jobs in difficult circumstances . . . but was there no chance of a place in the new housing scheme at Meadowfields?

Ten days later, a brown envelope arrived in the post and Findo's short life of luxury was over. He was picked up, hugged and squeezed, and the man with the pockmarked face summoned back.

"What's up?"

"It worked! They swallowed it. They've offered me a three-bed semi over Meadowfields."

"Lovely."

"So I don't need him any more."

"What?"

Findo's temporary mother sighed. "The baby. I don't need him any more. I've got the place; I don't want the baby now, do I? I've got a business to run. He's cute but too much work. Besides, he costs money."

"Get benefits don't you?"

"Yeah, but that's all sorted now. I don't need a baby to pick up the cheque."

"But what's it to do with me?"

"You can take him back. I don't know where you got him but I don't need him no more."

The tall man gave a leering smile. "It's not that easy."

"Why?"

"Well, you paid me to get him. I had to hand over money. They might not want him back."

"Get rid of him somewhere else then."

The tall man held up his hands. "Oh no. I don't do that sort of thing. 'Specially kids. It's not like drowning puppies. I can't just chuck him in the canal. Get caught doing something like that and it's no laughing matter."

The woman looked slightly embarrassed. She gave Findo a guilty glance. "I didn't mean like that. Couldn't you leave him at a hospital or something?"

"No."

"Why not?"

"Might get spotted. Besides, he's not my problem. You want to take him to a hospital, you do it."

The woman stared at the tall man then reached into her handbag. "Look, here's thirty. Take him away. Up to you what you do – take him to a hospital, give him back to his mother or leave him on a bus. I don't care, you can make sure he doesn't come to no harm."

"Not for thirty."

"Forty then."

"A hundred."

"No way. Fifty, final offer."

"Eighty."

"Fifty. In your hand, now."

"Alright."

An hour later, the tall man picked his way past the debris in the corridor and stuck his head around Bosnia's door. She was out but two of her brood were squabbling in the corner over a box of matches. The children looked up with slack eyes and no real interest.

The tall man strode in and deposited his burden on the soiled mattress in the middle of the room.

"Tell your mam the boy's back. He's not needed any more. She can keep the cot. No charge."

3. The fiercest guardian angel

Findo Gask's earliest years were given to staying alive: eating, sleeping, staying low and following his mother. Bosnia moved regularly. Her brood tagged along, mustered by their mother if she remembered. Other times, the children had to track her down. Fortunately Bosnia did not stray far. Squalid room followed squalid room – mostly in filthy squats – whenever she shifted territory.

By now, Bosnia had given up defrauding the benefits system. She had got progressively worse at maintaining identities and keeping papers showing her entitlements. Forgotten aliases gathered dust in the files of various agencies but as Bosnia she did not officially exist. Now, she made her money from selling herself to the desperate and unfussy, or through petty scams. She existed on sufferance, borrowing here and cadging there, living in part on what she had been and the few ties that lingered in remembrance of that past.

Once, Bosnia had been the hottest item in town – pert, sharp and sleek with a body made for giving. She had commanded the affections of the city's biggest men; the cocks of every walk were toys in her hands. Back then Bosnia had been able to choose, inevitably picking whoever could offer the most: cars, flats, money, clothes, drink, jewellery and drugs. But none of them gave her the attention she craved. And shut away in luxury while the man of the moment ran his fiefdom, Bosnia found ways to wile away the hours of boredom.

Soon, a little recreational entertainment turned to regular need. At times, Bosnia got her act back under control. But the crashes always followed and, with inevitable rhythm, got more frequent. By the time she had her second child, Bosnia was known as a regular crackhead. Her status began slipping. Her dignity and looks followed – although she never lost all trace of her former glory, the outline of the face and body that made her notorious there to the last.

In the months before Findo made his uninvited entrance into the world, Bosnia had been going through a relatively clean phase. But thanks to a dealer who remembered lusting over her during his teenage days in a local crew, it did not last. Offered a regular supply of good quality smack, Bosnia was happy to trade.

As a result, she did not notice when her eldest daughter sold Findo and was only mildly confused when he reappeared. The two younger children forgot about the tall man and never mentioned him.

Bosnia remembered having given birth but assumed a neighbour had taken the child. She vaguely wondered why but soon forgot as her baby son blended into the background.

Findo's chameleon-like gift for disappearing helped him through his first years, as well as proving an invaluable asset in his later career. More important to his survival, however, was Billy, his half-sister.

Billy was Bosnia's second eldest and – although they never knew it – her father was a cousin of Findo's sire. Billy was eight when Findo was born. She was small for her age and skinny but quick-witted and fast-moving, qualities shared with her youngest sibling.

Billy had seen their eldest sister, Natalie, sell Findo to the tall junkie but had not realised what was going on until the baby was gone. When Findo reappeared in the squat where the family were staying, Billy came home before Natalie and spotted the baby in the stolen travel cot. Putting two and two together, the girl guessed roughly what had happened, although not the reason.

Picking up Findo's cot, she carried it to the empty airing cupboard. Billy slid the cot onto the floor and swung onto the slatted shelf above. The cupboard was Billy's territory. It no longer had a door but a ripped sheet provided a curtain and with Billy that was enough. No one entered uninvited. She had made the space hers – and had now claimed Findo too.

Billy was always territorial. She could be generous but within limits, and Billy's boundaries were sacrosanct. Although small, she could generate ferocity at a speed that left few unintimidated. Her verbal venom alone was savage but Billy did not regard words as part of her armoury. If her tongue-spat warnings failed to register, she rarely bothered to repeat herself, moving straight to all-out aggression.

With Billy confrontations involved no half-measures. When she fought, every bit of her anatomy was a weapon – and any part of an opponent that could be kicked, punched, bitten, scratched, gouged, butted, elbowed, kneed, stamped on, twisted, crushed or otherwise harmed was a legitimate target.

Contrary to most impressions, Findo's sister did know when to back down. She just did not need to very often. Billy knew how to evaluate a situation, weigh up weaknesses, strengths and opportunities before most potential opponents even realised that she was a threat. She also knew that if she moved fast enough, screamed like a banshee and inflicted pain swiftly, savagely and with no holding back, few opponents stopped to consider that she was still less than four feet tall and weighed under sixty pounds. Billy's approach to conflict had a purity that was practically Zen-like and those who knew her rarely provoked her rage.

Which was why Natalie came no further than halfway across the room when she saw Billy sitting cross-legged in her cupboard with Findo beneath her.

"What's he doing here?"

Billy stared silently at her elder sister. She tolerated Natalie at best, well aware of her sister's greed, laziness and mean stupidity.

"Where'd he come from?"

Billy continued to stare.

Natalie shuffled her feet. "Billy," she whined. "What's he doing here?"

"Remember him then?"

"What? What you mean?"

"You remember who he is?"

Natalie blinked and a range of expressions passed across her face, none of them trustworthy. "What d'you mean, Billy? How am I supposed to remember some baby? I just wondered where he'd come from and what you're doing with him."

"Really?"

"Yeah. Look, I don't know where you got him."

Billy shrugged. "Yeah?" she said. "So how come you know it's a him?"

Natalie's mouth opened and shut a couple of times.

Billy pointed slowly at her sister. "You know who he is. You sold him to that Nick Seed."

"I didn't!" Natalie's denial was automatic rather than reasoned.

Billy shook her head. "He gave you forty quid. I wouldn't have thought you'd have forgotten."

"No."

"Don't lie to me, Natalie. You're too stupid to be good at it. You knew whose baby it was soon as you came in. You recognised the cot. It's your brother, the one you sold. Tell Her about it, did you?"

Natalie looked around anxiously.

"Give Her the forty quid, did you?" Billy continued. "Shall I ask?"

"No! I mean yes," blurted Natalie.

"Which one?"

"Don't say nothing to Her. Not about the money."

"Why?"

Natalie hesitated nervously then smiled blandly as an idea came to her. "Because she won't remember I give it her. She was out of it. She won't remember. If you tell her, she'll think I kept it. She won't believe me."

"So why don't I believe you?"

Natalie was stumped. "I dunno, Billy. Why you asking all these questions?" She smiled and made to step forward. "Let's have a look at him."

Billy moved lithe as a snake. She stood up on her shelf and rested her hands lightly on her hips.

"No."

Natalie stood uncertain. "Go on."

"No," repeated Billy. "He's mine. You ever touch him and I'll glass your fat face. Then I'll tell Her you sold him and kept the forty quid. I don't want you near him. And you can tell the others. He's mine and you keep away."

Natalie looked surprised. She was used to Billy and knew her sister well enough to realise the threat was no idle boast; she just could not imagine why her sister would want the baby.

"What you going to do with him?"

"Look after him," said Billy. "I know how you're supposed to look after babies. I'll make sure he's alright. This one's going to be mine, not hers." She smiled. "You can do one thing, though."

"What?"

"I want twenty quid of that money."

Natalie looked horrified. "I haven't got it no more!"

She frowned as it slowly dawned on her that she had proved her own lies.

Billy shrugged. "That's your problem. I still want it. I need it to get him some stuff. You can give me ten today. I'll take the other ten tomorrow."

"How am I supposed to get the money?"

Billy smiled and jumped down into the room, sending Natalie back towards the door. "That's your problem. But if you like your face where it is, just get it."

Findo's protector strolled calmly past Natalie. She slipped her head around the corner of the flat's main room. Bosnia was propped in the flat's one armchair, lighting a cigarette. Billy waited until her mother had seen her.

"Hi, Billy-babe."

"What's the baby called?"

"What?"

"The baby. The one you had a few weeks ago, what's he called?"

Bosnia looked blank for a while. "My baby?"

"Yeah, you came back with him, gave him to Natalie to look after."

Bosnia took a long drag on her cigarette, contemplating.

Billy saw her mother's eyes start to glaze over and realised she would have to be quick.

"His name. What's his name?"

Bosnia gave a little start. "Uh, his name. It was . . . Fin . . ."

She gestured vaguely, trying to pick an answer from the wreaths of smoke now surrounding her. "Findo. That's it. Findo Gask. That's his name."

"Findo Gask?"

"Yeah, that was it."

"Why?"

Bosnia looked uncertain. "I don't know."

Billy sighed and turned away. She walked back to her airing cupboard, passing Natalie without acknowledging her. Billy slipped back up onto her shelf and lay on her belly, peering down through the slats at Findo, who was fast asleep.

"Findo Gask, that's who you are," said Billy. "I'm Billy. I'm your big sister and I'm going to look after you."

And so, Findo Gask gained the protection of the very fiercest guardian angel. In the coming years, life was never as comfortable as during his first few weeks but Billy was rigorous in her attentions. Findo was fed, changed, clothed and – above all – sheltered. Whenever Bosnia did a flit, it was Billy who brought Findo. And each time the family moved into their next den, Billy made sure there was space for her brother when she secured her territory. She provided for him, helped him to walk and fiercely coaxed him to talk. She kept danger from him and, as he grew, taught him what she knew about surviving.

4. Natural born

Over the following years Findo Gask did not distinguish himself. Coached by Billy, he kept a low profile: staying quiet and out of the way. He learnt to appear when there was food but to not draw attention by competing too boldly. He discovered how to forage when the cupboard was bare, identifying potential donors of food aid wherever the family were living. He learnt to move quietly and make himself unseen. He found out the sort of people to which it was safe to speak and be seen by, and who to avoid at all costs. He also discovered how to identify his mother's moods, work out when she was no longer on the same planet and when it was best to sleep elsewhere.

Although they all lived together, Findo had little to do with his mother, older brothers or Natalie. Bosnia rarely interfered in his upbringing. Billy was the one he turned to if there was anything he needed. It was Billy who begged, borrowed or stole clothing for him. It was Billy who helped locate safe refuges and nursed Findo when he was ill. And when danger threatened it was Billy who stood in front – taking blows that could have been Findo's.

For the first six years, Findo's most notable trait was his ability to vanish. When trouble was brewing – family violence or external threat – Findo would just disappear. He would often be gone before the others even realised that something was about to happen. Whether it was sliding out the door, slipping into undergrowth, slithering under furniture or just merging with the background, Findo had a rare talent for not being there.

It was not until he was nearly seven that Findo Gask's talents first drew attention. It was a Thursday afternoon in November. The family was living in an old fairground caravan beneath a motorway flyover. The other children were out roaming, busy with their own affairs. Findo was sitting by the caravan steps, flicking pebbles at a broken bottle.

Then he heard rustling coming from inside as Bosnia woke from a long sleep and began fumbling around. Findo listened; ready to slip away if his mother sounded like she was going to emerge in one of her black moods. But it went quiet again and he returned to his game. A couple of minutes later, a window opened and Bosnia's mascara-streaked, bleary face emerged. She saw Findo and smiled.

"Fin-babe. Go get us some fags, love."

Findo looked round. He nodded without saying anything, stood up and set off. His mother did not think to offer the boy any money and it did not occur to him to ask.

The child's route followed the track away from the flyover. It ran alongside a small river, flowing black and sluggish between steep banks. Dead teasels and brambles choked the verges and a row of straggling hawthorns bent under the grey sky.

After a quarter of a mile, the track turned into the back of a small industrial estate. Findo trudged across oil-stained tarmac and the glitter of smashed windscreen glass, left behind from the estate's nocturnal role as racetrack and trashing-park. He walked past locked up starter units for small businesses that had never started. He skirted twelve-foot high steel fencing adorned with curved spikes and razor wire that protected a builders' yard. A burnt-out pub followed a derelict office building and then he was onto the main road leading towards a livelier part of town.

Findo walked past a few huddled bungalows and then came to the shops – a bookie's and a small takeaway. Next was a petrol station, with grilles on the kiosk windows and spikes that could lift out of the forecourt at the press of a button, bursting the tyres of cars being driven off without paying for fuel. It was rumoured the cashiers also had a loaded shotgun mounted behind a panel in the wall hatch. Beyond was a row of terraced houses with offices on the ground floor: a taxi firm, loan agency, heating firm and hairdressers, as well as several empty properties. The family had lived there for a while, squatting in a flat above an employment agency that had gone bust and done an overnight flit.

Findo continued. He passed a small convenience store and an off-licence, crossed a service road and followed an alley into Jubilee Square. The square was a concrete plaza surrounded by two levels of shops. The boy plodded wearily to the dry fountain in the middle. The doughnut-shaped trough was full of fag ends and other litter including a couple of broken, bloodstained needles. He sat down, ignoring the rank urine smell from the chipped and broken tiles.

Findo looked around, eyeing up the opportunities.

As Findo rested, he was spotted by a group of older children sitting on a fire escape in one the plaza's corners. Three boys, wearing hooded tops and baggy jeans, got up and made their way down to the square. They made their approach quietly, strolling casually across the grey paving. One boy slipped a butterfly knife from his sleeve. Two came at

Findo from the sides, the leader head on.

They stood around him in a pincer movement and stared down. None was older than eleven.

"Who're you?" said the boy in the middle.

Findo looked up. He saw their clothes and the knife in the hand of the boy on his left. "Findo Gask."

"Findo Gask?"

The boys laughed.

"What sort of name's that?" The leader grinned. Then his smile slipped away. "What you doing here, Findo Gask? Where you from?"

"I've come to get some cigarettes for my mum."

"Cigarettes? Good. Give you some money did she?"

"No," said Findo.

"No money? How you going to get some ciggies then?"

Findo shrugged. "Dunno. Find somewhere to take them."

The boy with the knife laughed.

The leader frowned. "I don't believe you. I reckon your mum gave you some dosh. A few quid for her ciggies."

Findo shook his head. "No."

"I don't believe you, Findo Gask."

"It's true. She never gave me any money."

"Didn't you ask her for some?"

"No."

"Why?"

"She probably hasn't got any."

Findo stared calmly back at the older boy. He was remembering what Billy had taught him. The boy was close enough for a kick in the groin. The boy with the knife looked alert but the third one, the youngest-looking, appeared more nervous. Findo was fairly certain that if he stopped the main boy in his tracks and went straight for the smaller one on his right, he would be able to make a break for it before the gang knew what was happening.

The leader put his hands together and flexed them. "Well, if you got no money, prove it. And if you haven't we'll have to tax you some other way." He flicked a hand at Findo. "Empty your pockets."

"No."

"What?"

The boy glanced at the one with the knife and began to reach out. Findo drew his leg back and prepared to swing.

"Hold it, Mickey."

It was the knife boy who spoke. The gang leader's hand stopped in mid-air and Findo halted the kick just inches from his groin. The boy who had spoken looked at the poised foot and grinned.

"I just remembered who he is."

"What do you mean? Who?"

"He's Billy's brother."

"Billy?"

"Yeah, Billy MacBeth. That's her kid brother."

Mickey drew his hand back slightly. He looked at Findo calculatingly. "That right?"

"Yes," said Findo, slowly lowering his leg.

"Why didn't you say?"

Findo shrugged. Mickey took a step back. He reached inside his top and fished out a crumpled cigarette packet.

"Here, have one. You don't have to pay no tax. Tell Billy I give you a fag."

Findo shook his head. "It's alright. You haven't got many. I'll get some more."

Mickey grinned. "You're a cool customer, nipper."

He gave Findo a nod then turned and strolled back across the square. His two henchmen followed, the boy with the knife flipping an ironic salute at Findo as he touched a finger to his forehead.

Findo watched them and then turned his thoughts back to business.

He stayed by the fountain for twenty minutes, watching people coming and going. He looked at the shops and at the ways out of the precinct. After a while, he got up and walked towards a small kiosk in one corner. The shop was a long, narrow cavern, with a counter immediately inside the door. The shopkeeper, a Turk with fierce eyes, sat hawk-like behind the till.

The Turk's position meant anyone coming inside had to go past him to get to the shop's goods – and to get out again. There was also a closed-circuit television camera at the rear of the shop, above the chill cabinet with the packets of five meat pies for one pound. There was a small television monitor above the counter and the Turk's eyes were constantly on the move, flicking from the monitor to the shelves at his end of the shop's twin aisles and to anyone coming near his shop.

Findo did not approach the shop directly. He aimed for the exit from the precinct, passing the shop from about ten yards, walking slowly and not looking in the Turk's direction.

But as soon as he was out of sight, Findo doubled back. He waited until a customer left the shop and then slipped along the wall, around a litter bin and through the door. He ducked quietly past the counter and into the shop's left-hand aisle, picking up a handful of Mars bars on the way. As he passed the Turk, Findo's head was a foot below the level of the counter and the shopkeeper – busy watching people outside – never saw him.

Findo moved calmly towards the back of the shop. It was packed with cheap goods. There was little floor space in the aisles and the central shelves rose almost to ceiling level. No one else was inside and the Turk, not having seen Findo, was watching the square outside.

Findo stopped at the back of the shop. He stuffed chocolate into the pockets of his jacket and looked around quickly. Then he reached up and pulled a packet of toilet rolls down from the shelf. He ripped the packet open and tugged out several handfuls of paper. Stuffing the thin tissue into a gap on a lower shelf, next to some boxes of sanitary towels, Findo reached into his pocket. He pulled out his matches, lit one and touched it to the paper. It caught quickly and the flames began to lick up. As they did so, Findo pulled out more toilet roll and added it to the flames, leading them towards the packets on the shelf above. The thin tissue burnt fast but the fire started to scorch the other goods on the shelves and a thin column of smoke was soon climbing up above the aisle.

Findo punched open the cardboard top of a box of Kleenex tissues and guided the flames towards the fresh fuel. Crackles began to be heard and the smoke thickened.

"Aiiii!"

The wail from the front of the shop was anguished.

Findo crouched at the end of the shop just long enough to be certain which aisle the Turk was coming down before running out the other way. Separated just by a few cartons of dried peas, tins of dog food and cereal packets, the two passed each other in the middle of the shop. Findo could hear the shopkeeper's heavy feet stamping past but the Turk was still ignorant of the boy's presence.

"What's this?"

There was a shout of disbelief from the back of the shop as the shopkeeper began flapping wildly at burning paper and pulling scorched cartons away from undamaged goods.

Findo dived straight behind the counter. He pulled himself onto the Turk's high stool, using the shelves behind the counter as a ladder. When he was up, he reached into the cabinet behind, ignoring the single packets and grabbed at the full cartons, stuffing three into his jacket.

"Hey!" The Turk's voice bellowed down the shop as the irate shopkeeper began to sprint back. "Thief!"

Findo did not stop to look. He stepped from the Turk's stool onto the counter, jumped out through the door and began running. He ignored the nearest exit from the square, which led to a service road lined with high walls and no easy place to hide, and sprinted for the corner to his left.

The boy was halfway across the square when the Turk reached the shop door and gave chase. There was a wild cheer from the gang on the fire escape but Findo never looked back. He charged straight down the short underpass and up into a car park. Clutching his booty to his chest, he weaved around the first couple of rows of cars then stopped between a rusting Sierra and an old Transit van.

Findo was ready to flee again but the Turk never appeared. The shopkeeper had stopped after ten yards, torn between desire to catch the thief and the more pragmatic need to guard his remaining stock. The shopkeeper would have loved to catch the boy and dish out some retribution but knew that if he followed Findo out of the square he would be lucky to have anything left in his shop by the time he got back. He also wanted to be certain that all the scraps of burning paper were extinguished. Fuming, the Turk stamped back to his shop, bolting the door behind him while he went to check the damage.

Findo stayed in the car park for nearly thirty minutes. After his initial escape, he moved warily through the vehicles. On the car park's far side, he rolled underneath an old pick-up truck. He stayed there watching, listening and eating Mars bars until the afternoon light began to fade and he was confident of escaping.

Emerging from beneath the pick-up, the boy flitted across the road and trotted swiftly home, unaware of the significance of the moment. For by successfully raiding the Turk's shop, Findo Gask's life had reached a milestone. Against unlikely odds he had got away with his first real theft. He was not quite seven but had outwitted a shopkeeper with over twenty years' bitter experience.

Findo had also been called a thief for the first time. It was an epithet that would come his way many times but for now he was still a novice – even if he had sailed through his first test in the art, scoring bonus points for audacity and imagination.

To Findo, however, the significance was lost. For him, taking from the Turk held little distinction from other forms of foraging. He would as happily have found the cigarettes in a skip or picked them from a tree. Other than the risk of violence, he was unaware of any difference; private property was not something Findo understood. In his world it was simple: you just had what you had – until someone else took it.

It was not that Findo was growing up in a complete moral vacuum, just that the subculture in which Bosnia and her children dwelt had fewer rules than the wider community. And most were of a fairly Biblical nature – like 'an eye for an eye' – with transgressors punished much more harshly and permanently than in the outside world.

Findo's early upbringing had been basic. Most of his education had been of the Darwinian school. Aided by Billy, he had learnt the rudiments of survival – appreciating his place in the pecking order. Beyond that there had been few niceties and no outside interference. To the system, Findo did not exist. His birth had not been registered and no social workers, health visitors or other guardians of the public good had ever troubled him. Theoretically, Findo was old enough to be at school but sending him had never crossed his mother's mind. And since the family lived in the kind of areas the police only entered in dire emergencies, there was little chance of Findo running into anyone from the education authorities.

Through Bosnia's mode of existence, Findo had picked up the idea of bartering but he had never been taught about money. He had seen his mother and older siblings with the stuff but had little idea of its purpose and had never been taken to a shop to buy anything in his life. Material goods were also few in Findo's world. Those that did exist tended to be consumables: food, drink and, for Bosnia, any narcotics or other recreational substances going. Luxury goods like furniture or electrical items tended to be as transient as Bosnia's male friends.

To Findo's mind, in stealing from the Turk all he had done was complete an errand. He had been told to fetch cigarettes and had done so. He had been given no instruction so had used his initiative. He had not consciously broken any laws of property because no one had told him they existed, let alone how they worked.

It was almost dark when Findo got home. There were candles alight inside the caravan and the sound of voices. Natalie was arguing with Rob, one of their three half-brothers.

Findo went up the steps and stuck his head around the door.

Natalie was wedged into one corner of the sofa, trying to stuff her face with crisps, while kicking Rob, who was trying to steal them. Otis, the youngest of Findo's brothers, was watching – ready to dart in and grab any that got spilt. There was no sign of Bosnia.

"Hey," said Findo.

All three looked toward the door.

"Findo," said Natalie. "Where you been?"

"Where is she?"

Natalie frowned. "What do you want Her for?"

Findo shrugged.

Rob saw his chance. Natalie's right knee had lowered while she spoke. Rob kicked his sister hard in the side of the thigh, lunged forward and grabbed the bag, which split. Prawn cocktail-flavoured crisps showered over Natalie but Rob managed to get the torn packet away from Natalie and buried his face in the foil, munching rapidly.

Natalie wailed and wobbled to her feet. She dived at Rob, pummelling him with her fat fists. Otis scuttled forward and quickly scooped up as many crisps as he could. He paused briefly to glance at Findo and pointed to the caravan's main bedroom.

"She's in there."

"Alone?"

"Yeah."

Otis turned back to his clean-up operation and Findo nipped into the caravan and made for the bedroom.

Natalie stopped punching her brother for a moment and stared suspiciously. "What you got there?"

Findo ignored her and darted through the door. Bosnia was sitting up in bed, idly filing her nails.

"Hi, Findo-babe." She looked at him quite brightly and Findo was relieved to see her smile. Bosnia's moods could swing erratically and entering her quarters unannounced did have risks. "What's going on out there?"

Findo shrugged. "Natalie and Rob are fighting." He unzipped his jacket and pulled out the stolen cartons. "I got your cigarettes."

Bosnia looked at him in astonishment, followed by delight. "Findo!" she trilled. "Where'd you get these? Are these for me? You wonderful little boy, come here."

She beckoned her youngest to her and enveloped him in a sweaty hug that smelt of Bosnia's personal fragrance of unwashed body, cheap perfume and nicotine. "How'd you get all these?"

Findo smiled at Bosnia, now busy ripping open a carton. "I got them up Jubilee Square," he said.

"How? Who gave them to you?"

"I got them from one of the shops."

Bosnia looked at her son with a mixture of curiosity and maternal pride, lighting a cigarette and inhaling greedily. "Did you? Well, aren't you the clever one? What a good boy you are."

5. Road rage

The trouble began just after nine in the evening. It started with a stop-and-search. Two policemen noticed a white Vauxhall Carlton veering erratically across the Castle Drive ring road. The officers followed from a distance, until the car suddenly swerved onto Tibbermore Road.

The police switched on their blue lights. They came up behind the car and flashed their headlights to pull the driver over. But the Carlton kept going at the same speed.

The officers got more alarmed when they saw the driver's arms waving above his head and his body twisting about in the seat. Unsure if they had a raving nutter, someone high on drugs or some kind of seizure victim, the police radioed for backup.

They followed the Carlton for another quarter of a mile until the patrol car driver saw the lights of another police vehicle coming off the ring road behind them. He put his siren on and pulled alongside the Carlton. The driver, a white male in his thirties, mouthed something and made a couple of frantic gestures before resuming his manic flapping and gyrating.

The police driver accelerated forwards and swung in front of the Vauxhall, forcing it into the kerb, where it bounced up onto the pavement before coming to a halt just in front of a lamp post. Seconds later, the other police car pulled up behind, boxing in the offending car. An officer got out of each patrol vehicle and began to approach the Carlton.

The door of the white car burst open. The driver leapt out, still waving his arms wildly. The nearest officer went for his baton, wishing the powers that be would hurry up and arm the police force with real weapons. His colleague reached for a can of CS spray. The Carlton driver suddenly slapped himself on the shoulder then gave a deep sigh of relief.

"Man! That fucking wasp." He gestured helplessly at the police. "Been fucking buzzing me ages."

"A wasp?" said the officer with the baton in disbelief.

"Yeah, fucking thing's been driving me mad." He waved at the police officers. "Just couldn't nail the fucker."

The policeman with the CS spray shook his head. "But why didn't you pull over? You could have stopped and let it out."

The Carlton driver leant back against his car and reached into his jacket, making the officer with the baton take an involuntary step backwards. The man pulled out a cigarette packet and put a hand-rolled cigarette in his mouth. Then he patted his pockets.

"You guys got a light?"

The policeman with the spray reached inside his tunic, noticing out of the corner of his eye the group of teenagers who had appeared just beyond the first police car. "Here." He tossed a disposable lighter to the car driver who caught it one-handed, lit his cigarette and flipped the lighter back.

"Cheers, man."

"So why didn't you stop or open a window, sir?"

The Carlton driver took a puff. "Couldn't fucking stop could I? I'm allergic to the fuckers. If that little thing fucking stung me it could have been fucking curtains for me. I swell up like a fucking balloon if one of them bastards get me. Had to fucking keep it off long as I fucking could. Couldn't undo the window because the handle's fucking bust."

"Why didn't you stop?"

"Oh, don't give me fucking grief. I'm allergic, like I said. I had to keep going. I got a needle at my place with some stuff in case I'm fucking stung. I'm not taking no fucking chances. I wanted to get home in case the fucker got me. Then I got a chance of finding my spike before it's too fucking late."

The policeman with the baton sniffed the air. "What's that you're smoking, sir?"

The Carlton driver looked at his roll-up in surprise. "This? Nothing."

He flicked it sideways, past the first police car towards the group of watching youths – now grown in number to seven. One teenager stepped forwards and scooped up the roll-up.

"Hey," said the policeman with the baton. "Give that here."

The teenager sneered and took an exaggerated draw on the smoke. "Piss off, copper."

The driver of the first car got out and looked at the gang of youths. The cars had stopped next to some waste ground near the western entrance to the Tibbermore estate. The policeman realised with alarm that he could see other figures making their way towards the scene. He reached inside and switched off the blue lights on his Mondeo.

Meanwhile, the officer with the baton, who had not taken in their situation, stepped towards the Carlton driver. "Right," he said. "Let's see what you've got there, sir? I want you to turn around slowly and put your hands on the car."

The Carlton driver gave a snort of disbelief. "What? I nearly get fucking killed and you want to search me? Are you for fucking real?"

"Look, sir, just do as you're told."

"Why? What you got to fucking search me for?"

"Just do as you're told, sir."

"Oh, for fuck's sake, stop calling me fucking 'sir'."

The policeman with the baton slowly drew his weapon. "Do as you're told and turn around."

His colleague with the CS spray nodded. "Come on. Do us a favour, don't make any trouble."

The Carlton driver laughed. "Fucking get you. I'm not making any fucking trouble. I just don't see why you have to search me because I nearly get killed. It's fucking ridiculous."

"Hey, guys?" The driver from the first police car flicked his head towards the tower blocks of Tibbermore. "Leave it, okay. I think it could be time to get out of here."

"What?"

"Oh shit!"

A beer can arced out of the evening sky and landed on the roof of the Mondeo, just missing the roof lights and spraying foam across the windscreen and bonnet. A cheer, taken up by a number of voices, came after it, followed by a volley of whistles and loud jeers.

The police should have known better. They had driven onto the edge of the Tibbermore estate on a summer night when there was no football on television. They had stopped a driver and then sat there with blue lights flashing instead of either letting him go or arresting him immediately and retreating.

Now the problem was not just going to go away. The local youths had taken the police incursion as a provocation. They were only too happy to help the situation escalate and see where it would lead. The gangs from Tibbermore were always ready for a fight – with each other or anyone else but particularly the police. And a full-scale riot was even better still.

Law and order always had a tenuous hold on Tibbermore and some residents saw public disturbances as a spot of free entertainment – for others they were a useful window of opportunity. A riot drew down a blanket of anarchy that concealed a multitude of sins: looting, arson, grudge attacks – and retribution.

Billy was on the roof of Tibbermore's John Smith block when the riot started. It was a still night and she was sitting with her back against a roof vent. Three candles were stuck on top of the vent and Billy was reading by their light with Findo sleeping next to her.

Billy had gone up to the roof, followed by her brother, in search of peace and quiet. For a while she had tried reading her battered paperback in the flat, ignoring the rest of the family. But she gave up when her two older brothers started fighting and screaming abuse at each other. Billy knew the fight could last for hours. Even if the violence did halt for a while, the tension would keep simmering all night and hostilities could begin again at any time.

There had been a time when Billy would have tried to enforce peace by joining the fight – often ending up beating both her brothers into submission. But she was starting to lose her appetite for spontaneous aggression. These days she was more likely to duck out of the way, taking Findo with her. And during the warmer weather of the past months, the roof had become a favourite escape.

Bosnia had got the flat by conning the local housing department, using the name of someone who had just been jailed in the Netherlands after being caught with a suitcase full of amphetamines and ecstasy. (Bosnia had tried asking for accommodation using a couple of her own names but given up when the authorities – despite trying to help – could find no traces of her existence.)

The family had moved to Tibbermore from the caravan under the flyover. They had been in the flat for nearly nine months now, which was a record as far as Billy could remember. But it was a spartan existence. The flat's electricity came from a meter fed by fifty-pence pieces and there were rarely any to feed it. The gas had been cut off after four months when no bills were paid and the first warning letters about the water supply had already arrived. Local burglars had kicked in the front door after the first week and, although that problem had been settled, the door had never been properly fixed and the broken bottom panel still gaped open.

Billy hated the block. She complained that the stairwells had more glue sniffers than steps and that the pigeons on the roof had a higher IQ than most of the inhabitants. Not that anyone took any notice; Billy hated everywhere she lived and found a reason for disliking most things on which she had an opinion.

So, when Billy came charging into the flat saying everyone had to leave, her other brothers and sisters took no notice.

"Listen," she said. "This is serious. There's a riot starting. We've got to get out quick."

Rob's eyes brightened. "A riot, excellent. I'm going to watch."

"No!"

Findo, now seven, watched from the doorway as she stamped her feet and gave Rob a withering stare.

"Listen, idiot. We've got to get out of here. Now."

Jimmy Ray and Natalie looked disdainful.

"What you on about, Billy?" said her sister.

"Why we got to go anywhere?" asked her brother.

"Look," said Billy. "You know what happens in riots."

"Yeah," said Rob. "Fighting, burning cars and chucking stuff at the coppers. Excellent."

Billy nodded. "But that's not all. People settle scores too."

Jimmy Ray nodded slowly. "Yeah. They do. Like that Nick Seed. There was a bloke in Livingstone kept messing him about. Last time there was trouble, he went in with two friends and some baseball bats. The bloke isn't going to walk again."

"Exactly," said Billy.

Natalie gave a petulant, impatient stamp of her foot. "But so what? Why do we care?"

"I know," said Jimmy Ray, who was not as dense as most people thought. "Davey Piper."

"What about Davey Piper?" said Natalie.

Billy shook her head despairingly. "He got out last week after doing six months."

"And?"

"He thinks She grassed him up."

"But She didn't."

Billy sighed. "That's beside the point. Look, Davey Piper got six months because he got caught with a load of stolen mobiles. He thinks She was the only one who knew he was holding them for the Muldoons. He knew she'd been picked up a couple of days earlier and let off without a charge, so when he gets nicked he reckons She must have grassed him up."

"But She didn't," repeated Natalie plaintively.

"I know that," said Billy, "but Davey Piper doesn't. He's out now and he's not the sort to ask questions. If he thinks he was grassed up, he'll just turn up and kick the door down first chance he gets."

"Yeah," said Jimmy Ray. "He's been staying down Benn block with Archie Cave. They were in The Lion couple of days back. He was mouthing off then."

"He won't just be mouthing off if we hang around," said Billy.

"What we going to do?"

Billy frowned. "I'm not sure."

She went to the front door and looked out. The flat was on the fifth floor and she could see across to a swarm of blue lights flashing at the entrance to the Tibbermore estate. It looked as though there were at least eight police vehicles drawn up just off Castle Drive. Billy could also see at least two vehicles burning at the scene of the original incident and a large mob facing the police.

"We haven't got much time," she said. "The coppers will probably drive them back into the estate soon. Then they'll start fighting around the blocks. That's when the trouble will really start." She turned to the others. "Is She with it?"

"Nah," said Jimmy Ray. "Been off her head all day and out for the count now."

"We'll have to get her out ourselves then," said Billy. "You lot get her and the others out of here. Go across the aerial to Livingstone and down to the back entrance."

"What you going to do?" said Natalie.

Billy smiled and grabbed Findo by the hand. "Sort out some transport."

The children crouched in the shadows just outside the back entrance to the estate's Livingstone block. Bosnia was slumped, half-conscious against the wall behind them.

"Where's Billy?" whined Natalie. "She said she'd be here."

The others ignored her and they were all silent for a while. They could hear distant shouting and occasional crashes and thuds.

Then the headlights of a vehicle suddenly appeared over the brow of the low hill behind the Tibbermore estate. It appeared to be following a footpath across the open ground. As it drew nearer the vehicle veered a few times, before slewing around in an arc and pulling up about ten yards away.

"Fuck!" said Rob. "It's the cops."

The driver's door of the police Transit opened and Billy leant out. "Come on, hurry up!"

"Fuck!" said Rob. "It's Billy."

"Come on!"

Natalie stood open mouthed but her older brothers grabbed Bosnia and pulled her upright. She stumbled like a zombie but managed to stagger across to the police vehicle. Billy helped haul her mother and the other children into the rear of the Transit before clambering back into the driver's seat.

"Wow!" said Rob, slipping into the passenger seat. "Where'd you get this?"

Billy crunched the Transit into gear and it lurched forwards. "The bus station, where do you think?"

Natalie leant forwards. "Billy, this is a police van, you can't use this. Anyway, you can't even drive."

"They see you?" said Jimmy Ray.

"Not until I was driving off," said Billy. "They were all too busy with their riot shields. They'd started lobbing a few petrol bombs and the cops were getting ready to charge." She swung the van round in a wide arc and headed back along the pedestrian path. "They didn't take any notice of me and Findo. We just looped round and came up behind. There was no one watching the van. A few coppers tried to run after me when we drove off but they stopped when I went back into the estate."

The engine screamed as she tried to change gear and missed. Billy stamped at the clutch and managed to ram the lever into third with a violent grinding. The van lurched a few times then shot forward again, bouncing over the hill.

"We'll have to be quick though. We're going to have to ditch this soon as we're clear of the estate."

"We could head down Chapelbank Road," said Jimmy Ray. "There's some new houses being built down there. I know a back way into the site."

6. Abigail McGee

Findo Gask was just over eight years old when he met Abigail McGee. The family had moved into a block of flats on the south side of town. The place had been abandoned after the previous occupants, a refugee family, fled one night. The eight Iraqis had endured six months of verbal abuse, burglaries, and obscene graffiti across their doors, walls and windows. That, and the general misery of life in one of the city's human dustbins, had brought them to the end of their tethers. The fact that it did not seem to have stopped raining for five months had not helped either.

A friend from the other end of the seventh-floor walkway told Bosnia about the flat. Sally Murray had helped lead the persecution of the Iraqis – driven by boredom and a bad experience involving a Pakistani taxi driver.

Sally was also the first to spot the door left open by the departed refugees. She made a quick sortie to see if they had left anything worth taking. Apart from a few open bags of rice and spices, which Sally dismissed as foreign food and threw out the window, the only other thing left was the front room carpet. Sally's was pockmarked with cigarette burns and various stains. This carpet was one colour and clean.

Unable to remove the carpet on her own, Sally quietly slipped out of the flat, pulled the door to and wedged it shut. She bumped into Bosnia later that day outside the High Spirits off-licence. The deal was done while the two women sat sharing a cigarette cadged from local thug Albie Hooper. Bosnia was living in a squat in the failed Meadowfields housing project but wanted out; a psychotic junkie called Mack had already attacked two other residents of the house.

Bosnia and Sally returned to Cowfield Heights via a hardware shop where they stole a new Yale lock. Back at the abandoned flat, a quick session with a Stanley knife (also pinched) and the women had the carpet up. After changing the locks, they lugged the carpet down the walkway to Sally's flat. They shoved the furniture to one side and spread the new carpet over the old one.

Sally sank into her favourite armchair. "That's it, eh?"

"Lovely. Nice and soft."

Sally cackled. "Yeah, fit to shag on." She reached down the side of her chair and pulled out her tobacco pouch. "Get a couple of lagers. There's some in the kitchen."

"Okay."

Bosnia wandered through to the kitchen. After a brief search among a pile of half-empty takeaway cartons, she found a four-pack nestling next to an assortment of beauty products from the Body Shop and Boots, collected on one of Sally's regular raids on the city centre. Back in the lounge, Bosnia cracked open cans for herself and Sally, who was busy rolling a joint.

"When you gonna get the kids then?"

Bosnia stared out of the window at the chimneys of the local power station. "Dunno," she said. "They'll be alright for today. Tomorrow maybe."

Only five of Bosnia's clan remained. Natalie had gone north. A man that she had met a few months earlier had taken her. Like her mother, Natalie enjoyed indulging herself. Unlike her mother, Natalie had never possessed the looks to be a prize and had gone straight to the street. She was not attractive enough to command a good price but had been a willing worker from the age of fourteen. At the age of eighteen, however, her limited attraction was already wearing thin and her new-found friend persuaded her to make the trip to Aberdeen, where he reckoned the oil workers, after months offshore, would be less fussy.

The oldest boy, Jimmy Ray, was out of circulation, serving a two-year stretch at a young offenders' institution. Jimmy would not be out for at least six months – longer if he did not behave himself. And with Jimmy the chances of getting parole for good behaviour were extremely slim.

That left Billy, who had reluctantly assumed charge of the rest of the family. Then came Rob, blond-haired and mean, followed by Otis, who was half-West Indian and sweet as treacle. Next to last was Louise, who was nine and hardly spoke, leading some to suspect – wrongly – that she was simple. Finally, came Findo, who talked nearly as little as Louise but, unlike his dreamy sister, took in everything.

A few days after Sally helped Bosnia find her new haunt, Billy and Findo were making their way slowly through the weeds and derelict buildings of an abandoned factory. The complex had once belonged to a firm making steel pipes but had been empty for more than thirty years. The factory stood on a loop in the River Allonby. It had been on the edge of the city, next to a planned ring road. But the business folded, the road was never built and the site was now miles from the motorway, the wrong side of hundreds of acres of grim housing estates. In healthier economic climes the factory might have had potential but, in a city with more development sites than developments, its future was as bleak as its surroundings.

Findo booted a rusting beer can left by another visitor. It sailed over a low wall and landed in a pool of oily water.

"You can't, Billy."

His sister scowled. "I can't stay here either."

They walked on silently, passing through a side door into one of the steel mills. The machinery had been stripped out decades ago and the building was now just an enormous, echoing cavern. Brick walls soared fifty or sixty feet to a piecemeal roof where blue sky showed through gaps torn out of the sheet-metal covering. A double row of pillars, church-like, ran the length of the mill, supporting the roof and the remains of some of the original gantries.

Findo and Billy trudged across the mill's floor, through rust flakes, pigeon droppings and dead leaves. They exited through the far end and headed across an area of open ground. Weaving around straggling brambles and clumps of buddleia, they walked slowly over the stone chippings and through a wide gap in a chain-link fence.

A couple of minutes later, they reached the base of a flight of steps leading up the side of a disused gasometer. The metal storage tank was almost a uniform rust colour now. Only a few patches of the original paintwork still lingered.

Findo stopped and looked at the side of the gasometer rising a hundred and fifty feet above.

"But why, Billy?"

She avoided his eye and sat on the bottom of the steps. "I've told you before."

"Tell me again, then."

Billy sighed. "You're impossible, Findo."

"I'm not. I just don't want you to go."

Billy reached out a hand and pulled her brother to come and sit next to her. "Findo, I know. If it wasn't for you I'd have gone a long time ago."

"Then why now?"

"Because I'm not sure how much longer I can take it."

Billy sat and looked towards the river. She put her arm around Findo and pulled him closer. Findo slipped his arm around her. His sister was crying but made no comment; he knew Billy was miserable but that did not make it any easier to let her go.

"Where will you go?"

Billy gave a thin smile. "Anywhere as long as it's out of here."

"But where? How will you get there?"

Billy sighed. "I'll take a train. South. I don't want to go to any cities. I want to see the countryside. I want to see the sea. I want to see clean places, animals, sunshine."

"Will you miss me?"

"Findo!" His sister pulled away. She twisted round and punched him on the arm.

"Ow! That hurt."

"Good. It was meant to. Don't ask stupid questions." Billy scowled but she was fighting back tears and smiles at the same time. "You're my little brother. I've looked after you since the beginning. I swore I would protect you before you were born and I only ever let you down once."

Findo nodded. "Fat Natalie got there first."

"But have I ever let you down since?"

"Not once," said Findo, finishing the routine as brother and sister high-fived each other.

"So don't you dare ask if I'll miss you," said Billy.

"Sorry."

"You should be. Not everyone's lucky enough to have me to look after them. And anyway, I've already told you – soon as I've got somewhere safe, I'm going to come back and get you. I'll take you away too. We can wave goodbye to this place and find a proper life."

"But what will I do when you're gone?"

"You'll survive, Findo. You'll be alright." Billy shrugged. "You're turning into a tough kid. I wouldn't leave if I didn't trust you to look after yourself. You know what I've told you. Keep out of the way, don't do anything you don't want to and look after yourself." She reached out and ruffled his hair. "I'd take you if I could but I reckon you're safest staying here. It could be tough to begin with. There's no point me taking you if we both end up in trouble. It's better if I come and find you when everything's sorted."

Findo nodded reluctantly. "But how long will it be?"

Billy shook her head sadly. "I don't know, Findo, I really don't. It might be a couple of months; it might be longer. I'm not going to make any promises because then I won't break them."

"How will you know where I am when you come to get me?"

Billy shrugged. "I'll find you. She never strays too far and there's plenty of people know her. I'll find you."

"Can you let me know when you're coming?"

"Sure," said Billy. "I'll write." She poked Findo in the ribs. "If you wanted, I could send you letters to tell you how I'm getting on. Tell you where I am and what I've been doing."

Findo nodded. "Will you?"

Billy nodded. "I could send letters to Eileen Dunn, she won't mind. She can get Mickey to find you. He'll let you know there's a letter."

Findo frowned. "But how will I know what they say?"

Billy laughed. "You could learn to read. Otherwise, you'll have to get Eileen to read them. Or Mickey, I think he knows how." Billy pulled Findo to her in an abrupt and savage hug. "Look, I've got some things to do. Some bits I need to sort out. See you later, okay?"

Findo bit his lip and nodded. He looked at the ground then reached up and threw his arms around his sister and buried his face in her neck. After about twenty seconds he let go and stepped back.

"Go on then."

Billy nodded and turned away.

Findo watched her. He knew he would not see her later. Billy was on her way. He had no idea when, or if, he would see her again. But neither could bear to say goodbye or prolong the parting.

She was halfway back towards the mill when he jumped onto the steps.

"Write lots of letters!" he called.

Billy's arm came up in acknowledgement but she did not stop or look back. Findo watched until she disappeared. Then, tears streaming down his face, he began to climb the long flight of steps leading up around the gasometer.

Billy MacBeth's heart was troubled as she walked away. She had no desire to leave Findo but knew that she faced an uncertain road. She had no idea where her journey would take her or what hardships and trials might lie along the way.

Billy was leaving for the simple reason that she could no longer stay. She hated her life; she hated the people around her. Most of all, she did not want to turn into one of them. For sixteen years, Billy had lived amongst poverty, crime, degradation, waste and ignorance. She had seen other children become drug addicts and convicts – or corpses. Some had turned mean, others spiteful. Many turned to petty crime, some to more serious offences. Others of Billy's generation, as they approached adulthood, had become the worst kind of whining cheats, not even trusting each other. Corrupted by the squalor of their environment, they had been dragged down to the level of their parents.

For Billy, the risk of being sucked into that morass, of becoming like her mother, was horrifying. But there was another, more immediate risk: Billy was nearly sixteen now. She was still small, still young-looking but men no longer ignored her and it was getting trickier to avoid their attention and stay as inconspicuous as Findo. And she did try; Billy never wore make-up, kept her hair cropped and wore the loosest, most concealing clothes. But it was not enough. She had inherited her mother's cheekbones and more beside – including a body that her sister Natalie would cheerfully have killed for.

Billy's defences were her tongue and reputation for violence. In most cases that was enough. But Billy knew that a sharp wit and obscene vocabulary would not deter some suitors; her barbed jests went over the head of many and her physical defences could be overwhelmed by a determined attack from a bigger, stronger man.

And Billy bitterly resented having to defend herself. Although she had grown up with a vicious temper and a natural ability for fighting, she had had enough. These days she avoided fights wherever possible – and felt dirty and sullied every time she was forced to resort to violence.

Now, Billy wanted a life free from oppression and privation. She wanted to make choices, not live by opportunism and threat. She had to leave the city before it was too late and she ended up becoming what she dreaded.

Findo only partly understood Billy's reasons for going but he had seen how she had become more withdrawn and bitter over the past year or so. No one else had noticed. They were used to Billy being sharp and aggressive. Few thought that her attitude might be an act, a shell to protect the creature inside.

For only a handful of people had ever really got to know Billy, to find out what she was like when the barriers came down. In public she never dropped her guard. But with her youngest brother, Billy did not pretend. She never tried to shut out Findo and he had seen the anger and resentment beginning to seep into her spirit.

Sharp tears ran down Findo's face as he climbed the gasometer; he wept for his sister partly because he was losing her, partly because he knew how miserable she must be.

The steps went up in long flights to circular walkways ringing the giant metal storage tank. Findo kept going past each landing. At the top, he stepped out onto the gasometer's slightly domed metal lid. A stiff breeze was blowing and Findo breathed deeply. The wind was coming up from the firth and carried the sharp tang of the sea – scents of salt and freedom. A few clouds scudded overhead but otherwise the March sky was clean and bright.

A handrail ran along the rim of the gasometer and Findo began to follow it clockwise. From this height he had a view across much of the city and beyond. To the north-east was the city centre with its high-rise offices, cathedral and grand parades of Victorian municipal architecture. To the east lay Cowfield Heights and the tower blocks of Tibbermore. Beyond was the sprawl of Clathy, a grey domain of dreary suburban life where office workers and lower management eked out drab lives. To the south-east – on the other side of the river – rose the leafier reaches of Chapelbank and Garvock Hill.

As he came round to the southern side, Findo stopped for a while. The loop of the river curved right around the base of the gasometer here. On the other side a landscape of hills rolled away from the city. Findo looked down at the river. He did not know what it was called. It was dark and sullen looking, sliding between thick mud flats. The fields on the opposite bank were waterlogged, poached by the hooves of bedraggled cattle. A thick wood, the trees still leafless, lay beyond.

Findo wondered what it would be like in the woods. He had never been out of the city and had little idea what lay outside it. Until now, he had never thought of going to see.

He glanced left and right to see if there was any nearby way to cross the river. No bridges caught his eye but something else did. On the other side of the gasometer, almost out of sight because of the domed roof, someone was sitting. Findo began to walk slowly closer. He could only see one figure, perched on the very edge of the gasometer.

He edged cautiously nearer. It looked like a girl, about the same size as him. She had long red hair and was bent over something. Findo was about fifteen feet away when she turned. The girl gave a little start and put something inside her jacket. She looked at Findo.

"Hello."

Findo stared back mutely. She was about his age, with a face full of freckles. Her hair was a torrent of loose curls, tied roughly behind her head. She was cleaner than Findo but her clothes did not look any better.

The girl stared back at Findo, weighing him up. "Well?"

"Well, what?" replied Findo.

"Aren't you going to say 'hello'?"

Findo shrugged. "What are you doing here?" he asked.

"Minding my own business."

"What business is that?"

"None of yours."

"How do you know?"

"Because I don't know you."

Findo smiled. He walked a little closer and sat down like the girl, holding the rail around the gasometer and dangling his legs over the edge. He bent over the bottom rail and peered over the thin band of rusted metal. There was only a thin strip of ground between the gasometer's base and the riverbank.

Out of the corner of his eye he could see the girl watching him. It was she who eventually broke the silence.

"What are you doing here?"

"Looking at the view."

"Which bit?"

"Huh?" Findo looked sideways. "What do you mean?"

The girl frowned. "Which bit of the view are you looking at? The whole thing or one part."

Findo shrugged. "Dunno. Whole thing I guess. I came up here to look at it all. I like to see the city from places like this. It's different. I can look at it and think which bits I want to see next."

The girl shook her head. "I like looking at the countryside. I come up here because I can see outside the city. I can see the fields and trees. Sometimes there's animals and birds. And I can see the sky."

"The sky?" said Findo. "But you can see the sky anywhere."

"Not so much of it. When you're down in the houses you only see the bits between the buildings. When I come up here I can see the whole sky. All the clouds and sun and everything."

"You been up here before then?"

The girl nodded. "Most days."

Findo frowned. "How come I've never seen you before?"

She shrugged. "Because I see you first."

Findo looked at her in surprise. "You've seen me before?"

The girl nodded. "Yes, a few times. You're normally with that girl. The tough-looking one."

Findo scowled. "How come I've never seen you?"

"Because if I see you coming, I go down the other side."

"Why didn't you go this time?"

The girl pouted slightly. "I didn't see you coming. I was too busy reading."

"Reading?"

"Yes, you know, books."

"Books?"

The girl sighed. "Yes, books. Like this."

She reached into her jacket and pulled out a paperback. It had a bright orange-red cover with a picture of a dragon on it. Findo nodded slowly.

"So you come up here to read?"

The girl gave him an exasperated look. "Yes. That's what you do with books. I come up here to read and get away from the city and look at the sky."

Findo grinned. "Could you teach me to read?"

The girl looked at Findo in surprise. She slid her book back inside her jacket and frowned. She started to speak a couple of times then stopped. Eventually she gave him a considering stare. "What's your name?"

"Findo."

"Findo what?"

"Findo Gask."

The girl only frowned briefly. Then she stood up, turned to Findo and stepped forwards. "I'm Abby McGee. Abby's short for Abigail but I don't like being called that."

Findo nodded and stared back silently.

After a long pause she scowled. "You're supposed to say you're pleased to meet me."

"Am I?"

"I don't know if you're pleased," said Abby. "But you're supposed to say it anyway."

"Why?"

She sighed and shook her red head in despair. "You just are, okay? Doesn't anyone teach you anything?"

Findo considered. "No. Not really."

7. Dog fishing

Findo Gask was a bad influence on Abigail McGee. Over the next seven years they shared much of their lives. For Billy had been right – although Findo had desperately wanted her to stay, he no longer needed her. At the age of eight he was already able to look out for himself. He no longer required a guardian angel; all he needed was someone to share his triumphs and despairs.

In Abby, Findo found the new companion he sought. She too was a misfit, lonely and isolated in a city of strangers. Although very different in upbringing and approach, she and Findo recognised each other as kindred spirits and – for a while at least – made each other's life complete.

Abby had arrived in the city about nine months before meeting Findo. She had come from a small town in northern Scotland, a fishing port where life moved to different rhythms. There, Abby had been happy. She had lived a carefree childhood, the kind of which many dream but few enjoy. Her home provided the warmth that no money can buy. Abby played, roaming the local hills and coast, went to school and was happy.

But hidden in the comforting blanket of family life was a thread of never-distant poverty that Abby was too young to appreciate. The family might have made it but for the intervention of unsympathetic fate. Abby's father was a fisherman and toiled hard to support his family. But then the night came, a couple of months after Abby's seventh birthday, when Andrew McGee and his boat did not return to port. Alarms were raised and a search begun. But on the second day, a small oil slick and bits of wreckage were spotted near a known foundering ground. Then the weather closed in and by the time the storm had blown itself out, hope was abandoned.

Abby and her mother, Suzanne, mourned and grieved with the fury of innocents wronged. They had been blessed with a life of happiness and love. Now that blessing was undone. Their world had been wrenched apart, daggers driven into their hearts.

Life went downhill rapidly. A week after the funeral, Abby's mother was told to pay a month's rent on their cottage in three days or get out. She also discovered Andrew's boat had been underinsured and the likely sum owing would be less than sufficient to cover their debts.

There was no one locally to support them. Andrew McGee had lost his own parents while he was still a boy. Suzanne was estranged from her own, middle-ranking professionals who had been horrified when their golden girl married a fisherman instead of a doctor, lawyer or teacher. She had never forgiven her parents for arriving late at the wedding and then her father's speech telling the assembled gathering that he was disappointed in his daughter and unimpressed by his new son-in-law. There was no way Suzanne was going to turn to them for help.

Rather than hang on to be made homeless, Suzanne fled. She could also no longer stand staying in the same town. She could have managed to grit her teeth and suffer the indignity of the local benefits office apart from the fact that it was only a street away from her father's veterinary practice. She might have been able to get part-time work but in a small town that would have involved working alongside the wives and relatives of other fishermen and enduring the well-meaning sympathy that would constantly bring back her loss. And everywhere Suzanne turned, she still saw Andrew. He was in every building, on every bit of harbour wall; every place within that town held a memory of the life they had shared and would never have again.

First, Suzanne went north to her grandmother. But the old lady was unwell herself and had no room to spare in her tiny, windswept bungalow. After a month Suzanne realised she was making them all miserable and making life impossible for a seventy-six-year-old who was too kind to complain.

Next they travelled south, Suzanne hoping to lose her pain along the way. On a train they met a stranger, a man of kind words and easy promises, who took them in and brought them to the city. But when Suzanne refused to forget Andrew and consider new arrangements, her saviour turned unpleasant, then obsessive and abusive. Suzanne fled, ending up in bed and breakfast accommodation with Abby. But the rejected saviour followed, now turned stalker. They hid for a few months in a refuge. Then the authorities offered a flat on the other side of town. It was lost in a street identical to twenty others, one speck in a sea of terraced homes.

Abby hated it. She did not blame her mother because she knew how much Suzanne was suffering. But every day she looked around at the grimness of her surroundings, the grey emptiness of their neighbours' lives and pined for open skies, clean air and the simple harmony of the life that was gone.

Until she met Findo, Abby's escape was books. She immersed herself in make-believe, in happiness and in places that were anywhere but here. Findo changed Abby's life because he took her out of herself. He came from an existence that, for her, was a fantasy – although Findo's world was dreadful, it was also incredible. In addition, Findo managed to make her smile; he gave her excitement and helped her stop living in her past.

Findo intrigued Abby. She thought he was exaggerating when he said that he could not read. Then, when she realised that he hardly even knew the alphabet, she was amazed. But she was undaunted and helping this strange boy to read became her quest.

They met regularly on top of the gasometer, or inside what had once been the steel factory's boardroom if the weather was bad. Abby first taught Findo his letters, chalking and spraying the alphabet around walls and across the gasometer's metal dome. She showed Findo how to write his name – a move that would later have far-reaching consequences. She gave the lessons, while Findo stole the material they needed: pens, paper, paint cans and brushes.

But Findo's lessons had to fit around Abby's own schooling. She had a place at the local primary school and attended regularly. Findo was curious and a little jealous but not enough to take up Abby's offer of going in with her. He looked from outside a few times but the learning on offer was not enough to tempt him past the security cameras put at the gate to deter drug dealers and child molesters. He looked at the high perimeter fences, the regimented rows at the end of playtime and the doors that would swallow hundreds of children for hours at a time. None of that was for Findo. Abby was his personal tutor and he preferred their arrangement to anything the state might have offered.

The lessons had been going for about a month on the day that Findo won Abby's heart. They had met in their usual place – a loading bay where finished pipes had once been lifted onto lorries. It was a dull April Sunday, dry but overcast, with a cool wind slicing around the empty buildings.

Findo had a new jacket, thick fleece with cotton inner shell and waterproof outer. He had stolen it from a city centre department store a few days earlier and was immensely proud of it. The jacket was too big for him but had lots of deep pockets – ideal for secreting all kind of items away.

Abby looked up as she reached the bottom of the loading platform where Findo had been waiting.

"Hi."

"Hi."

"Where we going today?"

"Up?"

Abby nodded. "Okay, but if it's too windy I'm not staying up there. My jacket's not as warm as yours."

Findo looked worried. "I could get you one. They've got all kind of colours."

Abby smiled but shook her head. "No. My mum would want to know where I'd got it from."

Findo shrugged. "Tell her I gave it to you."

They began walking towards the gasometer.

"But then she'd want to know who you are," said Abby. "She'd ask where you'd got it and why you were giving it to me."

Findo looked slightly surprised. "Well tell her I got it from the shops because you were cold."

"But she'd realise it was stolen."

"So?"

"She wouldn't like it."

"Why?"

"I don't know. She just wouldn't."

Findo shrugged. "Up to you."

They had just come through the empty mill building and started across the open ground toward the gasometer when Abby stopped. She gave a little gasp.

Findo grinned. "You like it?"

Abby stared in amazement.

The top section of the gasometer had been transformed. Vibrant letters twenty feet high had been sprayed onto the metal sides of the tank. Rainbow writing in swirling shades of red, green, yellow and blue spelt out 'Findo Gask' on the left-hand side of the gasometer. To the right, the graffiti continued with 'Abby McGee'.

"What do you think?" asked Findo.

"How did you do it? When?"

"I did it Friday while you were at school. I found some old metal rods in a shed and taped the paint cans to the top. It took loads of cans to do it all. Do you like it?"

Abby looked uncertain. "I think so. I like the colours. But what if someone sees my name up there?"

"So what?"

"I could get in trouble."

"Why?"

She shrugged. "I dunno. Some people don't like things like that. Where we used to live there was a bus shelter and the local boys were always spraying rude things on it. My mum told me not to read stuff like that when I asked her what it meant. I don't think she liked people writing on things."

Findo frowned. "What about the walls where we painted the alphabet and stuff?"

"That's different," said Abby. "No one's going to see that." She stared up at the enormous letters on the side of the gasometer. "You can probably read my name from the other side of the city."

Findo shrugged. "That's alright. I'll paint over it if you want."

Abby took his arm. "You don't mind?"

"No," he said. "It's your name, it's up to you." He grinned. "But I'm leaving my name there. I want people to see that. I'm going to write my name everywhere."

By midday Abby's name was gone. Findo had blanked it out by repeating his own name around the gasometer. After that they climbed to the roof of the tank and sat on the side out of the north-easterly wind, looking over the river.

"I'm hungry," said Abby. "What have you got?"

Findo reached into his jacket and delved into the pockets. He pulled out several bars of chocolate and a couple of plastic packs of sandwiches. He read carefully. "Prawn may-o-naise on soft brown bread and chicken and av-o-cado salad on malted brown."

Abby's eyes lit up. "Can I have the prawns? I love prawns."

"Sure." Findo handed her the package and ripped open his own. They sat in companionable silence for the next few minutes. Once the sandwiches were gone, Findo spread out the chocolate.

"We can share the Twix," he said. "Do you want the Mars or the Snickers? I don't mind because I like them all."

But Abby did not answer. She was staring down at the river. "What's that?"

"Where?"

"Down on the edge of the water. It looks like a bag but it's moving."

Findo followed the line of her arm. A white plastic sack lay in the mud of the opposite bank of the Allonby. The river water, rising slightly with an incoming tide, was just starting to lap around the bag. As Findo watched, the bag gave a kind of shudder. Then they heard it. A distant, muffled yelping.

Abby leapt to her feet. She looked aghast. "It's a dog! There's a dog in that sack."

Findo nodded. "Someone probably tried to drown it."

"That's terrible!" said Abby. "How could they do that?"

Findo shrugged. "Maybe it's a puppy. People do that when they want to get rid of them. Put it in a sack and chuck it in the river. But they should have put a brick or something in the sack to make it sink. It must have floated down here and got stuck."

Abby's eyes were wide. She began to turn towards the nearest steps down from the gasometer. "We've got to rescue it."

Findo saw the passion in her eyes and nodded. He grabbed his chocolate bars and followed Abby. They descended quickly, Abby almost leaping down the rusty flights of steps in her haste. At the bottom, they raced across the loose chippings to the river, stopping at the rusted wire that marked the edge of the steep bank.

Where they stood was about a dozen feet above the river. Below, a rough bank of grass and weeds descended nearly vertically. At the bottom lay beds of thick, glutinous mud with the river beyond. At the moment the Allonby was about twenty feet wide and fairly slow moving, beginning to be pushed back by the tide rolling into the estuary to the west. But the water level was rising; within the next four hours it would cover the mud and the river would be four times as wide.

The sack with the wriggling contents lay on the other side of the river.

Abby stared wildly around. "What do we do?"

Findo tugged off his new jacket, following it with his shirt. He stepped through the wire and began to climb down the bank. Grabbing handfuls of grass and kicking his trainers into the soft earth, he clambered down to the thin beach of gravel and stones at the bottom.

At the edge of the mud he reached out with one leg and probed. His foot sank. Findo pulled his leg back and took his trainers off. He threw them up the bank to Abby.

"What are you going to do?"

He shrugged. Findo knew the nearest bridge was half a mile away. "I'll see how deep it is."

He stepped onto the mud, his feet sinking into the glistening ooze. Findo advanced cautiously. By the time he was halfway to the water the mud was over his knees. As his feet came out of the mud, loud sucking, slurping sounds accompanied each step.

"What's it like?" called Abby.

"Muddy," said Findo.

At the sound of their shouts a sharp yap came from the bag on the opposite bank, followed by a series of eager whines.

Findo glanced across at the bag then tugged his right foot out of the mud and planted it in front of him. As it sank in, he pulled up his left and stepped forward. This time his foot sank less than an inch before meeting something hard. Findo frowned and tested the obstruction carefully before bringing up his right foot and stepping up onto it. He scraped at the mud with his feet and then grinned.

"It's an old car."

He walked gently across the roof of the buried vehicle. Beyond were just another couple of yards of mud and then the water. Findo stepped down off the car roof, avoiding where the windscreen would be in case it was broken. He sank into the mud almost to his waist. But the mud was much softer and more fluid and he could practically wade through it for the last stretch.

"Can you swim?" called Abby.

Findo bit his lip. "Not sure. I'll have a go."

He slid forward into the river with a shiver. Billy had taken him to a swimming pool a few times. It had been a year or so ago. Findo had revelled in the luxury of the warm, clean water (losing a couple of layers of grime in the process). His sister had showed him the basics of how to swim and they had spent over two hours in the pool each time, only leaving when they were kicked out. On the last occasion Findo had managed to swim a couple of widths and he hoped he could remember how to do it now.

He tucked his cupped hands under his chin and reached out in a clumsy breaststroke, kicking wildly with his feet. The river current was gentle on the surface, almost stilled by the rising tide. But the water was bitterly cold and Findo's teeth were quickly chattering. He fixed his eyes on the opposite bank of the river and ignored everything else, concentrating on his target.

Abby watched nervously. From above, Findo's progress looked painfully slow and his pale torso vulnerable in the dark water. But the twenty feet gradually shrank to fifteen and then he was in the middle of the river. For a moment he seemed to come to a halt and his arms paused. Then he reached out again and slowly, slowly got closer to the opposite bank.

Findo was only slightly off-target when he got close enough to reach down and feel mud beneath his feet. He turned upriver and thrashed his way for the final stretch towards the sack. His splashing set off a burst of frantic yapping from the bag, which began to wriggle and twist as if alive itself.

Findo slithered into the edge of the bank. He paused to get his breath, shivering violently. The bag jerked and twitched.

"Steady on," said Findo. "You'll put yourself in the water."

He waded through the mud and reached for the sack, which started to almost dance as his hand touched it. Then Findo glanced back across the river at Abby. He considered for a moment.

"I can't get back again," he called. "Not with the sack."

Abby clenched her hands together under her chin. "What are you going to do?"

"I'll have to go round. You know how to get to the Newmills railway station?"

She nodded. "I think so."

"I'll meet you there. I'll get across the railway bridge."

Abby grabbed Findo's clothes and trainers. "I'll bring your stuff."

Findo nodded and turned his attention back to getting out of the river. He picked up the bag, which wriggled but was quite light. It was an animal feed sack, knotted at the top. He swung it gently up the bank and pulled himself after it, half over the mud, half through the mud.

In the second field, Findo found a cattle trough. He put down the sack and dipped his hands in the water. He sluiced his face first then washed the worst of the drying mud off his arms and body. He was bitterly cold and his feet hurt but he was used to discomfort and glad to be out of the river.

With the worst of the filth off, Findo crouched down and tugged at the knot holding the feed sack closed. It opened without too much trouble and he pulled the bag open. A pair of puppies looked up with loving eyes. There was a third one but it was still and cold. Findo picked out the dead puppy, ignoring the pushing and pawing of its littermates. He looked around and then lobbed it into the leaves of the nearby hedge.

Findo turned back to the sack, reached in and picked up a pup in each hand. They came eagerly, licking and nuzzling him, using every fibre of their being to tell him how wonderful he was and how much more they would love him if he fed them, immediately. Findo hugged the wriggling puppies. They were damp but still warm. He cuddled them against his chest then lowered them back into the feed sack. "You'll have to stay there for now," he said. "I can't carry you in my arms and I need to find Abby and my clothes. Then you can get out."

8. Shopping therapy

Findo and Abby walked slowly along Dubmore Road. Abby's head was bowed and Findo knew she was trying hard not to cry. Behind lay the St Francis Sanctuary. Rummaging around inside the home's kennels were Duke and Dragon, the two puppies Findo had saved from drowning.

Abby sniffed. "Who do you think they'll go to live with?"

Findo thought for a moment. "Some rich family from up Garvock Hill."

"Will they be happy?"

"Oh yeah. They'll have baskets and sleep next to a fire. They'll get taken for long walks and fed steak every day."

Abby gave a little smile. "It is best, isn't it?"

Findo nodded. "Course it is. You know what your mum said. They need lots of space and we didn't have anywhere to keep them. They'll be happier."

"You don't think they'll end up stuck in that kennel and no one wanting them?"

Findo shook his head. He booted an empty Irn-Bru can lying on the pavement and watched it ricochet off a lamp post into the path of a passing bus.

"Nah," he said. "The man at the home said they'll be picked straight away. They're both young and cute. Anyone who sees them is bound to want them straight off. They'll see what good dogs they are." He shrugged. "Anyway, even if they stay there for a bit they'll be looked after. They get all the right food, walks and that. And they get taken to the vets and given all the injections and stuff they need so they don't get worms and things like that."

Abby sighed. "I still wish we could have kept them."

She had her head down and her hands stuffed in a jacket identical to Findo's; he had stolen it for her and kept it in a secret hiding hole at the old steel factory. Abby's hair was pulled back in an unruly ponytail and Findo could see the scowl on her face.

They continued in silence until Findo noticed a sign up ahead. He grabbed Abby's hand and suddenly steered her off down an alley towards a large, new shopping complex.

Abby looked up in surprise. "What's up?"

Findo gestured at the steel and glass edifice rising from the car park ahead. "I'm hungry," he said. "Let's go shopping."

As Abby followed Findo through the parked cars, her spirits lifted slightly. Over the past week Findo had begun to teach Abby a little about his life and how he fended for himself. It had been an eye-opening experience for a girl whose parents had tried bringing her up according to basic principles of honesty and responsibility.

Previously Abby might have recoiled at the idea of following Findo's example. But he had conquered her misgivings on the day when he blithely launched himself into a cold river to save two dogs from drowning. For Abby had realised that Findo might not have done anything if he had been there on his own. He had gone through the mud and across the river because of her. She had seen something awful and he had acted, careless of his own safety, to make her happy. Now, he was her hero.

Findo, unthinking diplomat, never mentioned the third puppy. On the day of the rescue he had clambered across the Newmills rail bridge with the plastic sack tucked carefully under one arm. Ignoring the angry shouts of a railway worker and the stares of bemused passengers, he had trotted onto the station platform and padded barefoot into the street outside. There he met Abby and quickly swapped his burden for trainers and clothes before leading them away from the station.

The children had made their way to Abby's house. Findo was introduced to Suzanne – who rushed him straight into a bath and his clothes into a washing machine. Abby's mother had been somewhat taken aback when her daughter arrived home with a filthy street urchin and two dogs in a sack. But she too was impressed when Abby explained what Findo had done. She was also cautiously relieved that Abby appeared to have made a friend.

Suzanne's initial reaction to Findo was wary. She was unsure whether he was the right kind of companion for her daughter. But aware of how lonely Abby had been – and that parental disapproval can have the opposite effect to the desired one – she kept quiet.

Abby was also careful not to tell her mother too much about how Findo lived, and the puppy saviour himself volunteered no information. But Suzanne was not stupid. She observed the boy's clothes: his worn and grubby underwear and too-expensive jacket. She watched his mannerisms: the way his eyes darted around but did not meet hers, how he did not speak until certain of his ground, the way he avoided touching things while Suzanne was looking. And when she persuaded him into the bath, Abby's mother noticed Findo's malnourished, scrawny and filthy body (only the top layer of which was riverine in origin). She also observed various scars and bruises, although her interpretation of their cause was more sinister than the truth.

Findo stayed that night on the McGee's sofa – he assuring Suzanne that his mother would not worry and she happy to take his word for it. He slept that night in comfort – in more luxury than he had experienced since the first few weeks of his life. And in the morning he woke to clean, dry clothes and breakfast at a table where food was waiting and no one tried to take it from him.

The puppies were housed in a cardboard box in a corner of the kitchen. Their long-term fate was not discussed on the day of their rescue or the next morning as Suzanne readied Abby for school.

"Will you look after the puppies?" she asked her mother. "They're called Duke and Dragon."

"Are they? Well don't worry, they'll be here when you get home."

The children left soon after. Suzanne did not mention school to Findo and he – now old enough to be learning the difference between his world and that of the rest of the population – kept his mouth shut. He set off with Abby, leaving her at the school gates with the promise he would be there at the end of the day.

And so they had settled into a routine: Findo collecting Abby from school and walking her home. They spent the evenings with the puppies, who had a carefree, pampered life in the flat – although Suzanne was careful to make sure Abby did her share of cleaning up the dog's mess, changing their bedding and feeding them.

Findo did not stay again during the week but turned up at breakfast each day – even bringing his own box of Coco Pops on the Tuesday. The following weekend they spent even more time playing with the puppies, going out only for a shopping trip when Findo led a nervous but excited Abby through a supermarket as he stole things he thought the dogs might like.

The pair of them could have gone on like that indefinitely if Abby's mother had not found the strength to intervene. Against Suzanne's instincts, she had been unable to find the heart to break the facts to Abby during the first week but knew that if she did not do something soon it would be too late. And so, on the second Wednesday evening, Suzanne had gently explained the situation to her daughter and Findo.

Abby's mother had herself been busy that week, contacting several animal charities for help and advice. She laid out the details slowly and carefully. Suzanne did not dictate but simply explained what two young dogs were likely to need in the way of food, exercise and medical care. Then she highlighted their own circumstances and the other options before summing up the situation.

"We can't afford to feed them and we won't be able to help them if they get ill. We're also not supposed to keep animals in the flat and it's only just about big enough for the two of us. But apart from that, two young dogs need lots and lots of exercise. If they don't get it they won't be happy. You have to go to school and I need to get a job. It wouldn't be fair to shut them up in the flat all day. That would be nearly as cruel as throwing them in the river." Abby's mother had glanced sideways at that point. "I know Findo was really brave to save them, it was wonderful what he did, but I doubt if he would be able to look after two dogs on his own all day either."

Findo said nothing.

"You've both been very kind and given these dogs a chance of a happy life. Now you have to decide the best way of making sure they get that happy life."

For a minute, Abby had stayed stubbornly silent. But ultimately, she was not selfish enough to ignore the truth. Sadly, she agreed it would be best for the dogs to hand them over into proper care. Suzanne suggested they keep the dogs in the house until the weekend and so it was that the two children had delivered the puppies to the St Francis Sanctuary the next Saturday.

Abby staggered up to the uniformed security guard standing inside the supermarket's foyer. "Hey, mister?"

He turned round, neck stiff to support the dignity of his braid-rimmed cap. He looked slowly down at Abby. With unsubtle calculation he took in her age and likely social standing.

"What?"

Abby dumped the two carrier bags by his feet and stood up with obvious relief. "My mum told me to get a trolley and take these to the car but they're too heavy. Can I leave one next to you while I go and get one? I won't be long." She tossed her mop of red hair back and gave the man her best winning smile.

He nodded reluctantly. "Okay."

Abby picked up one of the bulging bags and turned towards the entrance. "Thanks," she said.

"Be quick," added the guard. "I can't wait if I get called away."

Abby gave a grin over one shoulder. "Don't worry."

She moved towards the exit, swinging her load in an exaggerated fashion. She paused for a moment before stepping past the electronic security barrier with a little hop, the bag suddenly looking much lighter.

A loud siren blurted out and the lights on top of the detectors began flashing. Abby's mouth dropped and her eyes opened wide.

Then she gave a little wave at the staring security guard and began to walk off.

"Oi! You little toerag."

The man broke into a run, surprisingly swift for his apparent bulk. Abby fled, disappearing around the corner with the security guard in hot pursuit.

Findo followed a few moments later. He ignored the bleeping security alarm and strolled out of the supermarket unchallenged, a new knapsack over one shoulder.

Findo turned in the same direction as Abby and the security guard. He strolled along a footpath that ran back towards Dubmore Road. To begin with the path followed the outside wall of the supermarket. Beyond the building was a spiked metal fence separating the car park from a piece of derelict land.

Findo saw Abby's carrier bag dumped on the ground just before the corner of the supermarket. Two large Savoy cabbages, various other vegetables and a CD were strewn across the pavement. Findo stepped past and walked on.

A few yards further on the security guard was stood by the spiked fence. There was a narrow gap where building and railings met. Of Abby there was no sign. The man glanced briefly at Findo, who ignored him. There was a bleep from the radio on the guard's belt and he spoke into it briefly before turning and stamping back towards the supermarket.

They met at the side door to St Colomba's Church. Abby was waiting. Her eyes were bright and she grinned at Findo. "That was excellent!"

Findo smiled. "Worked alright, didn't it?"

Abby nodded. "But he could run faster than I expected. I thought he looked fat but he nearly caught me."

Findo looked alarmed. "Really?"

Abby waved a hand. "Oh, don't worry. I'm the fastest in my class. He wouldn't actually have caught me. But I was glad it wasn't any further. He was only a bit behind when I went through that fence." She laughed. "You should have heard him. He tried to get though the gap. He didn't stand a chance but he kept trying and swearing. You should have heard what he called me!"

Findo grinned. "Yeah? Well, get used to it."

"Anyway," said Abby. "Let's see what you've got."

She patted the stone step beside her and Findo sat down, swinging the stolen bag onto his lap. He pulled the top open and reached in.

"Let's see," he said. "Belgian chocolates, some spicy roast chicken, three packets of Pringles, peanuts, more chocolate."

Abby laughed. "Didn't you get anything apart from food?"

Findo looked a little hurt. "I got some socks."

"About time, your feet stink. You should try washing them too."

Findo pulled a green and red object out of the bag. "What's this?"

"Oh, I put that in," said Abby. "It's a mango."

"A mango? What's that for?"

"It's fruit, silly. You eat it!"

Findo scowled. "Well I didn't know. I've never heard of a mango. How am I supposed to know it's fruit?"

Abby smiled. "Don't worry. I thought you might remember."

"Remember what?"

"Mango. It was in that can of fruit stuff you had last week. Mango and something."

"Oh that," said Findo. "Yeah." He looked at the fruit with new interest and turned it in his hand. "So what do you do? Peel it, eat it whole or what?"

Abby frowned. "Not sure. I've never had one before. I've seen them in shops but I've not actually tried one."

Findo reached inside his jacket and, after some searching through his pockets, found a slender flick-knife. He pressed the button and the blade shot out. Holding the mango away from him, he shaved off a layer of skin, revealing the soft orange flesh beneath.

He put the fruit to his nose and sniffed. "Ummm. Smells good." Findo cautiously bit the piece of skin he had removed. "Bit tough."

This time he slid the knife in deeper and cut off a thick chunk. He laid the knife to one side and took a tentative taste, followed swiftly by a much bigger bite. He chewed rapidly and stared at Abby with big eyes.

"Oh yeah!"

9. Petrol heads

Findo suddenly sat up and stared at the television. Abby glanced at him in surprise. It was a few weeks later and they were in the living room at the McGee's. Abby had been watching the local news. Until now, Findo had shown no interest. He had been slumped back in the sofa, staring off into some world of his own.

"What's that?" he demanded.

"What?" said Abby.

On the screen of the small portable set, one of the city's members of parliament was being interviewed. Clement Dallaway was a Tory – a fact that surprised many people who knew the city's reputation as a grim symbol of urban decline. But the existence of a true-blue outpost in a sea of enemy red was not so surprising when the makeup of his Dubmore Valley seat was taken into account. Although Dallaway's seat included the Tibbermore estate – where he polled very few votes – it also took in the more exclusive domains of Garvock Hill and the rural area to the south of the city.

Dallaway, wearing a comfortable sweater and oilskin jacket, was standing outside his palatial residence on the edge of Garvock Hill. Around him was a broad sweep of gravel, leading to the Georgian façade of Harlequin Hall, with its balustrades, statuary, terraces and closed-circuit television cameras. Leaning on the kind of long stick used by a gillie with two spaniels frolicking brainlessly around his feet, Dalloway was droning on about his family's long history of benevolence to the less fortunate and its dedication to helping neglected and abused children.

"That," said Findo, pointing.

"What? What are you talking about?"

"The car."

Abby squinted at the screen. "Where?"

Findo jumped off the sofa and skidded across the carpet on his knees. He jabbed with a sticky finger at the television picture. "There. Can't you see it?"

Behind Dallaway and to his left could be seen a row of stables and a coach house. The wooden doors to the coach house were open and inside was parked a Land Rover. Next to it, just visible, was a tiny sports car. The windscreen of the vehicle barely reached the top of the Land Rover's wheel arches.

Abby frowned. "Dunno. Looks like a miniature car."

Findo pushed his face up against the television. "But it looks real."

"Well of course it's real," said Abby. "You can see it."

"That's not what I mean. What I mean is it doesn't look like a toy car. It looks like a proper sports car, just really small."

Abby shrugged. "So what."

Findo swivelled around and grinned. "I want one!"

The two children walked slowly along the lane leading up to Harlequin Hall. They passed a gate leading into a field full of cars. Two uniformed guards with radios on their belts stood at the entrance to the paddock. Inside were ranks of parked vehicles: sleek saloons and sports cars, gleaming executive estates and mud-spattered four-wheel drive vehicles with stickers advertising membership of country sports organisations.

Abby took Findo's hand as one of the guards stared at her.

"Do you think this will work?" she hissed once they were out of earshot.

Findo shrugged. "Dunno."

He led Abby on between the neatly trimmed hedgerows, taking care to try and keep his shoes out of any dirt. A little further they came to the main drive leading up to Clement Dallaway's home. Another two security guards stood beside the gates. Findo and Abby walked straight towards the drive.

As they reached the gates one of the men stepped forwards but his movement was half-hearted and he did not completely block their passage. He looked down at the children.

"Can I help you?" he asked.

"No," muttered Findo, "we're okay."

Abby stared at the man and looked him up and down in the kind of dismissive fashion that she had seen in television dramas. "We're here for the garden party," she proclaimed.

The security guard stayed where he was. "On your own?" he asked.

"Don't be silly," said Abby. "We're too young to be on our own. Mummy and Daddy are inside. We went to look at some ponies."

Findo ignored the guard and tugged at her hand.

"Come on," he said.

The security guard stepped back and the pair walked briskly past, up the drive. The gravel crunched beneath their feet as Findo and Abby exchanged glances, then looked away so as not to laugh.

Clement Dallaway's garden party was an annual affair. His mother had started the event in the 1950s and he had taken over after she left the house for a discreet nursing home, where her fondness for gin was less likely to cause embarrassment.

By now, the party was an important fixture in the local social calendar. It attracted most of those from the area who enjoyed, or aspired to, a similar lifestyle to the Dallaways'. Invitees were nearly all above a certain income bracket and included various minor celebrities, landowners and party supporters. The only names on the guest list to fall beneath the income threshold were either those whose breeding gave them the kind of pedigree that money cannot buy but were unfortunately in more straightened circumstances than their ancestors, or those whom Clement Dallaway wanted to impress or otherwise influence. The only other – rare – exceptions to the rule were those guests who knew how to behave in the company of their betters and could offer a certain cachet to the occasion by way of their personal attraction: whether looks, notoriety, fame or talent.

Nominally the gala was in aid of charity, although most of those attending could not have cared less whether it was raising money for the Ku Klux Klan or the local branch of the Guides. Every year half the proceeds went to a national children's charity and half to a local cause. This year, being the event's fiftieth anniversary, however, Dallaway was giving all the proceeds to help build a new children's hospice – to be named after his dear (although not yet departed) mother. The event also promised to be bigger, better and more glamorous than ever, which was why the MP had appeared on the local news and why a crew from the television station were on hand to record the golden jubilee for posterity.

Findo and Abby ducked behind the television crew's outside broadcast vehicle. Abby looked around at all the cables and roof-mounted satellite dish with interest. She smoothed down her dress and looked at Findo expectantly.

Abby was wearing her best dress, together with a hat that her mother had worn on her wedding day. She had smuggled the clothing out of the house that morning while Suzanne was busy cleaning the kitchen. Abby had met Findo at their usual rendezvous by the old factory, where she had also changed and pinned her rebellious hair into a semblance of order before jamming the straw hat down on top.

Findo's transformation was even more remarkable. Everything he wore was new, stolen the previous day from one of the city centre's more upmarket department stores. He was wearing a neat checked shirt, corduroy trousers and a quilted green body warmer. He had shiny brown leather shoes (the first time he had ever worn anything but trainers) and, to top it all off, a grey-green flat cap.

Abby had been flabbergasted when she first saw him but Findo had just shrugged off her surprise.

"If we're to get in, we've got to fit. There's no point going if they chuck us out straight away."

Abby had frowned. "But you look . . . wrong. It's not you."

"I don't care," Findo told her. "They had a picture of someone wearing this stuff in a magazine in the shop. He was standing outside somewhere a bit like this, so I reckon I might stand a chance."

To begin with, the children wandered around together, unsure what to do next. The doors to the coach house that they had seen on television were closed and a caterer's truck was parked in front of them. A couple of stable doors had their top halves open but neither of them were sure about trying to sneak past a horse at close quarters.

At first they tried circling the coach house to see if there was another way in but were halted by a high wall around the rear of the stable complex. There was one gate but it was firmly locked and all they could see beyond was a pile of horse manure and a kennel housing a disconsolate lone spaniel.

Foiled for the time being, they made their way back round to the front of the house. Abby took Findo's hand again and they went up the steps to the main entrance. The doors to the house were closed but a terrace ran along the front of Harlequin Hall. It led past a line of mullioned windows too high for the children to see through. On their right, gargoyles and Grecian stone figures adorned the long balustrade.

At the end of the terrace, the corner of the house met a long yew hedge. An open gate led through into the gardens. They followed a brick path through a parterre enclosed by clipped box hedges. Then a gravel walkway led through a rose arch and round a fern-fringed ornamental pond before bringing them to the back of the house.

Ahead, a rockery led down to a lawn surrounded by marquees. The tents enclosed about half an acre of grass dotted with tables and chairs. At and around the tables was a throng of sipping, nibbling, chatting, posing, strolling men and women in elegant summer outfits. A few children – all equally expensively attired – either stood obediently by parents or flitted between the adults, weaving in and out of people, table, chairs and marquees.

The marquees were arranged in a horseshoe. At the far end was a stage with a six-piece jazz band playing discrete muzak. Down each side of the lawn were three long marquees. The sides were rolled up into looped swags of canvas, held in place with blue ribbons and posies of flowers. Inside the marquees stood long tables covered with crisp white linen. Behind them, lines of liveried waiters served from platter after platter of meats, salads, quiches, tarts, vegetables, canapés, pies, cakes and all kind of savoury and sweet delicacies.

Findo glanced around the lawn. Then he saw what the tents contained. His eyes went wide and his mouth dropped. He stared in disbelief then pointed. "Abby."

"What?"

"All that food."

She had been watching the people rather than looking at what was inside the marquees. "Oh, wow."

Findo began to salivate. "They've got more food than a supermarket." He frowned. "Who's it for?"

Abby shrugged. "Dunno. The people here I suppose."

"No way," said Findo. "There's not enough people. There's loads of food. I've never seen that much before. Look, there's that tent and that one and that one. They're full of food. There's no way they could eat all that."

Abby smiled. "Well . . ." she said slowly, "it looks like they're trying. Maybe we should go and help."

Half an hour later both children, particularly Findo, were feeling sick. They had made their way warily down the rockery, ready to be challenged at any minute. But no one took the slightest notice and they had simply entered the throng and merged into the crowd. Slipping past knots of talking adults, the pair edged their way into the space between the tents – where Findo was amazed to realise that, apart from one marquee housing a long bar, both sides of the horseshoe were serving food, not just the three tents that he had seen from above.

After a short period of careful observation, the two children had followed a couple of women into one of the catering tents and picked up plates. Findo – in a transport of delight – made his way down the tables, piling his plate so high that he could hardly carry it, trying not to miss out on anything. The pair then quietly carried their booty behind the marquee where the grass was a little longer and the only other people were the occasional waiter who popped out for a quick smoke or other caterers on errands. The children were ignored, which suited them fine.

It took Findo a while to work his way through his plateful but eventually he managed it. Abby was a little more restrained but still polished off a dozen canapés, eight chicken satay sticks and a small mountain of shell-on tiger prawns. Belching loudly – to the amusement of two fag-sharing caterers – Findo pulled himself upright so he could go in search of a drink.

Abby stayed where she was and Findo returned a few minutes later clutching two glasses of iced lemonade, plus another plate. Apart from two pork pies and some more satay sticks, this one was mainly piled with pieces of cake.

Abby stared at the plate with a mixture of resignation and pleasure. "More food?"

"Yup."

"Did they just give you more?"

Findo nodded. "Didn't seem to matter. They just give you whatever you want." He sighed. "I could live here. This is heaven."

It was mid-afternoon before the children could think again of Findo's mission. They made their way cautiously through the space between two marquees and peered into the area of tables. Again, they went unnoticed. Most guests had finished eating, although a few gluttons were still picking in desultory fashion at remnants of their feasting. A handful of people were dancing lazily to the jazz band, the majority sat around talking and drinking, while waiters flitted from table to table with trays of drinks.

Findo and Abby glanced towards the house. There was another, wider terrace at the back of Harlequin Hall with several sets of French windows opening onto it. One was open, as was the main door in the centre of the house.

"Come on," said Findo.

"Are we going to go in the house?" asked Abby, as they approached the fan-shaped flight of stone steps leading up from the lawn.

"Might as well," said Findo. He pointed to the high wall running from the right-hand corner of the house. It stretched for several hundred yards until it met another yew hedge. There was a wooden door set in the wall but it was closed and a group of men were standing nearby talking. "Not sure we can get in that way." At the top of the steps Findo turned to Abby. "You scared?"

"No." She grinned. "This is fun. I want to see what it's like inside."

Clement Dallaway had slipped away from the party. His wife, Alice, was holding court in the centre of the lawn with a group of admirers. Dallaway's personal assistant, Katrina, was down near the front of the stage checking on arrangements for the charity auction that would be held once sufficient alcohol had worked its way into the systems of his guests.

In the meantime, Dallaway had business to attend to. He found Tasmin Perry waiting in the morning room. She was sipping a coffee and leafing through a copy of *Horse & Hound*. A liqueur glass sat next to the coffee cup and her briefcase was by her feet.

"Ah, Tasmin, my dear," said Dallaway. "I'm sorry to keep you waiting."

She rose to her feet and offered him a cheek to brush his lips against. "Don't worry, Clement. I've been well looked after."

He smiled. "I should hope so."

Dallaway took a seat on the sofa beside her. He glanced appreciatively at the sleek grey skirt, silk shirt and elegantly shod feet. He noted the sheen of pale hair on her tanned arms and the way her ash blonde hair was pulled back in a tight ponytail that curved around her smooth neck. Most of all, however, he admired Tasmin Perry's long, slim legs.

She let him look for longer than was strictly necessary before leaning forward to pick up her briefcase. As she did so, the pale cream silk of her shirt hung open, giving Dallaway a brief glimpse of more tanned skin, curving into white lace.

Perry smiled as she flipped open the catches on her lawyer's briefcase. She pulled a thin plastic folder from within and removed a sheaf of papers. She handed it to Dallaway. "This is a record of the transaction. As you can see, the money was transferred to the holding company in the early hours of this morning, British time."

Dallaway nodded, skimming down the figures – the dollar signs and accompanying numbers taking his mind from the other figure beside him.

Perry was about to hand the MP the next sheet of paper when Dallaway saw her glance sideways. He turned and saw the two children in the doorway. One, a redheaded girl wearing a slightly odd-looking hat, smiled at him.

"Hello, Mr Dallaway," she said.

He smiled back automatically while wondering what on earth the brat was doing in the house. Parents had been asked to keep their children away from the hall.

"It's a very nice party," she continued.

Dallaway nodded graciously. "Thank you, my dear," he said. "Now, what are you doing in here? Where are your parents?"

Abby pouted. "They're talking," she said. "It was really boring so we decided to go for a walk."

The MP smiled. "Well, I don't think you'll find anything interesting in here. It's just a boring old house. I think you'd have much more fun in the garden."

Abby shook her head while Findo wandered a few yards into the room. He looked around, staring at both Dallaway and Perry. The lawyer gave him a smile but Findo just looked back expressionless.

"No," said Abby. "It's much more interesting in here. It's a really lovely house."

Dallaway frowned. "Yes," he said, "but I'm sure you'd be happier outside."

Abby shook her head more fervently. "Oh, no. This is really nice in here."

"Yes, but won't your parents worry if they look for you?"

"No," said Abby. "I told you, they're really busy talking. They wouldn't notice what we did."

"Well," said Dallaway, "I'm sorry to interrupt your wandering but I need to talk to this lady here, if you don't mind."

"Oh, that's okay," replied Abby kindly. "We don't mind. You won't bother us."

Tasmin Perry bit her lip as she watched the MP's discomfort. Dallaway shifted awkwardly on his seat and held up his hands in entreaty, wishing there was someone he could call on to remove the children. The problem was that all his staff were supposed to be outside and he did not want anyone seeing the solicitor in the house unless strictly necessary. It occurred to him that he should have remembered to post someone at the door to steer away uninvited explorers like this infuriating child.

"Look here," said Dallaway, "I really think you should go outside."

"You still got that car?" Findo's interruption was so unexpected that Dallaway did not notice the boy's unrefined accent.

"What car?" he asked.

"That toy car," said Findo.

Dallaway shook his head, bemused, but Abby gave him a bright smile. "He means the little sports car. The miniature one you've got."

"Oh, that. You mean Oliver's little Maserati."

Abby nodded in blissful ignorance. "Yes that's the one."

Dallaway glanced briefly at the woman next to him as he made a quick calculation. "Would you like to see it?"

"Yes," said Findo instantly.

"Please," added Abby.

"Okay." The MP stood up and walked to the door. "Right, children, follow me." He glanced back at the woman watching him from the sofa. "Excuse me, Tasmin," he murmured. "I'll be back as soon as I can."

She picked up her glass of liqueur and raised it mockingly. "Have fun, Clement."

Dallaway led the children quickly through the house, along wide corridors in immaculate country home taste. They turned into an enormous farmhouse-style kitchen where appliances gleamed against shining tiles and polished wood. Abby drank it all in as she passed, lingering and trying not to rush, while Findo stayed tight on Dallaway's heels like an impatient terrier.

From a rack on the wall, the MP selected a bunch of large keys. He opened a side door and ushered the children into a paved courtyard. Off to the right the courtyard opened into a larger area enclosed by a row of kennels and other outhouses. A gate beyond the kennels led into a small orchard. Opposite, however, was a wooden half door leading into the stable block.

Dallaway herded Findo and Abby towards the wooden door. He leant inside and pulled back a bolt then swung the door open. He pointed down a long stone passageway that smelt of horses and hay.

"Go straight down there and you'll find the coach house. Oliver's Maserati is in there. You can have a good look but don't touch anything. I don't want you fiddling with the Maserati or anything else. Okay?"

Findo nodded and set off down the corridor without a word.

Dallaway turned to Abby. "See over there?" He pointed towards the orchard. "When you've had a look at the car, you can leave that way. There's a gate on the other side into the car park field. You can go back around."

Abby smiled. "Okay, Mr Dallaway. Thank you very much."

The MP frowned. He could not quite put his finger on it but there was something about the girl that did not look right. "Who are your parents, my dear?"

Abby began to follow Findo down the corridor. "My mummy's Anne," she said over one shoulder.

"Anne who?"

"Arbour," replied Abby, saying the first name that came into her head.

Dallaway stared after her. The name did not ring any bells but that was not particularly surprising. In his life he met all kind of people. He remembered the names of those who could be useful – or dangerous – to him. The others he just smiled at blandly and forgot.

Turning away, he went back into the kitchen, locking the door behind him as he hurried back to find Tasmin Perry and her papers.

It was dim inside the coach house. Motes of dust hung in the air and the gloomy, quiet, still space had a serene, almost church-like atmosphere.

Abby found Findo already sitting inside the miniature sports car. It was a complete replica of a proper Maserati – even down to the engine beneath the bonnet. It was a real rich boy's toy, built for the kind of parent whose only way to affection was to purchase it through ever more expensive gifts for children probably already beyond impressing. Findo was running his hands over the wheel, the dashboard and the gear lever.

"This is amazing," he said to Abby. "It's like a proper car but everything's just smaller." He gestured around. "It's really fancy. I've never seen a car like this before, big or little."

Abby bent down and ran her hand over the bright red bodywork. She gave Findo a grin. "He said we mustn't touch anything."

"Bit late for that."

Abby opened the passenger door of the two-seater and slid in next to Findo. The car was a quarter the size of the real thing but there was just the right amount of room in the cockpit for the two children.

"Does it go like an ordinary car?" she asked.

"I don't know," said Findo. He bent down and busied himself underneath the steering column. After a brief inspection, he sat up again. "It's got the same wires and everything. I reckon it should start like any other car."

"How fast do you reckon it would go?" asked Abby.

Findo shrugged. "Dunno. We'll have to take it out and see."

Abby looked around. "How we going to get out?"

Findo considered for a minute and then reluctantly climbed out of the driver's seat. "Let's have a look."

There were two main ways in and out of the coach house: sets of opposing wooden double doors on rollers that opened onto the drive at the front and the stable yard at the back. Both were bolted shut. Findo glanced at the passageway leading back towards the house but judged it was probably too narrow for the car, even taking its reduced dimensions into account.

He went over to the front doors and tried the bolt holding the two doors together. It was large but had been oiled and slid back without too much trouble. There were another two bolts going from each door into the brick floor and the wooden lintel above. Findo looked up at the top bolt. It was about seven feet above the ground and impossible for him to reach.

"Abby." Findo hissed her name, suddenly conscious that there could be people on the outside. "How do we open these ones?"

Abby considered. "Try sitting on my shoulders."

"Okay."

She lowered herself into a crouch and Findo, who was slightly lighter, climbed onto Abby's shoulders. She stood up slowly, while Findo helped by pulling himself up on the door. By the time she was standing straight, Findo could just stretch out and reach the two top bolts. He pulled them down slowly, trying to be as quiet as possible.

Abby lowered him to the ground with relief and Findo bent to lift the bolts holding the doors at their base. When they were up he looked at Abby and, taking a deep breath, tugged cautiously at the right-hand door. It rolled back easily and light poured into the coach house.

Findo stopped when there was a gap of about six inches and peered out. The catering truck was still parked across the entrance. There was a gap of about three feet between the truck and the wall — room for a person but not for a miniature Maserati.

"It's blocked," he said. "We'll have to try the back."

"Hold on," said Abby. "Let me have a look."

She slid past Findo and squeezed out through the gap in the doors.

"Mind you don't get seen," said Findo.

Abby shrugged. "Why? Mr Dallaway let us in here. We're allowed to be here." She gave a giggle. "Anyway, anyone sees us they'll just think we're with all these posh people."

She stepped out round the back of the catering truck. The drive looked empty and she walked round to the front of the truck. Abby stood on tiptoe but was unable to see anyone in the cab. She was about to go back into the coach house when she noticed the television crew's van parked a little further down the drive. There was a man in the front reading a paper and eating sandwiches from a plastic box.

Abby walked down to the van and waved at the man, who rolled down his window.

"Hello, love," he said. "You looking for something?"

"Yes," said Abby. "We need to move that van."

"Why's that then?"

"Mr Dallaway is going to need to get out of the coach house and it's blocking the doors."

The man scratched his stubble. "You need to find someone from the catering firm. I'm just driving this for the TV station."

"Could you drive their van?"

"Well, I'm sure I could drive it," he replied. "But I'd need the keys. Besides it's nothing to do with me. They might not like some stranger touching their stuff."

"Oh." Abby scowled. "We only need to move it a few feet."

The man sighed and put his paper and sandwiches to one side. "Tell you what, love," he said. "Let's have a look and see if they've left the keys in it. If there's no one else about I'm sure they won't mind if we move it a little way." He jumped down from his van and followed Abby to the front of the caterer's truck. "You're in luck," he said. "They've left the keys inside. I'll just hop in and shift it for you."

Abby grinned. "Thanks."

She slipped back around the rear of the truck and into the coach house to where Findo was standing in the shadows.

"What's happening?" he asked.

"I found someone to move the truck."

"You what?"

"He was in the television van. I told him Mr Dallaway needs the truck moving. He's going to do it for us. He's in there now."

Findo's eyes gleamed. "Brilliant!" He made straight for the toy sports car. "You open the doors and I'll start the car. Jump in as soon as I've got it going."

Abby nodded and grabbed hold of the nearer door. She pushed it further back and then turned to the other one, shoving the two doors apart until there was a good six-foot gap. A couple of abortive roars came from inside the coach house as Findo tried to hotwire the car but the sound was masked by the noise of the caterer's truck starting up. The Maserati's engine caught just as the truck outside began to roll forwards. Findo crunched the car into gear and jerked forward a few feet, stopping with the nose just inside the coach house doors.

"Coming?" he asked Abby.

She jumped into the miniature car and squeezed in beside Findo.

"Hold on," he said and lifted his foot off the clutch.

The car shot forward, missing the right-hand door of the coach house by only a couple of inches. Findo swung round the back of the caterer's truck, which was just coming to a halt, and turned down the drive in a broad arc. Gravel crunched beneath the tyres of the little sports car and Findo wrenched the car into second gear.

Abby watched with innocent trust as the car rocketed down the drive, almost clipping the stone wall around an ornamental flower bed. She glanced at Findo. "How d'you learn to drive?"

"Mickey Dunn taught me."

The Maserati picked up speed as it raced down the drive away from Harlequin Hall. The engine was still in second gear and whined in protest but did not falter. The needle on the speedometer was indicating about forty miles per hour and the rev counter was swinging into the red. Loose gravel sprayed to either side of the car.

At the bottom of the drive, the two security guards turned round in surprise as they heard the dwarf Maserati screaming towards them. It was still over a hundred yards away and one of the men stepped forward, while the other stood gaping.

Findo headed straight down the middle of the drive. His lips were pulled back into a snarling grin as he hunched over the tiny steering wheel. Abby had one hand on her head, clamping her mother's wedding hat onto her red locks. Her other hand gripped the door of the open-top car with white knuckles.

As they hurtled closer, the guard who had stepped forward raised a hand. He held it palm out and opened his mouth as if to speak. Stepping forward again, he began to wave frantically at the Maserati. But as the distance closed to thirty yards, then twenty – with the Maserati not showing any sign of slowing down – the man's waving faltered and he started to edge towards the side of the drive.

Findo shot past the two guards and through the open gates. He spun the wheel and the Maserati's rear end slid sideways on the gravel as the car slewed round into the lane. For a moment, Abby thought Findo was going to loose control but then the car settled onto its new course and accelerated away up the narrow road. Still in second gear, they whined between the high hedgerows, past the turning into Dallaway's car park field and towards Dubmore Road.

Half a mile later they were at the junction. Findo skidded to a halt and looked around. There was no sign of pursuit as yet and the main road ahead was fairly busy. A few motorists looked in surprise at the two children sitting in the scaled-down sports car.

"Hang on," said Findo.

He slammed the car back into first gear and they shot out of the junction on the wrong side of the road. He got the car into second again and then, with only a couple of brief lurches, found third gear. The Maserati roared happily and surged forwards. Findo accelerated past a taxi going in towards the city and swerved onto the left-hand carriageway just in time to avoid a head-on collision with a lorry that was coming towards them, flashing its lights and hooting loudly.

The stolen sports car raced on through Garvock Hill, past large detached houses in leafy gardens, past the entrance to Garvock

College and the row of boutique shops in Trinity Parade. Findo narrowly missed a collision with a bus by the Royal Standard Hotel then swung left into the road signposted for the hospital. Still at breakneck speed, he set off down Fortress Hill, heading back towards the security of his own territory.

10. The name of the thief

And so, the child grew. Findo Gask inherited a legacy of ill chance. He was seeded in degradation and grew amongst hopelessness, failure and apathy. But the hostility and indifference of his environment also provided Findo with the freedom to follow his own path.

By the time he was ten, Findo was already starting to become notorious. Inside the tower blocks of Tibbermore, in back-street pubs, in squats and other houses of ill-repute, on street corners and behind closed doors: there were many who knew his name – and his exploits were starting to draw the attention of the wider world.

Findo Gask's name had become known partly because he had spread it himself. The day that he painted his name in twenty-foot high letters across the gasometer was the trigger for a campaign of self-promotion. For although he did not like drawing attention personally, Findo quite wanted the world to know his name. And reasoning – quite accurately – that no one else was going to tell it, he began to leave his autograph wherever he could. Sometimes it was simple graffiti, but often it was a calling card. He would leave his name at the scenes of thefts, scrawling his tag across shop floors and walls in indelible marker pen or spraying it in paint across their windows.

He also liked to leave his mark on stolen objects once he had finished with them. The Maserati stolen from Harlequin Hall disappeared into an abandoned warehouse near Newmills Railway Station, emerging each night to tear around the streets like a tiny Batmobile. Findo was nearly caught several times but became expert at leading the police on merry chases before driving the dwarf car beneath parked lorries or down narrow alleyways where his pursuers could not follow.

The hunt for the miniature sports car and its phantom driver became a summer sensation that tickled the fancy of the media nationwide; the fact that the midget Maserati had been stolen in broad daylight from the stately pile of the city's Tory MP was the icing on the cake.

But Findo was too wise to push his luck forever. After a week, he parked the Maserati in an ornamental fishpond outside the city hall and left it there – his name painted across the bonnet and down both sides; an image that made it onto network television news and into most daily papers.

At the time, however, few people were sure who or what Findo

Gask was. Hardly any realised it was the name of a person. Some thought it was the name of a gang, pop act or some Celtic fringe group. (Most confused of all were the residents of the actual hamlet of Findo Gask, who wondered why the name of their home had been sprayed across a stolen car.)

But apart from his escapades with the Maserati and efforts to leave his mark on as many places as possible, Findo was also gathering fame for his thieving. Within his community he was already known as the boy with the lightest touch. He had a reputation as a thief who could lift anything a child could carry. And his depredations were not restricted to any particular area of the city. Findo ranged far and wide, by day and night, entering shops, offices, factories and any other building he fancied – although rarely people's homes.

Findo mainly stole for himself but was not above a challenge and rarely disappointed when he did take the bait and steal to order. However, although Findo's name was spreading and his reputation growing, few would notice him in the street. He was nothing in particular to look at: a boy, smaller than average and nondescript in looks. Only his eyes gave any clue to the character behind them – and that was something most people overlooked because Findo rarely raised them to meet another's gaze.

And although Findo liked to leave his name across buildings and objects, he preferred avoiding attention in person and was dull company for strangers. His natural instinct was to err on the side of caution, viewing anyone new as a threat until they demonstrated otherwise. With someone he did not know or like, Findo kept quiet, mumbling when spoken to and lowering his head. This was partly a survival technique from his younger days, partly a matter of choice. Findo was happy for people to talk about him but had no desire to talk with them.

His gift for making himself indistinct was a trait that served him well throughout his life and one that he perfected as he grew older. Findo was adept at vanishing, whether in a crowd or with a handful of people. He could slip from a room, slide into a corner or just merge with his surroundings as the circumstances dictated. And once he decided to make himself invisible, few people broke the spell. Even from his youngest days, Findo Gask possessed a rare stillness and calm, weaving about himself a negativity of presence that was his greatest armour.

The theft of the Maserati, apart from bringing Findo Gask's name to national attention for the first time, was also a watershed for other reasons. Until that day, Findo's experience of the world was strictly limited. He grew up in a closed community, an underworld that excluded as much as it was excluded. The flats, pubs and streets where Bosnia dragged her family were inhabited by people whose lives were confined to deals and cheats and getting by on the tightest margins. They were inward looking, with low expectations, limited ambition and no vision beyond the day to day. They were also Findo's yardsticks, the measures by which he understood human existence and its interactions – and he had no reason to suspect there were other ways to live.

Even when Findo first began to move further afield and follow his own direction, the vast majority of those he met conformed to the stereotypes he had already encountered – those that survived and those that stood in their way.

The city as a whole was poor. There were pockets of affluence but – although he sometimes sought richer pickings in these grounds – Findo had no contact with the people who lived there. On his wanderings, he saw people who wore smart clothes, children who went to school, diners who ate in restaurants, workers who had career prospects and drivers who owned their cars but they might as well have been a different species. They were ephemeral, wallpaper to the grit of real city life.

From time to time, Findo got to see television but the gloss and glamour of its programmes were far removed from his reality. He would watch the box and stare in fascination when something captured his attention. But it was only entertainment. It bore no relation to his world and, as far as Findo was concerned, there was no difference between *Star Trek*, *Eastenders* or Michael Jackson's music videos: all were fantasy. Television was a box of illusions, good for idle watching but with no more relation to the real world than the stars in the sky.

Findo's world stretched from the river on the south to the ring road and motorways that surrounded the city on the other points of the compass. He knew that the universe itself was larger; he had crossed into Garvock Hill a few times and seen the fields on the other side of the river – even trudged across them when he rescued the puppies. But although he could see and touch these places they were not of his world. They were as foreign as the sea to a desert nomad; he knew he did not belong there. He was a child of the city and could not really comprehend the idea of straying beyond its confines.

When Billy left, her departure had sown a few seeds of uncertainty but the effect had passed. His sister still wrote regularly but her letters came from so many different places that Findo was unable to follow, or comprehend, their significance. In truth, he had never really understood what it was she wrote about; all he cared was that she was still writing and was out there somewhere.

But when Findo Gask visited Clement Dallaway's garden party he realised that he had got it wrong. The people who lived in the fantasy worlds of television, magazines and the other side of brightly lit glass were real. And they had things of which he had never dreamt. They had more food than they could eat. They sat in sunshine, wore bright new clothes and danced to music played just for them. They drove the cars that slid by Findo's world without stopping or looking. And they lived in enormous houses, homes big enough to hold a dozen families, stuffed with flowery furniture, thick rugs and shiny ornaments. They had everything Findo had never known he lacked.

And now he knew he was missing out.

The impact of the discovery was significant. For the first time, Findo began to think beyond feeding, clothing and amusing himself. He wondered what else there was, what other things there were for taking and how to get them.

One result was that he began to widen his horizons. Instead of tackling the most obvious and convenient targets, he started to explore more widely, both within the city and its environs. He also studied his own territory in greater detail. Over the next few years he worked assiduously to learn every feature of his home turf. He walked every street and alley, looking for passageways, learning routes and memorising layouts. He explored parks and gardens, public spaces and private grounds, searching for exits, entrances and hiding places. Within a year, Findo Gask was a walking gazetteer, with greater knowledge of the city than any taxi driver or urban planner.

As well as the exterior of the city, he also studied the interior. By day and night he entered buildings both open and closed. He worked his way through offices, shops, workplaces and now homes too, seeing what each contained. Sometimes he would tackle a street methodically, going from building to building – a method that took him to places that he had never previously even noticed existed. Other times he would flit, as fancy took him, from one side of the city to the other, entering properties at random. He found ways into all kind of premises, entering in all manner of ways, honing his skills with each challenge.

His explorations even took him below ground. A chance find led him into a section of Victorian sewer tunnels. The discovery opened up a whole new range of possibilities. The city's history stretched back to Roman times – and over the centuries many people had dug down into the rock and soil on which it was founded. There were sewers, watercourses, crypts, cellars and shelters – some with connecting passages to be found by those who looked.

And it was through these investigations that Findo would come across a hiding place that became his home and escape from the perpetual transience of Bosnia's existence. His explorations also led him to a new passion: maps. He collected and stole plans of the city from past and present, using them to learn more about the terrain around him and the ways, obvious and hidden, into places of interest.

One of the other changes in Findo's methods was that he became far more selective. Until he was ten, his thieving had been petty and utilitarian. He had no strategy or plan, stealing when he needed something or it took his fancy. He also stole simply because he could. But that began to change. His explorations were often just that: Findo would enter buildings and wander them without taking a thing (although mentally noting down their contents for future reference). And rather than respond to a need, Findo began to plan. He also started making specific trips to equip himself for particular needs; collecting groceries in bulk and gathering clothes by the outfit.

If asked, he would have been hard pressed to say why he had changed his approach. It was something of which he was only vaguely aware. But what he was doing was preparing. He was learning and studying, improving his skills. He was getting ready – doing the groundwork for when his operations moved up another level.

11. Elder philosophies

It was towards the end of his eleventh year that Findo Gask was responsible for launching a gang war that tore apart the city's underworld. But in the months preceding that event he also met one of the people who was to have a profound effect on his life, helping forge what he was to become.

And it was Abby's idea to introduce her to Findo.

They were lying in Murdo Gardens, a small park behind the city museum. It was mid-August and early morning. Suzanne McGee had a new job as archive assistant for the council's archaeology unit. Abby – off school for the summer – had walked her mother to work then met Findo around the corner.

Findo no longer came to breakfast at the McGee's house. Even before the incident with the Maserati, Suzanne had harboured her doubts about Findo. She was suspicious about how he lived, what he did and, crucially, what he might get Abby into. But she had avoided confronting the boy for her daughter's sake. Findo was the first and only friend that Abby had made since her father's death and Suzanne was loath to interfere, knowing too well the fragility beneath the new, surface happiness.

But when Suzanne saw the abandoned sports car shown on television she recognised Findo's name sprayed across the vehicle and knew it was time to intervene. The news report said when the car had been stolen and Suzanne knew her daughter had been out with Findo all that day.

Abby's mother did not act immediately. She made no rash moves, made no attempt to forbid Abby from seeing Findo, knowing that would have been counter-productive. Instead, Suzanne took her daughter on a long walk a few days later. They went to the top of Clathy Hill and sat on a bench overlooking the city. Abby's mother spoke for a long time. She talked of the way that she and her husband had grown up, what they had meant to each other and how they had tried to live: their likes, dislikes and personal beliefs. Then she spoke of Findo and hazarded a few guesses about his upbringing. Mrs McGee made no attempt to disparage her daughter's friend but made sure Abby understood the differences in her upbringing and that of Findo. She told Abby that she would never try to stop her from seeing Findo but that Abby had to make a choice: to either live Findo's life or that of her parents.

Abby went silent for a long time and Suzanne gave her daughter time to think. She knew Abby's silence was not stubbornness; the girl had inherited her own trait of careful thinking and considered judgement. Then Suzanne suggested that, if she wanted to respect her parents, Abby could stay friends with Findo but ensure that she did not get involved in any activities of which they would disapprove.

Abby nodded slowly. "Okay," she told her mother. "But I might forget some times."

"I understand," Suzanne replied. "I don't expect you to be perfect all the time. But you can't use that as an excuse. I just expect you to remember how me and your father would want you to behave."

"Okay. I will."

Then, to Abby's astonishment, Suzanne sealed the bargain with a totally unexpected action. Reaching behind her neck she unclipped the slim gold chain holding her St Christopher. It had been given to Suzanne just before her eighteenth birthday by her then fiancé and was her most treasured memento of Andrew McGee. That afternoon she hung it around Abby's neck.

"Why . . . you can't . . . not this."

Suzanne shook her head. "I want you to wear it. You know how much it means to me. Your father gave it to me as a way of telling me how much he loved me. I couldn't wear an engagement ring because my parents wouldn't have let me so Andrew gave me this. Now I want you to wear it. Whenever you feel it, remember what we've talked about. And if you ever can't keep your side of the bargain you've got to promise to give it back."

Abby had her fingers on the gold chain as she watched Findo. He was lying on the grass on his stomach, frowning at a book about the city's military history. He had stolen the slim volume from a branch of Waterstone's a few days earlier. The book, by a local historian, was an account of the city's mid-eighteenth century role as a staging post for English-led forces engaged in putting down insurrection in the Scottish Highlands.

Findo was trying to make sense of an account of the doings of Lord George Murray and the Duke of Cumberland. The two English generals had passed through the city shortly before the Highlanders' struggle reached its nadir on the killing fields of Culloden. The author had used the visit as an excuse to recap at length on the political situation of the time in Scotland and northern England (hoping perhaps to mask the fact that the city's significance to the military campaign had been marginal).

Findo was not interested in Jacobite history. He had picked up –
and stolen the book – because its cover promised an account of the
construction of the city's fort. But rather than skim past the irrelevant
sections to find what he wanted to know, Findo was trying to read the
whole book – with the result that he was fast becoming bogged down
and near to despair.

The problem was not just Findo's own lack of education. The
book's text was far from crisp and it was weighed down by turgid
descriptions, the heavy prose laden with details that few readers
would have considered illuminating – from the exact composition of
individual baggage trains to the precise marching orders followed by
regiments on their way north. But determined not to be beaten, Findo
was trying to wade through it all, not realising he was wasting time on
an unnecessary challenge.

Findo had stolen the book after a chance discovery. A week earlier,
while exploring near an old church, he had come across a small area
of public space that he had not seen before. A tarmac path ran along a
flat strip of grassy ground as it curved around the hillside. The open
area was nowhere more than fifty feet wide but ran for about a
quarter mile, ending up near the main hospital.

The strip of land was clearly used mainly by people exercising –
and toileting – their dogs but had one intriguing feature: a wall about
twelve feet high that ran without break around the hill. The wall was
built of brick and completely sheer. It was covered with moss and a
few clumps of grass grew from cracks in the mortar, but was
otherwise featureless.

Where Findo first came across it, the wall ran dead straight for
about a hundred yards. Then came a section that stuck out like a
spearhead before disappearing into a grassy bank, after which the wall
turned at about forty-five degrees to follow the side of the hill, again
running straight and sheer.

Findo had wandered the length of the wall for some time,
wondering what it could be. He found the answer at the hospital end,
where the grass ran out and the tarmac path joined the road running
down towards the city centre. A small plaque explained that the wall
was part of Fort Hawley, a castle and military barracks dating back to
the last years of George II. The plaque gave no further details and
Findo was unable to find any other traces of the castle that day –
leading him on a hunt for answers.

Findo flung the book down with an angry exhalation and rolled over to look at Abby. "It's no use. Books are a waste of time."

Abby smiled. "No they're not."

Findo snorted. "They are. That book's supposed to be about the fort but it just keeps going on about Lord this and Lord that and how they were supposed to be on one side but were all scheming and kept pretending to be loyal to one lot then switched sides every week. Or it goes on about Duke So-And-So and how he was related to the king and what he got up to in Germany before he came here. Or about what sort of rations the soldiers had to carry and how many biscuits each one had, and that they were mostly rotten but they had to eat them anyway because if they complained they'd get flogged."

"Sounds like you've learnt a lot."

"Yeah, but it's all rubbish. I couldn't care less. I want to know about the fort."

Abby shrugged. "Why don't you look in the index?"

Findo frowned. "What's the index?"

Abby looked at him. She sometimes forgot how little Findo knew about things she took for granted. His confidence masked the many holes in his learning – but then there were some matters where his knowledge far outstripped hers.

She considered for a while. "I've got an idea."

"What's that?"

"You ever been to a library?"

Findo shook his head warily. "Should I?"

Abby shrugged. "Doesn't matter. But I know someone who might be able to help." She stood up. "Come on."

"Where we going?"

"To see Mrs Reid. She'll help you find out about the castle."

The pair made their way across city by bus. Abby insisted on paying and Findo let her, happy to go along with the plan if it meant he found out what he wanted to know.

They changed buses near the municipal swimming pool at Alexander Cross where they sometimes went and caught the number thirty-six towards Newtown, the area of the city where Abby and her mother lived. Findo climbed to the top of the near empty double-decker bus and quickly bagged the front seat. He slumped back and settled down to enjoy the ride; when Findo took buses he normally stayed on the bottom deck so he could get off again quickly when asked for a ticket.

But he was unable to enjoy the unaccustomed luxury for long. As they came into Corporation Road, Abby prodded him to his feet.

"Come on. Off here."

They scuttled down the spiral staircase. Neither bothered to push the bell-press and they jumped off as the bus was pulling away from a pelican crossing.

"Where we going then?" asked Findo.

Abby grabbed his hand and towed him along the pavement. "This way."

She led him past the chain-link fence outside a nursery school and turned onto a drab concrete forecourt. Behind was an ugly 1960s-built block with blue panels and large glass windows set into concrete block walls. The flat-roofed building looked in need of some care; the window frames were peeling and two broken windows were boarded up with sheets of plywood.

"What's this then?"

Abby steered him past a flowering cherry tree set in a concrete tub. The top of the tree had been snapped off level with its stake but a couple of twigs still bore small sprays of pale pink flowers.

"It's a library."

Findo looked with a mixture of curiosity and trepidation as they drew nearer. "So, it's full of books is it?"

"Well, it's a library. What do you expect?"

He shrugged. "Dunno."

Abby pushed open the first set of doors and led Findo in.

"Do they mind us just going in?"

Abby laughed. "Come on."

She shouldered open the next door and pulled Findo inside. They went straight past the front desk and headed towards a separate room off to one side. Findo stared at the shelves of books.

There were only a few people in the library – most of them looked at least sixty although there were a couple of younger men and one teenage girl with thick glasses engrossed in the titles on the science fiction shelves.

Abby led Findo into the reference section. A large desk was covered with piles of books, magazines, microfiches and a computer. Looking down at the mess was a tall woman with iron-grey hair and a soft smile. She looked up as the pair entered.

"Hello, Abby. How're you?"

"Fine thank you, Mrs Reid." Abby pulled a somewhat reluctant Findo forward. "Mrs Reid, this is my friend Findo. He needs some help."

"Well that's what we're here for. Pleased to meet you I'm sure. What is it you need to know?"

Findo glanced around. There was an atmosphere in the library that was unfamiliar. He met Mrs Reid's gaze only briefly before looking away.

"Does it cost much?" he asked.

"Does what cost much?"

He shrugged awkwardly. "To use the library."

Mrs Reid gave a warm smile. "I see. We have got some work to do with you, young man, haven't we?" She winked at Abby. "I think it's a good job you've brought him to see me, dear. If we'd left it any longer it might have been too late."

Frances Reid was an unusual woman with a complex history. She had been born in the early 1920s and lived a remarkable life. Over the coming weeks Findo learnt her story in instalments. He was hooked by the tale and Mrs Reid used its chapters as a reward.

Frances Reid's mother, Mary Glover, came from a staunch line of communists. A militant suffragette, she had also trained as a nurse and spent three years during the Great War serving her country by stitching up and patching wounded young men so they could return to the trenches and get slaughtered properly.

It was in the hospital that Mary met her husband-to-be. Captain Clive Willoughby was the elder son of a country parson and had been shot in the shoulder. Clive was lucky; the bullet – fired from behind by an over-enthusiastic teenager – passed through and did little more than dampen his ardour. A wily sergeant insisted on guiding his officer to a hospital several miles behind the front line – enabling them to miss the rest of the battalion being wiped out during an abortive assault on the German lines.

The couple were married a few months after the end of the war. Frances was the couple's third and last child. But to the dismay of Clive's family, motherhood failed to dampen the political ardour of their firebrand daughter-in-law. Their beliefs took the family – including the young Frances – to spend nearly a year in the new Soviet Union. The visit was a qualified success. The couple were both intelligent enough to see past the rhetoric and realise how brutal life under the new regime was for the average Russian. But the disappointment only served to rekindle Mary's, and now Clive's, passion for seeing communism work elsewhere.

Back in England, the Willoughbys, although opposed to the Stalinists, became active members of the British Communist Party. Over the next decade their children were brought up on a life of travel, meetings, strange beds, late-night talks and handing out leaflets to complete strangers. Frances, then an appealing child with curly blonde hair and big eyes, had a talent for waylaying passers-by and persuading them to take away tracts on how to throw off the chains of capitalism and seek unity with their fellow man through honest toil and cooperation.

Then came the Spanish Civil War. Again, the couple were united. Clive had no hesitation about laying his life on the line to defend Spain's recently elected Second Republic. Mary was horrified by stories of the Catholic Church and other nationalists using the conflict as an excuse for a crusade against women's freedom. The family set off together, children in tow, travelling across France by train and over the border towards Barcelona.

Mary and the children went no further than Catalonia, safely away from the front. But the war brought another opportunity. Mary had become interested in filmmaking; some of the first documentaries had recently been produced by the British film industry and she was interested in how the medium could be used to put across the socialist message. Aided by Frances and her son Fred, now in his teens, Mary set about recording life in Catalonia. Using a second-hand newsreel camera that a friend acquired for her, she and her young crew soon became a familiar sight on the streets of Barcelona. Mary's first aim was to show how international socialism was unifying behind the cause – the arrival of military supplies and food aid from Soviet Russia and the gathering of young volunteers come to fight in the International Brigades. But she also filmed more peaceful scenes, going out into the towns, villages and countryside to record how the Catalans lived in this brave, and dangerous, new world.

Then, in 1937, war reached out to Mary Willoughby and her children in Barcelona. Clive had travelled to Madrid to help defend the city against Franco's fascist forces. When the Republican government withdrew to Valencia, he stayed behind. On 8th February, as Franco tried to encircle Madrid, a nationalist bullet found the parson's son. He died instantly.

The news did not reach Mary and her children until nearly a month later. For a while she tried hoping it was a mistake and that her husband would turn up, back from the front unharmed. But March turned into April and May brought no miracle. The spring also brought vicious internal fighting in Barcelona when political tensions reached breaking point, with differences among the Republican coalition being settled in a bloodbath that left over five hundred dead. Mary accepted that she had lost her love. She had also had enough of Spain and the infighting that caused the left's eventual defeat.

The family returned to London. Fred joined his grandfather's printing business but Mary took Frances to Southampton where they boarded a boat for the United States. Mother and daughter made their way to Hollywood, where Mary had contacts in the film industry through her political connections. They lived there for nearly twenty years, only leaving in 1954 after Mary was blacklisted during Joseph McCarthy's anti-communist witch-hunt. Mary went south to Mexico. Frances – then in her thirties – went further, travelling to Australia where she met Ralph Reid, a millionaire farmer and owner of some of the biggest sheep stations in New South Wales. It was as unexpected a match as that of her parents had been but they were married three months later.

For the next twenty-five years, Mrs Reid lived in Bourke – a pretty but isolated town that became the Australian byword for anywhere remote. It was a simple life and one she loved. Ralph Reid was a good man but unfortunately a poor judge; when he died of a stroke in 1979, Frances found he had not left her rich. Despite the vast size of his holdings, Ralph Reid had wasted most of his inherited wealth on unsuccessful investments. The resulting debts accounted for almost the entire value of his property. Frances did not attempt to save their farming empire; there were no children and Australia held no value with Ralph gone. She sold up and – for the first time in forty-one years – headed home.

Back in England, Frances spent a little while deciding what to do. She had never kept in touch with the Willoughby side of the family and the Glover family had been a victim of the Blitz. She had distant relations but no immediate family. The remnants of Ralph Reid's fortune would keep her in moderate comfort but not forever.

Drawn by the city's reputation as a militant hotbed, she moved to Findo's hometown and began to study as a librarian. She bought a small house and, after completing her training, started working for the city council. The job was ideal. It gave her direct contact with people – for, after growing up in her mother's shadow and spending a quarter-century among the gum trees and sheep of the Australian outback, Frances had found her vocation: the gospel of information. She still believed passionately in the revolution but knew it would never come while nine-tenths of the population had no idea what it was missing. People had to be made to think and the route to questioning was knowledge. Television had become the new opium of the masses but books still made people use their own brains and create their own thoughts.

Frances, despite missing much of a conventional education, had spent most of her life with a book close to hand and found it hard to imagine not reading, whether to widen her learning or for entertainment. Books contained information and ideas and, for Frances Reid, the right to knowledge was sacred. But she was constantly amazed by how few people even seemed to understand its importance. She was also horrified when she began to realise how – in a country that still regarded itself as the centre of the civilised world – so many people were so badly educated. Not long into her new job, Frances came to the conclusion that many in the city, particularly its poorest and most hard-pressed inhabitants, were at least as ignorant of the world as the average Australian farm labourer, itinerant Californian worker or Catalan peasant.

That was why when Findo was brought through her door one morning in August, Frances Reid asked no questions but took up the cause of his education with the same passion that had always fuelled her life.

12. Finding refuge

Fort Hawley proved a red herring. Work on the military complex began in 1757 and lasted, on and off, for over twenty years. Originally, detailed plans were drawn up that included extensive fortifications surrounding large barracks, officers' quarters, training grounds, armouries and storerooms capable of holding enough supplies to support a large army through several months of campaigning. If built, the fort would have dramatically increased the city's status, turning it into a key military stronghold. The defences were planned on an ambitious scale and following the latest design, a system developed a few years earlier at the school for military engineering at Mézières in France.

But less than half the defensive walls and ditches were ever constructed and most of the buildings got no further than being marked out on the ground. The project was finally abandoned in 1779 when the site was sold off to raise funds for the war against the rebel colonists in North America. The land was bought by the Earl of Garvock who used the site to build the grand house that later became the city's further education college. The earl incorporated some of the part-finished ditches and walls into the grounds of the house, creating a system of fishponds and ornamental water features once quite famous.

The stretch of wall that Findo had discovered was the only remaining segment of Fort Hawley's walls still to be seen – the only other surviving portion of fortifications having been buried beneath the science wing built at Garvock College in 1963.

Frances Reid broke the news to Findo during their first afternoon of study together. The librarian had not heard of Fort Hawley previously but it did not take her long to find the information. She even managed to find an old copy of the plans, showing the design of the fort. An accompanying map showed how the fort was strategically placed, protected on two sides by the steep ground dropping down to the curving river. (None of them appreciated the significance of the fort's position; on the opposite side of the river from the city, it had been placed there not to protect the inhabitants but to guard against potential enemies marching south into England.)

Findo was disappointed but Fort Hawley was soon forgotten.

"You know there was another castle?" asked Mrs Reid.

"No."

"Another one?" said Abby. "Where?"

Mrs Reid shook her head, closing the book in front of them. "I'm not sure. There's nothing in here, this history is all far too modern, but I remember reading about it somewhere. Let me go and see if I can find the book it was in."

Findo ducked through the broken window, trying to avoid the fragments of glass that still stabbed out from the frame. Once inside, he stood up cautiously. The movement disturbed several pigeons. A couple of feathers tumbled through the shadowed air as the birds fluttered among the guano-spattered beams above.

Findo ignored the pigeons and looked at what lay before him. He was on the upper floor of an old pumping station, built on a pocket of low-lying land beside the River Allonby where the city's main water supply crossed the river. The Victorian building had been in use for over ninety years and was only finally decommissioned in 1973, when a new pumping station was built a quarter mile away. Since then, the stone-and-brick edifice had been left to go derelict.

No attempt had ever been made to demolish the pumping station; the site was no use for anything else and the building too solid to be easily knocked down. It had been stripped out when it was decommissioned. The water board had bricked up most entrances to the building and fixed a metal plate across the only remaining door, the key to which had been lost a few years later.

The pumping station's site was roughly triangular. To the west was the river. About fifty feet above and behind on the north-east side ran Stewart Road, the dual carriageway into the city centre. And to the south were the enormous masonry stumps of the city's fourteenth-century castle.

Findo had got to the pumping station's window by crawling along an old cast iron pipe that came out of the bank below Stewart Road. The pipe disappeared into the wall of the building at first floor level. However, a rowan sapling growing from a nearby crack in the brickwork had allowed Findo to swing himself round into the recess of a nearby window.

Now, he weighed up the prospects. The floor inside was more or less intact but had gaping holes in places. The wooden planks were sodden and greenery sprouted from some of the most rotten sections. Broken roof tiles lay amongst the bird-droppings and wind-blown litter. Through the holes in the floor he could also see the main room below: a gloomy, wet and empty hall, stained with rust and moss.

But Findo had not come for the pumping station. He had come for the castle. Not much was left standing but what there was sounded much more promising than the fort.

Findo had spent most of the morning surveying the ground. The ruins stood beside the roundabout where Stewart Road joined the Castle Drive ring road. Despite being a scheduled monument – hailed in the city's tourism propaganda as a historic treasure – what remained was hardly impressive. The two surviving towers were nearly full height but their entrances had been closed up decades ago and the only features to be seen from outside were a few wind and rain-eroded window slits. Between the towers was a section of wall that was about twenty feet high but had lost its battlements long ago. The only other part of the castle still intact was an arched gateway that now stood alone in a flowerbed full of limp flowers, fag ends and empty beer cans. Nearby, a grating covered a litter-filled pit that had once been a well.

The castle had been built in the early 1300s, the work of Robert de Warenne, younger brother of one of northern England's more powerful barons. At the time, the city had been a small town, built around a market and handful of wharves used by merchant and fishing boats that came up the Allonby when the tide was high. The castle was a useful base on the main north–south route and briefly became a minor outpost of Plantagenet power. Before being finished in 1323, it withstood one minor siege. Over the following century the castle saw action a couple more times but was never severely tested. And by the time Scotland and England were unified under the Stuarts, its importance had declined, overtaken by larger, more strategically placed fortresses.

Its moment finally came in 1640, during the conflict that was the precursor to the English Civil War. Following Charles I's attempts to impose Anglican forms of worship on an unwilling Scotland, the Presbyterians first rioted, then raised an army and attacked the north of England. In the campaign that followed, the castle was seized by rebels, then attacked by royalist forces come to put down the uprising. The siege lasted days; the castle was held by only a handful of Scots and the commander of the English forces, Sir Francis Ripon, was disinclined to mess around. Using cannon brought up river by boat, the royalists blew down the gates and stormed the castle in a dawn assault, putting all inside to the sword.

Ripon was unwilling to spare the manpower to garrison the captured building. Instead, he decided to spoil the castle. Its fortifications were mined and the resulting explosions shattered the keep and blew out most of the walls. The damage was never repaired and, over the next two centuries, the ruins were regularly plundered – treated by the city's residents as a convenient source of building material.

Now, a casual observer looking at the castle would have assumed that the freestanding gateway, two towers and single stretch of crumbling wall were all that still existed. But Mrs Reid's research had revealed that there was more than immediately met the eye. The history section in the city guide had led her to the annual reports of the municipal archaeology unit, stored on the library's microfilm archive (something that mesmerised Findo when he saw how much information could be held on a single roll).

The publication for 1962 – when work started on the ring road – contained a detailed survey of the castle, as well as the result of various digs around the ruins and details of finds now stored in the city museum. The report also provided plans of what remained of the castle, with cross-sections of the towers. The diagrams showed a corridor running inside the base of the wall and four adjoining rooms, including a large kitchen, although it was unclear whether these were still accessible.

Findo's own reconnaissance had also shown promise. He had crossed the Allonby at Byrnebridge then followed the river back, through a dank plantation of conifers, to the bank facing the castle. From there he had been able to see that the walls were much higher on the outside, rising over forty feet from the tide-stained rocks at the edge of the river. There were also several more windows to see – as well as an opening into the broken side of the northern tower. The hole was about twenty feet above ground but looked as if it was only a few feet from the pumping station built beside it.

Findo stepped forwards carefully. The wet planks were slippery and there was nothing to hold onto. He shuffled around one particularly rotten-looking spot and tried not to think about how far it was down to the floor of the hall below.

He had decided to take the direct route across the pumping station floor rather than follow the edge round. Although the walls gave the impression of protection he was not fooled – if a section of floor did collapse it would make no difference where he was standing. The route around the walls was also longer and there were holes in the floor to navigate whichever way he went.

It was about fifty feet to the window opposite but Findo knew he had to get across the building somehow. He had tried getting around the pumping station at ground level but the back had been built right into the bank and the front stuck out into the river. Except by swimming, there was no other way to get to the base of the castle tower.

Findo was about halfway across the floor when he came to a halt. A small wilderness covered the section of floor ahead – tufts of grass, weeds and fungi grew from the wood beneath a large hole in the roof. He stared warily at the patch. It was too wide to jump and Findo was uncertain of keeping his footing even if he made it to the other side.

He looked around. Immediately to the left of the rotten section was an open hole, while to the right the floor was covered with a pile of loose slates that had cascaded from above.

Findo edged towards the slates. He thought about trying his footing on them but noticed a metal bar lying a couple of feet away. He crouched down and, balancing on his fingertips, reached out with one foot and hooked the bar. He dragged it closer and picked up the three-foot length of rusted pipe.

Still crouched, Findo reached towards the slates with the bar. He prodded the centre of the pile – then drew back hastily as it disappeared. The thin sheets of stone had been balanced over another gap in the floor, held in place by a broken strip of roof lath. There was a rattle, followed by echoing crashes as the slates fell through the hole and shattered on the hard floor way below.

Findo swallowed. He looked at the hole that would have claimed him if he had tried walking across the slates. Once his pulse had finally slowed down again, he edged forward and crouched closer to the edge of the gap where the slates had been. It was only three planks wide and the wood either side looked firm. Eventually, he stood back up and took a long look at the stretch of floor leading to the opposite window. Then – gripping the metal bar in both hands as a balancing rod – he took the gap in one large stride. He did not stop but let his momentum carry him on and ran full pelt for the safety of the window recess. Heart hammering, he made it and sagged down onto the solidity of the lintel.

The way into the castle itself proved much less daunting, despite being in mid-air. The window on the far side of the pumping station opened onto the damp space separating the side of the nineteenth-century municipal building and the foundations of the fourteenth-century castle. Below lay a drop of over twenty feet onto slimy, broken rocks. But the gap between the buildings was barely three feet wide and almost directly opposite a section of broken stonework, damaged when a couple of blocks were blown out from the base of the tower when it was mined by Ripon's royalist forces. The breach created had been further eroded by rainfall over the centuries. It was the opening that Findo had seen from the other side of the river and that had inspired him to make the trip across the pumping station's rotten floor.

Findo jumped across to the castle without hesitation; physical risks had never disturbed him in the same way as the violence that had surrounded his childhood. He pulled himself quickly into the gap in the stonework, scraping one hand across the masonry as he grabbed for a hold. His feet found their place among the stones and he began to climb.

The way up was easy. The missing blocks had left regular corners behind and the eroded backfill provided additional cracks and crannies. It took less than a minute to climb up through the notch in the stonework and then Findo was sliding through the wall itself and into the gloom of the castle's interior.

Inside the tower, Findo slid his hand inside his jacket and pulled round the bag that had been slung across his back. He tugged the top open and felt his way through the contents until he found the camper's head torch stolen the day before. Findo took it out, fitted the straps around his head so the light perched above his forehead and twisted it on.

The torch beam revealed a scene of devastation. Concealed within the tower lay heaps of broken masonry. The jumble of shattered stonework covered the entire thirty-foot base of the tower.

Findo gazed around in surprise; it was not what he had been expecting. The ragged opening through which he had climbed had originally been an arrow slit overlooking the Allonby. Inside was one of the rooms where Sir Francis Ripon's men had placed the barrels of gunpowder used to blow up the castle. Some explosives, however, had not been well laid and, consequently, had not been enough to destroy this tower. Rather than splitting open the walls, the blast had been mainly directed upwards. The explosion had ripped through the interior of the tower, demolishing the three floors above and bringing them crashing down – as well as blowing out the stonework around the arrow slit. The weight of the falling masonry had collapsed the floor of the lower room, sending the rubble into the cellar beneath. What was left was a cellar full of broken blocks, and a hollow tower, capped only by its roof and a single upper room that could no longer be reached.

Findo turned his head slowly, the beam of light following his gaze upwards as he studied the soaring space and the devastation that had been wreaked to create it. He spotted several small openings in the curved wall of the tower, as well as the stumps of broken buttresses, shattered staircases and the hanging mouths of stranded fireplaces. In the eastern side of the tower he also noticed two bricked-up doorways that would once have led around into the next section of wall.

Only when he had finished inspecting the rest of the tower did Findo look across to see what lay on the south wall. He was not disappointed. A pile of battered masonry partly obscured his view but he could still see the open doorway leading into darkness.

He picked his way across the litter of rubble with eager glee. The blocks had settled over the years and the going was relatively easy. Even without Findo's torch, it was not entirely dark in the tower and a thin covering of moss and lichens grew over some parts of the stone. It only took a couple of minutes to cross the room and then he was standing in the doorway that led south.

The corridor ahead curved slightly. It was only a couple of feet wide and not much more than five feet high but plenty big enough for Findo. With a last glance back at the interior of the tower, he set off. The flagstones beneath his feet were level and dry, covered only with a thin layer of dust. There was no light in the passage apart from the beam of his torch and the air was deathly still, with a coolness that made the boy shiver slightly.

Findo turned his torch beam from side to side as he cautiously followed the passage. The wall on his right was constructed from massive blocks of sandstone, each about four feet in width. On his left, however, the wall was built from much smaller blocks of a coarser finish. The ceiling above was square, made of slabs of rock similar to the passage floor.

He had gone about twenty paces when he saw the outline of a doorway to his left and hurried forward. The opening had a low arch and went forward for a couple of feet but then Findo was forced to a halt. A solid sheet of concrete confronted him. He stared at it in frustration for a moment then shrugged and turned away. Whatever had been there was obviously no longer accessible, presumably buried beneath the flowerbeds next to the roundabout.

He continued along the gentle curve of the passageway. A little further on he came to three steps where the corridor rose to a new level and turned more sharply to the left. Just beyond that point a narrow staircase led up to the right. At the top was a small chamber containing two arrow slits. Findo turned off his torch and looked through each in turn. The openings looked down over the Allonby and its opposite bank, one upstream and one downstream. He guessed

101

that he was midway between the two towers, at a point he had noticed from outside where the wall bent slightly to follow the direction of the small cliff on which it was built.

Findo looked around with satisfaction at the small chamber then dug into his bag and pulled out a can of Pepsi and two Mars bars. He sat with his back against the wall between the two arrow slits and ate his lunch. Once he was finished, he stuffed the empty can and the wrappers through the northern arrow slit, pushing them out to drop onto the mud at the base of the castle wall.

His next discovery was more unexpected. He was walking along the next stretch of corridor when his light caught a pale object lying in the middle of the floor. Findo paused, uncertain. He advanced warily for a few paces, trying to make out what it was, before suddenly realising that he was looking at a discarded newspaper.

For a moment he was disappointed, thinking that the castle was not as untouched as he had hoped. But when he picked up the damp, folded paper he realised that its presence only confirmed his hopes. The paper was a copy of the *Daily Herald*, dated 2nd May 1962 – with a front-page story about the arrival of Prince Charles as a pupil at Gordonstoun School. Findo looked at the date, realising that it coincided with the end of the archaeological dig at the castle and the start of work on the new road system.

He put the paper back down where he had found it and moved on. A few paces further on was the entrance to another concrete-sealed doorway. Just beyond, a flight of steps led up to a final section of corridor. Findo followed it to the doorway into the second tower – where he stopped and laughed.

13. Rogan josh

The wail of sirens had become increasingly familiar around the Meadowfields estate since the housing project was built eleven years earlier. Once, the scheme had been seen as an answer to the problem of the city's high-rise slums, already infamous as a breeding ground for criminals and drug addicts. Some had seen areas like Tibbermore as a cancer gnawing at the city's heart and believed the only cure was their complete excision; but more liberal minds thought the answer was to create a healthier environment where those with the greatest need could learn the values of community and citizenship.

And so, Meadowfields had been built, a new estate of mixed housing complete with play areas, community facilities, its own shops, health centre and church. To begin with it had looked as if the idea might work. Young families and single parents were the first to gain places in the project's low-cost accommodation. The first residents were reasonably receptive to the ideals of the scheme's proponents but better housing alone could not compensate for unemployment, poverty and ignorance. Budget cuts at the city council also meant that although the estate did get two community workers there was little money to support the services they were supposed to provide. The community centre stayed an empty, bare hall and the crèche never got the toys and play equipment promised.

Then other arrivals followed the first wave of occupants. Not all of these got in following honest methods and their presence quickly began to change attitudes, police statistics and the look of the estate. Stolen cars began to appear in previously quiet streets. Discarded needles littered the play areas and other public places. Graffiti adorned the walls of public buildings, then private houses. A brothel opened in one house, then came stories of crack dens and shebeens operating from others. A petrol bomb wrecked the corner shop operated by a Pakistani couple after they refused to pay up when offered an 'insurance deal' by two local men. Soon after that, grilles appeared over the windows of the shops, the community centre and the church. The health centre, which had been burgled fifteen times in twenty-eight days, was closed down when the authorities decided to reorganise services.

Now, the sound of five sirens ululated through the air as police vehicles converged on the estate. Two were in direct pursuit of a Mercedes sports car; the other three had already moved to block the road ahead and force the stolen vehicle into a cul-de-sac.

The Mercedes was a bright red SL 320 soft-top. The convertible had been reported stolen only half an hour before being spotted by a police patrol cruising the Castle Drive ring road. The Mercedes was tailed for a couple of miles as it looped around the north of the city. Then, as a backup vehicle joined the first police car, the patrol team attempted to get the driver of the Mercedes to pull over. Their rulebook manoeuvres were pointless; the window of the sports car slid down and an arm directed a one-fingered salute at the policemen before the Mercedes accelerated away.

During the ensuing chase, the Mercedes went the wrong way around the Campfield roundabout before hitting speeds of up to seventy-three miles per hour as it shot down the middle of Albert Parade. The car swung into the pedestrianised section of Harris Street, forcing shoppers to dive for safety. After that, the pursuing officers lost the Mercedes for a while but it was spotted again by a police helicopter.

The chase resumed along Stewart Road, the Mercedes going counter-clockwise at the roundabout by the old castle, before heading west towards Meadowfields. However, that move – a regular route for the city's car-jackers – had been predicted and, by the time the Mercedes turned into Willow Avenue, three police vehicles were ahead of it.

The SL's 3.2 litre, V6 engine purred with power as the Mercedes accelerated to over one hundred miles per hour along Willow Avenue and the convertible soon left the two pursuing police cars way behind. But rounding the bend by the Oak House pub, the driver saw the roadblock and slammed on his brakes. The Mercedes fishtailed wildly on the damp road before the driver regained control. The sports car accelerated again and swung on screaming tyres into Rowan Close. The cul-de-sac was nearly a quarter of a mile long and the Mercedes was lost from view but the officers at the roadblock sighed with relief.

Two vehicles immediately set off in pursuit, followed by one of the cars that had chased the Mercedes into Meadowfields. The other vehicle from the roadblock drove on along Willow Avenue and took the next turning into Beechwoods Drive, ready for any attempt by the driver to escape on foot. The fifth police car did a U-turn and went back onto Stewart Road to patrol the southern edge of Meadowfields. The helicopter hovered overhead; ready to guide the forces on the ground.

The Mercedes skidded to a halt in a parking bay between two groups of houses. Mickey Dunn got out and calmly lit a cigarette. Then he unscrewed the petrol cap on the Mercedes, bounced the corner of the car and walked to the corner of the nearest house. He took a long drag on the cigarette and flicked it at the sports car, the cigarette hitting the paintwork just below the open fuel cap.

Mickey ducked around the corner just as the embers at the tip of the cigarette ignited the rising vapour. The explosion that followed shook the air and a ball of flame engulfed the Mercedes.

As the burning car settled down on its flaming tyres, Mickey trotted into the shared gardens behind the nearest houses. He could hear the sirens of the approaching cars and began to move faster, running for a wooden fence at the back of the next parking bay along the close. There were two vehicles, both wheel-less and raised on blocks, sitting in the bay. Mickey jumped on the bonnet of the nearest and leapt for the fence. He pulled himself over and dropped into the garden of the house on the other side.

An Alsatian barked from the property to the right but Mickey ignored it. He ran up the garden, hurdling an abandoned child's trike and various other toys scattered across the grass before diving down the passageway at the side of the house. There was a tall gate at the far end of the passage and Mickey stopped. He opened the wooden door carefully and peeked out.

The door led to the front garden, which opened onto Beechwoods Drive. Mickey moved out cautiously, closed the door and crouched behind a dustbin. He concealed himself just in time. A moment later the police car that was patrolling this escape route drove slowly by. Mickey watched it go, waiting until it was out of sight before sprinting for the other side of the road. He dashed into an alleyway that led between two houses and began to jog along the path – not realising that he was being watched from the helicopter above.

Mickey's route took him around the end of another close and into Fox Place, a terrace of houses at the northern end of Willow Avenue. He stopped for a moment by a block of garages and listened. The sound of sirens had ceased for the moment and all he could hear was the noise of the helicopter, chirring away in the grey sky above. The machine was about a quarter of a mile off to the south-west and was moving northwards in a wide arc. Mickey watched it for a couple of minutes and then strolled up to the third house in the terrace and rapped on the door.

Otis opened the door cautiously then nodded when he saw who it was and gestured inside with a flick of his woolly head.

"Alright, Mickey?"

"Sound, Otis. How's tricks?"

"Ah, you know."

"Yeah."

Mickey dug in the pockets of his puffer jacket. "Got the tape of that new album you wanted, the Soup Dragons one."

Otis grinned widely. "Cool."

Mickey continued to check his pockets. "Oh fuck."

"What's up?"

"Haven't got the fucking thing."

Mickey shook his head and patted Otis apologetically on the arm. "Sorry, mate. Must have left it in the car."

Otis shrugged. "Don't matter. I'll go get it if you want."

"Er, no," said Mickey. "Not much point." He slapped Otis around the shoulders. "But don't worry. I'll get you another. No problem. Anyway, how come you asked me? I thought your brother would be the one to get anything like that."

"Findo?" said Otis. "Nah. He's hardly around these days; don't see much of him at the moment. He turned up this morning but that's the first I seen him all week."

"How's that then?" asked Mickey. "What's he up to? Got a girlfriend stashed away somewhere?"

Otis shrugged. "Who knows? He wouldn't tell me if he had. He never lets on about anything." Otis nodded towards the kitchen. "Want a brew?"

Mickey nodded. "Yeah, that'd be good. Jimmy Ray about?"

"Nah," said Otis over one shoulder as he disappeared off into the kitchen. "Gone off to Carlisle with some blokes he met in the nick. Said something about a job. Should be back Tuesday or Wednesday."

Mickey nodded and pushed open the door to the lounge. Inside, Findo and his sister Louise were sitting on the floor playing cards. There was no sign of any other members of the family. Mickey reached into the back pocket of his trousers and pulled out a crumpled envelope. He tossed it to Findo.

"There you go. Latest letter."

Findo grabbed it eagerly. "Thanks."

"What's that, Fin?" said his youngest sister. "Is that from Billy?"

Findo stuffed the envelope inside his shirt and nodded slowly. "Yeah." He looked up at Mickey. "You after Jimmy Ray?"

"Was but Otis says he's not here."

"Yeah, back Tuesday or Wednesday if he doesn't get caught."

Mickey smiled. "You reckon he might?"

Findo shrugged. "Well, he's not too bright is he? And I saw one of the guys supposed to have set up this job; he made Jimmy Ray seem smart."

Mickey laughed and was about to say something when the sound of shouts from outside caught his attention. He dived at the window and got there just in time to stop Louise from pulling back the net curtains.

"Hold on." Mickey peered through the thin material. "Shit!" he said. "Cops."

Two police cars had pulled up in the road at one end of Fox Place. A third vehicle was stopped a little way up the road in the other direction. Four officers were already on the pavement and one was talking into his radio and looking up at the sky. The shouting was coming from three teenagers a little way further down Willow Avenue who were doing loud imitations of pigs and police sirens.

Findo glanced out of the window. "They after you, Mickey?"

The teenager grinned. "Reckon."

"What for?"

"Nicked a Merc," he said gleefully. "Real beauty. Wankers chased me right through town. I dumped it down Rowan Close, near Susie Piper's place." He frowned. "Bloody jelly must have spotted me. Told them where to come."

Mickey watched the police outside. They were gathering together and starting to head towards Fox Place. The burly officer in the lead was carrying a sledgehammer.

"You'd better hide, Mickey," said Louise.

Mickey shook his head. "Nah, love. No point, they'll have your door down in two seconds if you don't answer it."

He headed for the backdoor, pushing past Otis who was just coming in with a handful of mugs of tea. "Looks like I'm off, mate," said Mickey. "But you're about to get some new visitors – they might fancy a brew."

Otis looked blank.

"But if you've got any stash upstairs you might want to flush it," said Mickey, pointing to the shapes coming up the path. "That's the bizzies out there."

Otis dropped the mugs and shot upstairs. Mickey nipped smartly into the kitchen and opened the back door just as a loud knocking came from the front. Mickey ran across the small courtyard at the rear of the house. He opened the wooden gate set into the wall and stepped through into a service alley.

"Oi!"

"Round here!"

The shouts came from either end of the alley. Mickey looked left and right in despair. He was trapped. Then an arm pulled him back into the courtyard and he looked round in surprise as Findo reached past him to close and bolt the gate.

Findo grinned. "Want to get out of here?"

"Yeah!"

"Follow me."

Findo jumped onto a stack of empty beer crates and pulled himself onto the roof of a small shed in a corner of the yard. Mickey heard the kitchen door opening and followed smartly. He reached the top of the shed just in time to dodge hands that grabbed for his ankle. Findo helped tug him up and then turned away. He leapt clean across the alleyway, landing on the flat roof of a garage block opposite and ran off across the wet asphalt.

Mickey ignored the shouts as he followed Findo. He raced across the roof, pulse pounding as the joy of the chase began to fire his limbs into motion.

Mickey caught up with Findo at the far end of the roof and skidded to a halt. Glancing back over his shoulder, he saw the policeman who had tried to grab his legs standing on the roof of the shed, about to follow them onto the roof of the garages.

"Here," said Findo. "Help me with this."

A long scaffolding plank lay along the edge of the roof. Findo had started to pick it up and was sliding it out over the ten-foot gap that separated the garages on which they stood and the next, identical block. Mickey bent to help and together they lifted the plank and shot it forward so that it rested across the gap. Findo ran over it, the plank dipping gently.

"Come on."

Mickey's eyes widened. "What the fuck!" He ran across, just keeping his balance as the plank bowed under his greater weight.

As soon as Mickey was over, Findo grabbed the plank and threw the end over the edge of the roof so that it fell onto the tarmac below. Mickey held one finger up at the policeman running towards them.

Findo did not wait but ran on across the next roof, heading for the far end. "Come on!" he shouted.

Mickey followed and they reached the end together. Findo grabbed the edge and dropped down, hitting the wet grass below with a thud. Mickey joined him a second later and together they dodged behind a burnt-out Transit van. Findo crouched down and began to reach under the edge of the wreck.

"What now?" asked Mickey. "They won't give up that easy."

Findo pulled out a crowbar and swivelled around on the balls of his feet. "Don't worry. Another minute and we'll be gone." He shoved the blunt end of the crowbar into the edge of a round manhole cover. "Help me with this."

Mickey frowned and slid his fingers under the lip of the heavy metal plate as it slowly lifted from its position. He lifted the manhole cover up to reveal a concrete shaft going straight down.

"What we doing?"

Findo grinned. He shoved the crowbar inside his jacket and slipped past Mickey, lowering his feet into the shaft. "Going down." He climbed in rapidly, quickly disappearing into the shadowy tube. "Make sure you put the lid back once you're in."

Mickey shook his head in amazement and prepared to follow. He fumbled awkwardly for his first footing and then found the ladder of offset plates sticking out of the side of the shaft. Once he had got his body inside, Mickey reached up for the manhole cover and dragged it over his head. Just before he lowered it into place, he heard the sound of running feet somewhere on the other side of the Transit.

It was pitch dark for a few seconds and Mickey was starting to curse Findo quietly when a light appeared from below. He looked over one shoulder to see Findo standing beneath him with some kind of lamp strapped to his head.

"Hey," said Mickey. "What's that on your head? You look like a fucking miner – except someone's nicked the helmet and just left you the torch."

Findo shrugged and reached up. "I'll turn it off if you want."

Mickey scrambled down the last few rungs and stepped down beside Findo. "Nah. It's alright. You keep it on, mate."

He looked around. The shaft above them was about fifteen feet high. It had brought them down into a small concrete tunnel that ran past at a gentle slope. A steady trickle of water flowed along the middle of the curved floor.

"Where are we?"

"Storm drain," said Findo. "Goes up through the estate." He gestured to his left, down the tunnel. "We'd better move though, just in case they work out where we went."

Mickey followed, ducking his head slightly to avoid the ceiling. "Where we going, then?"

"The river," said Findo. "There's a bigger tunnel bit further down here. Goes right down to the river, comes out the other side of

Stewart Road, not far from Byrnebridge. It'll be dark in a bit. You can get out and nip over the river. Go find an alibi or something."

Mickey laughed. "You are fucking something else, Findo."

Five minutes later they stood together and watched the stream pouring through the grille. The water cascaded over the concrete lip, tumbling over some filthy stones and a dumped shopping trolley as it flowed down to join the Allonby.

Mickey took out a cigarette and lit it. He offered one to Findo, who shook his head. "Don't want to try?"

"Promised Billy I wouldn't."

"She alright then?"

"Think so. Sounded okay in her last letter but that was a few months back. Don't know what's in the new one."

Mickey nodded. "She still on the move?"

"Guess so. She said something about going to France last time she wrote."

"You ever think about going off?"

Findo shrugged. "Sometimes. Not sure I want to. Wouldn't mind seeing Billy again though."

They were silent for a while as Mickey smoked. When he had finished his cigarette, he flicked the butt out into the stream. It hit one of the metal bars of the grille and bounced off in a shower of sparks.

"What you up to tonight, then?" asked Mickey. "Going to see your girlfriend?"

"What girlfriend?"

"I dunno. Otis seemed to think you'd got one. Said they never see anything of you any more."

Findo shrugged, his expression lost in the gloom inside the tunnel. "Got my own place now. I don't go back much. Just go round sometimes to see Otis and Lou."

"What about the others?"

"What about them?"

Mickey grinned. "Well, Jimmy Ray's alright."

Findo gave a snort. "He's a thick twat with a nasty temper. He's a miserable bastard when he's sober and even worse when he's drunk. Only time he's alright is between the second pint and the fifth one – or when Otis gets him stoned. Apart from that, I keep out of his way."

Mickey laughed. "Yeah, suppose you got a point. He can be a bit risky. Still, he's useful if you need someone like that."

Findo frowned. "What did you want him for?"

Mickey touched the side of his nose. "Muldoon had an offer for him. Apart from that, couldn't tell you. Anyway, what about this place of yours? How come you got a new gaffe?"

Findo shrugged. "Just wanted my own place. Bit more peaceful than sharing with her, Jimmy Ray and Rob."

"Your own place? What you got?"

Findo smiled. "Oh it's just an old building, nothing much."

"What, some sort of squat?"

"Yeah."

Mickey watched Findo for a couple of minutes then grinned. "Don't give much away do you?"

Findo shrugged and looked at the darkening sky outside. "So, what are you doing tonight?"

Mickey smiled and rubbed his stomach. "Eating curry."

"Curry?"

"Yeah," said Mickey. "Meeting some mates down Packhouse Street later. Then we're off to the Taj Mahal for a curry."

Findo frowned. "You like curry then?"

Mickey laughed. "Do I like curry? Too fucking right! Can't beat a good rogan josh, especially after a few lagers. Lots of pilau rice, some naan breads and loads of onion bahjis. I love rogan josh."

"Is that a hot one?"

Mickey shrugged. "Nah, sort of medium – quite spicy but not one of those ones that blow your head off. Not like a vindaloo. Some of my mates have them but they're too much. Rot your guts too. Me, I like rogan josh. Tandooris are alright too and I like a good balti but lamb rogan josh is the best." He looked at Findo. "What about you? You like curry?"

"Not particularly."

"What's your favourite then?"

Findo paused, considering. "Deep-fried Mars bars."

"What?"

"Deep-fried Mars bars. They do them in the chippy down Corporation Road."

Mickey shook his head. "That's gross." He laughed. "Fucking hell! Deep-fried Mars bars. You're weird, Findo."

Mickey moved forwards, stepping carefully as he made his way across the sloping brickwork that ran down the side of the underground watercourse. He reached the point where the stream emerged into the Allonby. The metal grille that covered the entrance to the tunnel had thick bars reaching from floor to ceiling. But a section of brickwork next to the right-hand side of the grille was missing and there was just enough room for Mickey to squeeze out through the gap. He pushed through and scrambled up onto the bank.

Above was a low wall running along the side of Stewart Road. A couple of hundred yards downstream was Byrnebridge and Mickey could see the steady flow of cars and lorries crossing the Allonby. The streetlights were already on and only the faintest hint of daylight remained in the sky.

Mickey looked back down at Findo. "Why don't you come? You can show me your place then come out for a beer and a curry. I reckon I owe you something after today. My mates will kill themselves when I tell them how you got me away from the cops. They'd love to meet you."

14. Dangerous takings

Cold air poured into Findo's lungs. He drank it greedily, closing his eyes and turning his face up to the damp night.

After about twenty seconds, he stepped away from the doorway and into the alley. It was wet and dark; the only light came from the city glow reflected off the clouds and a streetlamp down at the alley's left-hand end. Puddles glimmered faintly and the dim shape of a row of wheelie bins loomed against one wall, their position given away by the stale smell from the empty bottles inside.

Findo stepped uncertainly forwards, weaving slightly. His face set into a scowl as he tried to fix his concentration in one place so that his head would stop spinning.

Mickey watched from the doorway behind, a sympathetic smile on his face. "You alright, kid?"

Findo nodded slowly.

"Wanna chuck?"

Findo considered the idea. "Maybe."

"Go and lean against the wall. Don't fight it. You'll feel better."

The boy made uncertainly for the opposite wall, reaching for it when he was still a couple of yards away. Arms outstretched, he propped himself against the bricks and looked down at the dark tarmac. He swallowed a couple of times.

"Go for it," said Mickey.

Findo stood propped a while longer then turned to speak to Mickey. He opened his mouth but then caught a whiff of the smell from the bins. He turned his head just in time to avoid his arm and vomited against the wall. Partly digested crisps and lager splattered against the brickwork, splashing down around his feet, accompanied by the acid smell of bile.

Mickey chuckled and disappeared back into the pub. He returned a minute later as Findo was levering himself away from the wall. Mickey walked over and held out the pint of water. "Get some of this down you."

Findo took it gratefully and glugged several mouthfuls, then spat. He rinsed his mouth again then drank some more water.

Mickey took back the glass. "Better?"

Findo nodded silently. He took several deep breaths and looked around. The world seemed to have stabilised a little and, although weak at the knees from throwing up, he felt a little more comfortable.

"Any more water?"

Findo shook his head. "No."

"You want to come back in?"

"No."

"Hang on then."

Mickey disappeared back into the Turk's Head. He was back a little while later without more water. He grinned at Findo. "Guess you're not a big drinker yet."

Findo shook his head. "I was okay after one."

Mickey nodded. "Maybe it was the crisps, eh?"

Findo shrugged. "Could be."

"Still," said Mickey, "if you will eat stuff like prawn cocktail I'm not surprised. That and deep-fried Mars bars – you eat some weird shit, Findo."

Findo closed his eyes and took some more deep breaths then began to walk slowly up the alley, away from Packhouse Street. Mickey followed, watching Findo's cautious, slightly exaggerated gait.

They were in Hobbes Town, the area just to the west of the city centre. Behind them lay the main road leading from Alexander Cross out towards Tibbermore and East Park. It was just after nine o'clock on a wet Monday evening in mid-December and Packhouse Street was starting to get busy. The fast food outlets were still quiet but the pubs and bars dotted along the road from Alexander Cross to the Castle Drive ring road were beginning to fill up. The drinking was so far fairly controlled – if reasonably urgent – and the hubbub of voices yet to be broken by the screams and yells that would erupt with increasing regularity as the night wore on.

The alley beside the Turk's Head made a dog-leg turn and then reached a side road running parallel with Packhouse Street. Opposite was a small, unlit lane that led past a collection of mismatched buildings before disappearing into a tunnel beneath the main railway line.

As Findo watched, a doorway up the lane opened, spilling a pool of light into the gloom. Two large men carrying a limp bundle stepped out. They swung their arms back and launched their load into the air. The shape hit the ground with a thud and groaned as it rolled over. One of the two men stepped forward. He jabbed one finger at the figure at his feet.

"Now piss off and get out of here before he changes his mind. You've got two days."

The body in the road got up slowly, then scrambled to his feet and dodged as the man in the doorway swung a lazy kick. "Remember –

two days. That's all. You get the money here by the end of the day or we'll come and collect."

Findo watched as the evicted man broke into a shambling run and headed off towards the railway tunnel. The pair who had slung him out went back inside and closed the door.

Mickey gave a low laugh. "Poor fucker. Wouldn't want to be in his shoes."

Findo looked round at him. "Why? What was going on?"

Mickey pulled a face. "That's a Muldoon place. They do most of their business from there."

Findo looked at him with interest. "Really?"

"Yeah," said Mickey. "It's like, their main office. I don't know who that was they chucked out but he obviously owes them money and that's not good."

"What'll they do?"

Mickey snorted. "If you don't know, then you don't want to know. Just take my advice and never get in debt to the Muldoons. They're alright to work for; they look after their own. But don't ever take anything from them that you can't pay back – with interest." He looked at Findo's eyes. "And I'd stay well away from their place too. Don't go poking around – they don't like strangers nosing about, even kids."

Findo crouched in the wet grass at the side of the railway. He glanced in both directions as he listened. He still felt a little unsteady but the familiarity of a reconnaissance in enemy territory was helping to focus his mind.

He could hear traffic from Packhouse Street, voices and a clatter of empty crates from the rear of a pub somewhere. A dog barked in the distance. But no sound came from the railway.

He looked both ways along the track again then darted forward, jumping each rail as he came to it. There were only two lines and it was a straight section of track with no wires or points to avoid. He crossed quickly and dropped into another crouch on the other side.

A rough, weed-covered bank led down to a low wall dividing the railway from a derelict carpet store. Findo could see no windows but a fire door beckoned. He scuttled down the bank and hopped over the wall next to the building's emergency exit, jumping down onto a concrete walkway that ran along the side of the building.

Findo ignored the emergency door for a moment and checked the walkway. At the corner of the building was a long flight of steps leading down to the carpet store's front car park. The steps ended at a wire gate set into a fence. Strands of barbed wire ran along the top of the fence and there was a heavy chain linked around the gate.

Satisfied, Findo returned to the fire exit. It was closed and he started probing for weaknesses. The search did not take long. The owners of the building had cut corners; rather than use a proper external door at the emergency exit, they had used an interior door. It was a cheap one and the plywood outer surface was coming adrift. Findo pulled a long screwdriver from his jacket and dug under the left-hand corner of the plywood. The pins holding the thin sheet to the door's inner frame popped in a row and he was soon able to get a hand underneath, then a second, making sure his fingers slid between the points of the thin nails.

He worked his hands around the bottom and sides until half of the plywood was coming away. Then, holding the sheet to one side, Findo stretched his leg through the gap and delivered a series of sharp kicks. It only took a minute or so to force off the inner side of the door as well. Findo wrenched the outer sheet a little further and wormed his way behind it. With the outer surface of the door pushing against his back, he pulled away the remnants of the door's honeycomb cardboard interior and kicked at the inner sheet of plywood until it was hanging almost free.

And then he was inside, standing in a dusty corridor above the main storage areas. There were a couple of empty rooms to the right with open doors and streetlamps shone through their grimy windows, casting a washed-out orange light into the passage.

Findo glanced at the fire door. The plywood on the outside had bent most of the way back into place and he knew there was little chance of anyone spotting his entrance by daylight, let alone on a December night. He walked quietly through the carpet store's second floor. The building was empty and Findo looked around thoughtfully, marking it down as another potential hideaway. Below him was another layer of offices and then the ground floor showroom – now boarded up. The rear of the building was a warehouse, with loading bays at the back.

The corridor went past a staircase leading down to the first floor but Findo ignored it; he needed to stay high. Straight ahead were some toilets. The corridor also turned left, ending in another fire exit. Bolts had been fitted to the door but they opened easily enough. Findo carefully pressed the release bar and opened the door cautiously.

Outside was the flat roof above the building's warehouse section. Puddles lay across the surface. Findo could see skylights, a row of roof vents and the housing of an old air conditioning unit. It was darker on the roof than inside; there were no streetlamps in the lane at the rear and the offices blocked the light coming from the road at the front.

Findo opened the fire exit further and slipped out. The adjoining building was built right against the warehouse but was higher and had no windows along its side. He padded quietly along the wall of the bigger building, enjoying the security of the shadows but after a couple of hundred yards came to the back of the carpet warehouse without finding any way up, or into, next door.

He turned and went back along the roof, then crossed to the far side of the carpet store's offices. A metal ladder led up to the roof of the building's front section and Findo climbed it quickly. He hopped over the low parapet onto the roof and looked around warily but there was no sign of danger and he was now too high to be seen from the street below. Even so, he stayed hunched as he walked to the side of the carpet store.

He was now higher than the adjoining building but there was only a drop of about two feet onto its roof. He climbed over carefully and lowered himself down. Treading softly, he made his way to the front of the building and peered over.

The street was empty apart from a few parked cars on the far side. There were no pedestrians in view. At the front of the building a small pool of light spilled from a single ground floor window. None of the other windows had lights inside. It was the same as when he had looked from the street earlier. The lit window and door next to it advertised a taxicab company and were the only indication that the building was occupied.

After another good look, Findo backed away from the edge. He turned and began to make his way down the middle of the flat roof. Just as above the carpet warehouse, there were various vents and skylights set into the damp surface. But unlike the carpet store – and despite the fact that the light from the cab firm's entrance was the only sign of life from below – he could see a glow coming from several of the skylights.

Findo padded towards the nearest illuminated skylight. As he got closer he trod very lightly and lowered himself to kneel besides the glass cover. The surface was filthy but he could still peer through.

Below was a large room containing sofas, armchairs – and seven men sat around a television. Findo could not see properly but it looked as if the men were watching some kind of match, probably football. Most had cans of beer in their hands and brimming ashtrays were propped on the arms of the furniture. Apart from the television stand and the arc of seats, the room looked empty. There were several doors that Findo could see but they were all closed.

Findo studied the men. One was enormous. He looked tall but also had the kind of girth that made doorways look small. He had arms to match the thighs of his companions and hands that could crush a face. Four of the other men had close-cropped hair and Findo could see tattoos on exposed muscles. One had a long scar across his rodent face. All seven were engrossed in the game but none were passive spectators. Findo saw hands clenched, fingers drumming on chair arms, crushed beer cans and savagely extinguished cigarettes.

After examining each in turn, Findo backed away. He knew the type; in time his elder brothers would fit comfortably into groups like that. He ignored the next skylight and headed for the rear of the building. He went first to the back of the roof and glanced over. It was quiet and dark in the lane below, no sign of the pair who had slung out the Muldoons' debtor earlier.

Findo turned. There were two skylights nearby, as well as a slat-sided box housing an air conditioning unit. Light was coming from the right-hand skylight but the other was dark.

Findo crept to the right and looked down. This room looked more businesslike. The room had a large desk in the middle and filing cabinets and other items of office furniture around the walls. There were several telephones on the desk, one being used by a middle-aged man wearing a faded denim shirt. He was leant back in his chair, a cigar in one hand and a glass of whisky sitting nearby. He had long, receding hair that was a mixture of blond and grey. He was looking around the room as he spoke into the telephone and Findo stepped back just as the man tilted his head back and swept his gaze across the ceiling.

Findo stayed still, just on the edge of the shadows, but the man's eyes moved on and he hunched over the desk again, still talking intently. The sound of his voice came up through the glass but it was too muffled to make out the words.

Findo took another quick glance around the room. He noticed the floor-length, heavy drapes at the window, which explained the darkness from outside. He also spotted what looked like a shotgun propped in a wastepaper basket behind the desk. There were a couple of maps of the city pinned on the wall and an expensive looking stereo system in one corner. Apart from that, it was all fairly functional.

The room beneath the other skylight was some kind of store. Shelving reached almost to the ceiling, making it easy for Findo to climb down. Opening the skylight had been simple; the only thing holding it closed had been a small catch. One flick with the blade of his penknife had been enough to knock it out of place.

When he reached floor level, Findo stood and looked around. He still had the head torch that he had used to guide Mickey through the tunnels beneath the Meadowfields estate. By its beam, Findo could see around the shelves. There was not much on them: a loose-stacked pile of cigarette cartons, some crates of beer and a few boxes and bundles.

Findo had a look in one box. It contained a number of smaller packets. Findo took one and opened it. A shower of bullets fell around his feet and he froze. The metal jackets clattered on the lino floor. Moving with exaggerated caution, Findo put the part-empty carton back into the box and used his right foot to push the loose bullets out of the middle of the floor and underneath the shelves. He stood and listened carefully. There was no sound from the other side of the storeroom's door.

Findo crept towards the door. There was no light coming underneath the bottom and the keyhole was dark too. He gently tried the handle but the door was locked. He tried to peek through the keyhole but it was either pitch-black on the other side of the door or the key was in the way.

Findo frowned and turned back to investigate the rest of the storeroom. There were several bundles covered by a loose cloth on the second shelf, next to the door. He pulled the covering back and let it hang down; underneath lay five shapes, each in its own wrapping. He pulled back the edge of one piece of oily cloth and stared at the machine gun that lay beneath.

He reached out slowly and stood for a while, touching the cold metal warily.

"Come in, come in and sit down, Victor."

Findo jerked around. The voice had come from the other side of the storeroom door. Light was also now coming in around it and he could hear the noise of several people in the room outside.

"Judge, get us a fresh bottle of malt will you. There's some in the cupboard."

Findo's eyes flicked around in horror. He had no idea if the speaker was referring to the storeroom or some other cupboard. He looked up. There was no time to try and get back up through the skylight. He quickly dropped down and rolled underneath the bottom shelf, sliding past a box of canned beer and behind the cloth that now hung down beneath the guns.

He was just in time. The key turned in the lock a few seconds later and the door opened. Heavy feet entered the storeroom and Findo could hear the man's ponderous breathing.

"Ah."

The sound of a box being moved came from somewhere on the opposite shelves and then the man turned. There was a rattle from the floor only inches from Findo's head.

"What the . . ."

There was a grunt and the rustle of cloth.

"What's up, Judge?"

"Ah, someone's dropped some slugs on the floor. I'll have a word with the boys."

"Make sure you fucking do." The voice had a harder edge and sounded like it was used to being obeyed. "I don't want no fucking mess. We ever have to pull out of here fast, we don't want anything left lying around could give the fucking bizzies a hand, do we?"

The deep voice from next to Findo rumbled assent. "No problem, boss. It was probably Nails. He's a sloppy cunt sometimes. I'll give him a little lesson."

"You do that. And make sure he learns – otherwise I'll give him his next lesson and he won't forget that one."

The one called Judge chuckled.

The other speaker gave a sigh. "Sorry about that, Victor. Housekeeping, eh? Bloody pain sometimes but you can never afford to let your standards slip, otherwise who knows when it will come back to haunt you."

"No need to apologise." The new voice sounded different; there was an accent but Findo could not place it. "We always have to be vigilant, Mr Muldoon. Only fools take chances. I prefer to make sure that my gambling is confined to the racecourse."

The first man laughed. "Ah but, Victor, even there you fix the fucking horses."

Findo breathed a sigh of relief as he heard the man beside him walk back into the main room. A short while later he heard glasses clink down on a table and the glug of liquid being poured out.

"For you, Victor."

"Thank you, Mr Muldoon."

"Hey, call me Danny."

"As you wish, Mr . . . Danny."

"And your man."

"No. He does not drink."

"Sensible. You don't want to get your gun too oiled, eh?"

The man called Victor gave a polite laugh. "Indeed."

120

"So, Victor, before we get down to business, a drink. To new partnerships."

"New partnerships . . . Danny."

There was a brief silence and Findo looked around. The door to the storeroom was still open and he could see light coming around the cloth hiding him. He stretched his body forward and craned his head towards the narrow gap between the material and the wall next to it.

He could only see part of the room. The man from the room with the telephones sat in a black leather armchair in front of a low glass table. Findo studied Danny Muldoon carefully. He looked in his mid-forties. He was average height with a stocky build and had none of the signs of a man going to seed. As well as the denim shirt, he wore black jeans, a heavy belt and a pair of gleaming cowboy boots with metal tips. His shirtsleeves were rolled up and Findo could see brawny forearms resting on the arms of the chair. In one hand, Muldoon held a heavy cut-glass tumbler. A cigar was in the other.

Findo could see part of a figure standing behind Muldoon. It looked like the big man from the room with the television. Of the other two occupants he could see very little. A pair of suited legs, wearing polished shoes, came from one armchair. Over the top of another, Findo could see black hair pulled back into a tight ponytail.

"So, Victor, still happy with the price?"

"Of course, Danny. I do not change my word once we have an agreement. The first payment is in the case. When we take delivery of the goods, we will provide the balance."

"Lovely."

"And, of course, once this consignment has been distributed, I will be happy to discuss repeat arrangements."

Muldoon laughed. "That's what I like to hear. Makes sense to work together. There's plenty of business for both of us. We don't want to be watching our backs – we should be out there making money."

"Certainly. There is no profit in pointless warfare."

Muldoon gave a crocodile smile. "Pointless warfare, no."

Findo watched as he tossed down the rest of his brandy.

"Okay then, Victor. Tell you what. Step into my office and we'll make a few phone calls, get a bit of merchandise shifted. Once you're happy that we've delivered our side of the bargain, you can sign on the dotted line and we'll both be happy."

"Sign?"

Muldoon laughed. "Words, Victor. I don't think either of us will be signing anything – just a figure of speech. What I mean is; we make the transfer, you hand over the cash. That's it. Both sides of the bargain kept." He turned and walked away. "Oh, you don't need to lug that around with you. Shove it in the cupboard, Judge. You can give Victor the key if he wants."

Findo slid further back underneath the shelf as he heard footsteps approaching. Something heavy was placed on the floor only a foot or so from his nose and then the door to the storeroom closed and the darkness returned.

Findo listened until he was happy that all was quiet. He turned his head torch back on and slid out from under the shelf. He was about to start climbing up to the skylight when he saw the briefcase sitting just inside the door. He hesitated only a couple of seconds and then crouched down next to it.

The case was not locked and Findo laid it flat then popped the catches. His breath caught as he looked inside. The case was packed with twenty-pound notes.

Findo reached in and touched the money. It felt crisp and new. He pulled one of the bundles out. It was about two inches thick, a solid wad of money. There was another layer of notes under the first.

The boy licked his lips. He could see ten stacks of notes and there were at least two layers. There were also more bundles stuffed down one end of the case.

Findo took out another wad of money and ran his fingers over the edge. He hardly breathed as he stroked the notes. Then, without giving himself time to stop and think, he stuffed the two bundles inside his jacket. He stood up. Then crouched back down and grabbed several more bundles. Another handful followed and then the inside of his jacket was stuffed.

Findo looked at the briefcase. It was over half empty. He considered picking it up, then saw a gym bag on a nearby shelf. The bag had a towel inside but was otherwise empty. Findo grabbed it and emptied the rest of the banknotes into the gym bag. He slung it over one shoulder then crouched down, closed the briefcase and stood it back up where it had been.

Climbing back out of the skylight was slightly more awkward with the money inside his jacket and the bag over his shoulder but the shelves were solid and he made it without any real problem.

Up on the roof, Findo hesitated – doubt making his heart lurch – but realised it was probably as risky to go back as it was to flee.

He moved quickly but carefully across the roof of the Muldoons' building and over onto the carpet store. A few minutes later, he was crouched by the side of the railway track, heart hammering in his chest. Hidden in the shadows and skeleton shapes of dead weeds, he thought about what to do. He had no idea what to do with the money, or even whether he really wanted it, but he knew he had to put it somewhere safe. The castle was the obvious place but it was on the other side of the city – and he was not so innocent as to expect that he would be safe walking across town late at night with a heavy bag. There were several dangers, from casual assault and robbery by those who saw him as easy pickings to the police, who would probably take him for a thief or runaway. Less likely but most dangerous was the risk of being stopped by the Muldoons' men.

Findo was still thinking about his options when the sound of a train drew his attention. He crouched lower and watched as the locomotive rolled slowly past, pulling a long line of freight wagons and tanker cars. The eastbound train was nearly past him when he heard a squeal from ahead and saw the wagons and cars jolting as they braked to an even slower pace.

Findo ran out and jumped onto the line behind the end of the train. It was still moving but slowly and he followed in its tracks, listening to the sound of the brakes. The train gradually reduced speed until it was practically crawling along and Findo sprinted up behind it. The last car was a tanker and he ran around onto the stones beside the line and began to jog parallel with the train. Next came a flatcar, carrying what looked in the orange light like machinery covered by a tarpaulin. The third wagon was a boxcar and the doors on its sides were open.

Findo ran alongside and slung the gym bag up, although keeping hold of the strap. He grabbed the lip of the opening and jumped, getting one elbow onto the edge. The train was moving now at little more than walking pace and he swung one leg up and onto the wooden floor of the wagon. After that it just took one good heave and he was on board and rolling over into the boxcar.

He was still wearing his head torch and he turned it back on. Half of the car was stacked with wooden crates holding what looked like cabbages. The remainder was empty. Findo allowed himself a smile and sank down into the corner, turning off his torch as he slumped to the floor in a mixture of exhaustion, exhilaration and disbelief.

15. Action, counter-action and reformation

The first major response to the disappearance of the money was a petrol bomb thrown through the window of a Chinese restaurant off Albert Parade. The attack happened in the early hours of Tuesday morning. The last diners had left an hour earlier but four staff members were still inside.

There was no warning. A brick was hurled through the window to smash the glass, followed by the petrol bomb. The explosion sent gouts of fire across the carpeted floor, over furniture and up the walls. Paper lanterns hanging from the ceiling incinerated in a flash and shrivelled into balls of ash. Lacquered chairs burst into flames as they were washed by the blast from the crude bomb. As the foam stuffing in the benches along the walls caught fire, toxic fumes were added to the smoke filling the restaurant.

One of the waiters, a youth of seventeen, was refilling the shelves behind the tiny bar when the attack happened. Luckily for him, he was bent over when the petrol exploded. Although closest to the blast, the teenager had the presence of mind not to run to the back of the restaurant. Instead, he leapt over the bar, past a table that was just starting to burn and straight out through the front window, escaping unscathed.

The other three in the restaurant were not so lucky. Some of the burning petrol splashed down the corridor into the kitchen. The flames ignited the oil in a deep fat fryer. Smoke billowed up into the confined space and the two cooks, one of whom had been caught on the arm by the flames, suffered serious smoke inhalation before getting the locked back door open.

The other waiter, who had been in the restaurant's back office, joined them in the small rear yard after stuffing the night's takings into his tunic. He escaped the restaurant safely but slipped while climbing the wall that surrounded the compound behind the building. The broken glass on top of the wall cut him badly on one leg and he broke his arm in two places when landing in the street on the other side.

The first police unit arrived within four minutes. They were followed eight minutes later by a fire engine, although the crew were unable to do much more than stop the fire spreading – the inside of the restaurant was already gutted. A paramedic team arrived seconds after the fire crew and immediately began treating the injured waiter, while waiting for a second ambulance to take the two chefs to hospital.

It was clear straight away that the emergency services were dealing with an arson attack and the police set about hunting for witnesses. They found one, although his account did not give them much to go on. A van driver dropping off the next morning's newspapers had seen two men get out of a dark coloured saloon, throw the brick and petrol bomb, get back into the car and drive away.

While the officers were talking to the witness, radio reports began coming in of several more major incidents.

First was an attack on a corner shop in the Newmills area. Intruders had smashed in the door of a mini-market then broken their way into private rooms at the back and assaulted a group of Asian men with clubs and knives. Some neighbours also claimed that shots had been fired – although the victims themselves had denied that any guns had been used or present.

It appeared that none of the victims – who ran various businesses around the city – wanted to press charges or even discuss the matter with the police. None would even admit to having been seriously hurt. One man, with blood dripping down his face from a head wound and an arm hanging limply by his side, told police that it had been an unfortunate mistake and that no serious harm had been done.

The men attacked were all Muslim and the initial fear was that this was a race attack but the idea was soon revised when CID told senior officers that they already knew the location. The rooms behind the shop were known to be a gambling den. The premises were also suspected of being a meeting place for Asian members of the city's underworld.

The next incident took place half an hour later when a stolen van was rammed through the window of a taxi firm in the Hobbes Town area of the city. A group of men – thought to be Chinese – then stormed the premises. Wielding machetes and various other weapons, including nunchakus and baseball bats, they burst through the taxi firm's offices and into premises behind owned by the building contractor William Muldoon and Sons.

The police were not certain what took place inside the building. The staff at the taxi firm all fled. When armed officers – responding to further reports of gunfire – entered the building they found no living occupants but did discover an Asian man in a stairwell. He had been hit in the head with the blast from a shotgun and was unquestionably dead. The police also found traces of fresh blood in several other places. One trail led to an open door at the rear of the building. There were also bullet holes in walls and spent cartridges, bullet casings and discarded knives littered around the maze of rooms inside the building.

Investigators at the crime scene made a number of discoveries. One was a selection of ammunition for various weapons stored in an upstairs cupboard. Another was a downstairs room containing sophisticated weighing equipment along with traces of cannabis, cocaine and heroin. A plastic bag lying on the floor contained the remains of several ecstasy tablets, although the pills were badly adulterated.

They also discovered two other rooms of interest. One, on the ground floor, contained a chair equipped with handcuffs and other restraints. There were various old stains on the floor around the chair, later identified as various bodily fluids. In an office on the top floor were the remains of a large-scale map of the city. The map had obviously been ripped down in a hurry and part had been left behind. Mainly covering the East Park area, it had rings and other markings around various properties, although there was no key as to what they meant.

Before the first December sunlight had begun to colour the sky, a major incident room was being set up at the divisional police headquarters at Alexander Cross. Senior officers and detectives had been roused from bed and dragged in for a 7 a.m. briefing. Duty rosters were revised and preparations made to draft in extra officers, both to staff the joint inquiry team and to provide backup if more incidents took place.

There was no immediate link between the first three incidents – apart from the fact that each location had known criminal links. However, the type of attack, the victims involved and the level of violence used suggested that these were no normal disputes and the senior detectives reviewing what was known so far could see all the makings of a major gang war breaking out.

The divisional commander, Chief Superintendent Ross Kirkbride, went over the key facts at the morning conference. There had initially been some doubt about whether the firebomb attack on the Tiong Shan restaurant should be looked at alongside the other two incidents. None of the staff members were known to police and the Tiong Shan was not known as being the venue for any criminal activity.

But then a detective inspector from the district's drugs squad revealed that his team were already investigating the Tiong Shan and three other restaurants around the city. Each had been identified as possible fronts for heroin dealing. Investigations had established that a company called Jurong Enterprises owned three of the businesses, including the Tiong Shan. The holding company listed one of its directors as Cheng Ho, an accountant believed to be one of the lieutenants of Victor Hong – thought to be the man behind over eighty per cent of local trafficking in hard drugs.

There was no clear link between Hong and the gambling den in Newmills. Although the men attacked had all been Asian, they were of Indian origin and, in the past, the city's Pakistani, Indian and Chinese communities had tended to keep to their own territory – whether for legitimate or illegitimate business dealings.

The attempt to storm the building in Hobbes Town was much more clearly gang-related. Although supposedly unoccupied except by the taxi business, the premises were owned by a company with a notorious name. The head of the family firm, William Muldoon, had been convicted eleven years earlier of the murder of two people and attempted killing of a third and was currently serving life in high security.

Muldoon, now in his late fifties, had once been the most infamous gangster in the city. As a teenager he was jailed for nearly beating to death a man twenty years his senior in an unprovoked attack. Over the years following – as he built up an empire based on robbery, extortion and prostitution – Muldoon collected a string of other convictions, ranging from grievous bodily harm to fraud. He was also suspected of being involved in many more crimes, including leading a string of armed bank raids, although these suspicions never even reached court.

Muldoon's reign had only come to an end when he tried to wipe out a rival family. At the resulting trial, it emerged that Muldoon had invited his father's old partner, Tommy Wallace, to meet him at a fishing lodge for peace talks after a series of violent territorial disputes. Muldoon went to the venue alone as a gesture of good faith. At the lodge, he welcomed Wallace, his daughter and son-in-law and plied them all with food and drink. During a break in the talks – which appeared to be about to reach an amicable resolution – Muldoon left the room, supposedly to relieve himself. But he returned with two shotguns and immediately shot the old man and his son-in-law. The jury heard how he then raped Wallace's daughter, Kate Docherty, before shooting her as well.

Muldoon then walked from the lodge, set fire to the building and drove calmly back to the city, where he picked his own wife up from the hairdressers' and went home for a family meal. But Muldoon had been careless. Wallace's son-in-law, Steven Docherty, was not killed by the shotgun blast that hit him and had crawled out of the building before it burnt down. He turned queen's evidence against Muldoon and, despite two attempts on his life, survived to get to the trial and bring down his wife's killer.

For the police at the morning briefing, the story of William Muldoon was history but the activities of his sons were another matter. When the old man was jailed, Danny and Barrie Muldoon had taken over the family's legitimate business dealings. And although neither had been convicted of the same kind of crimes as their father, the name of Muldoon still carried weight in the city's underworld. Between them, the boys were thought to have carried on and expanded all of their father's criminal activities, as well as moving into drug dealing and smuggling various other forms of contraband, including illegal immigrants.

The evidence from the building in Hobbes Town made it obvious that the taxi business had been a front. The premises had clearly been used as a centre of operations for various activities – although, other than their firm's ownership of the building, there was nothing to link the two Muldoon brothers personally to what had been going on.

Now, the evidence of a full-scale, armed assault on the building suggested that whatever was happening was serious. A rival gang would not make the decision to storm one of the Muldoons' bases lightly. There were two likely motives. One was a reprisal for an attack on the other gang's territory or property. The alternative was that the rival operation felt sufficiently confident to challenge the Muldoons for supremacy and attempt to remove them from power. Neither possibility was reassuring for the police, who knew that events could still be far from over.

While the police were discussing the situation, Findo was waking up. There was a thin frost across his sleeping bag but he was warm and cosy inside. He blinked slowly at the pale light coming in through the castle window and stretched.

The movement woke an ache in one shoulder, and the twinge of pain abruptly drove all sleep away as it brought back what he had done the previous night.

Findo stared up at the dim ceiling as the memory dawned. In the cold light of morning it seemed hard to believe. He knew enough about the Muldoons to know that he should have heeded Mickey's warning to keep away from the building near the Turk's Head. Breaking into the headquarters of the worst gang in the city was bad enough; stealing from them was pure madness.

Findo glanced at the doorway leading to the stairwell. He would have to check the bag; make sure it was true and not all a dream. Part of him hoped it was a dream – otherwise, he was not sure whether to feel proud, amazed or just sick with fear.

The situation reached crisis point half an hour later. Barrie Muldoon had just dropped his two children off at school in Chapelbank. He was driving along Connor Terrace when a grey car pulled out in front of his blue Isuzu Trooper and appeared to stall.

Muldoon did not suspect anything until he heard the motorbike coming up behind. Looking in the rear-view mirror, he saw the full-face helmets of rider and pillion passenger. He also caught a glimpse of a long object being carried by the passenger.

Muldoon slammed the big four-wheel drive vehicle into reverse and stamped his foot down on the accelerator. The 2.8 litre turbo diesel engine roared and the Trooper shot backwards. The motorbike was just a few yards away when Muldoon twisted the steering wheel and swerved backwards at it. He missed the motorbike – which darted up onto the pavement – but hit a parked car and ground to a halt with a loud crunch of breaking glass and folding metal.

He tried to get the Isuzu back into forward gear but was too slow. The motorbike had already skidded back round into the road and was now stopped in front of him. The grey car was gone. Barrie Muldoon stared in anger as the motorbike's pillion rider lowered the shotgun and aimed straight at him.

Ross Kirkbride was about to bite into a bacon roll from the canteen when there was a rap on his door. Detective Inspector Paul Sweet walked into the divisional commander's office.

"Sir."

"Paul. Something new?"

"Two things."

"Bad?"

Sweet gave a wry smile. "Depends on your view. One's certainly serious, the other's useful but unexpected."

Kirkbride pushed the roll aside and leant back in his chair. "Okay. Fire away."

Sweet nodded. "Right. First thing, Barrie Muldoon has been shot. Ambushed after dropping his kids off at school in Chapelbank. Happened about ten minutes ago."

"Where and how?"

"Connor Terrace, gunman on the back of a motorcycle. There was probably another car involved as well. It's quite narrow along there, parked cars on either side. Witnesses report a car pulled out in front of Muldoon's vehicle. Sounds like he must have twigged what was going on because it appears he tried to reverse up the road and ram the bike as it came up behind him. But Muldoon hit a parked car and the guy on the back of the bike let him have both barrels."

"He still alive?"

"At the moment but it's touch and go. There's a fair chance he won't make it."

Kirkbride scowled. "This is going too far. Chopping each other up behind closed doors is bad enough, warfare on the streets in broad daylight is another."

Sweet nodded. "We had a look in Muldoon's car. He had an Uzi in the glove compartment."

Kirkbride snorted. "Probably a good thing he didn't have time to use it." He frowned at Sweet. "So, what was the other thing you had to tell me?"

The DI nodded. "This is a bit more curious. Five minutes after the shooting we had an anonymous tip-off. Told us Danny Muldoon is holed up in an industrial unit near Jubilee Square. Said the Muldoons also use this spot as an arms cache and that we might find some interesting merchandise on the premises."

Kirkbride raised an eyebrow. "Do you know the place?"

Sweet shrugged. "I know where it is. We've got no intelligence on it but that doesn't mean it's not true. We didn't know quite how much was going on over in Hobbes Town."

Kirkbride nodded. "What about the map?"

"Sir?"

"The map we took from Hobbes Town. Didn't that cover East Park?"

Sweet's eyes widened then he frowned. "Damn!" he said. "Didn't think to look. I'll get onto that."

"Might be an idea."

The DI nodded. "Yes, but I've sent units out already. I've told them to hold back for the time being but to mount surveillance on the building."

Kirkbride shook his head. "No."

"No?"

"No. Send them in."

"Straight away?"

Kirkbride nodded. "Get as much manpower as you need. Make

sure you've got armed response. Take some dogs as well, including sniffers. Go in hard. Find any illegal weapons or other contraband and arrest everyone. Especially Danny Muldoon. If he's there, arrest him. If not, find him. I want him in custody as soon as possible. I don't care what you charge him with but take him out of circulation. I don't know what this war is about or who started it but it's going to stop."

Sweet smiled. "Understood. There is another thing though."

"Yes?"

"Our informant also told us where to find Victor Hong. And suggested that if we hit the Fu Ji Chinese restaurant in Trinity Parade we might find something interesting. Told us to look inside the fortune cookies."

Kirkbride flexed his fingers and stared at Sweet. "Hmm. Have we got someone playing both sides off against each other?"

"Seems like it."

"No idea who our source is?"

Sweet shook his head. "No. He asked to talk to Dave Bishop. Wouldn't say who he was and Dave said he didn't know the voice. Used the name Roadrunner though."

"Roadrunner?"

Mickey Dunn looked over his shoulder several times as he walked along Willow Avenue. When he reached Fox Place, he hesitated for a while before crossing the road.

Mickey rapped quickly on the door of the house and opened it before anyone could answer. He stepped into the hall and looked around. It was still early and he was not sure anyone would be up yet.

"Hey. Anyone home?"

The lounge door opened and Rob glared around it. His expression relaxed slightly when he saw who it was.

"Mickey."

"Rob."

Rob stepped back into the room and Mickey followed him in.

Bosnia sat in one chair. She was smoking a cigarette and staring vacantly at the window. Mickey noted the pallor of her face and dark hollows around her eyes. Her hair looked lank and her skin waxy.

Rob was the only other one in the room. He was wearing a football shirt and shorts and nursing a mug of coffee and a cigarette.

"You after Jimmy Ray?"

"He back?"

"Nah. Haven't heard anything either."

Mickey nodded and glanced quickly around the room. "Findo

about?"

"Findo? What you want that little shit for?"

"Nothing important."

Rob gave a short smile. "I heard about yesterday though."

Mickey's eyes widened and his mouth opened nervously. "What?"

Rob continued flicking through the porn magazine on his lap. "Getting you out of here when the cops came. Made himself useful for once."

Mickey gave a weak smile. "Yeah, he did well. Thought they were going to have me that time." He watched Rob for a moment. "Don't know where he is now, do you?"

Rob snorted. "No fucking idea, mate. He doesn't bother living with his family. Too fucking up himself. He's got some little bolthole somewhere. Little cunt don't come round here if he can help it."

Mickey nodded. "Yeah."

There was another pause, Bosnia still gazing blankly at the window while Rob looked at pictures of two teenage girls performing oral sex on an older man.

"You heard about last night?" asked Mickey.

Rob did not even look up. "No. What's that then?"

"Big trouble between the Muldoons and Victor Hong."

Rob flicked the magazine shut and looked up with new interest. "Yeah. What happened?"

Mickey gave an awkward shrug. "Dunno the details but Hong's men tried to take out the Muldoon place over Hobbes Town."

This time it was Rob's jaw that dropped. "You must be joking."

"No." Mickey shook his head. "They put a van through the window of the cab place. There was about a dozen Chinks went in. They had all this ninja gear, knives, clubs, and the works, even a couple of swords. But the Muldoons' lot were tooled up. Supposed to have killed three Chinks and wounded a few more."

"Fuck!" Rob whistled, his eyes gleaming.

"Still, Hong's lot did some damage. I heard the Judge got cut up pretty bad."

"What was it all about?"

Mickey shrugged. "Not sure. But some Chinky down the city centre got firebombed last night too. Two Muldoon blokes got knifed up near Jubilee Square and something went down over Newmills too."

Rob shook his head. "Oh, man," he said with delight. "It's going to be fucking war."

Findo flexed his shoulder gently as he lit the fire. He had landed awkwardly when jumping from the train. The rest of the journey had gone smoothly – and saved him the risk of walking across town. After climbing aboard the boxcar in Hobbes Town, he had stayed hidden as the train rumbled through the city centre. He had waited until the freight car had crossed the River Allonby at Newmills before getting off, leaping clear just as the train started to pick up speed again after its slow crawl across the bridge.

It should have been an easy drop but one foot had come down on a loose stone and he had tumbled down the embankment. Luckily the gym bag hanging over one shoulder had taken most of the impact but his shoulder had still taken a knock.

As the flames began to lick up around the kindling in the hearth, Findo moved his arm gently and then gingerly probed the bruise. It was tender but nothing to worry about. The ache was not enough to really bother him and would fade in a day or so.

He sat back onto his campstool and watched the fire as it caught, eager flames eating through newspaper and turning shavings and splinters of wood into burning embers. Findo held his fingers out for the meagre warmth. It was cold inside the stone-walled room. Even when he had first found his way into the tower in the summer it had never been particularly warm. The ancient stones seemed to hold the chill of centuries. Now it was December, being in the room sometimes felt like living inside a fridge.

But Findo was happy. He had left his family and, however cold and grim his new nest sometimes felt, it was calmer, quieter and safer than life with Bosnia and her mismatched clan.

He reached out and laid a couple of dry pine sticks across the thinner twigs that had already caught fire. The branches were quite dry and soon began to blaze, pushing the bubble of warmth further into the room. The light from the flames also began to illuminate more of the ancient chamber.

Findo breathed in the scent of wood smoke and smiled. From beside his stool he picked up a fresh mango, stolen a couple of days ago from a supermarket in the city centre. Taking his knife from his pocket, he began to slice off the green and red skin and bite into the bright orange flesh, savouring the rich, sherbet-like flavour of the exotic fruit.

Mickey was walking along Packhouse Street a few hours later when a car pulled up alongside him. The black BMW 535i slowed to match his speed and the rear nearside window slid down.

"Mickey."

The teenager jerked round in surprise. The BMW pulled into the kerb and stopped. Mickey looked at the open window then walked towards the car.

"Get in."

"Hey, Colin. How's things?"

"Get in, Mickey."

The young car thief looked surprised. "What's up?"

"You need to talk to me."

"What about?"

"Don't disappoint me, Mickey. Get in the car."

16. The root of evil

Abby walked past the roundabout. She glanced up at the ruined castle's southern tower as she went past. Although there was nothing to see from this side, she could not help looking. She was still fascinated by the idea of Findo hidden inside the grey walls. His refuge was so public, yet few people were even aware that the tower was there, let alone the rooms inside.

At the top of the bank by the pumping station, she paused. Abby looked around. It was a wet, cold Saturday morning – the last before Christmas – and few people were on foot. But like the castle, she was too commonplace to be noticed and the traffic on Stewart Road buzzed past heedless of a young, redheaded girl looking down at the River Allonby; the drivers and passengers whipping past had more pressing interests. Tyres hissed on wet tarmac and a thin drizzle drifted in the chill air, whipped around by a gusty wind blowing from the estuary to the west.

The river looked full and ugly. It rolled past in a brown flood, sub-surface currents creating fast-shifting patterns of ripples. The Allonby was in spate, fed by over thirty hours of heavy rain that had only ended the previous afternoon. The tide was going out and the river's mud banks should have been exposed but the water level was still well above its normal height.

Abby could see tangles of litter and debris caught in the lower branches of the trees in the plantation on the other side of the river. At high tide the Allonby must have burst its banks by a good couple of feet. She frowned as she realised how high the water must have come and wondered if any had got into the castle.

After watching the water for a little longer she walked on to where the wall curved round to the left. An old metal gate stood across the top of the narrow drive leading down to the pumping station. Brambles wove through the gate's wire grille and a pile of wet litter had collected in the corner.

Abby grabbed the metal pole supporting the gate and swung over the low wall. She trotted quickly down the concrete roadway, disappearing from the sight of anyone on the road above. At the bottom, she walked briskly across the small car park – where the usual covering of leaves and rubbish had been washed away and replaced with a thin layer of fresh mud. She ignored the sealed door and walked towards the back of the building. A length of string hung from a window above and Abby gave it several firm tugs.

It was several minutes before Findo's head appeared in the opening above. He gave Abby a glance then looked around warily, peering up at the bank above. "You on your own?"

Abby scowled. "Pleased to see you too, Findo."

He gave an apologetic smile and flicked a bundle out of the opening. The rope ladder dropped against the wall next to Abby and she grabbed hold of it.

"Come on up." Findo's head disappeared from sight again. Abby shrugged and began to climb. Findo was waiting at the top, crouched away from the window.

"Hello," said Abby.

He smiled wanly. "Hello."

She gave Findo a hard stare. "What's up with you?"

He shrugged and pulled up the rope ladder, dragging it away from the window. "Come inside."

Abby followed Findo into the pumping station. A line of planks led them through the building, lying across the original floorboards and away from any potentially dangerous sections. Off to one side, the cord that Abby had pulled to get Findo's attention ran diagonally across the room from a small screw eye fixed into the window frame.

At the window on the other side, another plank spanned the gap between the pumping station and the notch in the castle wall. Findo stepped to one side. "You first."

Abby nodded and stepped cautiously onto the plank, Findo steadying her from behind. She tried not to look at the rocks sticking up from the mud and water below. When she had shuffled forward a few feet – Findo's hand still on her coat – Abby lunged forwards and grabbed for the blocks of stone to either side of the notch. She pulled herself between them with relief and scrambled up through the gap.

Abby stopped when she reached the rubble-strewn base of the first tower. Looking down into the daylight, she watched while Findo crossed behind her, then pulled back the plank that had become the castle's modern-day drawbridge. He propped the length of wood up and climbed up to join her.

She looked at him as he picked up his head torch. "You don't normally bother with that."

"What?"

"Lifting the plank up."

Findo shrugged. "Don't want to take any chances."

Abby frowned at Findo. He seemed subdued and more nervous than usual. "What is it?"

"Come on." He gestured across the tower, the beam from the torch following the movement of his head. "I'll show you."

Findo took Abby's hand as he led her across the ruined interior of the tower. Beside them hung the same cord that stretched through the pumping station and across the gap between the two buildings. At the other side of the ruined tower they continued into the corridor that ran inside the main wall and through to the south tower. At the corridor's far end they ducked underneath the large set of metal wind chimes that hung from the ceiling, secured to the same cord that dangled outside the pumping station.

Findo led the way into the first room. The large chamber covered most of the floor of the tower. Three arrow slits looked out over the river. One doorway led to a small alcove that contained a rough stone seat and a chute leading down to the Allonby; a packet of toilet rolls stood by the entrance to the room. There was a fireplace against the north-west side of the tower but it was empty.

A narrow stone staircase took them up to the next level and a small landing. Findo turned right and entered the room beyond. Abby followed, looking around at the familiar scene.

The chamber took up most of the tower. A window on the east wall looked out over the Allonby; a blanket was nailed into the wall above the opening but had been pulled back to one side to let in the light. Several maps of the city were taped up on the south wall. Findo's camping mattress and sleeping bag lay on the floor beneath the maps. A pile of books lay between his pillow and the room's fireplace. There was a pile of ashes in the hearth but they looked dead. Several blankets were spread on the floor in front of the fire and a supply of extra blankets was piled by the foot of the bed. Candles were dotted around the room, mostly just stuck to the floor. Other traces of Findo's occupation included a heap of clothes and some carrier bags containing supplies.

Abby gazed at the dead fire and shivered; it was no warmer in the room than it was outside. "I wondered what had happened to you. I haven't seen you all week."

Findo gave a slight smile. "I haven't been out for days."

Abby looked at him sympathetically. "You haven't been ill, have you? I did think about coming over but I know you don't like us coming and going much in daylight and my mum doesn't like me going out after dark."

Findo shook his head and walked over to sit on the foot of his bed. "No, it's not that. I've been alright."

Abby sat next to him and shuffled close, as much for warmth as from affection. "So what's up? How long have you been in here?"

"Four days."

"Four days?" Abby shook her head. "Why?"

Findo smiled. "I'll tell you if you've got some food."

Abby elbowed him in the ribs. "You'll tell me anyway, Findo Gask." Then she turned and looked at him with a frown. "Have you been in here on your own for four days? What have you been eating?"

Findo shrugged. "I was alright. I always keep some supplies here. But I ran out yesterday; I haven't had anything today."

Abby looked horrified. "Findo! That's awful. Why not?" She dug in her pockets. "I've got an apple. That's all though. I didn't think you'd need food or I'd have brought some."

"That's okay," said Findo, taking the apple and biting into it. "You didn't know."

"So what's this all about?" Abby asked anxiously.

Findo reached into the pile of clothes to his left. "This."

He laid the gym bag in front of Abby and pulled back the zip.

It was starting to get dark again by the time Findo finished telling how he had stolen the money. Abby stared at him for several minutes, impressed and infuriated by the combination of bravery and stupidity that the act entailed.

"So how much is there?" she asked eventually.

Findo shook his head. "I don't know."

"You don't know!"

He looked at the wads of notes stuffed into the open bag. "I didn't like to touch it too much. After I got back that night I managed to stuff it all in the bag and I hid it in a chimney upstairs to begin with. I didn't know what to do with it. I thought about chucking it out the window but then I thought someone might spot it in the river. I nearly chucked it all on the fire but I couldn't do it." He stared at Abby with a plaintive look. "I don't want it any more but I don't know what to do with it and I can't just burn it. It's too much."

Abby tugged her mop of red hair back and secured it into a rough ponytail. "Well, we might as well see how much is there." She reached into the bag and took out a couple of bundles. "Do you reckon they're all the same?"

Findo shrugged. "I don't know. Probably. They all look the same."

Abby squeezed the two wads of notes. She handed one to Findo. "Let's count them. See if they are the same."

Findo took the money reluctantly and began to slowly peel back the notes, counting much more laboriously than Abby. It still took her a couple of minutes to count her bundle and once she was finished Abby stared at it in disbelief.

"There's two hundred notes there. They're all twenties. So . . ." Her freckled nose wrinkled as she calculated. "My God! That's four thousand pounds, just in that bundle." Abby's eyes widened further as it began to sink in quite how much money was in the bag. "How many are in your lot?"

Findo shook his head, still counting under his breath. Eventually he folded back the last note. "I think I got to one hundred and eighty something but I got lost a couple of times."

Abby shrugged. "So that's probably two hundred as well," she said, confident of her own counting. "How many bundles are there?"

"Dunno." Findo picked up the bag and shook the contents out on the floor in front of them. They stared at the pile before picking up a bundle.

"I know," said Abby. "We'll stack them on the floor next to each other. That way we can see how thick they are as well and if some are much bigger or smaller we'll be able to see."

They worked together, stacking the piles of notes on the floor. There were sixty-two identical looking bundles, plus one that was half-thickness.

"Oh my God! Oh my God!" Abby started to giggle. She turned and began to pummel Findo, shoving him down onto the bed. "Findo! That makes two hundred and fifty thousand pounds. That's a quarter of a million. You've stolen a quarter of a million pounds!"

A smile began to spread across the boy thief's face and he chuckled as he twisted away to avoid Abby's fists. She stopped punching him and they stared in each other's faces in silence for a moment before both breaking into laughter. Findo's eyes closed and tears began to pour down his cheeks. He rolled onto his back next to Abby and his breath jerked in and out in silent heaves as laughter choked him.

Finally, the hilarity ran out for both of them but the tears continued to pool around Findo's eyes. He turned, blinking. "Abby. I'm scared."

She reached out a hand and took his.

"I don't know what to do," said Findo. "If they find out I took the money they'll go mad. I don't know what they'll do to me – they'll probably kill me."

Abby looked fearful. "Are they that bad?"

Findo nodded, gripping Abby's fingers tight. "I think so. I've heard about things the Muldoons have done to people before. And they hadn't done nothing as bad as this. Rob told me once about this bloke who mugged a dealer who was working for the Muldoons. He saw this dealer selling stuff in the pub, followed him out at the end of the night and robbed him in an alley. But the dealer saw his face and found out this bloke was doing some work on a building site. The Muldoons sent some men round the next day and they stuck this bloke's feet into some concrete and laid into him with baseball bats until he told them where the money was. Rob said this bloke was in hospital for weeks."

Abby looked sick. "That's awful."

"I know, but that wasn't it. A couple of days after the man came out of hospital he got whacked by a hit-and-run driver and ended up back in intensive care. The Muldoons did that because when they went to get the money it turned out he'd spent some of it."

The two children sat in silence for a while. Abby put her arms around Findo and hugged him tight. She stared at the pile of money in front of them while Findo stared at the pile of dead ashes lying in the hearth.

After a while Abby released her grip. "But, Findo, there's no way they can know it was you."

He shrugged. "I don't know."

Abby grabbed his shoulders and turned him to face her. "Listen. The only person who even knew you were in that part of town was Mickey and you told him you were going home. Isn't that right?"

"Suppose so."

"Well then, you're safe. No one's going to suspect you. You said no one saw you break in. How are they going to even know you were there?"

Findo smiled weakly. "Because the money's gone."

Abby shook her head. "But think about it. First of all, apart from Mickey, no one knows you were in Hobbes Town."

"And his friends."

"Okay, his friends as well. But that doesn't matter; they all think you went home. Mickey saw you being sick. You told him you were going, they're not going to suspect anything." Abby shook Findo's shoulders. "And that doesn't matter anyway. If you got in and out without being seen they might not even realise that anyone broke in. The Muldoons might think one of their own men took the money. They probably don't even know who you are. They've got no reason to suspect you even if they did. Okay?"

Findo nodded slowly. "Maybe."

"So all you need to do is get rid of the money. You can't spend it because someone might suspect something if they knew you had loads of money. So, we've just got to get rid of it."

"Okay," said Findo. "But how?"

Abby thought for a while. Eventually she began to smile. "Well," she said, "you don't want to just throw it away because that seems wrong somehow now that you've got it."

Findo nodded. "So what do I do?"

Abby grinned, freckled face wrinkling. "We redistribute it."

"What?"

She nodded. "Well, you know what Mrs Reid says. How we should all be equal and how wealth is so unfair."

"Yeah."

"So, let's do something about it," said Abby. "Let's take the money and give it away."

Findo's eyes widened. "How?"

"I'm not sure," said Abby. "We can't tell people who it's from but there's a quarter of a million there. We could share that between a lot of people."

They waited until late evening before starting their operation. They had gone to Abby's house first – after she finally managed to persuade Findo to leave the castle. Mrs McGee was working today and then going straight out on a Christmas social for the staff at the city museum. She was not due back until late.

The children had walked through back streets from the Stewart Road roundabout to Corporation Road and along to the house in Denmark Street where the McGees lived. Once there, Abby had taken the opportunity to sit Findo down to a proper meal. She had also brought a bag of his clothes and stuffed them into the washing machine while he was banished to the bathroom with a selection of soaps and shampoos.

Later in the afternoon, Findo had gone out on a final errand, returning with packs of envelopes stolen from a branch of W H Smith's at the precinct near Newmills Railway Station.

It was just past 8 p.m. when they slipped out of Denmark Street – late enough but not so late that their presence on the streets would draw attention. They each carried a bag; Findo had dumped the stolen gym bag just in case and borrowed an old knapsack that a teenage Suzanne McGee had used when slipping away on illicit camping trips with her husband-to-be. Abby had her school bag.

Abby had managed to persuade Findo not to do anything in the Newtown area, even though he had wanted to leave some of the money for her mother. Instead, they walked south-east, brushing along the edge of Cowfield Heights, skimming through Newmills and along St Patrick's Road towards the bridge across the Allonby into the Chapelbank area.

They did not stop at every house, looking instead for those that looked darkest and saddest – or where children could be heard inside. Working together, the two eleven-year-olds quietly slipped envelopes through letterboxes and left as silently as they arrived. The envelopes were fat and their bags soon grew lighter. Even so, they surprised at how little time it took to put two hundred and fifty envelopes, each stuffed with a thousand pounds, through the doors of complete strangers.

17. Christmas bonuses

The redistribution of a quarter of a million pounds to the citizens of the city was a seasonal gesture as unexpected as the Queen's Christmas speech being delivered naked.

The impact of finding a thousand pounds lying on the doormat in an unmarked envelope affected people in different ways. Many recipients were more worried than delighted by the money's arrival. Quite a few took the cash and hid it, assuming that a wrong delivery had been made and nervous of a knock on the door from someone wanting to remedy the mistake. Some just burst into tears after opening the envelope and counting the notes inside. A very few took the mystery as evidence that miracles did happen at Christmas and surprised their local ministers by turning up at church to give thanks.

But most of the two hundred and fifty households involved simply took the money and spent it – nearly as quickly as it had arrived. These were people who did not believe in looking a gift horse in the mouth. Money came, money went – you enjoy it if you have it and worry about consequences afterwards.

None of these people had ever had a thousand pounds fall on their doormat before (literally or metaphorically). They did not expect it to happen again. Ever. And they were as broke as the next person. So they did not ask questions or wait for someone to come and ask for it back. They did worry about where the cash had come from and if anything else was going to happen – but not so much that it stopped them spending the money and making the most of it for the short time it was in their hands.

If an unexpected and unlikely windfall could be seen as a problem, then spending the money was one way of getting rid of the problem. A lot went on drink, some – but not that much – on paying off debts and dues. Some families splashed out on extra food and other last-minute luxuries for Christmas; a few children suddenly found themselves with the presents they had really wanted but never dreamed of getting. Other money disappeared on new clothes, bits and pieces for the house, or a flutter at the bookies – one man even managed to multiply his windfall more than tenfold with a lucky bet on the outcome of a seasonal football derby. (He immediately spent part of his winnings on a second-hand van and set off to drive to the south of Spain, never to return.)

However, the thought that others might have experienced the

same unexpected good fortune hardly occurred to those going on their personal buying spree. But the sudden spending of a thousand pounds by scores who never normally had any money to spare did draw attention. Initially, it was just gossip about a friend or acquaintance that had suddenly come into some money. The beneficiaries of the redistribution made all kinds of excuses about where the cash had come from – few told the truth.

But a handful did. And people began to put two and two together – sometimes making five as fictions emerged alongside the facts. The story spread and soon all kind of conclusions were being leapt to about anyone seen with more money in their wallets than usual. Rumours bred and gave birth to half-truths and lies. Whispers turned into full-throated debate and by the time it got to Christmas Day a new urban myth had been born.

In homes, pubs, clubs, workplaces and in the streets, the tale was told of how thousands of people across the city had received anonymous gifts of cash. The money was supposed to have arrived in the middle of the night with unmarked notes showering through letterboxes. The amount varied, ranging from hundreds to thousands. Some said it was drug money (true) from underworld villains with a guilty conscience (untrue). Other rumours were that someone from a telephone sales firm that went bust over the festive period had raided the company account and given the money away. Or that some mad millionaire – dying according to most stories – had decided to renounce his wealth. Another explanation was that a disillusioned city council employee had emptied the coffers before collapsing with a nervous breakdown.

There were nearly as many stories as bank notes involved but – to begin with at least – very few people thought of Findo, who was still lying low.

At police divisional headquarters, rumours of millions of pounds being stuffed through city letterboxes were treated with a fair degree of official cynicism. There was no evidence of any wrongdoing and, however unusual, it was not actually illegal to give away money. But behind the scenes, officers who had started to piece together the story behind the gang war that had led to the killing of Barrie Muldoon began to suspect more than coincidence.

Fortunately for the police, the eruption of violence that took place just before Christmas was stopped before it spiralled out of control – greatly helped by the tip-offs provided by the anonymous informant calling himself Roadrunner. But the city's force had been left with plenty to do and think about. So far, only two bodies were known about, although Chief Superintendent Ross Kirkbride and his team had little doubt that there would be more – once they knew where to look.

For the time being, however, all was quiet. The tip-off that sent police to the industrial estate in East Park had been well-timed. When armed officers burst into the premises they had caught Danny Muldoon and several of his men in the process of torturing a young associate of Victor Hong. Luckily, the police raid had been swift enough that Muldoon had not had time to think of silencing his victim. The young Singaporean turned out to be in the country illegally but spoke fluent English and once an agreement had been made that he would remain in the country pending any trial rather than be instantly deported, he was quite ready to give evidence against Danny Muldoon.

Nineteen members of the Muldoons' gang were now in custody as a result of that raid and others prompted by information from Roadrunner. Charges against the men involved offences relating to violence, possession of illegal weapons and drugs, and the handling of stolen goods. It was likely that a good number of other charges and further arrests would follow.

Victor Hong's growing empire had also suffered a major setback. Hong himself had vanished and was assumed to have fled the city; although whether he had left the country was open to debate. Apart from the firebombing of the Tiong Shan, three other restaurants had been closed following drug seizures. Two shops owned by members of the Pakistani community had been shut down as the result of similar busts. Nine men of Southeast Asian and Indian subcontinent extraction were awaiting either deportation or trial on drugs-related charges. Again, mostly thanks to information provided by Roadrunner.

In all, the gang war had been vicious but short. The long-term effects would not be known for some time but Ross Kirkbride was satisfied that, for the time being at least, the power of the Muldoon gang was broken and the rise of a new pan-Asian drug supply network had been curtailed.

But the Chief Superintendent had no doubt that the vacuum left by the fall of the two gangs would not be empty for long. Presuming a vacuum still existed.

18. Pause for thought

The end of the old year and the start of the new brought an enforced calm. Ice-laden winds swept down from the north and swept all but the mad, desperate and foolhardy from the streets. Bitter chills gusted down silent roads. The last of the fog left by the earlier wet weather was frozen wherever it lingered, leaving a sparkling rime across houses, trees, gardens, cars and anything that stopped moving. Pavements and streets glittered dangerously.

As the end of the festive season arrived, thermometer levels dropped further and meteorologists checked records. Crusts of ice formed along the edges of the Allonby, pipes shattered and crystals of ice swelled up from the ground like some Arctic crop. Admissions to the hospital soared as cars slid, pedestrians fell and cold thinned the old and the weak. Three homeless men were found frozen together in the doorway of a shop along Albert Parade. Children watched for snow but none came. The sky stayed clear, by day so pale it was nearly white and by night ablaze with stars. Emergency supplies were taken to the elderly – extra blankets and warming meals – and the few shoppers venturing out for the January sales were more interested in duvets and blankets than cut-price fashion.

In his office looking down across Alexander Cross, Ross Kirkbride watched the occasional car crawl by with relief. The pubs and clubs along Packhouse Street were virtually deserted and few people were stirring. The Chief Superintendent looked at the cold sky and gave a silent prayer of thanks for the respite the weather was giving his officers. With his feet as close as possible to a portable electric heater, he continued skimming through transcripts of interviews with those in custody.

Sitting wrapped up at home in Newtown, Abby stared out through patterns of frost at the empty road. She worried about Findo but her mother had forbidden her from venturing out on her own.

Alone in her terraced house just off Dubmore Road, Frances Reid studied the writings of the French anarchist philosopher Pierre-Joseph Proudhon. The library should have reopened days ago but the city council had decided to keep it closed and save heating costs while concentrating on emergency action to combat the big freeze and keeping essential services going.

Mrs Reid thought too of Findo but did not worry too much. She had experienced hardship and deprivation in her younger days and knew what it was to go hungry, shiver with cold and hide from enemies. She had no doubt it would be tough for the boy but was confident of Findo's ability to survive and respected the fact that he had chosen his own road.

Around the city others were also interested in how the young thief was faring. Some were actively looking for him but had no idea where he was holed up and searched in vain.

A keen-eyed observer passing the ruins of the city's castle might, if they had known where to look, have spotted a faint haze of heat above the south tower and the occasional thin trickle of smoke. But that was all there was to see and none even noticed, let alone made the connection with, the elusive Findo Gask.

Inside the ancient chamber of the one-time Plantagenet stronghold, Findo was snug and secure. In the days immediately after he and Abby had got rid of the money, before the story of its miraculous Christmas appearance began to spread, Findo had made a number of trips out from the castle, laying in his holiday supplies. It had been good timing. The two Muldoon brothers were out of circulation – one for good – and their gang disbanded as a result of the police raids. (Victor Hong was in fact still in the city, although lying next to his bodyguard under several feet of concrete in the middle of a new roundabout in Clathy High Street.) But – most importantly – no one had yet made the connection between the boy with the lightest fingers in the city and the disappearance of a quarter of a million pounds.

After shivering and starving his way through the day before Abby came to find him, Findo had two priorities when he went foraging. Food was easy; a few trips to the supermarket supplied him with most of his basic needs – chocolate and exotic fruit, along with biscuits, cakes, and various tinned and packet goods. Festive treats like mince pies, sausage rolls and a couple of Christmas cakes were added to his pantry. He also acquired a supply of bottled water and cans of soft drinks. On a night-time trip to Garvock Hill, he broke into an outdoor pursuits shop where he stole a camping stove and cooking equipment, along with a new five-season sleeping bag, more socks and a supply of dehydrated food.

His heating needs were supplied by several sources. He made trips to the plantation on the other side of the Allonby to collect large bundles of firewood. A building site on the edge of the Meadowfields estate provided him with further timber for burning, collected from various off-cuts left by the builders, as well as lengths of good wood supposed to be for the construction work. He also managed to remove part of a dry section of floor and a couple of window frames from inside the old pumping station.

Working mainly at night, Findo carried his firewood along the pavement that ran beside Stewart Road and threw it over the wall above the gap between the walls of the castle and the Victorian building. Over the space of three days he built up a useful pile of wood that he later gathered up and carried into the castle. He also took several bags of coal from a yard near Byrnebridge.

At the building site, Findo also ripped the window from a Portakabin being used as an office. He brought the metal-framed sheet of glass back to the castle and managed to wedge it into the single window in his stone-walled chamber. Bits of heavy cardboard and strips of wood and blanket were tacked and taped to the soft stone so they blocked the gaps around it. The same material was used to block up the arrow slits. Findo also fixed a heavy blanket so it hung across the door into the chamber. It took him a while to insulate the room to his satisfaction but once he had finished the effect was quite noticeable; the fire did not draw so well and let more smoke into the chamber but it was a lot warmer.

By Christmas Eve, Findo was prepared. He had planned to lay low anyway but the arrival of the big freeze gave him another reason not to venture out. When the first ice began to appear along the mud beside the Allonby, he lowered the curtains across his door and windows, lit the fire and retreated inside.

For the next ten days Findo hardly ventured further than his firewood supply. Apart from one supermarket foraging trip a couple of days after Christmas, his exercise was confined to walking between the two towers and climbing to the ruined chamber that lay above his own room. From there he could scramble up to the broken platform above and peer out through the remains of the battlements.

Findo spent most of his time by the fire: eating, sleeping and reading. He spent hours with a book in his hand. He would sit hunched in front of the fire, surrounded by a ring of burning candles, totally lost in whatever world he was reading about.

For although he had still never attended a day's schooling in his life, books had become a crucial part of Findo's life. They provided the escape he had never had before. They let him see beyond the city and expand his horizons without the limitations of television – and Findo had taken to reading like a fish to swimming. Since he was tiny he had always had a preference for avoiding reality. But as a child – lacking any kind of education or other normal stimulus – he had been given little to go on and his fantasies had lacked depth or subtlety. Now, with his mind being opened by the worlds – both real and make-believe – in the books he read, Findo was beginning to realise that imagination had few or no limits.

His reading had also done more than just give him an escape pod from everyday life. It had also – with the aid of some delicate encouragement from Frances Reid – helped teach him how to learn. Through the books that he picked and she suggested, Findo had begun to accumulate a little knowledge of a wide range of subjects, including history, geography and political philosophy.

And although some of his subject matter was hardly conventional, Findo was fast making up for lost time. It was now only just under three years since he had first asked Abby to help him to learn to read but the delay in starting his education did not seem to have caused any problems. He devoured knowledge and revelled in his imagination, letting his flights of fancy take him where they would. Even what could sometimes seem turgid to others was painless to Findo, for the simple reason that he only read what either interested him or represented a challenge. He also had total freedom to study how and when he chose. It was a haphazard sort of process and there were some areas of his education where Findo's knowledge was minimal at best. On the other hand, he could explain the background to the Spanish Civil War better than some A level history students.

Findo generally liked reading novels the most. But sometimes a story would lead him to a subject of which he knew nothing and he would appear at the library looking for the answers. Sir Walter Scott's *Ivanhoe* had led him to the history of the crusades and Robert Louis Stevenson's *Treasure Island* had sparked an interest in the South Seas.

But at the moment he was lost in fantasy. Shut away in his candle-lit tower, he was avidly working his way through the *Chronicles of Narnia*, while living off Pot Noodles, bags of crisps and his new addiction – Fry's Chocolate Creams. He was enjoying the Narnia books because he appreciated the way that anyone, even outsiders like the fat kid that no one liked, could become someone with respect and importance. But his favourite so far was *The Hobbit*. The idea of a ring that could turn you invisible seemed perfect to Findo and he had taken a great liking to Bilbo Baggins – it would have been hard for him not to sympathise with a fellow professional burglar.

19. Out of hibernation

A slight thaw came a few days into January, just before Findo's twelfth birthday. The clouds rolling in from the west brought a few flurries of snow in their vanguard but their thin dusting of white was followed by a rise in mercury levels. It was still far from warm but, for the first time in over nine days, the daytime temperature went up above zero. Although the ice remained in the shadows and the hollows, on rooftops and roads the worst of the frost started to melt.

The change in the weather was welcomed by many, including Findo. He had just finished *The Voyage of the Dawntreader* and was ready to re-emerge into the world for a while at least. He was tired of candlelight and Pot Noodles and needed fresh air. He wanted to see Abby and check she was okay. He had not seen her since a couple of days after they got rid of the money and he missed her company. After days of reading about others' adventures, he was also ready for some excitement of his own. The worst of his fears of retribution had receded and he was bored. It was time to get out and do something. His fingers were itching for something to steal and he was eager to get back to his explorations.

Findo emerged at the window of the pumping station, blinking at the brightness of the daylight. He looked around to check no one was looking over the wall or from down by the river. When he was satisfied that the coast was clear, Findo clambered down his rope ladder to ground level. Once at the base of the wall, he hauled the ladder back up out of sight using the long loop of nylon cord attached to the ladder's bottom rung. The cord ran up and over a roof beam inside; by pulling on it, Findo was able to raise the ladder up so it disappeared back inside the pumping station – leaving just the loop of cord dangling outside for when he wanted to get back in.

He set off first to see Abby, making a quick detour through a branch of Sainsbury's for breakfast. He ate as he was walking, wolfing down bites of bacon, lettuce and tomato sandwiches, washed down with Tango. It was still quiet on the streets. Although the worst of the ice had gone, most drivers were still taking it cautiously and pedestrians trod as if expecting their footing to go at any minute.

By the time he reached Denmark Street, the fresh air and exercise had brought a warm glow to Findo's face and he felt livelier than he had for days. He walked briskly up to the McGees' front door. He was uncertain whether Abby would have gone back to school by now but it was a Tuesday and he was reasonably certain her mother should be at work.

But there was no answer to his knock and the house was dark. Findo waited for a couple of minutes, knocked again and then pushed open the letterbox and peered through. The hall was gloomy and he could not hear anyone stirring.

Findo stepped back and crouched down in front of the door. He lifted the metal foot scraper and looked underneath. A neatly folded plastic bag was tucked under one corner of the grille. Inside the damp plastic was a sheet of notepaper.

Findo pulled it out and read:

Dear Findo,

I hope you had a nice Christmas in the castle. Thanks very much for your present, it was really cool, I love bubble bath and I've already used some of it up. I have got a present for your birthday but I don't know when I'll be able to give it to you.

My Mum's got me a new bike for Christmas. Well, it's second-hand really but it's got some new bits and it's bright red and excellent. I love it and I can't wait to show it to you.

We've had to go away because my Great-Gran is not well. We got a phone call on Boxing Day to say she had been taken to hospital. I don't know what's wrong but I really hope it's nothing bad because she's really nice and I'd hate it if anything happened to her.

My Mum's not looking forward to going because her mum and dad will probably be there and she still doesn't talk to them. I don't like them either but I think my Mum's more worried than me.

I don't know when we will get back. We're going by train today – which is Friday. I expect we'll be there for the New Year but I don't think we'll be having much of a party. I'll leave a message at the factory when I'm back. I'll see you again soon.

Lots of love
Abby xxx

Findo read the letter a couple of times then folded it and slipped it into an inside pocket. He turned away from the McGees' house and set off back down Denmark Street. He went next to the library but that was still closed and he could not see a sign to say when it would re-open.

Findo headed next in the Chapelbank direction, towards a side road that would take him through to Frances Reid's house in Dubmore Road. It was still cold and he had his collar folded up around his ears to keep them warm.

He was on his way along St Patrick's Road when a white car going the opposite way did a sudden U-turn and pulled up alongside him. Findo did not see the car turn and only noticed it when it stopped just in front of him.

The passenger window wound down and a head poked out.

"Oi, shithead!"

Findo looked up in surprise.

"Where you off to then?" demanded Jimmy Ray.

Findo shrugged. "Just to see a friend."

He wandered over to the car and crouched down next to the door. Jimmy Ray scowled at him. "Where you been all fucking Christmas? Why didn't you come and see us?"

"It was too cold," said Findo.

"That's fucking true. I couldn't even defrost the locks to get in this car." His brother glared. "You could have walked."

Findo shook his head. "Nah. Anyway, it wasn't worth it."

"Wasn't worth it?"

"Well, did you miss me?"

Jimmy Ray stared at Findo for a minute then laughed. "Cheeky fucking brat."

Findo smiled back. "Well, did you?"

Jimmy Ray shook his head. "Well, I fucking didn't and I don't think Mum noticed; she was off her head for a week. Had some twat round she'd picked up at a club but then he fucked off and she started on the vodka and snakebites. Otis spends all of his time stoned and Louise just moons around like some fucking space cadet."

"What about Rob?"

Jimmy Ray shrugged. "He's done a vanishing act too. Probably just shacked up with some bird, though. What about you? What you been up to?"

"Not a lot," said Findo. "First time I've been out for about a week. I've just been sitting around, eating and stuff."

"Yeah? What sort of stuff?"

"Reading."

"Reading?" Jimmy Ray sneered. "You fucking queer. Reading? Haven't you got a telly at your gaffe?"

Findo shook his head.

"I could get you one," said Jimmy Ray. "Brand new, video as well if you like. Won't cost much."

"No electricity," said Findo.

"No electricity? You in some shit-hole squat or something?"

"Sort of."

Jimmy Ray stared at him. "You going to tell me where it is?"

"No."

"You fucking sure about that?"

"What do you want to know for?" said Findo. "It's not like you miss me."

Jimmy Ray shook his head. "I can't make up my mind whether to give you a good kicking or just tell you to fuck off." He suddenly jabbed a finger at Findo. "Oh yeah. Just remembered. Mickey's after you."

"After me?"

"Yeah. He's been round about three times. Didn't say why but he was asking after you each time. Maybe he's got a job for you. I hear he's in with this new crew that have taken over from the Muldoons."

"Taken over from the Muldoons?"

"Yeah, where you been? They're fucking history now." Jimmy Ray leant back away from the window and gunned the engine of his Ford Escort. "Anyway, can't waste all fucking day talking to you, shithead. Got places to go. I'll tell Mickey I saw you."

The white Escort shot away from the kerb, forcing another car to swerve out of the way and narrowly missing an oncoming van. Findo watched it go and shook his head. His family might not have missed him but the feeling was mutual; he had enjoyed the Christmas just past more than any other.

It was nearly midday when he got to Frances Reid's house but again he was disappointed. The curtains were closed and there was no sign of life. It was only when Findo started walking back up Dubmore Road that he remembered the librarian saying that she was going to take some time off in January to go and visit Cuba. She had signed up for a cycling tour and was not going to be back until later in the month.

Findo thought for a while about getting into her house – he could look after it while she was away and make sure no one else burgled the property – but decided he did not feel right about breaking into a friend's home.

He set off instead up Dubmore Road, heading for the city centre. He had been thinking about whether or not to stay in the castle and wanted to check out some alternatives. Back before Christmas he had found a way into an empty office block near the Campfield roundabout. He had only got round to exploring part of the building and also intended inspecting a nearby warehouse that had been gutted in a fire two years ago and boarded up since.

Findo lowered himself over the wall and dropped the last four feet onto the tarmac. He landed with a thud and crouched where he was for a minute or two as he listened for any shouts.

He was in a parking compound between the office block and the burnt-out warehouse. The walled area was used by the managers from the biscuit factory and the high-tech business park on the other side of Warner Drive. There were car parks around the factory and offices but those drivers who valued their vehicles tended to prefer to pay the extra cost; it was less painful paying to have their precious motors locked up rather than see them speeding off towards the motorway for a high-speed chase.

Not that the compound was entirely safe. Mickey Dunn had once persuaded a rather dim security guard that he had been sent over to wash the Jaguar owned by the managing director of a new computer software firm. Three minutes later, the gleaming saloon rocketed out just as the guard was about to close the gates behind another car; neither the Jaguar nor the sacked security guard were ever seen there again.

But Findo was not bothered about cars. He was interested in the compound because it appeared to offer the only way into the derelict warehouse. He had spent the afternoon roaming the empty corridors, offices and storerooms of the office block but had come away empty-handed. The building had been well and truly stripped before it was vacated. Even the light bulbs and most of the carpets were gone. The water supply had been cut off and there was nothing else to attract him to the premises.

Findo had scratched the building from his list of potential refuges. Apart from the lack of facilities, there was another, even more important problem with the office block – it looked as if others had also found a way inside. There was graffiti along a number of internal walls and a fire had been started in one corridor. There was an old mattress in one office and other evidence of human occupation, including empty drink cans, cigarette butts and a couple of discarded syringes. Findo had experienced enough squats in his time with Bosnia to have no desire to share his quarters with strangers, let alone those from the same circles as the rest of his family.

Now he wanted to take a look at the warehouse. From the outside it did not look promising. There were still black streaks up the walls from when the place had been torched by arsonists. On an earlier reconnaissance, Findo had found that all the windows and doors were boarded up with heavy-duty plywood. But he also remembered that the building had been used to house electrical appliances rather than anything particularly flammable and from the top of the office block had been able to see that the warehouse roof was still intact.

The only possible way in that he had been able to spot was up a metal fire escape leading from a small courtyard. The one entrance had been bricked up and the top of the wall above it was protected with barbed wire and broken bottles. But there was another wall between the courtyard from the parking compound that was both lower and had no wire or glass on it.

Findo moved at a crouch, scuttling behind the cars parked at the back of the compound. Some were only inches from the wall with no room to squeeze by and he had to slide across their bonnets.

He made it to the opposite side of the parking area and crouched by the nose of a Vauxhall Carlton. The wall dividing the compound from the warehouse's courtyard area was about eight feet tall. Getting over was no problem; Findo was confident that if he got onto the Vauxhall's roof he would be able to reach the top of the wall and scramble up. Dropping down the other side did not scare him. The trouble was that he had no way of knowing if there was anything in the courtyard that he would be able to use to get back up and over the wall again.

Findo pulled a Twix from inside a pocket and ate it while pondering the problem. After a while, he stuffed the last bit of chocolate into his mouth and stood up. The only answer was to get up on the wall and look. He would risk being spotted by the security guard but there was no alternative. Until he could see into the courtyard there was no way to know whether the route was possible. The only other option was to come back with some rope and other tools but Findo did not want to wait.

Findo climbed up and knelt on the bonnet of the Carlton. By peering over the roof he could just about see the little kiosk by the compound's gate. There was no sign of the guard. Findo stood up a little bit higher and scanned the lines of parked cars. Still no sign of the guard. He wiped his hands on his jeans and stepped quickly up onto the roof of the Carlton. Leaning over the narrow gap between the car and the wall, he grabbed the top of the brickwork and launched himself at it, swinging one leg up. His foot caught and he pulled himself up, rolling onto the top of the wall and lying along it.

He stayed still, hoping the movement had not been spotted. No alarm sounded and he twisted his head to look down into the courtyard.

It was full of rubbish: pools of water, dead leaves, plastic bags and all kinds of other litter light enough to be lifted by the wind. Clumps of weeds grew from a blocked drain and the first scrubby plants had found a hold in cracks among the concrete. A couple of broken pallets lay in the middle of the courtyard and there was a stack of old plastic chairs in one corner. Some plastic sacks containing what looked like old paperwork had been thrown against another wall, spilling part of their contents across the ground. An old dustbin with holes rusted right through its sides stood nearby. Close to the base of the fire escape lay a section of metal drainpipe that had come away from the wall; fragments of shattered cast iron were spread around the spot where it had hit the ground.

Findo lay on the wall, listening out for any sound that he had been spotted while he studied the courtyard. The fire escape itself looked okay. The metal was rusty but still intact and came right down to the ground. The warehouse was on four floors and there were doors leading off the fire escape at each level, although Findo could not see whether they could be opened from the outside. The metal ladder also zigzagged its way right to the roof of the warehouse, which was mostly flat. Two ground floor windows looked onto the courtyard from the warehouse but were protected by heavy bars set into concrete surrounds.

Initially, Findo thought that was it. But then he spotted the door behind the pile of discarded office chairs. It was closed but there was a glazed panel in the top half. The glass was reinforced by wire but Findo knew from experience that it could still be broken.

He studied the contents of the courtyard again before swinging his feet round and dropping down into the enclosed area. Either the old pallets or the stack of chairs should be enough to give him a sufficient boost up over the wall on his way out.

Findo did not leave the warehouse until after six that evening. It had been dark for a couple of hours by the time he slipped over the fence at the front of the now empty parking compound and dropped onto the pavement running along Warner Drive. A fresh frost was already glittering on the pavement and he set off at a quick pace; it was a good couple of miles back to the castle and he was looking forward to settling back down in front of his fire. After a day's fresh air and exploration he was also ready to curl up with a book again and start reading the next Narnia book, *The Silver Chair*.

He was part-way along Albert Parade when he was spotted.

Albie Hooper was on his way out of the city centre's branch of Burger King when he saw Findo marching briskly along. Albie shoved a bag containing three burgers into one pocket of his overcoat, his portion of fries into the other and set off in pursuit, ignoring the squeal of brakes and gestures of a bus driver as he strode across Albert Parade.

Findo walked on oblivious with his head down, pulling his coat tighter around his scrawny frame. Albie converged on him a few hundred yards before the traffic lights at the Stewart Road junction. The first Findo knew of the big man's presence was when a hand gripped his collar and swung him into the air. The boy's feet flailed as they lost their contact with the ground and he twisted like a worm on a hook.

"Hello, Findo." Albie set him down again but kept hold of the boy's collar. "How you doing, nipper?"

Findo squirmed, glancing sideways, behind him and past Albie. "I'm alright."

Albie steered the young thief into the doorway of a closed travel agents'. He gave Findo a gentle push as he released his collar, sending the boy into one corner of the door. Albie leant against the shop window beside Findo, effectively sealing off his exit.

"Haven't seen you around much, Findo. Where you been?"

Findo shrugged. "Staying in. Keeping warm. Not doing much."

"Is that right?" Albie grinned at him. "Not what I heard."

Findo frowned. "What have you heard?"

"Oh, talk," said Albie. "About what you've been up to. Is it true?"

"How do I know?" said Findo. "I don't know what you've heard."

"So you have been up to something then?"

Findo frowned and shut his mouth in a tight scowl.

Albie grinned again. He reached into his pockets and pulled out the bag containing the burgers. He looked at Findo's expression and laughed. "Hey, don't look at me like that, you'll scare me." He offered a cheeseburger to Findo. "Hungry?"

Findo took it warily. "Thanks."

"S'alright," said Albie, talking around a quarter of a burger. "Enjoy it."

Findo ate in quick bites that he gulped down. When he was finished he screwed up the wrapper and flicked it onto the ground. Albie rammed the last of his second burger down his throat and pulled the cardboard carton of fries from his other pocket. He offered them to

Findo and they ate them together.

Once the food was gone, Findo gave Albie a smile. "Thanks for that."

He stepped forward to go past Albie and continue down the street. A heavy arm shot out and barred his way. "Nah."

Findo went to duck past the arm. "Look, I've got to get home."

Albie laughed. "No you haven't."

"I have."

"Yeah? Home to who?"

"Just home."

Albie shook his head sadly. "Come on, Findo. I've just shared my dinner with you. What sort of way's that to say thank you?"

"Okay." Findo stepped back into the doorway. "What do you want me for?"

"I don't."

Findo frowned.

"Someone else wants to see you. Been looking for you for a little while."

"Who?"

"Ah, you'll find out."

20. Career development

Findo looked around nervously. He had been collected from Albie by two men he did not know. They had picked him up by car from Albert Parade and brought him to a garage off Chapelbank Road. The men had not said anything on the way and now they ushered him through to a room at the back of the garage.

They closed the door, leaving Findo in a small waiting room. Cheap armchairs were arranged against two walls and there was a drink-dispensing machine on top of a filing cabinet. A low table was littered with dog-eared magazines. There were a couple of dirty ashtrays on the table and a calendar on the wall from a tyre company, January's glamour-girl oozing across the bonnet of a gleaming sports car.

There was one other door leading from the room but it was closed. Findo stepped cautiously closer and bent his ear towards the door. There was a faint murmur from beyond but it was impossible to make out what was being said or how many were talking.

Findo glanced quickly around again. There were no windows and no other ways in or out apart from the two doors. He moved back to the first door and crouched by it. Through the keyhole he could see part of the workshop beyond. There was a car on the hoist above the pit and another waiting to be serviced. The overhead lights were on and apart from the pit – which was too obvious anyway – there were no shadows in which to hide. The roller door at the front of the garage was shut. There was an open side door but Findo could see one of the men who had brought him here standing just outside smoking a cigarette.

Findo thought quickly. He could only think of two options and took the second one, lying on the floor and sliding under two of the armchairs. He reached up and tugged them slightly closer together then squirmed as far out of sight as he could.

He was just in time.

The second door opened and Findo saw a pair of feet appear in the entrance. There was a pause and then he saw their owner move briskly to the other door and open it.

"Hey! Steve! John!" The voice was abrupt. It sounded irritated.

"Yeah?" The reply came from somewhere on the other side of the garage.

"Where's the kid?"

"What?"

"Where's the kid? I wanted him in here."

Findo heard more footsteps approaching at a trot.

"Well, come on, where is he?"

"You're joking, aren't you?"

"No. I'm not fucking joking. Where's the kid?"

"But we left him in here."

"Well, you're fucking idiots then! Where is he now?"

A third voice joined the conversation. "Little bastard must have sneaked out."

"Then find him! Stop talking and get a fucking move on or he'll bloody well vanish again."

"Right," said the second man. "Well he must be in the workshop. We've been standing in the entrance. He couldn't have got past us."

"Yeah? Well, you're not standing there now, are you?"

Findo lay still, hardly daring to breathe. He watched the feet of the two men who had brought him to the garage as they dashed back into the workshop and began to search for him. Unfortunately, the man from the office did not join them. He stayed in the door to the workshop watching, with his back to Findo.

After a while he gave a deep sigh. "Any sign of him?"

"No."

"Can't see the bastard."

"You'd better go looking then."

The man turned back into the waiting room, slamming the door behind him. He returned across the room – then stopped. Findo watched him turn. It looked as if he was leaning against the doorframe.

Then he heard a deep chuckle. There was a pause and Findo closed his eyes.

"Well," said the voice, "you going to come out from there or shall I call my boys back and ask them to get you out?"

Findo lowered himself cautiously into the chair. The man walked back round to the other side of the desk and sat opposite. They stared at each other for a while, each evaluating and calculating. Eventually the man lent forwards.

"So you're the famous Findo Gask, the boy who stole the Maserati and takes anything else he fancies. Got quite a reputation you have – I hear the police reckon there's a whole gang of you. Funny; you're smaller than I expected, look younger too."

Findo said nothing.

"Being little must make it easier to get in and out of places though."

Findo stayed silent. The man continued to stare at him in a considering fashion. "I suppose looking young's probably an advantage too. Look young and innocent and no one takes any notice of you. Is that right? A little, insignificant lad like you could slip in and out of all sorts of places. Keep quiet, keep your head down, act shy, that sort of thing."

Findo looked down at the desk.

"Do you speak then?"

Findo gave a miniscule shrug.

"I hear you do a lot of slipping in and out of places."

Findo shrugged again.

"Like, let's see, an office building over in Hobbes Town?"

Findo stayed silent, trying not to show any reaction.

The man leaned closer. Findo could feel his breath; it smelt of mint. "That doesn't trigger any memories? You don't remember breaking in a little while before Christmas? Got into some offices and found a briefcase with a lot of money in it?"

Findo gave a small shake of the head.

"That's a shame," said the man. "Your friend Mickey seemed to think it might have been you. I was hoping it was; I wanted to congratulate you."

Findo looked up in surprise. The man sitting opposite grinned and laughed at Findo's expression. He tucked his hands behind his close-cropped head and lent back.

"Congratulate me?"

The man's expression became serious again. He had a narrow face and quick, sharp eyes. "Yes – if you're the one who took the money. Are you?"

Findo shrugged uneasily. "What money?"

The stranger laughed again. He grinned at Findo and held out a hand across the table. "Go on, shake it."

Findo took the man's hand and shook nervously.

The man chuckled. "You're smart, Findo Gask. You're delivered to my door and you still almost manage to trick me into thinking you've got away. And now I've got you, you're still not saying anything. You don't trust me and that's good. Even when I act like your friend you don't take any chances." He nodded. "You'll go a long way. If you get bored with thieving, try poker. A face like yours could do well." The man leant back into his chair and swung his feet up onto the desk. He was wearing heavy workman's boots scuffed from use. "Now look," he said. "I know we've probably put the wind up you but don't worry. I honestly don't mean you any harm. I know you don't even know who I am but, without meaning to, you've done me an enormous favour."

The man folded his hands together across his chest. "My name's Colin Speed. I'm no friend of the Muldoons or Victor Hong so don't worry about that."

Findo frowned. "Who's Victor Hong?" he asked quietly.

Colin Speed smiled. "The man who used to control most of this city's heroin supply. The man you stole a cool quarter million from."

Findo's eyes widened and Speed laughed. "You don't even really know what you did, do you?"

Findo shook his head.

"Do you know one of the Muldoons is dead and the other one's been locked up?"

The boy's mouth opened silently.

Speed nodded. "Maybe I should explain what happened," he said. "You see, that Monday when you went to the Turk's Head with Mickey Dunn and his friends . . . You do remember going there?"

"Yeah."

"Good. Well, Danny Muldoon and Victor Hong were negotiating a deal. You see, Hong was supplying smack and other stuff through his restaurants and other places. He'd also got the Pakis and others like them on his side. Got quite a big network. The Muldoons had tried to muscle in a few times but Hong's men were tough enough to stand up to them." Speed spread his hands. "So, although the Muldoons wanted to be top-dog, they also wanted to do business. They'd taken control of a racket down at Port Annan docks and were starting to bring in some big shipments of heroin. And rather than get into a turf war with Hong, they proposed a deal. He was going to be middleman and buy the gear from them in bulk. It meant Hong stayed in control of the outlets but the Muldoons got to shift all their gear without having to get their hands dirty doing any of the dealing." Speed cocked his head at Findo. "With me so far?"

Findo gave a small nod. "Think so."

"Good. Well, I don't know exactly what happened in there but it sounds like they were closing the deal over in Hobbes Town. Hong was handing over the cash and, in return, the Muldoons were delivering the first consignment of smack to one of Hong's restaurants."

Speed grinned. "But something went wrong," he continued. "The money disappeared. Hong had brought a briefcase with him but when Danny Muldoon opened it, it was empty. You see, that's when it all started to get messy. Danny Muldoon thought Victor Hong was trying to pull some trick on him and Victor Hong thought Muldoon had double-crossed him. They both go crazy accusing each other and it turns into a bloodbath instead of a new partnership. Mad, eh?"

Speed was interrupted by a knock on the door. "Yes?"

One of the men who had brought Findo to the garage stuck his head round the door. "We can't . . ." The man's jaw dropped when he saw Findo. "How did he get here?"

Speed laughed. "We were all nearly too slow for this one, John."

Speed's henchman gave a perplexed scowl. "Where'd he get to then?"

The man behind the desk laughed. "He hadn't gone anywhere – he was hiding under the chairs. Almost had us all fooled." He winked at Findo. "Next time I get you to bring him to see me, take a sack to put him in."

The man called John shook his head in slow admiration. "Slippery little bastard," he said. "Wouldn't think it, would you? Looks all innocent."

"Oh, he is," said Speed. "Maybe not harmless but innocent. That's what makes him so good." He pointed at Findo. "You hungry, lad?"

Findo shrugged.

"Well I am," said Speed. "Go and get us a takeaway will you, John. I fancy a bit of Indian. Nip down the Bombay and get a load of grub. Get some for you and Steve and our young friend here. A few beers as well wouldn't go amiss."

Findo stuffed the last piece of naan bread into his mouth and lent back. The metal cartons in front of him gleamed. The three men watching grinned.

"Bloody hell!" said John. "You could eat for the fucking Olympics, you could."

His mate Steve nodded. "Don't the bastards feed you at home?"

Findo shrugged and belched loudly.

"Hey!" Steve waved a beer can in the air. "Let it out."

"You enjoy that then, Findo?" said Colin Speed.

The boy nodded. "Yeah." He looked around at the empty dishes. "Thanks."

"That's alright," said Speed. "No worries. I believe in looking after my friends. You stick with me Findo and we'll make sure you're okay. Right, lads?"

The other two men nodded. "Aye," said Steve. "He'll treat you right if you're straight with him."

Findo looked from one to the other then stood up slowly and nodded at Speed. "Well, thanks for the food," he said. "I'd better be going now."

Speed raised an eyebrow. "You sure?"

Findo gave a quick nod. "Yeah, I need to get home."

"Okay," said Speed. "But make sure you don't bump into any of the Muldoons' gang."

Findo froze. "The Muldoons. But I thought you said . . ."

Speed lent back in his chair and picked at the remnants of a samosa. "Yeah. Barrie Muldoon's dead and his brother's behind bars. But that doesn't mean Danny Muldoon's out of action. Some of his men are still about and I imagine that if Danny Muldoon gets word who stole Victor Hong's money he's going to be pretty pissed off. Life could get pretty unpleasant for you Findo. So watch out; it would be sad if anything happened to you."

Findo sat down again slowly. "Does he know?"

Speed shrugged. "Wouldn't know. Doubt it though."

Findo glanced around but the other two men just looked back at him – there was no help there.

"Are you going to tell him?"

Speed laughed. "Findo, what kind of bloke do you take me for? Like I said, you did me a favour. I've got no desire to help Danny Muldoon; as far as I'm concerned he's a piece of shit and I wouldn't give a fuck if he got the same treatment as his brother. I'd sooner touch a rabid dog than trust anyone from that family. But thing is, I put two and two together and came up with your name. Now, I wouldn't tell them – and you can trust Steve and John here too – but it's not impossible that someone else could do the same."

Findo swallowed and blinked a couple of times. He felt cold and weak. "What can I do?" he said.

Speed stared him in the eye. "Well," he said, "there's no guarantee that anyone will think of you but then there's no guarantee that they won't. So, if I was you, I'd think about some kind of insurance."

"Insurance?"

Speed smiled. "Yeah, insurance. You see, Findo, you're a smart kid but you're still just a kid and you're out there on your own. Now, you're a good thief – from what I hear you're a star – but you're just an amateur. What I'd suggest is you kill two birds with one stone. Turn professional."

Findo frowned but kept silent.

"You see," continued Speed, "to me, crime is a business just like any other and I need people with talent. I was looking at expanding in the New Year anyway and thanks to you setting Hong and the Muldoons at each other's throats, you've created an unexpected opportunity to move things on faster than I'd originally planned. So, you see, I've got what you could call a staffing problem and I'm recruiting new talent. Now, if you agreed to work for me, I could put your talents to good use. There's plenty of jobs where I could use someone like you. I'd make sure you did alright out of it too; you'd get a good cut from whatever you did and you wouldn't have to worry about fencing anything. I'd tell you what I needed and I'd move the gear afterwards. I'll pay cash or goods, depends on what you want. You'd have good prospects with me, Findo. It would be like turning a hobby into a career."

He leant forward. "And the other thing is that I'd put the word out that you're working for me, Findo. If I do that, you can forget the Muldoons. No one's going to have a pop at you if they know you're working for me."

21. From little things

And so, Findo Gask's life entered a new phase as the boy thief was recruited into the adult world and made the transition from opportunist survivor to proactive adventurer.

Findo entered the world of the professional criminal hardened but still relatively naive. He had grown up among the city's dregs and dropouts, living a hand-to-mouth existence among addicts, prostitutes, petty criminals and other human cast-offs. It had been a thankless existence and one on which he had only recently begun to improve – principally through his own efforts. None of his family – with the possible exception of the now absent Billy – had ever provided him with a more positive role model and joining mainstream society was an idea that Findo had never been invited to even consider.

But while a loser in the social stakes, Findo was a winner in the roulette of genetic inheritance. He had passed lightly through the trials of childhood illness despite his circumstances and, although still small and scrawny, emerged from childhood tough and strong with an endurance level far in excess of his size.

Learning to read opened up doorways to escape routes from the city, showing him for the first time that – even if only in the realm of imagination – better worlds did exist. And as Findo grew a little older, reading enabled him to begin a belated education. Through books, magazines and comics he started accumulating knowledge and ideas – some more useful and reliable than others. Facts and thoughts seeped into the empty spaces in his head, sparking his brain into new life and expanding his horizons beyond the limits of city streets, gang turfs and places to steal a quick lunch.

But Findo's new awareness of worlds beyond the city's mean streets did not change his way of life. The only lessons provided by his childhood had been simple ones – like possession being nine-tenths of the law and getting your retribution in first. And with most people around him cheating the system in some way or other, it had never occurred to Findo that there was any difference between defrauding the Benefits Agency and stealing his dinner from Sainsbury's; to him, deceiving and thieving were as natural a way of foraging as searching for nuts and berries to a primitive hunter-gatherer.

What he did begin to realise was that different spheres existed even within the city. There was his world, Bosnia's and Abby's, as well as all the other worlds of the employed and the idle, the exploited and the exploiters, the rule-makers and the rule-breakers. All lived side-by-side, yet were so foreign to each other they could have been on different planets. It was a revelation that began slowly but accelerated radically after the two children gate-crashed Clement Dallaway's garden party. There, Findo had witnessed – in all its drunken, overfed and self-important glory – the kind of life that he had never thought was more than a figment of the imagination of the aliens who created television.

Previously, Findo had accepted that life was how it was; he had no reason to imagine alternatives. Awareness of other worlds brought with it the slow dawning of a feeling that was to be a significant facet of his life for years to come. It was not exactly resentment, more a belief that he was different: outside the webs of loyalty and obedience that bound others.

Alongside Findo's increased realisation of the complicated weft and weave of society's layers came an emerging conviction that he had as much right to a stake in the world as the next person. This was expressed in various ways. One was the thieving. With nothing given to him it was only natural to take. Initially stealing was a means to an end, a question of survival. Later, with his basic needs secured, theft became a form of self-expression – with Findo deriving as much satisfaction from the challenge as from the possession that resulted. That was one reason Findo Gask never went down the route of robbery. Another was that violence disturbed him; he associated its use with stupidity.

During the early years of his career, Findo asserted his claim on life by scrawling his name across the city. His territorial markings were proclaimed in spray paint and marker pen upon and inside buildings, over vehicles and across any other stationary object that took his fancy. Sometimes his tagging simply marked his passage; other times it was a calling card at the scenes of his depredation. Police officers became used to finding Findo's name daubed on the walls inside office buildings, shops and warehouses that had been reported burgled. It happened often enough that – coupled with the fact that they did not recognise Findo Gask as a name – the words came to be taken as some kind of gang moniker.

By the time he was recruited by Colin Speed, Findo was ready to move on. He had already established his independence by forsaking the family life offered by Bosnia and his half-siblings. He had been forced to provide for himself for years – now he had shown that he was also capable of finding his own shelter.

Colin Speed's organisation provided a new sort of security – as well as a kind of kinship. For although Findo began his professional career when he was just twelve, he was never regarded as a junior member of the team. He had earned his spurs the hard way and his bravado and expertise at the art of thievery had been known for years. His theft of the toy Maserati and the way he had disposed of it after eluding the city's police had already entered local mythology. The rumour that he had also stolen a quarter of a million pounds from Victor Hong then given it away started him on the route to becoming a folk hero.

For it did not take long for the tale of the emptied briefcase to begin to circulate. Colin Speed kept his word, as did his two lieutenants. They never breathed a word of what they knew, which was originally based only on a hunch (although Findo did tell them the full story one drunken night).

Speed had only made the connection with Findo by chance. The morning after the theft, Mickey Dunn had gone back to the Turk's Head to see if anyone wanted a car stealing. He had slept in late and the nervous conversation going on in the bar was the first Mickey had heard of the overnight outbreak of gang war. At first, he listened to the reports and rumours with interest.

Then the blood drained from Mickey's face as one of the drinkers, a teenage heroin dealer who did the rounds of the housing estates, told how the fighting had been sparked off when a deal being conducted in Muldoon's building near the back of the pub went sour. The teenager laughed as he recounted how a briefcase full of money was supposed to have vanished and Hong's men had later tried to storm the building to exact revenge and get the cash back.

Fortunately for Mickey, the only person to notice his reaction had been Speed's lieutenant, John Biggs, who was drinking at one end of the bar and listening to the gossip. John watched as Mickey's mouth dropped open and the young car thief suddenly turned around and left the pub. John reported back to his boss and Mickey was picked up later that day. Helped by a mixture of threats and promises – plus the fact that he knew Colin Speed was no friend of either the Muldoons or Hong – he was persuaded to explain his response. Speed then put out the word to bring in Findo.

It was Rob, already jealous of the reputation his baby brother was gaining, who spread the story. Mickey had told Rob what had happened, thinking that Findo could trust his brother. Rob broke his silence for the sheer pleasure of the provocation it caused – an act of treachery that backfired when he told the story for the third time in an

East Park pub called the Mayfield Arms. Two thugs who used to get regular employment from the Muldoon brothers were listening. On the grounds that Rob was Findo's brother, they jumped him when he left the pub. After giving him a good beating, they stamped on Rob's hands with heavy boots and threw him back into the pub through the window. Rob spent over a week in hospital and it took nearly three months until all the cuts and bruises had healed. He also had problems with his fists for the rest of his life and was never able to punch anyone as well as previously.

But Findo's fears of retribution eventually proved groundless. Although his name was already becoming legend, his face was far less known. He had never liked being the centre of attention and had turned self-effacement into a discipline. As a result, even plenty who had met him face-to-face would be hard pressed to say what he looked like or recognise him in the street. He was also rarely to be seen in the kind of drinking holes and other dens where he might have bumped into survivors from the Muldoon gang.

Not that there were many about. Chief Superintendent Ross Kirkbride's men had not had any trouble finding enough evidence to keep Danny Muldoon from ever getting bail and his subsequent trial saw him join his father in prison on a sentence that removed the family from circulation for decades. Barrie Muldoon, like Victor Hong and several of the brothers' henchmen, was dead. Most of the other principal members of the Muldoons' family firm were also languishing at Her Majesty's pleasure. A few of the more professional employees of the gang had accepted the change in management. Like Findo, they now worked for Colin Speed and could not care less about the fate of their old bosses. Those Muldoon casuals who were still out on the streets were mostly small fry who owed little allegiance and posed no danger.

The only real exception was the man called the Judge. He was the one who had executed Victor Hong on Danny Muldoon's behalf. On the night that the money disappeared and the mutual accusations and recriminations began, Hong and his bodyguard had been allowed to leave the premises in Hobbes Town safely – mainly because Danny Muldoon was as astonished as Hong by the sight of the empty briefcase. Despite his angry accusations, Muldoon actually found it hard to believe that Hong would have been so stupid as to pull such a blatant trick in order to get the heroin and could not rule out the possibility that one of his own men, as Hong alleged, must have taken the cash.

The firebomb attack on Hong's restaurant and the assault on the

Newmills gambling den were more of an automatic response from Danny Muldoon than a case of serious retribution. But once the assault launched on the Hobbes Town building by Hong's men had been fought off, Muldoon's short fuse blew. Furious, he dispatched the Judge and three handpicked assistants to find the Singaporean with clear orders. The Judge's team found Hong a couple of hours later at the city centre offices of his associate, Cheng Ho. The accountant managed to escape during the subsequent attack (and later did flee the city after carrying out some bank transfers involving large amounts of money). But Victor Hong and his bodyguard, along with one of the Judge's team, died that night.

The next morning, the Judge had been on his way to one of the gang's weapons dumps at a farm outside the city when Barrie Muldoon was shot. He was still at the depot when Danny Muldoon was picked up and soon after he got a message telling him to disappear. He did, catching a ferry from Stranraer to Northern Ireland and later, a flight from Shannon to New York, where he vanished from circulation.

But the Judge was no danger to Findo while in the United States and there was no other real threat within the city. Hong's organisation had melted away with his death and no one really mourned the passing of the Muldoons. Colin Speed's protection also carried weight. For although Speed was not as vicious or unpredictable as the Muldoons, he still had a reputation (deliberately cultivated) as being a hard man who was as tough with punishments as fair with rewards.

Speed's protection of Findo also extended further than if it had been just a case of him looking after his own men. The new boss of the city's underworld was at heart a sentimental man and had taken a liking to Findo. The boy's persistent elusiveness and slipperiness even when apparently caught had tickled Speed's sense of humour. And even though he could not quite understand it, he was highly amused by the way that Findo had given away the money stolen from Victor Hong.

Speed, who was the cousin of the junkie who had sold Findo as a baby, had also been telling the truth when he said Findo had done him an enormous favour. Behind the cover of a number of legitimate businesses including garages, a property letting firm and an auction house, Colin Speed had operated at the fringes of the city's underworld for many years. But he had never intended to be a minor player forever, he had just been biding his time, building up his strength through activities that he was careful to ensure did not draw the attention of others who might see his actions as an infringement on their turf. Speed had never seen the point in drawing enemy fire until he was ready to return it.

While in his twenties, Speed had spent some years living in London, Amsterdam and Newcastle, working for a variety of legitimate and thoroughly bent operations. Through the contacts made during those years, he had earned a reputation in certain quarters both around the country and internationally. Speed's expertise had been based on two key areas: the acquisition and disposal of specialist motors and of antiques and collectibles. He also dabbled in a few other areas of crime. However, these activities were more as a way of staying in touch with other fields of interest rather than being a serious pursuit.

On the day that Findo inadvertently launched the gang war between the Muldoons and Victor Hong, his future boss was not widely known in his home city. Although he generally worked out of it, Speed had always taken care to keep a low profile locally. Other than with a couple of police officers that he had been introduced to by a mutual contact, he had never made himself known to the forces of law and order. Most of Speed's network of operators was located around other metropolitan areas.

But that had been due to change: the city's secretive wheeler-dealer had slowly been getting ready to redraw the lines of power within the city.

Colin Speed's plans had been born of necessity. While he was as comfortable with the rough side of business as the smooth, his primary motivation was money not power. Ultimately, he was a businessman, wanting wealth not scalps. He even had his own pension plan – a fund he had been steadily accumulating in order to buy a house on a Caribbean island, complete with large powerboat and the other accoutrements of a serious sport fisherman with a certain lifestyle. And to get to that position, Speed was prepared to work. But that meant having a stable economy and secure options. Operating his more far-flung businesses was lucrative but risky, and the distances involved meant it was harder to be assured of control. So Speed had looked closer to home.

Over the previous year he had considered several options, including working with the city's existing players. Speed had no desire to rule the city's underworld just for the thrill of it; he just wanted to make money. And so, unknown to those involved, he spent months studying their operations, looking at what they controlled and how. Hong was the kingpin in a network of drug dealers linked to various ethnic communities but his outfit, although it could muster enough muscle to keep the Muldoons at bay, was only really concerned with the narcotics trade and, therefore, of less interest to Speed.

The Muldoons were the other real power. But as he gathered his intelligence it had become clear to Speed that the brothers were too volatile. The Muldoons had ruled by violence and intimidation but had never been particularly efficient. Worse, they were unreliable and not consistent. Ultimately that meant they were too unprofessional to try working with. Therefore they had to go.

He had begun to prepare the ground for his coup in the summer. He brought in some trusted employees from outside the city. Some began working for his legitimate cover businesses, a number found jobs on the fringes of the Muldoon gang. The connection with Speed – known locally only as a dodgy garage owner and landlord – was something about which their new bosses remained in complete ignorance.

By the time it got to Christmas, Speed was almost ready. He had built up an accurate enough picture of what the Muldoons ran, where they operated from, who worked for them – and how many men were likely to stand up and be counted when it came to a showdown. Speed also knew that when the day did come there would be no half-measures. Knocking out the Muldoons would have to be done in one go, fast. They would also need to be taken out of circulation permanently.

Speed intended letting the police do a lot of his work. He planned to wait until the Muldoons had a large operation going down somewhere. A tip-off would get the police into action – he had already told the right officers what pseudonym to expect from their informant. When the time came, he would let the police know where to find the Muldoons – using his insiders to cause just enough of a problem to draw the brothers out if they needed to be brought closer to the action. Speed had also made preparations so that the police would have all the incriminating evidence they needed – even if some of it had to be provided.

Speed had no scruples about giving the police the information to put away the Muldoons. He did not see it as betrayal. To have grassed up a fellow professional would have been unforgivable but the Muldoons were thugs. To Speed, they were the kind of scum to give crime a bad name. They took pleasure in harming people for the sake of it and were bad for business.

And if anything went wrong with his main plan, Speed knew there was still an alternative option. It would be more costly and was only something he would do if left with no choice but at least it had the benefit of being permanent – and would lead to few tears being shed.

But Findo had changed everything. He had come out of the blue: an unknown catalyst sparking a chain reaction.

The first Speed knew of it was when one of his men called him at two o'clock in the morning. A whispered voice on a mobile phone, speaking from inside a toilet at the Hobbes Town building, told him that the Judge had just been sent to kill Victor Hong. That was all he said but it was enough. Speed had been aware of the deal being put together – the possibility of Hong working with the brothers had added a new dimension to the equation that had already alarmed him.

But as soon as he heard that the Muldoons had unleashed their most feared weapon and put Hong under sentence of death, Speed knew it was his cue; with the daggers drawn there would be plenty of blood to flow – and it would take more than a few sticking plasters to heal the resulting wounds.

Speed also knew that neither side would back down or give up easily. The Muldoons were vicious but Hong's operation was more disciplined and it would take a fierce battle to bring it down. And once the gloves were off there would be no escalation – the fight would be to the death from the moment the first blow was struck. There was also no certainty about the outcome – if the brothers had been confident of winning they would never have considered working with Hong in the first place.

It was nearly three in the morning before Speed got more news. One of his police contacts, called out to deal with the sudden explosion of gang violence, phoned to ask if he knew what was going on. Shortly after, two of his own men reported in with more detailed (and accurate) information about the Newmills incident and the firebombing. Just before six o'clock, the insider from the Hobbes Town building slipped into Speed's office and gave a brisk account of all he knew of what had happened involving Hong and Danny Muldoon's aborted deal and the battle that had taken place a few hours later. Speed's man then gave a quick rundown of the Muldoon war council that had ended only twenty minutes earlier and what the brothers were planning to do.

Soon after, Speed started to make a few phone calls himself. He started with the police headquarters, identifying himself simply as Roadrunner.

While the various mopping-up operations carried on, Speed continued to pull strings from behind the scenes. His men vanished from Danny Muldoon's side just before the police net closed in. Visits were made to others around the city to inform them of the change in leadership, reinforcing the message with the aid of cash payments or beatings as appropriate.

By the time it got to the end of the day, Speed's coup was essentially complete. The last few pockets of resistance had either been removed by the police or his own men. The new boss was in control and the process had been much less painful than anticipated – thanks largely to a certain Findo Gask and his inability to keep out of places where he was not supposed to be.

22. Private property

John swung open the door and ushered Findo through. The flat was fairly small but airy and light. It was on the upper floor of a terraced property at the eastern end of Corporation Road, a few hundred yards from Alexander Cross.

On the ground floor was a betting shop, run by a bookie who had worked for Speed for years. Above were a couple of floors of empty offices. And at the top of the building was an attic flat. There were two main rooms: a living room and a bedroom, as well as a small kitchen and bathroom. At the front, a dormer window looked onto Corporation Road. At the back was a door onto a flat roof that stretched back over the offices on the floor below.

John led Findo around the flat. He pointed out the monitors in the bedroom and the living room. They were linked to two security cameras: one in the lobby, the other in the stairwell. He led Findo onto the flat roof and showed him the fire escape that descended to a courtyard at the back. Beyond were a couple of narrow lanes. One ran parallel with Corporation Road; the other went off at an angle towards Albert Parade.

Back inside, John strolled into the living room and went over to the fireplace. The surround and hearth were still in place but there was no fire. A single sheet of white-painted plywood sealed off the space beneath the mantelpiece.

"Here," he said. "I reckon you'll like this bit."

He took hold of a small brass pipe sticking out of one corner of the hearth: it looked like the capped-off feed for a gas fire. As Findo watched, the pipe and the whole sheet of plywood swung up to reveal a large, dark opening. John reached inside and flicked a switch. A light came on, revealing another room, the mirror image of the one they were standing in.

Findo smiled at the trick. "Neat."

John nodded. "Yeah, the boss used this place for a while. He's like you – likes to have an escape route handy."

Findo crouched down and looked through at the other, empty flat. "What's through there?"

John gestured through. "Check it out if you want. It's the same as this one, just not used. But you can use the staircase. Gives another way out. You can get out front or back."

Findo nodded but made no move to go through. Instead, he stood up again and wandered around the flat, opening cupboard doors and testing the furniture. There was a big sofa in the living room, as well as a television, video recorder and empty bookcase. The bedroom contained a double bed, pine wardrobe and chest of drawers. The kitchen was also fully kitted out with new appliances, crockery, cutlery, and even a few packets of basic foodstuffs.

John stood propped against the wall next to the living room door, watching Findo's prowling. After a while he laughed. "Well?"

"What?" Findo looked awkward.

John shook his head. "Nothing," he said. "Why don't you get the fucking kettle on and stop wearing out the carpet?"

Findo looked at him blankly for a moment then turned on his heel and headed back into the kitchen. Inside, he picked up the jug kettle suspiciously. He pulled off the lid and peered inside then moved to the sink. Findo turned the cold tap on slowly and watched the running water for a moment before sticking the spout of the kettle into the flow.

Now fifteen, Findo had been working for Colin Speed for more than three years, first as apprentice and then as fully qualified burglar.

Their first year had been cautious on both parts. Although Speed had been happy to take the young thief under his wing, he had remained aware of Findo's age and not tried asking too much too soon. Speed was an investor. He saw Findo as an asset to be nurtured. The boy's greatest quality – apart from his skills as a thief – was his anonymity. Except by name, he was virtually unknown. As long as he stayed that way, he remained a valuable tool. Speed had recognised Findo's potential and special qualities and was keen to preserve them – not see his freedom curtailed by the attention of the police, social services or any other agency.

Having a mentor was as strange to Findo as the concept of a regular employer. Initially he fought shy of Speed's control, wary in part just because it was such an alien feeling to have someone pay him so much attention. But over the months that followed their first meeting he finally grew to trust the city's new crime lord.

Speed was clever. He made no attempt to order Findo about, merely offering advice, telling him where certain items could be found and asking for help in their retrieval. He also kept his word: on the one hand never betraying Findo's role in the Hobbes Town incident, on the other making sure it was known around the city that the boy was under his protection.

Findo was also persuaded by Mickey Dunn to trust his new

guardian. The city's most prolific car thief had been one of Speed's first recruits from the local crime pool. And Mickey had soon come to enjoy working for the new boss. He was still stealing cars but doing it to order on a regular basis. Mickey's new employment also took him out of his hometown and to places across northern England and southern Scotland that he had never visited before.

There was a downside to the new arrangement. For the first time, Mickey had to be careful. In the past he used to take cars for the fun of it and a high-speed police chase was just part of the game. Working for Speed, however, he had to exercise caution, avoid attention and only drive like a lunatic when there was no other option. But on the other hand he was well looked after. Speed paid what he had promised and on time. Equally importantly for Mickey, he was treated with respect.

Gradually, Findo came to share Mickey's assessment. He also got on well with Speed's principal lieutenant, John Biggs. Like Findo, John was a quiet man who preferred staying in the background. He was in his fifties and on the surface seemed a fairly dull sort. But John's life story, although seldom told, was anything but ordinary. He had joined the army from school and saw active service while still a teenager. He was posted to Kenya during the last year of the Mau Mau uprising against British rule and was in Cyprus while the island's EOKA movement were fighting for independence. During the early 1960s he had a brief spell in the Congo as a mercenary, then returned home, got involved in a bungled bank robbery and spent the next eight years in jail. A couple of years after he was released (bored with working as a van driver), he left the UK and spent the remainder of his thirties travelling across Asia and Australia. In the mid-1980s, he returned to Europe and went to Amsterdam, where he met Colin Speed. The two worked together on several operations, smuggling first hashish and then cocaine through Britain's east coast container ports. Mutual respect became coupled with friendship and when Speed began to strike out on his own it had seemed natural for John Biggs to offer his services.

Findo only learnt that story in stages. He liked John for other qualities, including a dry sense of humour and one major weakness – science fiction. John was addicted. Sci-fi was his drug and he loved nothing better than tales of distant worlds, interstellar ships and alien artefacts. For John, the grander the space opera, the better. He was a fan of the old school and often to be found with his nose buried in a well-thumbed paperback by Heinlein, Clarke or Asimov.

Findo's exploration of the worlds of fantasy had already brought him to the edge of the genre. Under Frances Reid's direction he had attempted Aldous Huxley's *Brave New World* and tried the writings of H G Wells. John's tastes were not quite so worthy (and easier for Findo to share). For John, science fiction was about escapism; political and moral messages were fine but of secondary importance. He moved Findo's reading forward by more than five decades, to the cosmic wonders of sci-fi's golden age, as well as the more Byzantine fantasy worlds of authors like Robert Silverberg and Michael Moorcock.

John also showed Findo the pleasure of science fiction on celluloid. Tucked away in a flat in Cowfield Heights, Speed's lieutenant had a video library that put many shops to shame. He had obvious favourites like the *Star Wars* films and every *Star Trek* episode and feature ever created. But John's collection also contained dozens of classic (and not so classic) film ventures into the worlds of space travel, future lives and alien worlds. They ranged from early works like Fritz Lang's *Metropolis*, through obscure wonders like the hippy absurdity of *Dark Star* and its talking bomb, to more modern favourites like the visceral horror of *Alien*.

John Biggs also never tried teaching Findo anything or tell him what to do. He offered friendship but made no attempt to push it. He also never spoke unless he had something worth saying and he preferred quiet to noise and peace to excitement, having experienced enough action in his earlier life to value its absence. His tastes were straightforward but he had definite ideas of what he liked and cared nothing for what others thought. He had a wry sense of humour and was fundamentally a kind man and not easily offended – but could sulk when he was.

For those reasons, Findo quickly grew to like Speed's lieutenant and – by a process of trust by association – also became more inclined to accept his new boss.

Another factor that helped persuade Findo to trust Speed was the training. Early in their association, Findo was quizzed about what he knew about getting into buildings. Findo talked about climbing and drains and roofs but Speed pressed him on what he knew about locks and alarms. It took Speed a while to get the information from Findo, who only after persistent questioning admitted that he knew little and generally relied on speed and agility.

Speed had nodded, not surprised. A week later, he collected Findo in his black BMW and drove off through Garvock Hill and towards Dubmore. Soon they were further out of the city than Findo had ever been. Several hours later, they were still travelling. Eventually, they came to a small village. They continued on, taking a single-track road that finally ended at a grey farmhouse surrounded by nettles, rusted farm machinery and vacant-eyed sheep. Above them loomed a brooding swell of moorland.

Inside, Speed introduced Findo to Alan Sowerby, a small man in his sixties. Findo spent most of the next week with Sowerby in one of the barns behind the farm. From outside, the building appeared half-derelict – the lichen-stained walls looked as old as the fells above and the sagging stone-slab roof poised to fall in at any moment. But inside was another story. The walls were whitewashed and bright lights hung from solid beams. Long benches lined the main room and racks of tools stood ready for use.

It was there that Findo learnt some of the craft of his profession and came to know the tools of his trade. Alan Sowerby showed him how to pick locks, open a safe and – if necessary – blow it. He learnt about saws and blades, hard steel and soft, diamond drills and the many different types of window glass. He was shown how all manner of security systems operated, from simple electrical circuits to movement detectors and infrared beams.

Findo's first reaction at having been taken so far from his city was one of indignation and resentment. But his mood soon changed. Apart from when Sowerby sent him outside to stretch his legs and rest his eyes, Findo was hardly aware that he was away from home. He was fascinated. Sowerby was an expert in his trade and a rare breed; he had never been caught. He was also a perfectionist and had no truck with gambling. The only kind of bet Sowerby liked was a safe one, which was, of course, precisely why his forty-year career as a jewel thief had never been broken with a prison sentence.

Sowerby had retired now but like many ex-professionals liked to keep his hand in. He rarely travelled further than the local market town these days but there were others only too happy to come to him. For Sowerby offered his services as a consultant to those he knew and worked if he felt like it, happy to pass on any of his expertise in return for a generous consideration. There in the barn, on the farm his family had run for generations, he had set up his own kind of training centre. He had doors and windows set up in freestanding frames to which he could attach dozens of kinds of locks and other fastenings. There were a dozen safes, numerous security boxes and a host of alarms – any of which could be set up in all kind of configurations ready for his students to test their skills.

Sowerby's academy only normally took one pupil at a time and he was a hard taskmaster, demanding dedication and painstaking application. He did not suffer fools at all and was sparing with his praise. But once the entrance fee had been paid, he was free with his knowledge and no pupils who stuck out his course ever regretted it.

Findo loved it. He was less concerned about safecracking but wanted to learn everything Sowerby could teach him about locks and catches and alarms. He wanted to know it all. It was not a question of crime, simply a matter of knowledge. Access to Sowerby's skills was the key; it would help him gain access to all the places in the city that had so far frustrated his attempts to enter them. Then he could fill in the blank spots on the map.

Most of Sowerby's students came for a few days and stayed long enough to get a good grasp of a particular skill. Findo stayed for six days and when he left the old thief felt drained. Sowerby was used to having to push his students, drilling them time and time again until they had perfected the required moves. With Findo it was the other way around. The boy was not faultless but he was quicker than anyone Sowerby had taught before. He was also insatiable for the old man's knowledge. He probed and he questioned – and only stopped when Sowerby insisted they had a break.

They did not part as friends; their personalities were too different for that. But by the time Speed came to collect Findo, teacher and pupil had established a mutual respect. They did not see each other again – Sowerby died of a heart attack eight months later. However, Findo left with a growing confidence, coupled with a new awareness of the dangers that could lurk inside darkened buildings.

Back in the city, Findo was eager to try his new skills. Speed helped find him targets, although not too many to begin with. He kept Findo back from more serious operations but let him whet his appetite and hone his craft on a variety of solo challenges.

Findo did not care. He had little interest in the outcome of his endeavours; he just enjoyed the satisfaction of a test passed. The tasks dreamt up by his new boss added new spice to his continuing exploration of the city and the skills that Sowerby had taught him opened up a whole new range of possibilities for entering buildings that had previously proved impregnable.

During the first year of their association, Speed set Findo all manner of challenges – few for any serious criminal purpose. Some tests were straightforward, others more bizarre. Findo was sent to steal specific documents from the city council headquarters, to lift the pictures from the walls of an office belonging to a large insurance firm and to steal the chimney pot from the roof of a local judge. Sometimes he did not even have to take anything. On one occasion, Speed gave him the keys to a clapped out Morris Minor and told Findo he had to put it in the centre of the showroom of the city's Jaguar dealer.

Some tasks were harder than others; each had its own problems and moments of doubt and fear. A few took more than one attempt and one nearly ended in disaster when Findo had to flee a security guard after draping a string of sausages around the neck of a dummy in the window of the city's main department store. But Findo managed them all, one way or another.

He also continued his habit of leaving his mark at the scene of each challenge – although at John's suggestion his method became slightly more sophisticated. Now, instead of scrawling his name in pen or spray paint, Findo left a printed business card. Speed never liked the idea and tried to argue against it but Findo insisted; it mattered to him.

He always made sure the cards were displayed neatly but placed somewhere prominent. And although the idea of the cards themselves was John's idea, their messages were Findo's work. He had two sets printed, each bearing two quotes. The first read:

From each according to his abilities, to each according to his needs – Karl Marx
From you according to my abilities, to me according to my needs – Findo Gask

The second was even simpler.

Property is theft – Pierre-Joseph Proudhon
Theft is easy; property is mine – Findo Gask

The cards baffled the police, particularly when they were found at the scene of some of Findo's odder exploits. Knowledge of his name spread further, although the mystery of who – or what – Findo Gask was only deepened.

Over the next three years, Findo began to work for Speed on more serious matters. Mostly it was burglaries, some in the city and some a little way outside (but always with a card left behind). Some break-ins took place at business premises. Other times, Findo found himself entering private houses, often in pursuit of items like paintings or antiques.

Except on rare occasions, Findo only stole what he was sent to get. He ignored office safes that were not on his list of instructions and walked past jewellery boxes when he was after other items. He was a careful thief and Speed still used him sparingly. He knew Findo was good and like any wise operator he did not waste his best tool on a crude job that took little precision.

It was a partnership from which both benefited. Speed got what he wanted – without any messy complications to be sorted out once the main task was over. Findo was given money if he needed it, protection from rivals and enemies and the pleasure of assignments that gave him the kind of kick on which he thrived. He also began to enjoy being part of a close-knit team and to appreciate the respect shown for a job well done.

Findo had just switched the kettle on when the buzzer sounded from the lounge. He went back through and John pointed to the monitor mounted next to the entrance to the flat. The small screen showed Colin Speed standing in the lobby at the entrance to the bookie's shop.

"You going to let him in then?"

Findo looked up in surprise. "How?"

John pointed to the small box next to the monitor. "That's the intercom. Press the left-hand button to speak to whoever's down there. Press the other one to open the door. The one in the bedroom's the same."

Findo stepped across. He looked at the speaker grille then pressed the right-hand button. He watched as Speed opened the door and stepped through into the stairwell. As he did so, the screen changed, cutting to the feed from the second security camera. Findo now had a view from the top of the first flight of stairs. He saw Speed close the door from the lobby and start upwards. A few seconds later, the view on the monitor cut back to the outside lobby and Findo watched as two old men in worn suits walked past and disappeared into the betting shop.

John pointed to a pair of buttons at the side of the screen.

"There's a movement sensor that picks up anyone coming up the stairs and changes views automatically but you can override it if you want. Just press the top button for the lobby camera and the bottom one for the stair camera."

Findo nodded. "Okay."

John walked back over to the lounge window where he had been standing. "Makes it pretty hard for anyone to surprise you. Boss had it put in when he was using this place. Insurance in case the police ever got onto him and wanted to pay a surprise visit." He grinned. "He's like you, Findo. Likes to have several options."

Findo frowned. "What about the fire escape? They could come up that way."

John nodded. "Yeah, but they'd have to pull it down first. You have to lower the bottom section from above and we always keep it chained up. There's a key on a hook by the door onto the roof."

"They could use a ladder, though."

John laughed. "Yeah. And they could use helicopters and stun grenades! Come on, there's taking precautions and there's being paranoid. Of course you can't make it completely impossible for anyone to get in. That's not the point. The idea is just not to make it too easy."

There was a rap of knuckles on the flat door. Findo opened it and Speed walked in. "Afternoon, Findo." Speed nodded at John. "You given him the tour?"

"Yeah. I was trying to get him to make a cup of tea as well but I don't think he's got very far."

Speed shook his head. "Bloody hell. Don't tell me he needs house-training as well?"

"Looks like it," said John.

Findo raised his hands. "Okay," he said. "I'll make a brew."

Speed followed him into the kitchen. He watched silently for a couple of minutes as Findo searched around in the cupboards and found a teapot and three large mugs.

"Tea's in the jar there." Speed pointed along the worktop to a stainless steel container.

"Thanks." Findo chucked four bags into the teapot.

"Hey! Hold on," said Speed.

"What?"

"Haven't you learnt anything useful since you've been working for me? Make the tea properly."

Findo scowled. "What do you mean? I'm making it aren't I?"

Speed sighed. "Not properly, no. Heat up the pot first. Put some hot water in and give it a swirl."

Findo gave him a sideways stare. "Why?"

Speed shook his head. "Bloody hell. Because if you pour hot water into a cold pot then the water cools down too fast. Tea needs to be made with boiling water. So you heat up the teapot first. Okay?"

Findo nodded. "No problem."

They took the tea back into the lounge. Speed had found a tray from one of the cupboards and loaded it up with teapot, mugs, spoons, sugar bowl and a carton of milk.

As the three of them sat down around the small dining table, Speed pulled a packet of plain chocolate Hobnobs from his coat pocket.

Findo frowned. "Didn't they have any milk chocolate ones?"

"Yes."

"What d'you get them for then?"

Speed snorted. "Because, you cheeky little bastard, we've got better taste than you. I like plain chocolate and so does John. So you're outnumbered even if this is your flat."

Findo opened his mouth to speak then turned and stared silently at Speed, who grinned. "That shut you up, eh."

Speed took the lid off the teapot and gave the bags inside a stir. Then he poured a little milk into each mug and filled them up with tea. He added a spoonful of sugar to his and gave it a stir. He ripped open the packet of biscuits and popped one into his mouth whole then took a swig of tea. Speed gave John a wink and then sat munching and watching Findo.

After a long silence, Findo looked away. He reached forward and picked up his tea after adding four heaped spoonfuls of sugar. Eventually, he looked at Speed again. "What do you mean, my flat?"

Speed shrugged. "What I said."

"But I thought John said this was your place."

"It is," said Speed. "I own it. I own the whole building and next door. I did use the place a couple of times but I haven't been in here for a couple of years." He shrugged. "You see, I've got a few places like this. I keep them in reserve in case I suddenly need somewhere people don't know about. But I've been thinking about it and, you see, I reckon I don't need this flat at the moment. Not as well as the other two. I did think about renting it out but then I had a better idea." Speed grinned at Findo. "I thought it was about time you had a place of your own."

Findo looked bewildered. "Why?"

Speed and John both laughed.

"You don't fucking change, do you?" said Speed. "Now, some people would say thank you if I gave them a flat to live in. Not you though. You have to know why."

Findo shrugged awkwardly. "Yeah. Well?"

Speed gave another chuckle. "It's alright, Findo," he said. "Don't get offended. I don't blame you. You've got more sense than most people, that's all." Speed grinned. "You're dead right too. I'm not just doing this out of the kindness of my heart. I do have another motive."

Findo nodded slowly. "Okay, so what is it?"

Speed laughed. "I'm fucked off with trying to track you down all the time, that's what! You hole up in places like that old warehouse off Warner Drive. Half the time I've got no idea where you're living."

Findo took a cautious bite of a Hobnob. "Is that a problem?"

"Yeah!" said Speed. "Because, you see, sometimes I need you for some job and I can't find you. Now, I don't expect you to be hanging around waiting for my orders. Sometimes there's nothing going on for a few weeks and I don't need you. But most of the time, you just disappear. And even when we know where you're supposed to be living, half the time you're not there. Or you've found some lair that's impossible to get into unless you're in the fucking SAS or can climb like monkeys."

Findo sipped his tea and grinned. "Well," he said. "I'm like you, I don't like taking chances. If people can't find me, then I don't have to worry about unwelcome guests."

John laughed. "Yeah, but Findo – we're supposed to be your mates."

"You are."

"Yeah," said John, "but it can be a bit one-sided."

"How do you mean?"

"Well, you come round my place and we watch a film, have a couple of beers, whatever."

Findo looked anxious. "I thought you didn't mind."

John laughed. "I don't, you stupid sod. What I'm saying is we're mates, yeah?"

"Yeah, of course."

"So, you come round my place and that's good. Or you go and see Colin to find out if he needs you for anything. But we can't just come and see you if we feel like it. Half the time we don't know where you're living, the other half we can't get in to find out if you're there. We always have to rely on you coming to see us."

Findo nodded thoughtfully.

"So," added Speed, "I thought maybe I could solve the problem." He gestured around. "I've got this nice flat. No one's living in it and I'm not using it. So why not have it?" He shrugged. "You don't have to live in it if you don't want to. No one's forcing you. But it's yours if you want it. I own the building so it's all legit. There's no rent to pay, nothing like that. All the rates and bills are already taken care of. It's got all mod cons and there's a phone and answer machine so I can leave messages for you. But no one else is going to know you're here unless you tell them."

Findo nodded slowly. "What about the bookies'?"

Speed shook his head. "Don't worry. You can trust Phil downstairs. He's known me a long time and if he ever sees you going in and out he'll keep his mouth shut, he won't say anything to anyone – and if anyone starts asking he'll let me know." Speed downed the rest of his mug of tea and leant over for a refill. "And the offices below are empty so no one's ever going to hear you moving around up here."

He leant back. "It's up to you, Findo. Have the key. From now on this is your place. Use it how you want. You can live here permanently or occasionally – the only thing I'm asking is you come here every couple of days to see if I've left a message on the answering machine. You see, that way, I might finally be able to get hold of you when I need you. Okay?"

Findo nodded. "Yeah . . . and Colin?"

"What?"

"Thanks."

23. Candles and cider

Abby was walking along St Patrick's Road when she saw Findo. He was on the other side of the road, sitting on the wall outside the community centre. He smiled when their eyes met and flicked his head, indicating that she should cross over.

Abby glanced at the three girls with her. She had just finished school and was on her way home to Denmark Street. It was a route she had walked nearly every day after school for the past three-and-a-half years. Most of those times, except when Findo had been with her, she had been alone. But this year things were promising to be different.

Abby still did not make friends easily. At primary school she had stayed a loner, partly by choice. During her first years in the city she had still been mourning her father and resenting where fate had brought her. Then she met Findo. For the next few years they had been faithful companions and, although they did not spend so much time together these days, he was still her closest friend.

When she moved on to the local comprehensive, Abby's solitary habit had become hard to break. She had got used to being on her own and made little effort to seek out others or win their acceptance. She was accustomed to living in her own world and felt no need to surround herself in order to feel secure. At school she had also learnt the hard way that sometimes she needed to use her fists as well as her tongue if anyone upset her. Once the other children realised Abby had learnt this lesson, they were happy to leave her alone.

In class she was quick and intelligent but stubborn. She would argue with teachers if she thought they were wrong and press for more information when she found classroom explanations inadequate. Her independent streak and quick temper won her a few distant admirers (teachers as well as pupils) but still no friends.

Then, as she moved into her teens – and began to forget the past – Abby started to gain in confidence. As a result, she slowly became less prickly. The veil of red hair started to be pushed back as often to reveal a smile as a scowl. She talked to others in class and started to use jokes instead of sharp retorts to disarm antagonists. She would debate rather than argue and, tentatively at first, began to join in the kind of pranks from which she had once stayed aloof.

Her looks also changed. The rounder features started to melt away. Her face became sharper and more defined. And as her puppy fat disappeared, new curves arrived, ones that started to draw the attention of the boys in her class. Now fifteen, she was by no means the best-looking or most accessible girl in school but she was no ugly duckling either. For the first time in her life, boys tried to flirt rather than tease and provoke her. Sexual solidarity, coupled with Abby's own mellowed personality, led other girls to draw her into their ranks and suddenly she had friends.

Things had really taken off at the beginning of the current academic year. Abby was starting on the courses that would lead to her first real examinations. Classes had been reorganised and she found herself streamlined into sets of others with similar ability levels. Lessons were more serious and so were her fellow pupils. Abby found it easier to relate to those around her and flourished in the more academic atmosphere. On the other hand, she also began to realise that being right all the time did not make you popular and stopped giving the correct reply every time a question was asked to which she knew the answer. As a result, bonds with her classmates became easier to form and more comfortable to maintain.

The three girls she was with now were all in her art class. Their friendship had slowly formed during the first term and blossomed after Christmas. Now it was more than just a classroom relationship and Abby and the three others had begun to meet outside of school. Recently they had started to walk home as a group, discussing the day and their friendships and affections.

Abby looked again at Findo and smiled. She tilted her head to indicate that he should come over to her side.

Findo looked surprised. He stood up and for a moment Abby thought he was going to cross the road and join them. But then he started to walk along the pavement parallel with the four girls. He beckoned at Abby again.

She smiled back, shook her head. To begin with the other girls were too busy talking to notice but then Sadie spotted the signals being exchanged across the road. "Hey, Abby! Who's that?"

The other two looked around. They saw Sadie staring at Findo. He was still walking along on the other side of the road and looked away when he saw he had become the focus of the girls' attention. Nicola and Debbie exchanged looks with Sadie, raising their eyebrows and giggling.

"What's going on, Abby?" said Debbie. "Who's he?"

Abby bit her lip awkwardly. "He's a friend."

The other three laughed.

"Oh yeah?" said Debbie. "What sort?"

"Boyfriend?" asked Sadie.

"No." Abby shook her head. "He's a friend; I've known him for years."

"A friend?" said Nicola. "Just a friend?"

"Come on," said Debbie. "You can tell us. You can tell us everything."

"Yeah," said Sadie. "What sort of a friend?"

Abby shrugged. "I don't know." She glanced across at Findo. He was lagging behind the girls now, looking slightly wary. He smiled at her and gave another quick jerk of his head.

"What do you mean, you don't know!" said Debbie. "Come on, Abby. You must know what sort of a friend he is. You sure he's not a boyfriend?" She put an arm around Abby, who had gone bright red. "I think you'd better tell us everything. What his name is. What school he goes to. Where you met. Everything. You can't keep anything from us. We're your friends and we need to know."

Findo watched the four girls. They were walking in a tight huddle now, Abby talking slowly while the others gathered around, interrupting with questions and giggled comments. They also kept glancing over at Findo and giving him bright smiles.

After a few minutes, Findo finally caught Abby's eye. "Later," he mouthed at her and turned quickly away. He took a right turn up a street of terraced houses that led through towards Dubmore Road and the Alexander Cross junction. He walked briskly, troubled. He had expected Abby to come and join him. He was not used to her having other friends and was uncertain how to respond. He had not seen as much of her over the past year as in the past but he had never really considered that she might be spending time with other people. She had been part of his life for more than seven years now. He had never thought about that changing.

Findo worked his way around the edge of Cowfield Heights and cut through the area of Victorian streets that lay between the estate and Alexander Cross. He emerged onto Dubmore Road by the Tropical Dreams aquarium shop and turned left. He was going to go back to the flat but changed his mind at the last minute and continued up towards the city centre shops along Albert Parade.

It was about five o'clock when he reached the HMV store. He wandered in, fingering the wad of notes in his pocket. Colin Speed had been trying to encourage him not to shoplift, on the grounds of not taking any chances when it came to preserving Findo's anonymity. He had also just given Findo fifty pounds as payment for a dozen cases of fine wines stolen from an off-licence in Garvock Hill.

Findo wandered slowly through the shop, absent-mindedly staring at the racks of T-shirts, CDs, videos and tapes. He was not quite sure what he was looking for until he saw the display of new releases.

He picked up the Madonna CD and looked at it thoughtfully. He knew Abby liked Madonna.

It was about eight in the evening when Findo turned into the alley that ran behind the houses in Denmark Street. He had wanted to come earlier but decided to leave it a while in case Abby had brought her friends home. At the back of the McGee's house, Findo grabbed the top of the fence and pulled himself up until he could rest his elbows on the top.

"Hello."

Findo looked down in surprise. He had been hoping to be able to see if Abby was up in her bedroom. Instead, she was sitting on a kitchen chair in the yard behind the house. There was a book in her hand and a notepad on her lap.

"What are you doing?" he asked.

"Hello yourself, Findo," she replied.

He shrugged. "Hi."

Abby looked at him clinging to the top of the back fence. "Do you want to come in or do you want to talk over the fence?"

Findo frowned. "What about your mum?"

"She's not here," said Abby. "She's at an evening class. Doing some yoga. Won't be back for another hour."

Findo nodded. "Do you want to come to my place instead?"

Abby shook her head. "It's too late. I've got homework to do. I haven't really got time to go out tonight. Why don't you come in here for a bit?"

"I've got a new place," said Findo. "I wanted to show it to you. I think you'll like it."

Abby smiled. "Another one? I didn't know you were on the move again. You haven't been in the last place long."

Findo nodded. "I wasn't planning to move but something came up; a new place — a bit different from usual. It's not far, either. I thought you might like to see it."

Abby looked at him quizzically. "What's different about it?"

Findo grinned. "Come and see it."

She smiled back. "What about tomorrow?"

"Okay."

Findo pulled himself up and put a leg over the fence. He swung the rest of his body over and dropped down into the McGees' yard. He came and sat on the concrete next to Abby's chair.

"You could come over after school if you'd like."

Abby nodded. "Okay. Are you going to meet me?"

"If you want."

She gave him a sly look. "So why didn't you come over to see me earlier?"

Findo looked at the evening sky. It was mid-May and the heavens were still bright blue. "You were with your friends. I thought you wanted to be with them."

Abby sighed. They sat in silence for a minute.

"You could still have come over," said Abby. "They're alright. They'd have liked to meet you. They all thought you were my boyfriend."

Findo laughed but did not say anything.

"They're just friends from school," said Abby. "They're in my class for art and a couple of other things. I like them. They all live in Newtown and we walk home together."

Findo nodded. After a while he got up. "I'm going to head off," he said. "I'll meet you tomorrow, okay?"

Abby nodded.

"Come round for the evening," said Findo. "I'll get dinner." He turned to go then stopped just as he was about to climb back over the fence. "I nearly forgot," he said. "I got you a present."

He took the Madonna CD out of his jacket pocket and handed it to Abby. Her face lit up but was followed by a look of concern.

"Don't worry," said Findo. "It's not stolen. I got paid for some work I did. I bought it from HMV this afternoon. I even kept the receipt so I can change it if you don't like it. Just thought you might like it."

Abby reached out and took Findo's arm. He looked at her uncertainly. He seemed nervous, almost as if he was about to flinch away.

"Thanks," said Abby. "That's really nice. I do like it." She lent forward and gave Findo a swift kiss on the cheek and smiled at him warmly. "That's really sweet. Thank you."

She stepped back again, holding the CD. Findo looked into her eyes for a moment and then quickly turned again, scrambled up over the fence and was away.

Wednesday afternoon was a long time coming for both Findo and

Abby. Findo woke early and spent the first half of the day walking over to East Allonby, a village on the fringe of the city beyond the Clathy estates. Speed had asked him to case a large house on the edge of the village.

Findo got there mid-morning and walked quietly up the village's old high street. He found the house in question and followed the lane that led past it. A little way past the house was the village church. Inside, Findo found the door to the tower. It was locked but the key was hanging up in the vestry.

A few minutes later, Findo was standing on the roof of the tower. He could see the large redbrick house a few hundred yards away, partially hidden by trees. Findo studied the house for a while but found it hard to concentrate. He kept thinking of Abby. He wondered what she was doing, what she was thinking about – and who she was with.

The rest of the day was not much more productive and Findo spent the afternoon wandering slowly back from East Allonby, following the river as it wound its way into the city. By three in the afternoon he was sitting on the wall outside the community centre in St Patrick's Road and he stayed there, waiting, troubled by vague and inconclusive daydreams.

Abby had a similar problem. Classes provided more to distract her, but her thoughts kept returning to the question of Findo. They had been friends for so many years. She had never really thought about their friendship before.

She knew that her mother still disapproved of Findo but that was different. Suzanne McGee did not dislike Findo or even really blame him for how he was; she just objected to the way that he lived and the influence he might hold over her only child. Ever since the day when Suzanne took her daughter to the top of Clathy Hill and explained the choice between Findo's lifestyle and the wishes of her parents, a kind of nervous truce had existed between the two contenders for Abby's loyalty. Suzanne knew that Abby still spent a lot of time with Findo but was wise enough to trust her daughter. She also made no attempt to stop Abby seeing Findo or letting him come to their house.

Likewise, Findo had soon realised that Suzanne was disturbed by his presence and was intelligent enough to be discrete. He would only come to the McGees' house when he was fairly certain Suzanne was not there. Even then he would normally lurk around the house first, checking to see if the coast was clear and trying to attract Abby's attention without coming to the door. If he knew Suzanne was around he would melt away, disappearing back into the shadowy world she feared.

Suzanne, on the other hand, had developed a practice of never coming home earlier than expected. It was not something she had thought about consciously – and would have denied if challenged. But if she were out at something that finished early, she would dawdle in the street window-shopping, go for a solitary drink in a pub or stop and chat with neighbours rather than risk turning up earlier than expected and seeing Findo in her house. And if by chance they did meet in the street, the pair would exchange the polite greetings of wary strangers before hurrying away in opposite directions.

Abby had got used to Suzanne and Findo's careful avoidance of each other. It was just how things were. Both were extremely important to her. Suzanne was her mother and – since the death of her great grandmother two years ago – her only close relative in both senses of the word. Findo was her best friend: ally, confidant, co-conspirator and foil. But now she found herself wondering what else he was. Whether he was anything else to her – or had the potential to be anything else.

Until yesterday, the idea of Findo as her boyfriend had never occurred to her. The question from her friends had startled her. At first, the concept seemed ridiculous and unimportant. Then it left her confused. It perturbed her. It nagged and pulled at emotions she had not known were there. Emotions that did not even have names. Abby had no answer and did not know whether she wanted one – or what answer she wanted. But once out of the box where it had lain hidden and unbidden, the question rapidly gained in significance and weight. Now she had started to wonder, it would not go away. All of a sudden, she had to know – although Abby had no idea how to ask.

The three other girls watched as Abby darted across St Patrick's Road through a brief gap in the traffic.

Debbie Prince waved. "Hi, Findo!"

He raised his hand halfway in response and then turned quickly to Abby as she reached him. She stopped a few feet away.

"Hello."

"Hello."

They stood in awkward silence for a moment and then Abby dug into her school bag. "I got you something," she said. "A thank you for the CD."

Findo took the loosely wrapped bundle, trying to ignore the three girls still watching from the other side of the road. He turned without opening it and indicated up the road. "You ready?"

"Ready for what?" said Abby.

"Ready to see my new place."

She nodded and they set off together, walking slightly further apart than usual. They had turned off into the cut-though towards Dubmore Road when Abby glanced at Findo.

"Don't you want to know what I've got you?"

Findo looked at her in surprise. He had been staring at the pavement, lost in his thoughts but more conscious of Abby walking beside him than was comfortable. "Err . . . I was going to wait until we got there."

Abby shrugged. "Okay."

They walked on in silence again. Findo continued to look down. Abby's gaze shifted around, flicking from road to sky to her own feet. Occasionally her eyes lingered on Findo and a slight frown would crease her forehead.

"What have you been doing today?" she asked, as they turned the corner past the aquarium shop.

Findo was silent for a moment and she thought that he had not heard her. "Not much," he said eventually. "Been for a walk by the river."

"So where's the new place?" said Abby. "Is it far?"

Findo shook his head. "No. A few more minutes, that's all."

Abby looked at the traffic queuing ahead of them at the Alexander Cross traffic lights. "What's it like?"

Findo glanced at her and gave his first smile of the afternoon. "You'll see in a minute," he said.

Abby smiled back. "I didn't realise it was a surprise."

Findo grinned. "I told you this place was different. I think you'll like it though."

Findo led the way into the betting shop's entrance. Abby hesitated as they approached the door and looked at Findo.

"You're staying in a bookies'?"

Findo laughed. "Not exactly." He gestured towards the door. "Come on. Trust me."

Abby followed him cautiously. She had never been into a betting shop before. They were outside her experience. There was also something mysterious and possibly sleazy about them. The obscured windows and doors were designed to keep out prying eyes – like the sex shop in Packhouse Street. Abby was not sure if they fell into the same category or not. No one had ever said that going to a betting shop was bad but Abby knew gambling was one of those things that, though legal, some people did and others did not; she was not sure into which category she fitted.

Findo pushed open the outer door but instead of continuing inside, unlocked an unmarked door in the lobby. He ushered Abby through and carefully shut the door behind them. Findo said nothing and Abby followed him silently upstairs. At the top of the last flight of steps, he pulled out a key from a string around his neck and unlocked the door in front of them.

Abby stared around in amazement at the neat lounge. She took in the pale carpet, blue sofa and white walls. She looked at the pine table and chairs, the television and stereo in the corner. There was even a small bunch of freesias in a vase on the table.

Then she saw the map of the city pinned to a board that hung from the wall next to the door through to the kitchen. She saw the neat stack of paperbacks next to one end of the sofa. On the hearth was the old tin box that held all the letters from Billy. There were other telltale signs too – Mars Bar wrappers in the bin and empty Pot Noodle cartons on the side in the kitchen.

"Findo?" Abby stared at him. "Are you really staying here?"

He nodded, grinning with sudden pride. "Yeah." Findo waved around. "It's got everything – electrics, water. There's even heating." He grabbed Abby's hand and tugged her through towards the kitchen. "Look. I've got a kettle and a cooker and a washing machine. There's cupboards for food and drawers with knives and forks and stuff." He flung open cupboard doors. "Look, saucepans!" Findo suddenly whirled and pointed the other way. "I've got a toaster, too!"

He grinned and capered like an idiot while Abby stared at him, at first open-mouthed and then laughing too, sharing his delight.

"How?" said Abby.

But Findo ignored the question and took her hand again. "Come on," he said. "You haven't seen it all yet."

He led her back into the lounge and through the door into the bedroom. Abby stared in continuing astonishment at the double bed with neat duvet, the chest of drawers and open pine wardrobe, where she could see some of Findo's clothes hanging up.

"Bedroom!" he announced.

Then she was off again, being tugged through the bedroom.

"Bathroom!" Findo waved at the pale suite, tiled walls and chrome fittings. "Toilet, bath, basin and shower. It's got hot and cold." He flung back the plastic curtain and pointed at the showerhead. "And it's got a real fancy nozzle thing. You turn it and the water comes out all different ways." Findo grinned at Abby. "What do you reckon?"

"What, about the shower?"

201

He looked worried a moment and then grinned. "Nah, stupid. The flat. What do you reckon?"

Abby held up her hands in disbelief. "It's great but I don't understand. How come? Are you supposed to be here?"

Findo laughed and led her back to the lounge. "It's mine," he said. "I can stay here as much as I want."

"But, how come?"

He flopped down onto the sofa. "I know the man who owns the building. He owns the whole place – and next door. He wasn't using this flat and I do some work for him sometimes so he said I could have the flat. It's mine."

Abby stared around then laughed.

"What is it?"

She shook her head. "My present's not much use to you."

"Why?"

Findo reached over to the bundle, which he had put down on the sofa when they first entered the flat. He pulled back the paper. Inside were two large, multi-coloured candles.

"I thought you'd need them," said Abby. "I didn't expect you to be somewhere with light bulbs that work."

Findo grinned. He hefted the candles thoughtfully. "That's okay," he said. "They're nice. I like candles. I can still use them even if I've got electricity."

He stood up and went over to the blocked-up fireplace. He stood the candles up on the mantelpiece, leaning them against the wall for support.

"You'd better find a saucer or something to put them in," said Abby.

Findo hesitated a moment then nodded. "Yeah, suppose so." He turned back to face Abby. "Do you want something to eat? I've got some pizzas. I can stick them in the oven and heat them up – it's really easy. And I've got some cider if you'd like. It's in the fridge – keeps it nice and cold."

Abby laughed. "Okay."

A couple of hours later they were still sat on the sofa. Two empty plates lay nearby, smeared with tomato and melted cheese. Findo had placed the candles on small side plates and lit them. He had switched off the light above and the flames were busy sending a warm glow across the lounge's white walls and ceiling.

Abby raised her glass and took another sip of cider. "What's this music?"

"Dunno." Findo reached out and picked up the CD case. "Someone called Bob Dylan."

"Do you like it?"

He shrugged. "Not sure. Do you?"

Abby pulled a face. "Not really. How come you're listening to it if you don't know what it is?"

Findo shrugged. "It's John's. He's a friend of mine. Lent me this whole pile of CDs. Said it was all good stuff."

"You've got other ones then?" said Abby.

Findo nodded. "Bagful." He pulled himself up and moved across to the stereo system. "Here you go."

He handed a carrier bag containing about forty CDs to Abby.

"Okay," she said. "Let's see what you've got." She bent her head into the bag, flicking through the cases with one hand. "Nah . . . oh, no . . . hmm . . . ah!" She pulled a CD out. "Here you go. I know this one. My mum plays it."

Findo looked at the cover and stepped back over to the corner of the lounge. "Marvin Gaye? *What's Going On*? Okay."

He slid the disc into the tray and pressed play then came back and sat next to Abby again. She took another drink of cider and slid further down into the sofa. Her head was next to Findo's shoulder and, as she shuffled on the seat for maximum comfort, Abby's hair brushed against him. Findo's body stiffened slightly.

Abby felt the tension. She bit her lip slightly – and then lent her head firmly against his shoulder. They had sat that way many times before but she had never been so conscious of the position before. She sighed and let her body relax, absorbing the contact, wondering about it, if it felt right, if it felt good.

Findo was silent. His posture relaxed slightly but only so far. Abby lay still, a small part of her mind listening to the music while the rest raced far away. On the mantelpiece the candles burnt down and the dreamy smooth lyrics of the album's classic title track faded away. Without interruption, the second song drifted by and melted almost seamlessly into 'Flyin' High'.

Findo's muscles gave a little further and Abby snuggled against him, warm in the security of friendly flames, familiar company and songs that had been part of life from before she was even born. 'Save The Children' went by in its easy groove and then the tempo began to build for 'God Is Love', before slipping back a notch again for the next track.

Abby turned sideways, still propped against Findo, and kicked her legs up so that they hung over the end of the sofa. Her head slid down

Findo's side and ended up against his hip, not quite on his lap but not far away. Coils of red hair spilled in a pool around her face and Findo licked his dry lips and swallowed as he looked at her and then away, not daring to shift his body.

The music died for a second. Then the classic intro came – the piano with the first solo chords, joined a couple of bars later by the flute. The percussion broke in next, followed a few seconds later by Gaye's honey-drenched vocals. The slow-burn had begun – the smooth, climbing passion of 'Right On', one of the album's cornerstone tracks.

Abby's eyes closed and her mouth curled up in a peaceful smile. Up and down the music moved, soft verses followed by crescendos of horn and flute – finally drifting away into the soulful comedown of 'Wholy Holy'.

Findo watched Abby out of the corners of his eyes. He studied the line of her nose, the freckles scattered across her face, her pale lashes and eyebrows, the jut of her chin and the soft curve of her lips. His eyes also wandered further down her body, at the rise and fall of her small breasts and the legs hooked over the arm of the sofa.

Abby's head began to nod and her hands picked up the beat as the album reached its final track and the gentle funk of 'Inner City Blues'. She listened to the music with a satisfied expression, only finally opening her eyes about twenty seconds after the last notes had died away.

She turned on her side and pushed her body up with one arm. She looked at Findo and smiled.

"Abby?" he began.

She shook her head. "Kiss me, Findo."

24. Clinging doggo

Findo crouched in the back of the truck. There were three other men in the back. One was Albie Hooper; the other two were strangers. John Biggs was in the cab, driving. They were on Castle Drive, following the ring road west around the city centre. There was little light in the freight compartment and all of them were dressed in black from head to toe.

It was early morning, a little after seven. There was a faint drizzle falling outside and the sky was still grey. A few early commuters were already on the road, enough to provide a light flow of traffic but none of the congestion that would start in an hour or so.

Inside the truck it was silent. None of the men spoke. Albie watched Findo. The other two stared at their hands, each sitting with hands locked together on their knees, shotguns resting across their thighs. Albie's sawn-off lay by his side, one meaty paw clamping it to the bench on which he sat.

Findo stared at the hole cut into the truck floor, listening to the hiss of the tyres on the wet tarmac below. His mind was blank. It was too late to turn back and there was no point thinking about it. The plan had worked in practice. There was no reason why it should not do the same in reality.

The truck slowed and Findo stiffened. He looked at Albie, who shook his head.

"Not this one," said Albie. "That's Eastgate Road. Another one to go after this."

Findo nodded quickly and looked down again at the hole in the truck floor. Albie lent forward and peered through the gap cut into the front of the load compartment. Through the opening he could see into the cab and out of the windscreen. The big man nodded at the others.

"Still looks good. The security van's up ahead, between us and the cars. One more set of lights and then it's time."

The truck moved forward again and the hiss beneath them resumed. There was silence in the vehicle again. They drove on for a quarter mile before briefly slowing, then accelerating forwards.

Albie looked again at what was happening. "Okay, that was the other lights. Next lot, we stop." The big man looked at Findo. "Ready?"

Findo shrugged and sighed. "Dunno," he replied but dropped down and lay on the floor of the truck next to the hole. It was cut to his size and he lay on his back, parallel to the opening, with his head forward. He could feel one of the ringbolts that had been fixed into the floor, and the cord attached to it, digging into his shoulder

Albie reached down and squeezed Findo's shoulder tight. "You'll be alright, mate."

Findo stared blankly at the roof of the truck compartment. He was not sure he should be doing this. It was not his kind of thing but had been his idea; he had come up with the solution and promised Colin Speed he could do it. And if the idea worked, Findo's plan was a lot less risky than the public assault that had been the other option.

As he lay there, he thought of Abby. It was five months since that day in May when she came to the flat and they kissed for the first time. But it was still strange to Findo. He had discovered emotions that were new and disturbing. He did not know what they were – or who to ask for guidance.

Abby had spent last night at the flat. She came every Tuesday and Thursday, the nights her mother did yoga and had her Spanish classes. It had become routine without even being discussed. Findo had not mentioned this morning's raid. He knew Abby would be furious if she had any idea what he was doing. Partly for the risk that he was taking and the danger to himself, but also because she would disapprove of the idea of what they were planning.

Albie still had his eye glued to the gap in the front of the freight compartment. As the truck began to slow again, he prodded Findo with a foot. "Get ready. We're almost there."

The two other men slid to their knees at the end of the hole by Findo's feet. The hiss of wet wheels dropped in pitch and Findo slid his body over so he was hanging above the hole by his hands and feet.

"Okay," said Albie. "Light's gone red and we're all stopping."

"Remember the routine," said Findo.

The two men at his feet nodded and Albie reached down to pat his shoulder. The truck rolled to a halt and Findo felt himself lowered into the hole. A foot down, his back met the wheeled board suspended beneath the truck's chassis. He could feel the cords holding it against his ankles and upper arms.

"I'm on," he said.

There was a slight jerk and then he felt himself going down. A few seconds later there was a bump as he hit the road surface under the truck.

"Okay," called Findo softly. "I'm down."

He felt the pressure of the cords disappear as they were dropped to the ground and he reached up for the underneath of their truck. Findo propelled himself forwards. He was lying on a board like that which mechanics use to slide underneath cars. This one had been adapted. It was longer than usual and had bigger, smoother wheels, as well as a large handle at the foot end.

Findo slid quickly on, under the truck's cab. There was a brief strip of daylight and then he was rolling under the rear bumper of the vehicle ahead. He reached up to grab at the security van and get right underneath. Then he kicked up his feet into the positions they had practised on the test vehicle.

He could hear the engine of the van above and the smell of diesel and hot metal. There was the sound of gears being engaged somewhere in front of his head. Reaching down with gloved hands, he pulled out the clips on the belt around his waist and snapped them into place.

As he did so, the security van rolled forward a couple of feet. Findo went with the van, the board still beneath him sliding over the tarmac. He ignored the movement and stretched forwards. Pressing with his feet to bring his body as close as possible to the underneath of the van, he lifted himself off the board. As he did so, he clicked the hooks on his wrist supports onto their holds.

Findo closed his eyes as the security van moved forward a few more inches, halted and then pulled away from the lights.

The board stayed where it was in the middle of the road. Behind the security van, the truck that Findo had been in rolled gently forward. As it passed over the board, Albie's arm came down and he snagged the handle. Albie gave a loud knock on the front of the compartment with his free hand and the truck also pulled away from the lights, following the grey van ahead.

Beneath the security van, Findo hung on grimly. All he could do now was to cling and hope. It had worked fine in practice. There was no reason why it should not work now. Except for the unforeseen.

His legs and arms were tense as he felt the vehicle pull away from the traffic lights, picking up speed as it turned right around the Campfield junction. About halfway round the junction's central island the van slowed briefly as it approached the next set of lights but then accelerated forwards again.

It turned onto Warner Drive and began to move faster. The van was travelling at about forty-five miles per hour but the speed was meaningless to Findo. His senses were overwhelmed and it was all he could do to just cling on and endure. He held his head as high as he could, almost pressing it to the underneath of the van, dreading the impact that would come if anything went wrong and he slipped or the van went over an object in the road.. His eyes were shut tight to keep out the cloud of fine, oily droplets that washed around his body and across his face. The moisture sprayed up as the vehicle drove along the wet road and Findo could taste it on his lips.

He had also never expected it to be so noisy. There was a swooshing roar from the tyres around him. From above, the deep hum of the drive shaft came like the purring of a giant cat. In front, the engine ground away, changing pitch from bass rumble to whine and back down again as the van slowed and accelerated. The vibrations from the moving vehicle seemed to be running through his whole body and Findo was only too aware of the tarmac speeding past inches beneath his unprotected shoulders and back.

It felt like at least an hour but in less than ten minutes the van was turning off Warner Drive, swinging left into a small service road. Findo felt the turn rather than saw it, his hanging body swaying with the motion, forced sideways for a couple of seconds as it tried to follow the van's old course.

The vehicle pulled to a brief halt after about a hundred yards and Findo blinked to try and clear some of the road spray from his eyes. He counted slowly, trying to estimate how long they were stopped.

After about seven seconds he heard a rattle as the wire gates in front of the van rolled back and six seconds later they moved forward again. They moved relatively slowly, less than half the speed they had been going and Findo could visualise the short stretch of approach road they were on. He had seen it briefly at a distance about a week ago.

The entrance to the security firm's depot was off the side road. A pair of high gates, made of thick bars and topped with razor wire, was set into a twenty-foot high brick wall. Inside was a short approach road running between more high fences, with open areas to either side patrolled by guard dogs. Security cameras overlooked both the inner roadway and the area immediately outside the depot. At the end of the approach road was the solid steel door leading to the depot's inner compound.

Findo felt the van stop again and heard a low rumbling as the main door swung open. His heart was starting to beat faster and his fingers were trembling in a way that had nothing to do with the vibrations from the vehicle. He swallowed. He was used to tension and the fear of discovery – but never before like this.

The van moved forward again and Findo knew it was almost time. They halted again about ten yards further on and Findo heard the driver's door and then the passenger's open. Twisting his head, he saw booted feet step down onto the concrete.

He swallowed again. Now it depended on the accuracy of the information that Speed had been sold. They knew that the men in the security van had a remote control that could open the compound's outer gates. To get into the inner courtyard, however, they had to be let in by a guard in the gatehouse, who also had an override switch for the outer gates – as well as the panic button that would lock every door in the premises and set bells ringing and lights flashing at the police headquarters.

But the informant had also promised them there would only be a skeleton staff at the depot at this time of day. He had assured them that once the guard had opened the main door to let the arrivals in and shut it again, he would leave his post to help the team from the van – after they had a cup of tea.

Findo clung silently to the van listening, his head tipped back and on its side. The two men had stopped in front of the van and he wondered what they were doing. He could still see one pair of feet and had heard several small noises but nothing that he could make sense of. Then he heard a sudden intake of breath and saw a dead match fall to the ground. They were lighting cigarettes.

A door opened somewhere off to the right of the van and he heard a cheerful whistle, followed by another pair of feet approaching.

"Alright, Charlie?" said one of the men by the van.

Findo released the clips attached to his wrists and carefully stretched his arms and hands. The clips were part of the harness that had held him to the underneath of the van. Thick, padded bands around his waist and wrists were reinforced with lengths of rope with large clips attached to their ends.

"Not bad, lads. Good trip?"

"Yeah, you know," said the first speaker.

"Dark and wet," added a third voice. "Apart from that it was okay. Pretty quiet."

"Yeah," said the first man. "We made good time. Time for a quick brew before we unload?"

"Suits me," said the one called Charlie.

Findo dropped his aching legs from where they were wedged against the van's undercarriage. Using one arm to push his body up, he undid the clip at one hip then shifted his weight to open the other.

He paused a few seconds, listening to the three men walking off, then dropped onto his back. He lay for a moment against the damp concrete, feeling the solidity of ground beneath him again. Then he rolled over and slid out from under the van – rolling his balaclava down so that the black material covered his face, leaving just his mouth and eyes visible.

Out in the open, he pulled himself upright and looked around quickly. He was in a small yard, just as described. There were some parking spaces ahead of the van with offices beyond but the doors were closed and the windows still dark. On the far side of the compound was a garage area; Findo could see an open workshop and two parked security vans inside.

He pressed his back against the van that had carried him into the compound and twisted round to look the other way. The massive steel entrance gate with its big rollers was firmly closed. But to its left was the guard's cubicle, its door still ajar.

Findo bent down and peeped warily under the corner of the van. On the other side of the vehicle was the reception area where consignments were loaded and unloaded from the strongroom beyond. That was also where the drivers had a small room with a table, chairs and kettle. He could just see the base of the loading bay and the bottom of a door at the side. The door was open but he could see no sign of anyone in the entrance.

He pulled himself upright, swallowed and tiptoed quickly away from the van, heading for the far wall of the compound and the entrance to the guardroom. A few yards before the door to the control booth, Findo reached the point where he could see into – and be seen from – the loading bay.

He tilted his head very slowly to the side. The entrance where the three men had disappeared was empty. Findo drew a deep breath and sprinted the last few yards, flitting as silently as he could across the exposed section of wall. As he entered the guardroom, he grabbed the cubicle's door and quickly swung it back to the same position in which it had been left. Inside, Findo dropped to his knees and froze.

Silence. No shouts, no alarms, no running feet. So far, so good.

He looked around. It was a small room with a window looking out over the compound. Beneath the window was a desk with a control panel. There was a swivel chair, a telephone and a few oddments on a shelf but nothing else.

Findo shuffled over to the desk, keeping low. He used the chair to pull himself up. There were only a few controls on the panel, all helpfully labelled. There were buttons to open and shut the outer door and a similar pair for the inner door. In the middle of the panel was a monitor linked to the depot's security cameras and a control pad for switching view.

Findo raised his head a fraction and peeked at the screen. It showed the outside gates and the road immediately outside. He could not see John's truck but Findo knew it would not be far away.

He turned his attention back to the controls. To the right of the monitor was an intercom with a line of smaller buttons next to it. Each was labelled. There was one for the front gates, for the main office, the loading bay and several with names of members of staff. There was also a large red button in the top corner of the desk, with a plastic cover to prevent it being knocked by accident.

Findo looked at the guardroom's window but decided not to risk a glance out. Instead, he darted back to the door and crouched down again. He could hear voices but they sounded distant. Lowering his balaclava-clad head to the ground, he lent slowly forward until he could just see out into the compound.

There was no sign of the three men. They must be still drinking their tea. All he could do now was wait until they opened the van.

Outside, John would be waiting at the wheel of the truck. Findo could imagine the thoughts going through the minds of the men waiting. In some ways it was worse for them. They had no way of knowing whether Findo had been discovered. For all they knew, the police could already be on their way.

But there was no point opening the gates too soon. After much decision, Speed had decided they should wait until the guards opened the van and deactivated the security devices before making any move. It made the operation slightly more nerve-wracking but also greatly increased their chances of getting at the contents of the van safely. It would be a pointless exercise if they managed to get into the depot but the contents of the van's safe ended up sprayed with indelible dye.

And although the main haul was in the van, waiting increased the chance of extra pickings. There were bound to be other valuables inside the strongroom and the guards would open that too when they started unloading the van. Waiting also reduced the risk of heroics and the need for violence. For although the team in the truck were all armed, there was always the chance – unlikely but still a risk – that the security guards might refuse to cooperate. But if the safes were already open, the gang would not have to make the guards do anything. Then, the guns would only be needed to scare them into submission while John's team cleared out the safes and made their getaway.

Findo pulled his head back into cover and crouched still, listening. Various scenarios went through his head – the guards sneaking up on him as he waited, armed officers surrounding the depot and carting the others away in handcuffs.

But then, finally, he heard footsteps. Charlie's whistling carried across the yard.

"Right then," he heard one say. "I suppose we'd better get this lot off."

"Okay," said Charlie. "Let me just chuck my paper in the box. If I leave it here it'll walk."

Findo felt a chill run down his neck. He could hear boots approaching across the concrete. He glanced frantically around. There was no cover.

Just as the sound of Charlie's footsteps were a few feet from the door, Findo moved for the only hiding place possible – behind the door. He backed into the narrow space and stood up quickly. He pressed his back flat against the rear wall of the guardroom, breathing in so that he took up as little space as possible. There was a glass panel in the door but it did not take up the full width of the opening. By leaning towards the corner of the guardroom, Findo gambled that he would just have enough cover.

The door swung open and Findo held his breath. A folded copy of *The Sun* sailed onto the shelf next to the control panel. Charlie's cap followed it, then the sound of him walking away.

Findo felt his knees go weak but he knew he could not falter now. Moving as quickly and quietly as he could, he dropped to his knees again and went back to his crouched position by the door.

He saw a man in a blue uniform walking back to the van. Charlie was a big man with grey stubble. He moved slowly and Findo guessed that a lot of the bulk was now fat rather than muscle.

"What d'you reckon to the game last night then?"

"Oh, we were robbed. United should never have got that penalty. Ref was right out of order."

The men's voices came from around the van. Findo watched Charlie turn the corner and disappear. The conversation continued but the voices kept fluctuating in volume and Findo realised the security guards were walking in and out of the bay, discussing last night's football as they unloaded.

He moved swiftly to the control panel, punched the button for the outside gate and started to count. It would take a few seconds for John to see the gate open. Then he would have to pull off from where he was parked, drive in and get to the main entrance.

Findo was halfway to twenty seconds when he remembered the security cameras. The view on the monitor was still set on the outside gates and he raised himself up just enough to see the screen.

The gates were nearly open but there was no sign of the truck. Findo's mouth went dry.

But then it appeared. The back came first as John reversed the big vehicle, turning quickly into the fenced approach road. Findo hit the button to close the outer gates and punched the control for the inner gate. There was a whine from the electric motor and then another rumble as the heavy steel gate slid open on its rollers. Findo could also hear the roar of the engine from the approaching truck.

"Hey, Charlie?"

"What the fuck?"

The guards were confused by the sounds of the gate and approaching truck. Findo saw one walk from behind the van towards the main gate. Charlie appeared round the front of the van and broke into a trot, coming towards the guardroom. There was no sign of the third man.

"Down, down down!"

The cry came from the entrance to the depot and, as Findo watched, a big figure in black carrying a sawn-off shotgun strode through the still-opening main gate as John reversed in behind him.

"On the floor. Now!"

Albie was holding the sawn-off in one hand, brandishing it like a pistol. Charlie's head turned towards the masked intruder but he had not taken in what was happening and was still jogging uncertainly towards the guardroom. Findo saw Albie's aim move towards the running man and acted without thinking. He flung open the door of the guardroom and stepped out.

"Stop!" He pointed the torch at Charlie.

The big man gaped and wobbled to a halt as he looked at the balaclava-wearing figure standing in the doorway to his cubicle. Findo saw Albie's aim move back to the other side of the security van.

Charlie stared at Findo and his weapon. "What the . . .? That's my torch."

The main gate was completely open now and the truck was reversing all the way in. Albie's two companions were jumping down from the rear compartment, both brandishing their own weapons.

"Yeah," said Findo. "It is." He pointed over Charlie's shoulder. "But those are shotguns."

The guard turned slowly. He looked in horror as one of the other raiders came towards him. Charlie looked at the shotgun and quickly raised his hands. "Please." He spoke in a soft, terrified voice. "Don't shoot."

The man with the gun jerked his weapon in the direction of the loading bay. Charlie nodded and walked back the way he had come, still holding his hands high.

Findo darted back into the guardroom. He pressed the button to close the main gate and looked at the monitor. There was no sign of any activity outside. This was one of the other danger points; they were in, they just had to hope that no one had seen them and realised what was happening.

Findo looked at the control pad for the other cameras. He pressed one labelled 'front, left' and the view on the monitor changed. He was now looking at the road outside the security depot – but the camera was looking further into the industrial estate rather than out the way they had come. Findo could see the entrance to a builders' merchants' yard and where the service road ended at an empty plot that had never been built on. There were no cars or people in view.

He tried another camera, this one labelled 'front, right' but it was turned so it was looking down at an angle along the outside wall. Findo could see the pavement outside but nothing else. Then he saw the small wheel next to the camera buttons. It had arrows around it and Findo gave it a slow twist. As he did so, the view on the screen changed. The camera swung a fraction further to the left so it was now looking inside the depot's outer yard. Findo grinned to himself and twisted the wheel the other way. He also tilted it towards him slightly.

The camera turned back to the right and lifted up. Findo watched as the view on the monitor changed slowly to show the service road leading in from Warner Drive. The view was empty. There was no traffic and no one moving on foot.

He was still watching when a figure appeared at the door. Findo recognised John's eyes through the holes in the balaclava.

"Okay?" said Speed's lieutenant.

"Sure," said Findo. "Just keeping an eye on the road." He pointed to the screen. "Nothing moving at the moment."

"Excellent." John grinned. "I didn't think of using their cameras to watch our backs."

He was about to turn away but a car suddenly appeared on the screen. They both watched as it turned into the side road and drove towards the camera.

"See where it's going," said John.

"Okay," said Findo. "Don't worry, I'm on it."

He pressed the button for the other front camera and they watched as the old Volvo estate turned into the entrance to the builders' merchants'. A man got out and walked forward, disappearing from view. Findo turned the camera to follow him and they saw him open the gates at the front of the yard, then return to his car, get back in and drive inside.

John glanced at his watch. "Just opening up for the day," he said. "Okay, looks like we're nearly there." He turned away. "We'll just finish loading up and then we're off. When I give you a shout open the front gate first and then the main gate. Soon as it's starting to open you come and jump in the back of the truck."

Findo shook his head. "You go through first. Once the truck's through, I'll press the button to close it again. It takes a few seconds. I'll get out before it shuts. It won't look suspicious from outside then."

John paused, considering. "Alright. But be quick."

He was on his way out through the door when Findo called after him. "Are the guards okay?"

John laughed. "Don't worry. They didn't give us any trouble. They're all sitting in their tearoom with parcel tape around their legs and wrists. They won't come to any harm."

Findo nodded to himself. He watched through the guardroom window as John went back over to the truck. Albie was by the tailgate, throwing up heavy cotton bags being passed to him by one of the other men. Findo glanced at the monitor for the security cameras and turned the view back to the service road. It was still quiet.

He took off one glove to scratch at an itch on the back of his head and then remembered something. Reaching down inside his black overalls, Findo pulled out a small business card and laid it neatly in the middle of the guardroom's control panel.

25. Mirror, mirror

Findo did not leave the old steel factory until it was dark. Following the raid he had got Albie to drop him near his flat. But instead of going home he had continued past the bookies', heading down Corporation Road and through Newtown. He had taken the back streets, walking fast and with his head down, wary of every car that passed or pedestrian that glanced his way. His balaclava and black overalls had been left in the back of the truck but Findo buried his chin in his collar and let his hair hang down over his face, working his way through Newtown until he got to the abandoned steel mill.

It was over a year since Findo had last been to the site. It looked little different. Nature was slowly wearing away the remains of the factory but it was a gradual process. A few more bricks had fallen and some extra cracks had appeared in the expanses of concrete around the buildings. Another crop of weeds had grown up and the ever-encroaching brambles had got a few yards further into the site. But autumn had stripped them bare and now the loops of naked briars lay like bundles of brown wire, snagging wind-blown leaves and litter on their thorns.

The big gas register looked a bit rustier – and the letters spelling out Findo's name around its sides had nearly faded or flaked away – but its ladders were still sound and Findo had climbed quickly to the top. He stayed there for most of the day, looking down at the Allonby and the fields and woods on the other bank. He remembered that first time he met Abby and the day, over seven years ago, when he had swum the river to rescue the abandoned puppies from their sack – wondering for a while what had happened to the dogs and whether their life had been happy and easy.

Later, it rained and Findo withdrew inside. He wandered aimlessly for a while through the mill and other derelict buildings, ending up eventually in the loading bay where he and Abby once met almost every day. There was a pile of broken pallets in one corner and Findo sat there for a couple of hours, lost in a dream of Abby.

Abby had asked him a few days ago whether he loved her and the easy answer would have been 'yes'. But Findo had avoided a direct reply. He thought he knew why Abby was asking and part of him desperately wanted to give her the answer she wanted.

But he was not so naive as to be totally unaware of the

217

consequences of what she wanted to know and had been unable to bring himself to lie to her – at least not until he knew the answer himself. And since it was asked, the question had disturbed his thoughts whenever he stopped to think. Abby was precious to him. She had been part of his life for years. She was his confessor and his confidant. She had taught him to read and introduced him to Frances Reid. She made him smile and seemed to understand his moods better than he did.

But they were also very different. Abby's temper flashed hotter and faster than Findo's slow-burning emotions. She liked music that did nothing for him and in the last few years had begun to talk about things, like clothes and ambition, that were alien territory for Findo. She had begun to be interested in politics and things like animal rights and conservation.

Abby also still talked – although not quite as passionately as she had once – about leaving the city. In Abby's mind, it had only ever been a temporary port of call, an unnecessary evil to be endured until she could leave. Abby took it for granted that she would move away one day and live somewhere else. Somewhere 'real', she said. Recently, she had talked about the places she might go to when she went away to university. To Findo, however, the city was the only place that he could imagine living. It was his home. He knew its streets, estates, buildings, open spaces and hidden places better than anyone. He had a kind of love-hate feeling for the place but it was also an addictive relationship – and while he felt free to criticise the city freely, Findo took instant offence if anyone else did the same.

More important to Findo's relationship with Abby was the fact that she was finding it harder and harder to accept how he lived. When they first met, her feelings about theft had been vague and unformed. She was still a child and concepts like possession and the rules of society had hardly seemed significant. She had been concerned with more immediate matters – the loss of her father and being uprooted to come and live in a strange and unpleasant place. Being taken shoplifting by Findo had just seemed a novel and exciting form of entertainment. And stealing the toy sports car from Clement Dalloway's garden party had been the biggest adventure she had ever experienced.

But over the years that followed, she had begun to see Findo's life in a new light. Her mother's talk on the top of Clathy Hill some years earlier had made a big impression and – while she had not jumped to any instant conclusions – spurred Abby to think about her own values. She understood as well as anyone why Findo was like he was. She saw the pain beneath his skin. She recognised the hurt that burned deep inside better than he did. But Abby had no desire to share Findo's burden by adopting his rejection of anything that fell outside his own self-imposed confines. She tried hard not to measure Findo against her own standards but it became increasingly difficult. And as the childhood allies each followed their own paths, communications began to grow harder and harder.

For Abby, the first kiss had not simply been a matter of desire. She cared deeply for Findo. She was also drawn to him physically – he was a boy and not unattractive. He was dangerous but not to her. He was both more innocent and more knowing than any of the boys at her school.

The kiss had been an attempt to re-forge the connection between them, to try and pull him closer and keep him in her life. Because Abby realised – albeit unconsciously – that their lives had reached a critical point. They had to choose between each other and the paths they were following. Sooner rather than later, something would give. Abby had a sad premonition of what it was but had no intention of giving up easily. While she could, she was going to hold onto Findo and try and make him take what was – to her way of thinking – the right way.

And for those reasons, although the two teenagers were physically closer than they had ever been, emotionally they were growing apart. Findo could sense the separation but did not understand the problem as clearly as Abby. He was aware of a sense of unease but had no idea what was wrong. Findo, who found it much harder to analyse these things than Abby, just knew that he was confused and uncertain about what he felt, what he wanted – and how to behave.

The sun had set a good hour before Findo finally slipped out through the fence at the front of the derelict factory. Despite a day lost in thought, he was no closer to sorting out his feelings for Abby. But spending the time wondering about their relationship, and whether he was ready to take it further, had saved him from having to think about the morning's armed raid on the security depot. That was another mental minefield and he could only cope with threading through one at a time.

Leaving the abandoned industrial site behind, Findo set off through the bleak lines of terraced houses that ran off towards the east. He trudged through the area where the city's Newtown district met neighbouring Newmills. The rain had faded to a steady drizzle but Findo was happy to walk through the drifting clouds of fine droplets; their blanket dulled the light from the streetlamps overhead and helped further mask his passage.

After a mile and a half, Findo reached Jamaica Road. The street followed the railway north-east from Newmills station to where the line crossed St Patrick's Road near Abby's school. Findo stayed on the side with the houses. There were parked cars along the other side of the road but there was also a high wall at the base of the railway embankment. The north side offered less cover but there were breaks in the rows of houses and more chance of making an escape if Findo ran into anyone he did not want to see.

A few cars went past as Findo walked along Jamaica Road and he passed one other pedestrian, an elderly black man walking an even more elderly Jack Russell terrier. The dog was in a tartan jacket; its owner wore a long overcoat. Both were plodding along with their heads down and looked as miserable but stubborn as each other. They ignored Findo, who overtook the pair when they paused in the lee of a lamp post for a rest.

He reached St Patrick's Road without incident and paused on the corner to look around. There was more traffic here. St Patrick's Road ran north-west from Chapel Bank to where it joined Corporation Road in the middle of Newtown. There were various pubs, shops and petrol stations along its length and the road was also the main route from the south-west quarter of the city up towards the hospital. Despite the steady drizzle, there were also more people about on foot.

Findo glanced in either direction and flitted across the road. He tucked his head back down, turned right and started walking again.

It was gone seven-thirty in the evening when Findo reached Frances Reid's house. The librarian lived in a small, detached house at the southern end of Dubmore Road, a few hundred yards north of where the road crossed the Allonby. The house had been built just after the Second World War, slotted into a narrow plot between two larger Victorian properties.

Findo ignored the main entrance and slipped through a smaller opening in the dank privet hedge that screened the front of the house. He followed a line of slippery paving bricks down the side of the house and to the kitchen door. The kitchen was dark but Findo could see light coming from somewhere inside. He gave three quick raps on the door.

Mrs Reid appeared a couple of minutes later. She turned on the kitchen light while hooking her glasses over her ears. She gave a nod when she saw Findo and came over and unlocked the door.

"Come in, young man."

Mrs Reid stood to one side as he stepped inside. Although now over seventy, Frances Reid was nearly as vigorous and spry as she had always been. Her eyes and hearing were not as sharp as they had been but her mind and tongue worked as well as ever. Her joints were a little more reluctant to cooperate but she still walked several miles every day and swam in the municipal pool at least twice a week.

She also continued to work four days a week at the library, although only part time. She could have retired whenever she wanted. Apart from the small pension to which she was entitled, the last of the money from the sale of the farm in Australia had been carefully invested nearly fifteen years ago and still gave her a small but steady income. But Frances Reid had no intention of giving up her job while she was still mentally and physically capable of continuing. A couple of council managers had tried to suggest that she retire but she had always resisted the idea resolutely and, helped by the fact that she was extremely good at her job and paid very little, had managed to avoid the civic axe.

"Take your coat off," she ordered, as Findo entered the kitchen.

As he began to comply, Mrs Reid turned away and walked back out into the hall. "Lock the door again, please," she said. "Make yourself a drink if you'd like. I'll be in the front parlour."

Findo nodded. "Okay."

He hung his coat on a hook on the back of the kitchen door and turned the key again. He also slid across the bolts, top and bottom. Findo looked out into the hall and then at the kettle. He stepped to the door through into the rest of the house.

"Would you like a drink, Mrs Reid?"

There was a short pause before she called back. "I'll have a cup of tea, thank you.

Findo smiled to himself and set to work. A few minutes later, he carried the tray out of the kitchen, down the narrow hall and into the small lounge.

Mrs Reid was sat in an upright chair. There was a copy of Stephen Hawking's *A Brief History of Time* on her lap but it was closed. A record was playing on a small music centre to the right of the fireplace. One of Mrs Reid's hands gently rose and fell in time with the music.

She smiled briefly at Findo and gestured at him to put the tray on a table by her side. "I'll pour," she said. "You stand next to the fire and get warm. You look a little damp."

Findo nodded and did as instructed. He walked over to the fireplace. A coal fire burnt in the open grate. It was a small fire but the backs of Findo's trousers began to steam gently before too long.

Mrs Reid handed him his tea. He took the cup and saucer gratefully. Findo picked up the small china cup carefully, holding the handle tightly between finger and thumb as he sipped the hot drink.

Mrs Reid took a sip of her tea then lowered it back to her lap and resumed her conducting. Findo looked around the familiar room silently. It was quite compact, little more than twelve feet square. Apart from Mrs Reid's chair and the stereo system, there were two wing-backed armchairs opposite the fireplace and a round wooden table in the bay window. A brass pot sat on the table. Cascading from it was an enormous asparagus fern with tumbling sprays of spiky foliage. There was a Turkish rug on the floor and a number of pictures on the wall. On one wall were several black and white photographs from Australia – views of outback life, including stockmen at work and Aboriginal children at a muddy waterhole. Another wall had prints of Soviet posters, classic images of stylised workers in heroic poses, exhorting factory and farm comrades to strive harder in support of the great cause.

The alcoves on either side of the chimney breast were lined with shelves. Rows of books – works of literature, history and philosophy – filled the shelves. There was also a large collection of *National Geographic* magazines and several neat piles of other periodicals, including *New Statesman*, *New Internationalist* and a new publication called *Red Pepper*. Slotted under the shelves in the right-hand alcove was a small bureau, its drawers full of writing paper, old letters, pens, notebooks and other stationery.

The record on the turntable came to an end and the arm lifted off with a click. Mrs Reid smiled. "Ah, Sergey Prokofiev," she said. "One of my favourite Russians." She looked at Findo's blank expression. "But I see he didn't inspire you."

Findo shrugged and Mrs Reid frowned. "Findo! That is such a graceless response. I'd rather you say if the music is not to your taste."

He smiled apologetically. "I dunno," he said. "It's just . . . I prefer songs. Music with words."

Mrs Reid raised an eyebrow. "I could play you one of his operas if you prefer."

Findo winced. "It's alright."

The old librarian gave a chuckle. "Don't look so worried. I know how opera affects you and I'm not feeling that mean tonight."

She went silent and sat looking down at her tea. Findo frowned and stepped away from the fire, starting to feel the heat of the flames through the now crisp fabric of his trousers. He watched Mrs Reid uneasily for a while and then turned and stood artlessly looking at the books in the left-hand alcove.

After a while, Mrs Reid sighed. "So, you're in trouble, young man."

Findo looked round in surprise. "How did . . ."

She shook her head. "Well, I could have told by your manner but I didn't need to. I do still read the papers."

"The papers?"

"That's right," said Mrs Reid. "Folding things, print the news."

Findo looked confused. "What have the papers got to do with anything?"

She sighed. "No, I don't suppose you'd even think of looking in the paper would you?" The librarian indicated the bureau in the other alcove. "Today's paper is over there. Have a look at the front page."

Findo hurried over, looking even more worried than usual. He picked up the paper, unfolded it and began to read the main story. As his eyes moved across the words, his face went pale and his teeth sank into his bottom lip.

Mrs Reid watched him silently. When he lowered the paper, she gestured at one of the armchairs to her left. "Sit down."

Findo did as he was bidden. He lowered the paper and let it drop to the floor as he sat. The pages spilled across the reds and golds of the Turkish rug in front of them. Findo folded his hands across his lap. His hands were shaking slightly and the colour still had not returned to his face.

"Well," said Mrs Reid. "I think it's been quite a day, even for you."

Findo shook his head. "Why is it in the paper?"

Mrs Reid tutted crossly. "Findo. Don't be so obtuse. You can hardly expect a crime of that scale not to be reported. I don't know how they've got hold of your name but I doubt very much if it's entirely coincidence." She sat silently until Findo eventually looked up. "So," she asked, "were you involved?"

He said nothing for a while then eventually nodded. "I got them inside."

Mrs Reid said nothing.

"But why blame me?" he asked bitterly.

The librarian looked sad. "Findo, don't act innocent with me. I know what you're like and it's no use trying to deny the facts – they won't go away. You showed me those silly cards you had printed. Did you leave one behind?"

The boy nodded. "Yes."

"Well, there you are then," said Mrs Reid. "Did the other men you were with leave their autographs behind?"

Findo shook his head.

"In that case," she continued, "what else can you expect? If you tell the police that you were there, you're very foolish not to expect them to take notice." Mrs Reid sighed and turned to the tray by her side. "Would you like another cup of tea?"

Findo looked surprised then shook his head. "No, thank you."

"Very well," said Mrs Reid. She poured herself another cup and placed it on the saucer on her lap. "Now," she said, "it may have come as a nasty shock to you to learn that your name is all over the front of the newspaper but that isn't why you came to see me, is it?"

Findo shook his head.

"So, why are you upset?"

He took a deep breath and held it for a while before exhaling slowly and looking at his hands. "I didn't like it."

"Well, why did you do it?"

"I didn't know what it would be like."

"What did you think it would be like?"

Findo shrugged. "Oh, I don't know. I've never done anything like that before. I didn't really want to do it this time, well, most of me didn't." He looked up and Mrs Reid saw several tears on his face. "I've never taken anything from anyone before. I've never done a hold-up or anything like that. Not with guns and stuff."

Mrs Reid looked back sternly. "So why did you get involved?"

Findo looked awkward. "Well," he said, "they've been talking about trying to get into this place for a few weeks. Colin knew this money was coming. Someone who used to work there told him about the deliveries. You know, when the money comes in and when it goes out."

"Actually, I don't know," said Mrs Reid, "but go on."

Findo shrugged again. "This bloke . . . sorry, man . . . he told Colin and the others about the layout of the place and how the gates were operated. But they couldn't work out how to get at the money. You see, if they tried to hold up the security van in the open, there's a lot more chance of getting seen. And the other thing is if they forced the van open, there's all these alarms and stuff that get set off. They even have sprays inside that coat the money with ink that won't come off. If they opened the van up wrong, the spray gets triggered and then all the money's useless." He wrapped his fingers around each other and wrung them together. "And they can't get the drivers to open the van either because there's all these time delays and things like that. And they have these tracking things on the van so that even if you steal the whole van and drive off the police can follow it on their

224

radar or something."

Findo sighed. "So," he said, "the best way of getting hold of the money was to get into the depot but they couldn't work out how to do it without setting off any alarms. They talked about it for days but they weren't getting anywhere." He paused for a moment and then looked up at Mrs Reid. "But I worked out a way it could be done and I told Colin. They didn't believe me at first. They said it wasn't possible and that it was too dangerous but I said it was alright. So, we had a practice and it worked fine. But the others were all too big and awkward to do it." Findo gave a brief smile. "And they were too scared to risk it. So, I ended up doing it. I got them in. I opened the gates and let them in. And we did it. We got the money and we got out without anyone knowing we were there."

"Except for the three men that you held up," said Mrs Reid.

"Yes," said Findo. "Except for them."

"And that's what you didn't like?"

He nodded.

Mrs Reid shook her head sadly. "Findo. What did you expect?"

He shrugged. "I don't know."

She looked disappointed. "Did anyone get hurt?"

"No."

"But that's not the point is it?"

"No."

Mrs Reid took a sip of tea and considered the teenager sitting hunched in the chair next to her. "It was your decision, Findo. So you are going to have to live with it. I just hope that you think carefully. You can't ignore the consequences of your own actions. It's no use pretending that you didn't know what could have happened. If you don't like guns, then stay away from them. If you decide to get involved with guns you have to be aware of what they are; guns are tools designed for killing. That's what they do, they kill and maim and destroy."

Findo kept his head lowered.

"It's no good hiding your head, young man," said Mrs Reid. "No one forced you to do this. You decided to get involved. And it sounds like it's because you were showing off. You wanted to prove that you could do what the others couldn't. You wanted to prove you could get inside this security firm's compound. Well, that's all very well, but it was your choice. You knew why they wanted to get inside and you knew they would have guns. So, if you didn't like it, it's your own fault."

Findo had looked up again and she stared at him hard. "I really hope this isn't going to be how Findo Gask does things from now on."

He shook his head quickly. "No."

"Are you sure?"

He nodded firmly. "I'm not doing that again."

Mrs Reid looked unconvinced. "It's up to you, Findo. Only you can make that choice, but just remember that you're also the one responsible for the consequences. You're not involved in a war and you're not fighting for a cause, so what you do is entirely up to you. If you steal, it's for yourself. And if you use weapons and harm others, it's just to satisfy your own greed. So, if you go down that path, you must be prepared to live with that knowledge."

She sighed. "We live in a rotten world, Findo. There's a pretence of international justice but it's just a sham. Behind the façade it's a case of devil take the hindmost and grab what you can. I've seen it all over the world. Everything else is just illusion. Even the world's so-called greatest democracy is a sick joke. Poverty, injustice and hypocrisy are as rife there as anywhere. Utopia is a dream that we will never create while there are human beings in the world. The innocent try to fight for what's right but it's a lost cause. There are too many forces ready to trample anyone who tries to oppose the great god Profit or upset the balance of power. Either that, or they get their feet pulled from beneath them by the meanness and self-interest of those supposed to be on their side."

Mrs Reid looked sad. "I gave up pretending otherwise a long time ago, Findo. All we can do is create our own personal utopia and be true to that. You can make your own rules but stick to them. If we are to be our own judges then we have to be honest with ourselves; that's absolutely crucial or there's no point even trying."

Findo spent that night in Mrs Reid's spare room. She insisted he stayed, saying he was as safe in her home as anywhere. After breakfast, she readied herself for work but made Findo promise not to go anywhere until she returned at lunchtime. After some resistance he agreed, unwilling to push the boundaries of their relationship but grateful for the loyalty.

Their friendship had built steadily – principally because Frances Reid was the first person to show Findo that he had an intellect. More importantly, she drove him to use it. She taught Findo by feeding his curiosity and earned his trust by her lack of questions. It was not that she did not realise how Findo lived; rather that she saw his existence as evidence of the corruption of a system that could allow its most precious resource – its children – to grow up in squalor and ignorance. The old radical had resigned herself to living within a society that her own philosophy rejected and, as long as Findo did not harm others for his own gratification, she had no scruples about him stealing for a living.

For Findo, the elderly Marxist became special because she was the first person to really show him respect. He had been given love and affection by Billy and Abby but his relationship with Frances Reid was different. She accepted him for what he was and dealt with him on equal terms. She had offered him the same help that she would to any stranger who came to the library looking for information and, having established what he wanted to know, had made no attempt to judge him or his endeavours but simply helped seek the answers he wanted.

Since their first meeting, that relationship had become deeper and more important to both. As well as treating him as her equal, Mrs Reid had also started to challenge Findo, subtly at first and then more openly. She rejected his early reservations about his own academic abilities and refused to let him use his lack of education as an excuse for laziness – teaching him that he was as capable as anyone of learning. Her resoluteness about his capabilities and the mental discipline she imparted had played a significant part in developing his sense of self-worth and his right to independence of thought and action.

Findo spent a quiet morning, prowling the downstairs of the house to begin with. There were net curtains in the lounge window and he stood for a while behind them, watching the road through the gap in the privet hedge. He went to the kitchen door a few times but got no further than putting his hand on the key. Eventually, he returned to the lounge and browsed the bookshelves before picking up a pile of *National Geographic* magazines and settling down to immerse himself in rediscovered history, endangered animals and photo stories on exotic lands.

He was still reading when Mrs Reid returned just before two in the afternoon. She was carrying several carrier bags and handed one to Findo as she came in. "Here you are. Try them on."

Findo looked at the bag in surprise. It came from one of the sports shops along Albert Parade. "What's this?"

"If you have a look you'll see." Mrs Reid took off her coat and scarf and hung them neatly on the hooks inside the front door. "You can make the tea once you've had a look. I'll prepare our lunch."

With that, she walked off to the kitchen and began to bustle about, putting the rest of her shopping away and laying a selection of rolls, cheese and other sandwich fillings on a tray.

Findo opened the carrier bag. Inside were a new football shirt, a scarf and a woollen hat. He looked at them in puzzlement then walked through to the kitchen.

"Mrs Reid?"

"Yes, dear?"

"What are these for?"

She raised one eyebrow. "I'd have guessed that they're for wearing."

Findo looked confused. "But why?"

"Because people don't approve if we walk around naked," she retorted.

Findo looked even more confused and she smiled, her face crinkling up with a myriad of fine lines. "I'm sorry, dear," she said. "But it was a silly question."

He shook his head. "But you know what I mean."

Mrs Reid sighed. "Yes, I do. But I was hoping you might manage to put two and two together yourself."

"What do you mean?"

"Well," she said, "you don't normally wear football shirts and nonsense like that do you?"

"No."

"Well then, in that case people are less likely to recognise you if you start wearing one now."

Findo frowned. He held up the bright red shirt. "But . . . it's not very . . . subtle."

Mrs Reid shook her head and laughed. "No, it's ghastly. But it's the kind of thing lots of young people wear. I see them everyday. And if you don't want to be noticed, you might be better off wearing the same thing. You always wear quite drab clothes." She gestured to the shirt. "This is a different kind of camouflage."

Findo nodded. "I suppose so."

Mrs Reid shook her head. "There's no 'suppose' about it. You got your name all over the papers and the police might not know who they're looking for but there will be some people who recognise you and they're not all going to be your friends, particularly with a reward on offer."

"A reward?"

"Yes," said Mrs Reid. "It's in today's paper. The company are offering ten thousand pounds to anyone providing information leading to the conviction of those who robbed the depot. You're a wanted man, Findo Gask."

Findo left the house after lunch. He felt incredibly self-conscious as he stepped out into Dubmore Road wearing the bright red football shirt but no one gave him a second glance. The scarf was knotted tightly around his neck and he had the hat pulled right down on his head, all of his hair tucked up underneath.

He walked slowly up Dubmore Road, trying not to stare about too much in case he started drawing attention by acting oddly. As he drew closer to Alexander Cross, he turned off left, unable to nerve himself to walk around the junction in full view of the divisional police headquarters. Findo cut through a couple of side streets, emerging onto Corporation Road a few hundred yards from his flat.

Findo walked past the bookies' on the opposite side of the road. There was the usual number of pedestrians about for a Thursday afternoon but no obvious sign of anyone lying in wait. After a few minutes of dithering and indecision, he crossed over and walked swiftly into the betting shop. He unlocked the door at the bottom of the stairs and went in. He closed the door behind him and paused for a moment. It was quiet in the stairwell, no sounds to alarm him.

Findo set off upstairs, past the offices on the floors above and around the dogleg flight of stairs to his own door. He put his key in the lock and turned it.

As he did so, the door swung open of its own accord and an arm shot out. It grabbed him by the front of the shirt and yanked, catching him completely off balance. Blinking in surprise, Findo was hauled into

229

the flat and slung across the room to land on the sofa. He landed hard and sprawled across the cushions. There was no time to pick himself up before the man in the doorway was on him again. A knee thudded down onto Findo's chest, pinning him to the sofa. Hands grabbed his and wrenched his arms down by his side.

Ross Kirkbride stood in his office with his arms folded behind his back. He looked down at Alexander Cross, watching the traffic flowing in and out of the city centre. There were three others in the room.

"Okay, Snoopy, what have we got? Any theories on how this lot got inside?"

Detective Inspector Charlotte Brown was in charge of the investigation into the raid on the security depot off Warner Drive. She was new to the division but had already caught a number of collars. A graduate in psychology, she hid a tough, analytical mind under a soft and sometimes flouncy exterior. Following the logic of police humour, she had been christened Snoopy within a few days of first putting on a uniform. It was a name she liked; it had a couple of possible interpretations, both suitable.

She put her sheaf of paperwork to one side and lent back. "Okay. First of all, the raid: We think the Custodian van was tailed along Castle Drive. It was early; they reached the depot at 7.12 a.m. There can't have been much light in the sky and it was drizzling. We're trying to trace other drivers who may have been on the road but I wouldn't hold out much hope. We think that somewhere along Castle Drive, probably at one of the sets of lights, our stowaway slid underneath the truck and clung on for the rest of the journey. Sounds hard to believe but that's the only way we can see they did it."

Kirkbride nodded, still gazing out at the view. "SOCO and forensic go along with that?"

DI Brown nodded. "Yes, sir. There are marks on the undercarriage that could correspond with hooks from some kind of harness."

"Any idea where this stowaway got on board?"

Her brows knotted together. "No. That's one thing that we haven't worked out – but the exact location may be irrelevant. I'd guess it happened at one of the sets of traffic lights because I couldn't see it being something anyone would fancy doing for too long and they were on the motorway before that."

"So how did he get underneath?"

The young DI smiled. "Well, we've had a spot more luck there. Uniform turned up a burnt-out truck dumped over the other side of East Allonby late yesterday. Not much to go on but the interesting thing was that, before it was torched, someone had cut a hole in the floor."

Kirkbride looked at her over his shoulder.

Snoopy smiled. "Big enough for a person to climb through. We're guessing that the truck got in front of Custodian's van at one of the lights. The stowaway dropped through the hole, rolled underneath the two vehicles and attached themselves to the van."

"Okay," said Kirkbride turning round to face the room, "Sounds crazy but until we've got an alternative, we'll work on the basis that it's true. The two from the van, they didn't see anything?"

"No, sir. If they stopped a normal distance behind the truck they probably wouldn't have seen the tarmac in front of them. If the stowaway came out from underneath . . ."

"Have you asked them about the truck? Anyone cut them up? Stop in front of them?"

"No joy. One of them said there may have been some kind of truck on Castle Drive but he couldn't swear what it looked like. He also thought it had been behind them. Neither remember anyone blocking them in, cutting them up, stalling in front of them or anything like that."

One of the other two men in the room raised a hand. Kirkbride gave him a nod. "Paul?"

"I was just wondering, why do you think the stowaway came from in front?"

Snoopy shrugged. "We're not certain he did. I just think it's more likely. Whichever way it was, he'd have to be pretty quick. I'd have thought it would make more sense for the robbers to stop in front of the van. That way they could be certain it wasn't going to jump the lights or shoot off as soon as they changed."

"Okay," said Paul Sweet, "I agree that sounds more likely. I just think that if one of the Custodian men says he may have seen a truck behind them, we should bear that in mind."

"Or, of course," said Kirkbride, "we may be looking at more than one vehicle. The truck could be behind, while they use a car in front to keep the van from moving off too quickly." He paced across to his desk and turned. "Either way, the stowaway hangs on underneath. He gets inside, waits until no one is looking and sneaks into the control room where he opens the gates. How does he time that right?"

"There are security cameras all round the depot," said Snoopy. "Some look out over the service road from Warner Drive. It would be easy enough to look and see if the truck was in position, then open the gates."

"They could come in by foot," offered the third man in the room, Detective Inspector Dave Mayfield.

Snoopy shook her head. "No. All three from Custodian agree on that. They heard the gates opening and when they turned to look, the truck was already coming up the internal driveway. The first of the raiders apparently jumped from the back of it as it reached the gates."

Mayfield nodded. "Okay, but this must have been an inside job."

Snoopy shrugged. "Inside information, yes. Inside job? Not necessarily." She smiled at the men in the room. "We're looking at Custodian's personnel records – anyone who's left recently, that kind of thing, checking where they are now and what sort of alibi they have."

Kirkbride nodded. "Anyone not turn up for work since the robbery?"

"No." Snoopy shook her head. "Nothing like that. They don't employ that many either. We may be looking at an ex-employee and I'm sure someone sold them information about the layout of the place and how to open the gates. But I don't think we're looking at current employees."

"Okay," said Kirkbride. "What else?"

"We're trying to trace the truck," said Snoopy. "It was a Mercedes, recent model. The plates had been taken off before it was torched and the engine and chassis numbers removed. It was a professional job but we're crosschecking records to see if we can turn up a similar vehicle being reported stolen anywhere in the country. We'll also get in touch with owners of the same model and see if we can turn anything up that way." She gave a brief smile. "One other clue is that SOCO think it had been resprayed recently. The truck was blue but there was white paint underneath."

"What about a livery?" suggested Sweet.

His colleague raised an eyebrow. "Sorry?"

"Could it have been repainted to hide a previous livery? Particularly if it was stolen, it might have had the owner's details on it."

Snoopy nodded. "Yeah, thanks. I'll get them to have a look at that. We haven't got much in the way of paintwork left but they might be able to turn up something."

"Anything from in the truck or around?" asked Kirkbride.

Snoopy shook her head. "Not really. The raiders were all wearing balaclavas and black overalls. Usual sort of gear. There were some ashes in the back of the truck and we think their clothes might have been in there when they torched it. But there wasn't anything to provide any clues. We don't think they off-loaded the loot there either. The truck was torched down a track on the edge of farmland. There were no fresh tracks from other vehicles nearby. We think they must have unloaded the money somewhere else, then one person drove the truck to where it was torched and escaped on foot. Or possibly on a bicycle, there were tyre tracks from a mountain bike going off into a nearby Forestry Commission plantation."

She shrugged. "Quite clever really. There's a car park about a mile away. A lot of mountain bikers use tracks in the plantation for riding. It would have been easy enough to have a car waiting and there'll be so many tyre tracks around that there's no way of connecting any of them with the raid. We're putting out an appeal on the local news tonight – TV and radio – asking for anyone who saw the truck near East Allonby or anything else suspicious involving a blue Mercedes. But we're just going through the motions really. This raid was well planned and well organised. It's possible that they slipped up somewhere along the line but we're relying on luck there."

Kirkbride sighed. "So what else have we got? What other leads do we have?"

Snoopy grinned. "Well, there's still that card."

"Ah, yes," said Kirkbride. "Findo bloody Gask. I don't suppose you could get a print from the card?"

The young DI pulled a face. "A partial one. It'll help but it's not that good. However, we may be able to match it with others with a Findo Gask connection."

Kirkbride shook his head. "Okay. Well, keep up the spadework. It may seem like it's going nowhere but digging normally pays off eventually. Whoever planned this raid, they're not perfect. That truck came from somewhere and so did their information about the depot. If necessary, start pulling in every ex-employee and putting the fear of God into them. And in the meantime, keep checking the current ones as well. Someone talked and if we can find them we'll get a lot closer to this Findo Gask or whoever it is we're looking for."

Speed did not know whether to laugh or shout. He waved the front page of the previous day's newspaper under Findo's nose. "Are you mad!"

Findo backed away and said nothing.

"Why?" demanded Speed. "Of all places, why leave one there? Do you want to get caught? Do you want to see us all inside?"

Findo looked at the lounge carpet. His employer had arrived at the flat a couple of hours after Findo's own return. Dougie Page, the man who had been lying in wait for Findo, had summoned him. It was Page who had hauled Findo through the door and thrown him onto the sofa. He had not recognised Findo in his new football shirt and was in a foul temper. Page had spent all day and the previous night sitting around waiting for Findo, who he disliked anyway.

"I knew those cards would get you in trouble," said Speed. "What the bloody hell were you thinking of?"

Findo shrugged uneasily.

"Oh Christ!" said Speed. "What do I do with you?"

"Break his legs," muttered Page.

"Yeah?" said Speed. "That's not a bad idea." He laughed and jabbed his finger at Findo's head. "Maybe Dougie's right. I should beat the crap out of you. That way I might manage to knock some sense into you."

Findo shuffled backwards nervously. There was an intensity in Speed's manner that he found hard to handle and he was unsure whether or not Speed was joking.

Speed sighed. "I mean, listen to this." He held the paper out and began to read in imitation of a radio newsreader. "'Armed robbers escaped with over half a million pounds in cash after a dawn raid on security firm Custodian. Raiders brandishing sawn-off shotguns forced their way into a depot on the Warner Drive estate early this morning. After forcing three terrorised Custodian employees to open safes at the depot, the gang escaped with bags stuffed with over £500,000 in cash.'" Speed shook his head. "Is this right, John? You didn't really terrorise them did you?"

John Biggs was standing next to the fireplace watching Findo and his boss. "Oh, I wouldn't say that. Albie was quite nice really. If they thought that was terrorising, they should see him when he's in a bad mood." He shrugged. "You know how it is, Colin. Press get half a story and dress it up to make it sound how they think it should be. Facts aren't straight either. We didn't force anyone to open any safes; we waited until they'd opened them and then went in."

Speed sighed with exasperation. "I don't know, sloppy reporting." He lifted the paper again. "So what else do they say? Here we are: 'Police sources say the raid is believed to be the work of the Findo Gask gang. This notorious outfit have recently been linked with a series of crimes in the city, although this is the first time that they are known to have been involved in a robbery of this scale.'"

Speed shook his head in disbelief. "What are they on. 'Findo Gask gang'!" He laughed. "I dunno, 'robbery of this scale'. Well, of course they haven't. It's the biggest bloody heist anyone's ever done in this town. No one's ever done a security firm here before. Not for money like this." Speed chucked the paper to one side then grinned. "Well, I suppose we should look on the bright side. If anyone asks, me and John can say we don't know anything. After all, it was all the work of that nasty Findo Gask gang." He sighed. "Findo?"

"Yes?"

Speed's fist flicked up in a swift upper cut. The blow caught Findo on the side of his jaw and he fell back but John caught him, pinning his arms to his side.

Speed sat down on the sofa.

"Findo," he said, "you've been fucking stupid, and if you don't learn to think you're going to end up in serious trouble. You see, if the Muldoons had still been around and you'd done that while you were on a job for them you'd probably be propping up a motorway flyover somewhere by now. I've given you a lot of free rein, more than I would most people. Now, I just hope you're not taking the piss."

Findo flexed his jaw cautiously, running his tongue over his teeth to check they were all still in place. He shook his head.

"Because I do expect some discipline," said Speed. "You see, I'll look after you but you've got to show some sense and this time you've let me down badly."

Findo lowered his eyes.

"I'm sorry," he said. "I wasn't thinking."

"No, you weren't," said Speed. "And normally that would be it. I'd be finished with you." He sighed. "But in the circumstances, I'm going to be kind. If it wasn't for you, we wouldn't have got into that depot. It was your idea and it was you that got us in. You've seriously pissed me off but on the other hand I owe you. So, you see, I'm going to give you another chance."

Findo smiled weakly. "Thanks," he said.

"Yeah," said Speed, "but you don't get off that lightly. I'm docking your cut by fifty percent. I've also got to get you out of town for a bit – and that's going to cost a bit of money. You're a bloody liability right now. Your name's on the front page of the papers and the coppers are going to be looking hard for you. Only takes one person to grass you up. So, you're going away for a bit, Findo. Think of it as a holiday. Sort of paid leave. Just not negotiable."

27. And she was

The three men were about to leave the flat when the door buzzer sounded. Speed had just finished giving Findo his orders: he was to stay in the flat, not go out under any circumstances and wait until told what to do. He was also to lie low, keeping the curtains drawn and not answering the door – as well as watching out for anyone hanging around the flat, front or rear.

Speed frowned. "This had better not be trouble," he said. "Who's there, Dougie?"

Page was nearest to the door's security monitor. "Couple," he said. "Young. Don't look like cops."

Speed snorted. "The best ones don't!" He turned to Findo. "You expecting anyone?"

Findo shook his head. "No."

"It's alright," said Page. "One's that Mickey Dunn. Can't see who the girl is."

"Okay," said Speed. "Let them in. See what they want then get them to clear off." He gave Findo a hard stare. "I don't want visitors, either," he said. "Understand?"

Findo nodded. He thought of Abby but said nothing. So far, he had kept her existence secret from Speed and the others he worked with. She was a separate part of his life, one that he kept to himself.

Speed jerked his head sideways. "Go in the bedroom and shut the door."

"What?"

"Do as you're told. Mickey knows you live here and I can't help that. But I don't want anyone else seeing you. I don't know who this girl is he's got with him but I don't want her seeing you. Now, get in there and keep quite."

Findo nodded slowly and slunk out of the lounge. He closed the door behind him and flopped backwards onto the bed. He lay with his hands behind his head and stared at the ceiling. He was glad in a way that Speed had taken charge. He did not want to leave the city but realised that it made sense. He would be back before long and would just have to be more careful – talk to less people and start moving around more again.

He heard a knock on the flat door and the sound of Mickey's voice as it opened. There was a short conversation and then one voice, a woman's, rose above the rest.

"Listen, I'm his sister. Tell me where he is."

Findo hardly heard the rest. He knew the voice. It was different, older, but still the same person. He leapt to his feet and flung open the bedroom door. Speed turned and glared but Findo did not even see him. He looked past Page's shoulder and into the middle of the room.

"Billy?"

"Findo!"

She dived past the men standing around her and launched herself at him. Dougie Page half raised an arm as if to ward her off but he was too slow; Billy already had her arms wrapped tight around her baby brother's shoulders and was lifting him off the ground. Findo returned the embrace with equal ferocity and startled himself by beginning to cry.

"Billy!" He murmured in her ear.

"Findo, Findo, Findo." She squeezed him again and again. "It's so good to see you again," she whispered. "I'm really sorry it's taken so long."

"S'alright," mumbled Findo.

Eventually they separated and stood back a little. Both went silent as they took each other in again, appraising the changes that seven years had wrought. Both were slightly taken aback at the mutual intensity of their reunion. Findo was still crying. Billy was the only member of his family about which he had ever really cared – or been cared for by. And even though he had reluctantly understood her need to go, their separation had been savagely painful and left a terrible hole in his young life.

Seven-and-a-half years on, Findo was not so different physically. He had grown – and was as tall as Billy now, if no broader. His face was starting to mature and his voice was deeper. But other than that, his appearance had not altered significantly. He was still skinny, still dark and the shape of his face basically the same.

The changes in Billy's appearance were a little more dramatic. Through her teens she had tried everything possible to defeminise her appearance, including hacking her sleek dark hair into a short and ragged crop. That was gone; in its place was a tumbled mass of platinum blonde, held back from her forehead by a red bandanna. There was a large silver ring in her nose and other rings in her ears. Her skin was deeply tanned and there was a small scar on her left cheek. The cheekbones inherited from her mother were still there but even more defined now and the brightness in her eyes – dulled during her teenage years – had been rekindled to burn as strongly as when

238

Billy had been a small, savage child.

But it was not only Billy's appearance that had changed; her attitude was different too. When had Findo last seen her, Billy had been subdued and miserable, scared of her looks and resentful of the world that surrounded her. She had kept her gaze down to avoid eye contact and spoken in mumbles whenever anyone else was around. Now, that bitter and frightened girl was gone. Billy stood square and proud, holding herself with a poise that combined a dancer's elegance and a fighter's challenge.

There were some things, however, that were unchanged. She was still small and slender – but could crack her tongue with force when needed. Stepping back a fraction from Findo, she glanced over her shoulder at the men in the room.

"Right, you lot," she said. "We haven't seen each other for over seven years and I want to talk to my brother." She flicked her head. "Come back later if you want but for now you can clear off."

Dougie Page scowled. "Hey." He reached out to grab Billy's shoulder but he was too slow. Before he could touch her, Billy was no longer in the same place. Instead, Page found himself being spun round to face the wall. His right arm was twisted behind his shoulders at the same time with his thumb being bent painfully backwards.

Billy glanced at the other two men in the room. They made no move to interfere.

"Get off, you bitch!" Page snarled and spluttered with his face against the wall. Then, relying purely on brute force, he shoved back hard.

But again Billy was not where he expected – although she did keep hold of his thumb as she neatly sidestepped his reverse charge. Page stumbled back. Then, whirled round by a yank on his thumb and helped by a foot hooked around his ankle, he found himself thudding face down on the lounge carpet.

Billy stepped back towards Findo. "Before you get up," she told Page. "A couple of things you should know – I'm a black-belt in tae kwon do and I kick-box. And I grew up around Tibbermore so I know plenty of ways of putting you back on the floor and making sure you stay there that aren't in the book. Okay?"

Page pushed himself slowly up of the floor, looking at Billy and Findo with an expression of loathing. He mumbled something under his breath and glanced sideways at his boss. But Speed ignored Page and stared at Billy in admiration. John Biggs just raised his eyebrows. From the doorway, Mickey Dunn grinned.

The room was silent for a moment then Speed nodded slowly.

"Very good," he said. He glanced at Page. "Dougie, wait for us downstairs. We'll be down in a minute."

Page scowled but did as told and stamped off down the stairs, shoving Mickey aside as he went.

"I'm sorry about that," said Speed. "He's not a bad bloke really, just not too bright."

Billy nodded. "Yeah? I've met his sort before."

Speed smiled. "Well, I think we'd better leave you two to it. But can I ask one thing?"

Billy nodded.

"Your brother's got himself in a little spot of bother," said Speed. "He could do with lying low for a bit. Can you help make sure he doesn't go out?"

Billy shrugged. "If that's what he wants."

Speed nodded. "Findo will explain. Have a good time catching up. I'll call round again later this evening. Probably be some time after nine, if that's alright."

Billy shrugged. "Please yourself."

Speed smiled. "I'll bring some food for you both. A few beers as well."

"I prefer wine," said Billy. "White and dry, if you can cope with that."

Speed nodded but stopped again at the doorway. He gave Billy an apologetic smile. "One question," he said.

"What?"

"Your hair," said Speed. "Is it natural?"

Billy's tone was cold when she answered. "Why?"

Speed held up his hands as if to ward off any attack. "No offence," he said. "It looks good. I just wondered if you could turn him blond too?"

There was no thaw in Billy's glacial expression. "Would you like me to cook and sew as well?"

Speed backed out of the door quickly. "I'll bring wine when I come back."

"Don't rush."

When they were alone, Billy turned to Findo again. She held out her arms and pulled him into another hug. They stood like that for several minutes, only moving apart when Findo stepped back to take another look at his guardian angel.

"It really is you, isn't it?" he said.

Billy smiled. "Yeah, it's me, Findo."

"Seven years."

She looked rueful. "Better late than never."

He smiled. "Yeah."

Findo paced over to the fireplace, looking at her sideways as he went. Then he turned and stood staring at her.

Billy looked uncomfortable. "What is it?"

"You," said Findo.

"What about me?" She looked worried.

Findo grinned and laughed. "Everything," he said.

She smiled back. "Everything?"

"Yeah," said Findo. "Everything." He shrugged. "I know it's been a long time. I've never stopped missing you but that doesn't matter. You're here. You're back." He grinned. "Even if you look a bit different."

Billy looked down at the floor, embarrassed.

"But you look good," said Findo quickly. "You look fantastic." He laughed. "And that was brilliant what you did with Page. I don't like him much anyway. That was so cool the way he never even touched you."

Billy shrugged. "That was nothing," she said. "He didn't have a chance." She frowned. "But what was that guy saying about you being in trouble and having to stay in? What's happened? Is he a friend of yours or not?"

Findo waved a hand dismissively. "Oh, that's nothing. It's not that important. And Colin's alright. I work for him. But I don't want to talk about me. What about you? I haven't seen you for seven years and I haven't had a letter for six months. I was starting to worry. I want to know all about you. Where you've been and what you've been doing. And why you've come back now."

28. In search of safety

Findo already knew the outline of Billy's story. She had kept her promise to write – although the timing of the letters was never constant. Unwilling to disappoint the brother she left behind, Billy had avoided setting a routine that could be broken. She warned in her first letter that she was not going to write regularly and, although her letters were long, their arrival had always been erratic. A few times, Findo received a couple of letters in as many weeks. On other occasions there would be several months between each instalment of his sister's news.

The letters had always gone first to Mickey Dunn's mother. When Billy left the city, Eileen Dunn had been about the only person she trusted.

Eileen was the widow of an offshore oil worker, a tough and canny man who, before the helicopter crash that took his life, had salted away sufficient money and taken out enough insurance policies to allow his wife to buy their council house outright after his death. In fact, Mrs Dunn could have left the cramped three-bedroom terraced house where she had brought up Mickey and his three younger sisters. The money would have bought a substantial home almost anywhere. But Eileen Dunn had been born and brought up in East Park and had no inclination to move up either the property ladder or the social stakes by changing address. She was a hard, plain-speaking woman who – apart from where her own children were concerned – had a well-developed sense of right and wrong.

She had won Billy's trust by punching one of Bosnia's boyfriends unconscious. The man, a car mechanic and part-time drug dealer, had turned nasty one night when Billy was fourteen. Billy had reluctantly gone into one of the East Park drinking-holes with a message that Bosnia was unwell. Deprived of his expected company, the boyfriend had decided the daughter would do instead and tried to pull Billy onto his lap. When she refused and pulled away, he got angry and grabbed her by the hair, pulling her across the table. The mechanic slapped Billy hard across the face and demanded to know if she thought she was too good for him.

Eileen Dunn had seen what happened. She marched up and threw the man's pint in his face. When he stood up in rage to give her a face-full of abuse, Eileen drew back her fist and slammed it straight into his nose. The mechanic never troubled Billy again and gave up on

Bosnia shortly after. Eileen, who knew of Bosnia, took Billy to her house, which was just around the corner and cleaned up a cut left by the man's ring. Billy returned the next day to thank Eileen and stayed to help bathe her youngest daughter. Over the next few years, Billy became a regular visitor to the house – an oasis of relative normality and decency compared to her own family environment.

And when Billy fled the city, Eileen Dunn's was also the only reliable address she knew for sending the letters that she had promised Findo.

Sitting in Findo's flat above the betting shop on Corporation Road, Billy took them back to that morning when they had said farewell by the old gasometer.

Leaving the city, she had travelled light. All she took was a couple of changes of clothing stuffed into a shoulder bag. Plus something even more valuable: proof of who she was.

For Billy had been born in the days before Bosnia became Bosnia. Back then, Billy's mother called herself Nova MacBeth and was only at the start of the slide that took her from being one of the hottest properties in town to undesirable slum residence. And although the relationship only lasted a few more months – Nova just beginning a longer-lasting love affair with crack – when Billy was born, her parents lived together and her birth was properly registered.

One day, about seven years later, as Bosnia slept off a heavy drinking session, Billy was going through her mother's clothes and bags looking for money to buy food. She only found one pound, seventy-three pence. But stuck in the lining of an old coat, Billy found a small bundle of documents. There were sets of papers under various names, including several birth certificates – one for someone born in the city's maternity hospital thirty-eight years earlier called Shirley White.

The bundle also contained birth certificates for Natalie, Billy and Jimmy Ray. Billy took hers and kept it safe from that day. It was with her when she left the city and Billy knew it was far more valuable than any other kind of luggage.

After her farewell to Findo, Billy had collected her bag from Eileen Dunn's house and caught a bus to Dubmore. Although she had said she was going to take a train south, Billy did not want to waste her money and set off using only her thumb. She left with just over eighty pounds in cash. Some had been carefully saved over nearly six months as Billy tried to build up the courage for her escape. Ten pounds had been stolen from Bosnia's pocket that morning; another twenty had been a parting gift from Eileen Dunn.

It took Billy less than half an hour to get a lift. A businessman on his way back to Birmingham after a meeting stopped for her outstretched thumb. Billy climbed into the front of the Vauxhall Cavalier with more trepidation than excitement. But to her relief, the man did not even seem to register that it was a girl next to him in the car. He had given Billy a lift so that he would have someone to talk to on the trip south. And for most of the next few hours he talked non-stop. He had no interest in who Billy was or where she was going; she was simply his excuse to talk to himself about his job, house, car and family without feeling self-conscious.

The rest of Billy's initial flight from the city was equally uneventful. Her next lift was a lorry driver who took her from the Hilton Park services near Birmingham to Taunton. Again, Billy's presence was virtually ignored once she had been picked up. The trucker was a taciturn man in his fifties. He spoke to Billy only to tell her – with a certain satisfaction – that he was not supposed to pick up anyone and that his boss would be furious if he knew.

Billy was happy not to have to talk and settled back into the corner of the cab. She was content to watch the countryside roll past, every minute putting another mile between her and the city.

Next, Billy was dumped unceremoniously at the motorway junction just north of Taunton. It was dark now and she was in a bad spot to pick up a lift; most vehicles speeding up the slip road were going too fast to stop. But just when Billy was starting to despair, a retired schoolteacher on his way to visit his sister in Exmouth stopped for her.

This time, Billy had to answer some questions but they all seemed harmless and as they drove on into the South West, she gradually began to relax. As they left the motorway and drove into a service station at Exeter, where Billy had asked to be dropped, she let the man buy her a coffee. After a little bit of small talk, the schoolteacher left to continue his journey. Billy sat on in the warm canteen for a while longer, wondering what to do next. It was only when she got up to leave that she noticed something sticking out of the side pocket on her bag. She almost cried when she saw what it was; sometime while she was not looking, the old man had slipped two ten-pound notes into her bag.

But then Billy's luck turned. For the next couple of weeks she slept rough, unsure what to do or where to go. Drifting without plan, mostly on foot, she followed the coast south. At night she sheltered in bus stops, empty buildings and doorways. A couple of nights were spent in the porch of a church.

More by accident than design, she found a way to bring in a little extra money. She was sitting huddled on the promenade at Dawlish when a middle-aged woman threw a handful of change onto Billy's bag, which was lying between her feet. Billy was taken by surprise; she had been staring out at the grey, choppy sea and had not even thought about begging. She let the change lie there, unsure how to respond. But then it started to multiply, the initial donation acting as the magnet to draw more coins to Billy's feet. Other passers-by saw the money lying there and added their own. A few offered kind words as well – although one or two only threw a few words of abuse.

The day set a precedent and as she wandered the Devon Riviera, Billy began to live on other people's spare change. But it was not an easy life. Billy was lonely and miserable. Often she was cold and there were times when, having been caught by the rain, she was wet through and had to walk all day just to try and keep warm. She was moved on by the police a few times and after that began to hide whenever she saw someone in uniform, scared of being taken in and locked up. Apart from the police, there were other hazards to life on the streets. One shopkeeper who found her curled up on his doorstep hurled a bucket of filthy water over her. Adults would give her dirty looks and filthy language when they saw her begging. Children could be even worse; they seemed to know that she had stepped outside society's boundaries – she was no longer a proper person and, therefore, a safe target for behaviour that they would never dare try normally. And it was worse at night if she was not well hidden. Because she was on the streets, some men seemed to assume she would do anything. A couple of times she had to flee from drunken yobs who stumbled across her after a night out in Torbay's nightclubs.

And so, Billy kept moving on, reaching Brixham several weeks after arriving in Exeter. The fishing port's main claim to fame was that William of Orange landed there with his army when invited to come and claim the English throne in 1688. But Brixham's historical significance was lost on Billy and she arrived on a miserable day when curtains of steady drizzle were blowing in from the English Channel.

From a small café where she had bought a mug of tea, Billy looked over the harbour. Beads of rain ran down the outside of the windows while steam from the hot food and drying bodies inside the café condensed on Billy's side of the glass. She shivered. It was time to move on. She was not in the right place. Torbay was too developed, too ugly. The smaller towns like Brixham were prettier but half-hearted. They lacked something. She sensed that they had once been lively, thriving places but their vitality was now second-hand. They lived mainly on visitors; and out of season the hollowness showed.

It took Billy a couple of days to leave Devon. She stopped again at Exeter and spent a few hours on the green near the cathedral, watching people and writing the first letter that she sent to her brother.

Findo knew the facts of the story that followed — how a chance meeting with a group of travellers in the Blackdown Hills had led to her joining the camp and spending a summer living in a makeshift shelter in a small copse. He also knew the outline of her life over the next couple of years — buying an old van and moving around travellers' sites across the south of England.

But Billy's letters had left out some aspects of life with the travellers — and why she had never asked her brother to come and join her. Sitting face to face at last, she slowly let the story out as she drew their lives back together again.

It was the third and final site where it all went sour. Billy had moved there following rumours that the police were going to raid the site in Hampshire where she had been living and impound any unroadworthy vehicles. With no tax or MOT for her van, Billy left one morning, her battered Transit limping across the county border to a site on an old droveway just off the Winchester to Salisbury road.

The move was a mistake. The site was beautiful, tucked under a spreading beech wood against the side of a chalk down. Fields stretched down to the river. Rising on the other side of the valley was Salisbury Plain. The site had space and fantastic views. But the residents were very different from those on the sites where Billy had been before. They squabbled, bickered, stole from each other and had no respect for their own living conditions or the countryside around them. Parts of broken down vehicles were dumped in the hedgerows and left to rust. Healthy trees were hacked down for firewood and the wood used as a communal dump. There was also no discipline when it came to hygiene. Instead of the neatly dug toilet-holes on the other sites, the field edges and ground inside the trees had become one vast communal latrine — making walking anywhere a dangerous occupation.

But for Billy, now eighteen, the real problems began at the end of the year. Her van had given up the ghost and she was stuck on the site unless she abandoned her vehicle. To make matters worse, an unattractive Geordie called Stevie had taken a fancy to Billy. His approaches were unsubtle and not pleasant. Stevie also frightened off other admirers, including a shy young guitarist called Brad who had developed a crush on Billy. Brad came back from a busking trip into Salisbury one day to find his caravan had been trashed. Stevie was

247

sitting nearby smirking. He commiserated with Brad and told him that he had seen two kids running off but had not been able to catch them. His story was full of holes and Brad did not believe him for a minute but knew better than to challenge Stevie. Brad got the intended message straight away. Thankful that his precious guitar had been with him, he left the site that afternoon, heading back to his family's large house in the Buckinghamshire stockbroker belt.

Billy did not know what to do. None of the others on the site were going to intervene against Stevie, who had a vicious reputation. In other circumstances she would have dealt with Stevie directly and violently but Billy knew that one victory could just spark off an escalation. And if it came to sheer strength, she knew that Stevie would be able to overpower her.

Rather than flee on foot, Billy began to lock herself away inside the van. Again, her hair was hacked back to a ragged crop and she stopped caring for herself. It was a cycle that bred on its own misery and she stopped feeding herself properly. Soon, she had lost pounds in weight and flitted around the site like a pale wraith, avoiding conversation or any other confrontation that could trap her in the open.

She was rescued the following spring. The sound of a souped-up Volkswagen Beetle, bouncing along the droveway, heralded the end of her incarceration. The gleaming pink, open-top VW arrived on a glorious April afternoon. From it sprang Chloe Williams – Billy's angel of mercy.

Chloe was twenty-eight and as self-assured as a politician on the make. She came from a well-off family and lived on a sprawling farm on the edge of the New Forest. She was extremely bright but had too agile and restless a mind for her own good. After graduating with a degree that did no justice to her intellect but was still an impressive achievement in light of her partying record, she had not settled at anything over the previous seven years. She had spent a few years travelling the world, working in a Hong Kong law firm, a Palestinian refugee camp and a South African newspaper office. Recently, she had come back to visit her family after a couple of years touring France and Spain.

Now, she had come to buy an ounce of cannabis for a party. As Chloe got out of the car, she noticed Billy watching her through the window. Chloe had long blonde hair and moved with natural poise. She was wearing old jeans and a plain top but managed to make them look stylish just by being inside them. There was a self-assurance to Chloe that was a painful reminder of how Billy had once been and the antithesis of everything she was now. In many ways, Chloe was what Billy could have become if the younger girl had been granted a different life.

Chloe grinned at Billy. The intensity of the smile – focused fully on her – forced a faint response.

"D'you mind if I park here?" Chloe asked.

Billy shook her head. "No."

"Here." On impulse, Chloe handed the keys through the window and Billy took them automatically. "Just shift it if it's in your way. I want to see if the boys up there have got any blow to sell."

Billy was still watching the VW an hour-and-a-half later when Chloe came back down the track. Chloe knocked on the driver's door of the van. A few minutes later Billy was surprised to find herself sitting outside in the sunshine with Chloe. They smoked a joint together and she listened to Chloe telling stories about her travels. Chloe seemed in no hurry to leave and kept chatting; Billy did not realise that it was just an excuse.

Billy made an admiring comment about Chloe's car. A few minutes later they were driving off down the droveway to go for a spin and the rest of the afternoon passed in a happy blur. Later, they found a small pub in Whitsbury, a village south of Salisbury. Hidden away in the snug, they drank Adnams Broadside and dined on sausages, mash and onion gravy. Chloe bought Billy a second pint and the alcohol – the first in weeks – went straight to her head. Bits of her life story tumbled out and she poured out the truth about life on the travellers' site.

They did not go back that night. Chloe took Billy to her parents' home and found her a bed, bath and a change of clothes. The next day, Chloe left Billy sleeping in and drove to the site on her own. She had taken the keys to the van from Billy's bag and stripped its meagre contents, taking anything of possible value.

For a couple of minutes, Billy was angry when Chloe told her what she had done. Later, she broke down in tears and sobbed with gratitude.

Chloe changed Billy's life. For a couple of weeks, Billy lived in the family's farmhouse. Chloe and her mother made sure she was kept busy – and warm and well fed. Then Billy moved out to a caravan behind the stables. It was used from time to time by staff employed on the farm and was twice the size of Billy's old van. Billy was asked to help with a few jobs around the farm and before she knew it had a full-time job and her own home. She tried to refuse a wage but relented when told that they had already made deductions for board and accommodation and were paying her the going rate for farm staff.

It was a good year. Billy's work kept her busy and fit. Chloe was not around all the time; she flitted away for holidays and other journeys. But she was never away too long and returned regularly to take Billy out – on shopping and camping trips, as well as to pubs, clubs and weekend-long parties.

Billy's letters had not said much to Findo about her relationship with Chloe but her love for her saviour was evident in both words and manner as she went back over the story. And Chloe had earned it. She had turned up when Billy was in danger of spiralling into a depression that would have been as dangerous mentally as her neglect of her body was harmful physically. Chloe took charge of Billy's life but imposed no prices. She got Billy back on her feet and then let her make her own choices.

By the following summer, Chloe had been itching to move on. She bounced into Billy's caravan one Sunday morning and dived onto the bed as she announced her plan.

The two young women left England on the ferry from Poole a few days later. Chloe had planned everything. The cherished Beetle had gone; in its place was a VW camper van, bright yellow with a split windscreen and powerful stereo system. The two women crossed to St Malo and spent a few weeks following the Brittany coast before heading south. They were in no hurry and wandered from town to town, camping and checking out beaches, chateaus, markets and bars – a journey that brought them much closer together and solidified their relationship.

The exploratory road trip brought them to a farm in the hill country of the Tarn-et-Garonne region. The farm's owner was Richard Cruickshank, a distant relative of Chloe and ex-army officer. Through spells working with the Gurkhas, a few years based in Hong Kong and a brief spell as a military liaison officer in South Korea, Cruickshank had developed a fascination for many things Asian. After leaving the forces, his own travels and studies had focused that interest. He spent a few years in Japan, where he married, studied several martial arts disciplines and converted to Buddhism.

But his European blood pulled him home and, England now being too cold for his tastes, he settled in France. His new home, L'Arbre Figue, was part working farm, part ashram. Over the next eighteen months it was also home to Chloe and Billy. They lived in one of several rooms that Cruickshank had built with his own hands around a central courtyard. They worked on the land; picking plums, melons, grapes and apples, and looking after the sheep that provided the wool that was the farm's other main source of income. And in addition to learning about farming in France, Cruickshank began to teach the two women some of what he knew about yoga, tai chi and self-defence.

Chloe was the harder pupil. She was quick to learn moves but lacked the discipline to stop thinking and let her unconscious take control. Billy was different; she could blank out or focus depending on what was required. She had superb hand-eye coordination, good balance and a couple of years of farm work had honed her muscles nicely. And what Billy lacked in power, she made up for in speed and agility.

Cruickshank was quick to see her potential. Chloe had told him about Billy's upbringing and past experiences. Cruickshank did not believe any woman should have to accept the physical or emotional oppression that Billy had endured – or that defence should necessarily be passive. Over the next few months, he added to Billy's lessons and started to pass on some extra skills. Billy mainly learnt tae kwon do but Cruickshank also taught her a few less orthodox moves that appeared in no manual or rulebook.

They moved on again the next January – a few days after Findo, by now working for Colin Speed, had his thirteenth birthday. It was Cruickshank's idea. He felt that Billy had enormous promise as a student of the martial arts but needed better teaching than he could offer. He made no specific suggestions but suggested that if Billy was willing she should look for guidance at the source of whatever belief or discipline drew her.

When they left, Chloe already had her own money in an English bank account. Cruickshank also gave them a lump sum. It was a share of the profit from the farm's income over the time they had been there. Billy accepted the money in the spirit in which it was given.

Their first flight took them to Delhi. They went overland by train and crossed into Nepal at the town of Sunauli. A bus trip took them across the Terai and up towards the trekking capital of Pokhara, and the spectacular grandeur of the Annapurna range. The daytime temperatures were already beginning to rise and the two women collected trekking permits and headed off on the long climb up from the sub-tropical foothills of the Himalaya towards the cold heights on the edge of the Tibetan plateau.

It was the start of an incredible experience and journey of self-discovery for Billy. First, their Asian odyssey took her and Chloe to the vast, high spaces that were Buddhism's spiritual home. Then they travelled back into the Indian foothills of the Himalaya to visit an ashram at Rishikesh. But they found the yoga course taught there too commercialised and left after only a few days. They travelled across India until, by late May, the rising temperature and the approaching monsoon got too much. They got a flight to Hong Kong and then on to Seoul in South Korea to look up a contact of Cruickshank's.

In a village near the northern town of Ch'unch'on, they found Kojong Rhee. The Korean was then in his early seventies, small, bald and unprepossessing to look at. But in 1955 he had been serving in the country's army under General Choi Hong Hoi, the founder of tae kwon do. The general had founded the new school of fighting by combining the country's ancient Korean foot-fighting technique of tae kyon with Japanese karate. Rhee, already accomplished in both arts, became one of tae kwon do's most skilled practitioners and accompanied General Choi when he went to North America in the 1960s to demonstrate the new martial art's high kicks, twists and rapid sparring. For more than twenty years, Rhee had fought at the new sport's top level and coached many teams for international contests.

Now, Rhee had retired from the public arena and lived quietly in a small house in his home village – but he also ran a small school for select students. On the basis of Cruickshank's recommendation, he accepted Billy as a pupil. The two women spent the next seven months living in the Korean village. Billy proved a worthy student and soon progressed up the grades, achieving her black belt within six months.

But at the end of the year their money was starting to run out and – to Billy's disappointment if not Chloe's – they decided to leave. However, instead of going straight home to a winter in England, they flew to Thailand. They visited Buddhist temples, the northern jungles around Chiang Mai and the tropical beaches of the south.

It was while they were in Thailand that Billy also witnessed her first kick-boxing contest. She was hooked. The sport was similar in some ways to tae kwon do, with its high-speed kicking and punching. They went back to Bangkok, where Billy found a school that allowed her to join its lessons. Some of the Thais were sceptical about allowing a young British woman to step into the ring with them but soon changed their mind when they experienced Billy's speed and agility at first-hand. After a couple of months in Bangkok, Billy even entered a few tournaments and acquitted herself well, defeating a number of opponents who had been fighting for much longer than her.

That May, Chloe drew the line. She had gone along with Billy all the way until then. But it was by then well over a year since they had left France and nearly three years since they had left England. Although Chloe's love for Billy was undiminished, she was homesick. The realisation had come to her after a long spell of unease, sleepless nights and unaccountable tears in the quiet moments when Billy was training. Chloe knew she had to go home and one evening sat Billy down and poured out her heart.

Chloe had not wanted to give Billy an ultimatum and was dismayed when that was how it came out. And Billy was distraught – not because she saw Chloe's words as a threat but because she was furious with herself for having been so focused on her own mission that she had not seen her best friend's distress. The night turned into a party that mixed tears with joy. Two days later, they flew back to Heathrow and caught a train straight to the Williams' farm for a long awaited family reunion.

Later that summer, the two women returned to France. They flew to Toulouse and then went straight to L'Arbre Figue. They stayed a few months on the farm and Billy spent quite a few hours sparring with Richard Cruickshank. But she was also careful not to neglect Chloe.

Towards the end of the year, the yellow VW camper van re-emerged from the barn where it had been stored. After a thorough service, it was ready for the road again and the two women set off once again. This time they headed down towards the Pyrenees and into Spain. A ferry took them across to Tangier and they drove on again through Morocco. They headed south, past sweeping Atlantic beaches, the industrial sprawl of Casablanca and beyond the tourist resort of Agadir. They spent the winter on the coast at Sidi Ifni, a curious ex-Spanish outpost, perched above a windswept and often mist-shrouded stretch coast that was desolate and also beautiful. The town had been built in the 1930s and still preserved an unusual collection of Moorish-influenced art deco buildings. It had a strange atmosphere, part-ghost town, part-decaying film set.

In the spring they worked their way slowly north again. They travelled up through the Algarve and Europe's Atlantic coast until they were back in France. Near Bordeaux, they stopped at a farm and vineyard owned by a friend of Cruickshank and stayed for several months on a working visit. Then, as autumn approached, they headed back once more to Chloe's home.

But after a few weeks of life with the Williams family it was Billy's turn to realise that something was missing. In mid-October she realised what it was. Yet again the two women climbed back into the yellow camper van but this time they headed north. Billy had decided that it was past time to keep the promise made long ago; she was going to find her brother.

Billy was still answering Findo's questions when Colin Speed returned just before nine o'clock. When Speed walked into the flat, Billy looked at him as if she had forgotten who he was. But her eyes registered the cartons of Indian food and bottles of wine in the bag he dangled from one hand.

Findo also caught the aromas coming from Speed's bag. He had not eaten for over eight hours. But he had been unaware of how hungry he was until he smelt the food.

"Dinner!" said Findo. "What have you got? Any onion bhajis?"

Speed shrugged. "Maybe."

Findo sprang to his feet. "Excellent, I'm starving."

"Well get some plates and forks then," said Speed. "We can't eat this lot out of the boxes. And grab some glasses as well. Corkscrew too."

"Corkscrew?"

"Yeah, curly thing, use it for getting corks out of bottles."

"I'm not sure there's one here," said Findo.

"No corkscrew?" said Speed.

Findo shrugged. "Well you're the one kitted the place out."

Speed's composure slipped slightly and Billy smiled as she saw him give a little frown.

"Never mind," she said smoothly. "If you've got a wooden spoon or something with a long handle we can push the corks in. Just means we have to drink the whole bottle once it's opened."

Speed's good humour recovered instantly. "Oh, well that's a hardship then."

Findo came back with three plates and a handful of cutlery that he dumped on top of the table, ignoring the clutter of magazines and other junk already littering its surface. "You got any beers as well?" he asked. "I'm not sure I like wine."

"No," said Speed.

"You could try drinking some and then decide if you like it," said Billy.

Findo gave an unwilling nod. He shoved a couple of books to one side and started pulling the cartons of food out of Speed's bag, opening each one to check what was inside.

"Ah, bhajis!" Findo pulled out a chair and sat down to start eating.

Speed laughed. "What a host! We'd better join in bloody quick or there'll be nothing left but empty boxes."

Half an hour later, the food was gone. To Findo's incomprehension, Billy had stuck to the vegetarian options in Speed's selection. With the food, they had drunk one bottle of white wine and made a good start on the next. Findo was still unsure whether he liked wine but having guzzled a few glasses was prepared to give it the benefit of the doubt for now. And although Speed had tried to keep Billy's glass topped up, it was Findo who had drunk most: needing to wash down the piles of curry, rice and bread that he had scoffed with hardly a pause. Luckily, Speed knew Findo's appetite and had brought sufficient quantity as well as a choice of dishes.

Unusually, Speed had also splashed out on some of the more expensive items on the menu, including several with king prawns. To his disappointment, Billy had not touched these, although to his relief she had pronounced the wine to be quite drinkable. Speed made a mental note to slip a thank you to the assistant at the off-licence next time he was picking up his usual packs of lager.

Speed pulled a cigarette packet from his shirt pocket and offered it to Billy. She shook her head and Speed closed the packet.

"I don't mind," she said.

Speed looked blank.

"Smoke," said Billy. "If you want a cigarette, go ahead. Just open a window to let some air in."

Speed nodded. "Okay."

He went over to the lounge window. Billy looked at Findo.

"So," she said. "I've told you where I've been. What's going on with you? Why are you lying low?"

Findo looked down at his polished plate and mumbled something incoherent.

"Findo?" Billy's voice was sharp and he looked up smartly. "Who am I?" she asked.

"Billy."

"Yeah, your sister. The person who used to take care of you, in case you'd forgotten. Someone I'd have thought you would trust."

"I do trust you."

"So tell me what's going on or I'll put you on the floor and twist your arm behind your back like I did with your mate Dougie."

Findo grinned. "You wouldn't!"

Billy was round the table before Findo had even pushed his seat back. A couple of seconds later he was out of his chair and on the floor. His right arm was up behind his shoulder blades and one of his sister's knees was digging painfully into the small of his back. He flailed impotently with his free arm and tried to push up but did not have the strength to get Billy off him. Her other knee landed on the flesh of his free arm, pinning that limb also. A sharp nail jabbed in behind his left ear and pressed down.

By the window, Speed smoked his cigarette and watched thoughtfully.

"Billy!"

"Yes?"

"Get off. You're hurting!"

She shrugged. "That's the idea."

"What?"

She sprang back and went back to her chair. Findo got up looking awkward and confused.

"You didn't need to do that."

"Why not? You hurt me."

Her brother looked surprised. "I hurt you?"

"Yes," said Billy. "You won't tell me what's going on. Either you're embarrassed by what you've done or you're scared. You tell me. But either way it's the same thing – means you don't trust me."

"I do!"

"Then tell me," Billy said fiercely. "I came to find you not to judge you."

"Okay," said Findo.

He sat down again and pulled his chair up next to Billy. He took her hands in his. "I'm sorry," he said. "You're the last person I want to upset. I do trust you. It's just . . . Well, I wasn't expecting to see you. It's been a long time and I still can't believe you're really here again. It's hard just trying to take that in." He shrugged. "It would be amazing enough normally but now? It's almost too much to handle."

Billy frowned. "Too much?"

Findo shook his head. "I don't mean I don't want you here . . . It's just . . ." He squeezed her hands. "I'm a bit scared, Billy."

She reached up and stroked his hair. "So, what have you done?"

It was nearly midnight by the time Billy finished questioning Findo. After hearing an outline of the raid on the security compound, she got him to backtrack and give a quick account of his life since she had left the city.

"Okay," she said. "So you need to go into hiding. What's the plan?"

Findo shrugged and glanced at Speed who was back by the

window with another cigarette. Speed flicked his ash through the window and looked at them thoughtfully for a moment. "Well," he said. "That could depend on Billy."

She raised her eyebrows. "Yeah?"

"Yeah," said Speed. "I was planning on getting him out of the city for a bit anyway. I can't keep him shut away here for the next year even if I thought he'd stay hidden. But you give us another option."

Findo frowned. "The next year?"

Speed laughed. "What did you think? Did you reckon you could just lie low for a few days and then go wandering the city like normal? There are people out there who know your face. There's a reward out on the crew who did this job. Most friends are cheap, Findo. They'll sell you for the right price. You need to disappear for six months at least. Even if we get you a good alibi, we can't risk someone fingering you to the cops. You've left your mark too many places. Even if they don't get you for this job, they'll find something else."

He shrugged. "You're good at what you do. No doubt of that. But just as important, you've got no record at the moment. That's worth keeping." Speed sighed. "The other thing is, you've done a lot of jobs in this city, some of them pretty big. Whether it's this job or another, if the cops get hold of you, you'll be looking at a spell inside. And I don't reckon you'd like being locked up. Some people can handle doing a stretch but I'm not sure you'd be very good at it."

Findo looked down and seemed to shrink in on himself. Billy reached out a hand and squeezed his shoulder. "Okay," she said. "Sounds simple enough then. Colin's right; we need to get you out of here." She looked up at Speed. "What did you have in mind?"

Speed shrugged. "Depends. What are your plans? You thinking of sticking around or did you have somewhere else to go to? You see, I could get him out of here easy enough. I could probably get him out of the country. But the kind of people I know might not be so good at keeping him out of trouble and there's no point jumping out of one tight spot just to end up with the same problem somewhere else. You haven't been here for seven years and it doesn't sound like you'd be very traceable. Cops aren't going to know you exist so they're not going to look for you even if they could find you. I reckon you could make him disappear much better than me."

30. Yellow camper van

They were about fifteen miles out of the city when Findo suddenly twisted round in his seat and looked over his shoulder.

"What is it?" said Billy. She glanced in the rear view mirror in alarm. "Are we being followed?"

Findo shook his head. "No."

"Well, what is it then?"

He squirmed uncomfortably. "It's Abby."

"Abby?"

Findo nodded quickly. "Who's Abby?"

He shrugged. "My friend."

Billy shook her head and turned her attention back to the road. They were on the main road south of Dubmore – following the same route that she had taken seven years earlier. It was still a little while until dawn and the road was quiet; what traffic there was heading in towards the city.

They drove in silence for a couple of minutes. Then Billy spotted a turning on the right. She slowed and pulled into the narrow lane. A little way along was the entrance to a field. Billy pulled over and stopped the van. She turned the engine and headlights off then twisted round to face Findo.

"Right," she said. "Talk."

He looked out of the window at the empty fields and the damp hills silhouetted against the pre-dawn half-light.

"Who's Abby?" demanded Billy.

Findo looked at his hands. "A friend," he said slowly. "A good friend."

"Girlfriend?"

Findo frowned. "Dunno."

Billy snorted in disbelief. "What do you mean, you don't know!"

Findo looked at his sister and her expression softened when she saw the confusion on his face. "What is it?" she asked. "You haven't told her what you think about her?"

Findo shook his head. "It's not that," he said. "I've known her since you went away."

Billy looked surprised.

"I met her the day you left," continued Findo. "She's been my best friend for ages. We've done all sorts of things together. That car that Colin was talking about last night, the one from the MP's house?"

"I remember," said Billy.

"Abby was with me when I took that," said Findo. "She knows everything about me."

"But Colin Speed doesn't know about her?"

Findo smiled. "No one does." He shrugged. "After the car, her mum got a bit funny. She knew that was me and didn't like Abby being involved."

"How surprising," said Billy.

"Yeah, well," said Findo. "Anyway, after that, she didn't get involved in any nicking or anything like that. But we never stopped being friends. I always told her pretty much everything anyway. There was a time earlier this year when we didn't see each other quite so much; she started spending time with some new friends from school. But then I got my flat and we sort of sorted things out. I suppose we started being more like boyfriend and girlfriend."

"Uh huh." Billy nodded. "And now you've suddenly realised that you're about to disappear for who knows how long and you haven't told her you're going."

Findo looked miserable. "Yeah."

"So how much do you care about her?" said Billy.

"I don't know."

"Well, don't you think it's about time you decided?" The snap in her voice made Findo look up in surprise. Billy gave her brother an angry stare. "It's your decision," said Billy. "Depends on what she means to you and how much you care about her feelings. If she's your closest friend and your girlfriend, how do you think she's going to feel about you just vanishing? You need to think – and think quick – about what you're going to do. Are you going to just disappear? Are you going to call her and tell her what you've done or are you going to write and explain?"

Findo was silent for a minute. "I want to say goodbye."

Billy sighed. "Part of me's glad you said that. We might end up regretting it, though."

It was still barely light when the camper van drove into Denmark Street. Billy found a space and pulled in against the kerb. She killed the lights and engine and wound the driver's window down a little way so the windscreen would not fog up too much.

"So you reckon her mum leaves just after eight?"

"Yeah," said Findo. "Pretty much on the dot, I think." He was sat in the back of the van with the curtains drawn. "She works in the city museum and has to be in by eight-thirty."

"Okay," said Billy. "We've got about quarter of an hour then. Will you be able to see her from in the back without her spotting you?"

"Sure," said Findo.

They sat in the yellow van for nearly twenty minutes before Suzanne McGee appeared at the door of number fifteen. Findo spotted her from his hiding place in the back of the VW and crouched down. Billy buried her nose in a map but need not have bothered; Abby's mother was busy wrapping a scarf around her neck and did not spare the parked vehicle a glance.

Another ten minutes later the door to the house opened again. Abby came out with a school bag slung across one shoulder. She locked the door and set off at a brisk walk down Denmark Street.

Billy wound down the driver's window and waited until Abby was about to pass the van.

"Abby."

She came to a surprised halt and stared at Billy.

"Yes. Who are you?"

Billy smiled. "Findo's sister."

"What!" Abby smiled briefly and looked at Billy with new interest; a mixture of curiosity and calculation. But then a deep frown creased her freckled brow. "Well I don't know where he is," said Abby. "So I can't help you."

She started to walk on.

"Abby." Billy's tone was sharper and Abby stopped again with obvious reluctance.

"What?"

"I know where he is," said Billy. "He wants to see you. To talk to you."

"Well I don't want to speak to him."

Findo pulled back the curtain above the camper van's tiny sink. Abby saw the movement and met Findo's gaze. But she did not smile.

"I've got to get to school," she said.

"Abby!" Findo raised a hand to the window imploringly as Abby walked quickly away.

Billy turned in her seat. "Findo, stay there. Don't you dare move."

Billy opened the van door and stepped down onto the pavement. Through the windows, Findo watched as his sister hurried after Abby and fell into step beside her. A few yards further on they both stopped and spoke briefly. Then they walked on again but a little more slowly, apparently deep in conversation. At the end of Denmark Street, they stopped a second time. They spoke for another couple of minutes.

Then Billy suddenly reached out and gave Abby a quick hug

before they separated. Abby continued on and disappeared from sight, while Billy walked quickly back to the camper van. She climbed back into the driver's seat, closed the door and started the engine.

"What did she say, Billy? What's going on?"

Billy shook her head. "Wait a minute and I'll tell you."

She pulled out from the kerb and drove to the far end of Denmark Street. A short lane took them past a block of garages and a burnt-out car. Billy swung right again onto a road parallel with Denmark Street.

"Billy! What is it?"

"Wait, Findo."

She drove quickly back down past identical rows of terraced houses and turned left onto Corporation Road. As they approached the junction with St Patrick's Road, Findo saw Abby turning off on her usual route. She was walking quickly, her head down, not looking around.

But Billy did not follow her. Instead, she took the next left and cut up through to Stewart Road. Findo stared out of the van's back window as Abby vanished from sight and they drove away from her.

"Billy, stop."

His sister shook her head. "Sorry, Findo. She doesn't want to see you at the moment."

"But why?"

"Because she's angry with you."

"Angry?"

"Yes. Angry. Because she didn't know what you were up to and a couple of days ago she suddenly saw your name across the front of the paper."

"But that wasn't my fault."

"Findo!" Billy sounded irritated. "Don't be such a fuckwit! You did that robbery and you were stupid enough to leave your name on a card there. You were showing off and didn't think of the consequences." Billy shook her head. "Anyway, that's not the point. The point is Abby's upset because she doesn't like what you're doing and it makes it even worse when she sees your name in the papers. She's frightened, Findo. Frightened for you and frightened for herself and her family."

Findo frowned. "Why's she frightened for her family? Anyway there's only her and her mum."

"Doesn't matter how many of them there are," said Billy. "The point is she's frightened. She's frightened about what happens if you're caught. She's upset because her mum's angry and thinks Abby should turn you in. She feels she's not sure she knows you any more.

And you stood her up last night."

"Oh. Yeah."

"Yeah," said Billy. "You were supposed to see her last night and never turned up. You left her sitting on her own at home thinking the worst, wondering if you've been caught or if you've already gone on the run and left without saying goodbye. She's angry because she thinks you've been stupid and you've been thoughtless and because she's scared about what could happen to you."

Findo looked sad. "I've got to see her, Billy."

His sister shook her head. "No. No you don't. For one thing, she doesn't want to see you. If you pester her now you're just going to upset her more. You've tried to say goodbye. She knows you tried. The best thing you can do now is just leave it for a while. You can write though. I got her to agree to let you write to her." Billy glanced back over her shoulder. "She doesn't hate you, Findo, she's just upset and angry at the moment. If you really love each other you'll be able to work it out again some other time – just not now. Right now we've got to get you out of the city. It's disappearing time."

Findo was silent for most of the journey. To begin with, he lurked in the back of the van, not bothering to look at where they were going. Billy put a tape into the stereo and ignored him, leaving her brother to stew in his own fug of confused self-analysis.

They left the M6 at Penrith and headed west into the Lake District. A few miles along the A66, they turned off towards Ullswater and the heart of the National Park.

The weather had improved as the morning wore on and the early mist and drizzle cleared to leave a cool and breezy autumn day. Thin sunshine glinted on the wet landscape of trees, river, fields of damp sheep and fells rising all around them.

As they reached the edge of Ullswater, Findo finally left the back of the van and climbed through into the front. He watched the scenery get progressively more dramatic as they began to wind along the shore of the lake, past the waterfalls at Aira Force and the cliffs, tumbled boulders and twisted trees around the approach to Glenridding. There was little other traffic and the yellow camper van continued past the end of the lake at Patterdale, around the smaller expanse of Brothers Water and up into Kirkstone Pass.

At the top of the pass, Billy pulled over into the car park by the pub. They both got out and stood looking around at the peaks stretching away in all directions. Findo suddenly shivered as the cold wind sliced through his inadequate layers.

Billy grinned. "Come on, let's get a beer and something to eat."

By the time Billy drove down into Ambleside, Findo was in a better mood, though still subdued. They wandered for a while around the town, quiet now the usual summer infestation of incomers and holidaymakers had died away.

Before they left the city, Speed had handed Billy a wad of cash and a building society passbook that gave access to some of Findo's earnings from the past few years. As they strolled around Ambleside, Billy first sized up her teenage brother and then dragged him into several shops to kit him out with a few changes of clothing. She also insisted on buying him an expensive pair of walking boots and some waterproofs.

When he saw how much the items cost, Findo baulked and tried to suggest there were cheaper ways of getting the things that Billy had in mind. But he stopped protesting after Billy took hold of his arm and threatened to twist it behind his back.

It was only when they returned to the van and began to load their purchases that Findo thought to ask where they were going.

"Eskdale," said Billy.

"Eskdale? Where's that?"

Billy waved vaguely westwards. "Over there."

"Yeah, but what is it and why're we going there?"

Billy smiled. "Well, for one thing, to find Chloe."

"Chloe?" said Findo. He looked at Billy and shrugged. "Yeah, it'd be interesting to meet her."

Billy smiled. "Yeah. I hope you two like each other."

Findo shrugged. "One way to find out."

She took hold of his arm. "Be nice to her will you? And don't say too much about what you do or why we've left the city so soon. Please?"

Findo frowned. "Why we've left so soon? Were you planning on staying?"

Billy shrugged. "I didn't know. I had no idea how easy it would be to find you. I wasn't expecting just to find you and leave. I didn't know whether you'd be happy or miserable, whether you'd be glad to see me or not. You might have wanted to stay in the city. I was just going to take things as they came. I told Chloe I might be a week or so." She squeezed Findo's arm. "Don't say too much, okay?"

He smiled. "Don't worry. I don't just tell people stuff – you should know that. So anyway, what's Eskdale and what's Chloe doing there?"

Billy climbed into the driver's seat and started the van. "It's a valley over the other side of the Lakes. One of Chloe's brothers lives there. He works for a place where they teach climbing and other outdoor stuff. He's got a cottage near a place called Boot."

"Boot?"

"That's what it's called. It's nice, you'll like it."

"Yeah?"

"Yeah. You'd better like it because we're staying there for a few weeks."

With that, Billy put the van into gear and pulled out of the car park. She drove them towards Langdale and then up over Wrynose Pass. They emerged into a damp, bleak valley high in the fells. Acres of dead bracken stretched away towards rocky hillsides and the road ran alongside a swollen stream that rushed down over dark boulders. Between the bracken were areas of boggy grass, cropped tight to the ground by the vacant-eyed sheep that wandered everywhere.

A collection of grey buildings marked a lonely farm. There was a junction by the farm and Billy swung right and across the river. There was a short stretch of relatively gentle climb and then the narrow, single-track road jerked abruptly upwards. Billy dropped down into first gear as they began the assault on Hardknott Pass, the Lake District's highest road and the only direct route across to Eskdale.

31. To every action

Findo Gask's second departure from the city of his birth marked the end of another phase in his life. The previous four years had seen the young thief recruited into an apprenticeship as a career criminal – graduating with panache.

But it had not been an intentional path. Throughout his life, Findo had acted in response to opportunities or situations. He rarely planned beyond a few days ahead – the need had never occurred to him. And until Colin Speed took him on, Findo had only operated on a relatively small scale. He had burgled and stolen but – with the exception of the theft of Clement Dallaway's toy Maserati – none of his exploits had attracted any widespread attention.

Until the age of eleven, although famous as the boy who could pinch anything, Findo had not stolen anything 'big'. Generally, he took what he needed for his own care or comfort, or what someone else fancied. He stole food, clothes, televisions, toys, alcohol, chocolate, books, cigarettes, cheap jewellery, office equipment, cameras and anything else that could be found in a high-street shop or office. He also took cash from tills. As a result, although plenty of store detectives and police officers would have loved to get their hands around his neck, Findo had gained notoriety but no real enemies.

Mickey Dunn's escape from the police had been equally spontaneous. Findo had helped Mickey for several reasons. One was that Mickey did not want to be caught and that Findo knew how to spirit him away – and the opportunity to show off was too tempting to ignore. Another was that Findo had no reason to owe the police anything; he lived in a culture that saw them as the enemy and had no personal reason to think otherwise. And most importantly, Mickey and his mother had acted as both safety deposit and delivery service for the letters from Findo's sister – that alone was enough to gain his allegiance.

Chance, and a low tolerance to alcohol, took Findo and Mickey into the alley behind the Turk's Head. The effects of the drink – plus naivety and a continuing desire to prove himself – led Findo to tempt fate by getting into the Muldoons' headquarters. The break-in was easy enough. And once inside, having a bag containing a quarter of a million pounds dropped literally in front of him had been too much to resist. For a boy whose pride in his reputation outweighed his fear, leaving empty-handed was not a consideration. And if he was going to touch the money, there was little point stealing just some of it.

The explosion of violence that followed the disappearance of the cash was in some ways only partly Findo's fault; he was the catalyst but the coup had been waiting to happen. (Although when he opened the bag of money the next morning and realised the magnitude of what he had done, for the first time in his life it occurred to Findo that he might have gone too far.) What he did next seemed the only logical thing: he hid, leaving Abby to come up with the idea of sharing the stolen drug money between several hundred strangers.

It had been equally natural for Colin Speed to want to know who was responsible for stealing the money from under the noses of the Muldoons and Hong. And when Findo – still a few weeks short of his twelfth birthday – was delivered to him, Speed soon realised there was more to the boy than just his thieving. He looked beyond the scruffy surface and undistinguished appearance. He saw sharpness, quick thinking and agility; Findo's near escape from Speed's garage demonstrated that ability to think on his feet.

The fact that Findo's previous exploits had already earned him a name among the local underclass was also telling. The city already had more than its fair share of crooks, conmen and wannabe outlaws. To be standing out from the crowd at his age was quite a feat.

But in addition to this raw talent, Speed recognised something else to mark Findo as unique – an independence of thought and action untainted by concern for the opinion of the world at large. Findo was a free spirit. He had never been part of anything and lived by weighing threat against need and opportunity – a code of Darwinian purity that bore little relation to the conceits and constrictions of everyday society.

Findo had evolved into the creature he was mainly because of the circumstances of his birth and upbringing. But nurture was not the only factor. Findo had survived because of his own abilities, guided by his natural inclinations. For Findo, putting self-preservation and self-interest before other considerations was a matter of logic. His personal tribe – his circle of allies and comrades – was tiny and nothing had ever been put into his life from outside of that select group. Therefore, Findo saw no reason to do anything that went against his own instincts and interests. He lived in his own world and kept his own rules. He was aware of the existence of the wider world some called society but was not interested in its purpose or workings. He did not seek acceptance. He had no reason to. He believed in Findo Gask. He was the centre of his own universe; anything else was secondary.

That was in essence what Speed saw. He recognised the qualities in Findo because there were similar, though less primitive, elements in his own make-up. He knew straight away what Findo was and saw the potential for his use. Findo was a natural sociopath with the intelligence and physical ability to make him an ideal criminal.

When Speed took Findo under his wing, it had not really seemed as if a choice was involved. The threat of vengeance from the Muldoon gang had turned independence into a dangerous option. Findo took Speed's protection primarily because he had thought it was his only resort. Accepting Speed's offer of work and training had been a natural progression – and one that suited Findo. It had also been a fruitful path; the days spent with Alan Sowerby learning the secrets of his chosen craft, had been an opportunity for which Findo would have paid willingly if he had known it existed.

And as Findo learnt new skills and began to put them to profitable use for Speed, their relationship gradually deepened into mutual respect. While gratitude was not something Findo had ever really learnt, he accepted that Speed looked after him. Speed provided Findo with a home and a degree of comfort that he had never experienced before. In addition to discovering how to cut a dozen different kinds of glass and disable all kind of security devices, Findo also learnt about home comforts, square meals and dry beds.

As a result, Findo never had cause to want to leave Speed's employ. He enjoyed burglary. No scruples interfered with his pursuit of gain. Thieving was an exercise in skill and caution, a lone pursuit that tested him physically and mentally. He had started his career with Speed as an unusually good thief. Helped by extra practical knowledge, he improved rapidly. By the time he entered his teens, there were few physical barriers to keep out a determined Findo Gask. He was still as slippery as the day he was born but now smarter too. Although it had never been a specific ambition, circumstances and his reaction to them had led to this; he had become an excellent thief.

Now, aged nearly sixteen, part of his life had come full circle. Billy had left him when he was eight. He had found Abby the same day and she had got closer to him than anyone save his sister. Now, Billy was back but he appeared, for the time being at least, to have lost Abby. The world had turned and, yet again, it was time for Findo to respond to a new set of circumstances.

32. Fluid dynamics, ballistics and rope technique

The Lake District opened Findo's eyes to a world he had never experienced before. When he first left the city, Findo had also ended up in wild and remote hill country. But there had been little chance to explore; he had been there to learn and spent most of his time inside a converted barn. This time, however, he was positively encouraged to get out and enjoy the great outdoors.

Billy had shed her city inheritance years before. She retained no affinity for busy streets and crowded buildings. She was delighted to be away from her birthplace and back where there was space to breathe and room to feel the delight of insignificance.

At the end of the day on which they had left the city, Billy drove slowly down from the fells as the light faded away towards the Irish Sea. She parked the yellow camper van outside a small, white-painted cottage that huddled low in the corner of a sheep-cropped field. There were lights already on inside and the door opened as they were getting out of the van.

Findo hung back as a slim woman with blonde hair ran up to Billy and drew her into a hug. Billy returned the embrace with feeling, then stepped back and held the other at arms' length.

"Miss me?"

Chloe shook her head. "Not sure, what's your name again?"

They hugged again briefly and then Billy turned away and looked at Findo. "Chloe, meet my brother. This is Findo."

The other woman smiled and walked towards Findo. She began to hold out a hand and then shook her head and pulled Findo into another hug. "Hi," she said. "It's good to see you. I've been waiting a long time to meet you."

Over the next day, Findo also met Chloe's brother Mark, Jess his collie, Jennie his girlfriend, and two other instructors that shared the house. One was a dour Welshman called Evan Griffith, the other a bouncing Australian called Barnaby Summers.

To Billy's disappointment, Findo and Chloe did not become instant friends. No immediate bond or mutual sympathy sprang from their first meeting and it became increasingly apparent that the long-term prognosis was no more favourable. Not only were they very different in temperament, they also had no common ground on which to base a friendship.

After her initial burst of enthusiasm for the project fell on stony ground, Billy backed off. She made no more attempts to push them into an unwilling comradeship and concentrated instead on sharing her affections with scrupulous fairness. On the surface an awkward truce developed, which showed itself in stilted conversations and quiet sulks. If the option presented itself, Findo and Chloe preferred to avoid each other's company (and preferably forget the other's existence). Findo in particular nurtured an uneasy jealousy, resenting any time and attention the other demanded from Billy. From a positive point of view, there was no serious animosity or open warfare. On the other hand, it soon became clear that any relationship between Findo and Chloe would be based on no more than polite courtesy, adopted for the sake of the shared object of their affection.

For the first few days, Findo kept a low profile. He felt out of place; the environment was all wrong. Even apart from Chloe's presence, he found the cottage confining and crowded, while outdoors was empty and intimidating. High ridges of rugged hills rose to the north and the south. Back to the east was Hardknott Pass, its twisting hairpin road climbing to still more bleak fells. And although Eskdale itself felt sandwiched in by the hills, it was still all too open to feel comfortable. The sheep stared at him and black-and-white collies snarled from farm gates. There were few cars and the only traffic seemed to be made up of Land Rovers, tractors and quad bikes. There was nothing about the place to which Findo could relate. Even the pub felt wrong; people stared but there was no edge of violence.

The locals were stern-looking men and women who all seemed to wear flat caps, waxed jackets and mud-coated boots. They nodded and grunted or ignored Findo completely. By contrast, the instructors from the outdoor centre were gaudy and loud. They dressed in bright-coloured waterproofs with fancy logos and too many zips and Velcro fastenings. Men and women alike wore skin-tight leggings and boots. Coming inside they would shed endless layers of lurid fleeces and body-hugging thermal clothing. They also talked too much, drank endless cups of tea and were just too aggressively energetic.

To begin with, Findo slept on the lounge floor, while Billy and Chloe shared the spare room upstairs. There was a constant traffic of people coming and going and too many of the visitors wanted to try and engage him in pointless conversation about his life: how he knew the others, where he came from, what he was doing, why and when. After three nights, Findo could face no more of it and withdrew to the camper van. It was not so pleasant at night; there were too many strange noises and he felt vulnerable knowing that all the darkness

272

and emptiness was just outside. But it was better than being inside, waiting until the whole household had gone to bed before lying down on his own. The van was the closest thing to normality he could find and the best refuge from the intensity of life in the cottage.

After nearly a week in Eskdale, Findo was getting twitchy. He was an exile in a world that he did not understand. His only link with reality was his sister but after such a long time apart she was almost a stranger. He could not relate to the others at all and did not know what to do. There were no streets to roam and no buildings to explore. He missed the city, his flat and the ease of his own world.

He also thought a lot about Abby but did not know what to do about her. He had tried to write several letters but then given up the attempt. He did not know what he wanted to say or how to start saying it. The simple option would have been to send Abby a chronicle of what he had done but Findo was not sure that was what was needed. Not knowing what else to write, Findo screwed up his aborted missives and threw them away in disgust.

Findo tried to ask Billy what her plans were but his sister's answers were vague. She knew Findo was unhappy but asked him to be patient and give the place a chance.

Billy's reluctance to leave was partly because Chloe had promised to spend a few weeks with her younger brother, who she had not seen for several years. Billy was also greatly taken by Eskdale. She had not been to the Lake District before but felt at home straight away. She was comfortable with the open spaces and loved the grand vistas that unfolded all around. There was a simplicity to life to which she could relate. She liked being able to open the door and see a sky that could change from hanging grey gloom to bright sunshine and back to ragged, storm-tossed streamers of incoming cloud in the space of a day. There was an invigorating freshness to the air – even though she found it hard to forget that there was a nuclear power station and reprocessing plant only a few miles away at Sellafield.

During the first week, Billy roamed the scree paths along the melancholy side of Wast Water, hiked to Scawfell Pike and scrambled up the dramatic ascent to Pillar. She also explored the Ravenglass Estuary and drove to Coniston to walk through the abandoned mines. When the weather closed in, she visited the small towns around the edges of the National Park or sat for hours inside a barn that stood next to the cottage, meditating and practising her yoga. She also spent a few sessions sparring with Chloe, with Findo watching silently from a perch at the other end of the barn.

Findo joined the two women on most of their expeditions, mainly because there was little else to do but also so Chloe did not get Billy to herself all of the time. Billy also wanted her brother to enjoy himself and to get to know him again. But although on the fells his silence was not a problem, in the evenings and at more sociable moments his brooding presence began to unnerve even his sister.

Over breakfast on their eighth morning in Eskdale, Billy told Findo that she was going to walk to Langdale on her own and would not be back until late afternoon. Findo's first reaction was alarm at the prospect of being left with Chloe. But then Chloe said she was going to Carlisle with her brother. She and Mark left in the van ten minutes later. The cottage's other two residents had already disappeared and, after watching Billy set off, Findo suddenly found himself alone.

He watched television for a while, searched the videotapes on a nearby shelf without finding anything to his taste and mooched moodily around the cottage. Findo looked through some books in Evan's room but discovered nothing to capture his restless imagination. Eventually, he found his coat and wandered out into the late morning.

Findo walked down the valley, following the road with no destination in mind. After a while, he reached a junction. To the right was the outdoor centre and one of the stations for the Ravenglass and Eskdale Railway. Findo turned left and strolled towards Forge Bridge. He stopped in the middle of the bridge and looked at the river. It had rained heavily during the night and the Esk looked swollen and fast.

He was still on the bridge when Barnaby Summers came driving past. The Australian slowed when he saw Findo and gave a cheery wave. He pulled up on the bend just past the bridge and jumped out of his old Astra. There was a canoe strapped to the roof of Barnaby's car and he was wearing a wetsuit.

Barnaby stretched as he got out of the car then walked over. The Australian was in his late twenties and an irrepressible optimist. Life was an endless series of opportunities for Barnaby – and he took his chances with such gusto that the result was a life that seemed to veer wildly from unqualified successes to unmitigated disasters. But he threw himself into all his endeavours with such obvious enthusiasm and good-natured humour that even the victims of his failed ventures would generally, if against their better judgement, succumb to his charm.

"Hey, mate, how's it going? How's it look?"

Findo frowned. "What? How does what look?"

Barnaby bent over the parapet. "The river. How does the river look?"

"Wet?"

"That's a good start. Better than some of the ones back home then."

"Eh?"

Barnaby grinned. "Where I come from it's so bloody dry rivers only fill up when there's a really big storm. Rest of the time they're just rocks and bloody lizards. Not much good for kayaking."

"Kayaking?" said Findo. "What's that?"

Barnaby jerked his thumb at his car. "Posh name for canoeing." He grinned. "River's running well now. Can't beat 'em when they're in flood."

Findo looked sideways at the young Australian. "You don't go in there, do you?"

Barnaby nodded. "Too right, mate. Bit of white water gets the old ticker pumping. Can't beat a good flood."

Findo looked at the torrent cascading down through the narrow riverbed and swirling in sleek brown power around the bridge. "You're mad."

"Yeah," said Barnaby, "maybe – but it's bloody good fun. You should try it."

Findo's eyes widened but he also felt a gnawing excitement in his stomach that had been missing for too many days. "What, me? In that?"

Barnaby laughed. "Sure. Why not?" Then he frowned. "Well, maybe not in there."

Findo felt slightly disappointed.

"Not yet anyway," said Barnaby. "That's not really a beginner's kind of run. But if you fancy it, mate, I could give you some lessons. Teach you a few basics. I could find some spare kit and a boat from the centre." He grinned. "Tell you what, we do that and once you've got the basics I'll get hold of a two-man kayak and take you down a bit of white water. What you reckon?"

Findo looked thoughtfully at the river and bit his lip. Then he nodded eagerly. "Yeah. That would be good. Thanks."

From that moment on, life in Eskdale got much more interesting for Findo. After meeting Barnaby on the bridge, everything changed. A couple of hours later, dressed in a wetsuit, with a neoprene apron floating around his waist like a skirt, he found himself floundering in Wast Water, discovering just how bitterly cold deep lakes can get in autumn. Beside him, a small one-man kayak floated upside down.

Barnaby grinned. "Don't worry, mate. We've all been there. Balancing a kayak while you get in and out is one of those things that looks a darn sight bloody easier than it is." He waded into the edge of the lake and pulled Findo's kayak up onto the bank. "Okay, let's get the water out of this and then we'll have another go. But remember your paddle. It's your lever; it can give you a lot of support. Don't just wave it around in the air like you're trying to conduct an orchestra, use it like you mean it." He gave Findo a hand up out of the lake. "Not too cold?"

Findo shook his head stubbornly. "No."

"Good," said Barnaby. "And remember, this is the boring bit. Soon as you've got the hang of getting in and out of the boat it gets more interesting."

"Do we go for a paddle?"

The Australian chuckled. "Yeah . . . Got a little bit more fun to have before that though."

Findo scowled damply. "What sort of fun?"

Barnaby shrugged. "Well, thing is, mate, when you go kayaking it's pretty likely that somewhere along the line you're going to go over."

"Go over? What do you mean, fall out?"

Barnaby laughed. "Not that simple. You see, once you tip, you tend to keep going. And because you're wedged in nice and tight, with your spraydeck snug around the cockpit, you don't normally fall out. What happens is, one minute you're sitting up like a duck, next minute you're hanging down like a bat. Only problem is the boat's still on the surface and you're underneath trying to breathe like a fish. So, once you've learnt how to get in the boat, the next thing is to learn how to get out of the boat quick when you're upside down." The Aussie grinned. "After all, it's all part of the fun."

"Yeah?"

Barnaby nodded. "But don't worry, not many people drown at this stage."

To Findo's relief, the rest of the introductory lessons went quickly. Barnaby was a good teacher and patient with his student. At the end of the day both were wet and cold but Findo had mastered the knack of climbing in and out of a canoe that was floating at the lakeshore, as well as how to rip off a spraydeck underwater and pull himself out of the cockpit while suspended upside down.

The next day, Barnaby was not working and offered to continue the lessons, with the incentive of letting Findo try some white water canoeing at the end of the day. They covered more of the basics during the morning and, in the afternoon, Barnaby let Findo test his balance in a section of river that was tame for an advanced kayaker but still provided plenty of challenge for a novice. Despite getting plenty more dunkings, Findo was soon hooked. Barnaby was also impressed by how fast the teenager learnt – not realising how Findo's natural agility and wiry build had been honed by years of practising the kind of survival skills that do not get taught at even the toughest activity centres.

Over the following week, Barnaby spent much of his spare time teaching Findo how to kayak. They soon covered the basic theory and Findo learnt various techniques for paddling, turning and getting back into a boat in the water. They tackled a few river runs that were low-grade but still fast enough to provide a rush of adrenaline. One morning they followed the Esk down into the tidal section below the walls of the Roman fort of Glannoventa. There Findo got to play in the waves of an incoming tide and experience what it was like to ride through water where strong currents plucked at the canoe from different directions. Barnaby also introduced Findo to the Eskimo roll. The Australian instructor was delighted when his young pupil managed to perform a perfect three-hundred-and-sixty degree roll on only the fourth attempt. From that moment on, having mastered the art of self-righting, Findo never looked back. His confidence grew, as did his enthusiasm.

And as Findo's addiction to kayaking took hold, the others in the cottage gave silent thanks to Barnaby. In a matter of days, the teenager went from being a morose shadow skulking in the corner to becoming another of life's cheerful enthusiasts. At the pub in the evenings, Billy listened with amusement as her brother discussed the delights of kayaking with anyone willing to share his new passion. He was particularly fascinated with the idea of canoeing down mountain streams in flood – the sort of high-speed obstacle course they represented offered a thrill as immediate and physical as tackling a difficult burglary. Findo would talk sieves, strainers, pools and eddies all night. He also listened with the same insatiable thirst for knowledge that he brought to all interests that managed to capture his attention. Most of the other Outward Bound instructors were happy to indulge him. It gave them a chance to brag about the scariest floods they had ever paddled and digress into obscure discussions that would have bored most listeners rigid in a matter of minutes. But Findo would listen intently to debates about how the art of kayaking depended on knowledge of fluid dynamics or, in really high floods, an understanding of the principles of ballistics.

When Barnaby announced that he was going off for a week to meet some friends in London, Findo was crushed. Only pride kept him from begging to be allowed to go with the young Australian. For a couple of days the teenager lapsed back into the sullen persona that had irritated the other occupants of the cottage. But he was snapped back out his misery after Mark and a couple of friends offered to take Findo to Penrith.

"We're going for a play on the climbing wall over there," said Chloe's brother.

"The climbing wall? What's one of them?"

Mark frowned. "Well, it's a climbing wall, a wall for practising climbing on. It's got all kinds of different holds." He shrugged. "Come and see. That's the best answer. It's good fun. Make a change from being stuck here all the time."

Mark pointed through to the kitchen where Billy and Chloe were enveloped by recipe books, piles of vegetables and various aromatic smells. "You don't want to stay here; you'll only end up getting drafted as a kitchen slave. Best to leave them to it. Keep out of their way and then come back and eat the results later." He winked. "Or go to the pub for a pint and a pie if you don't fancy what they come up with."

Despite himself, Findo smiled. Billy had many abilities but cooking was not one of them. However, this had not stopped her in her quest to recreate various Thai curries and other exotic dishes that she and Chloe had eaten on their travels. The results tended to be met with polite comments by the cottage's other residents, before they made their escape in search of more palatable fare.

He followed Mark and the others outside, where they piled into an old van for the trip across the Lake District to Penrith. The journey proved worthwhile. At the other end Findo was introduced to the concept of an artificial climbing wall. He listened to Mark's briefing and watched the others for a short while – then, as the others looked on in astonishment, launched himself at the wall with the same casual abandon as an orang-utan taking a morning swing through the jungle. With apparent ease, Findo scaled the wall quicker than any of his companions had ever done. He made his way up fearlessly, using the smallest of grips, suspending himself by fingertips and stretching for holds that would have baffled many experienced climbers. He showed a complete lack of fear for heights, only struggling slightly with an overhang that was nearly too far for his reach.

When Findo was back down on the ground, Mark stared at him.

"Where did you learn to climb like that?"

Findo grinned. "Oh, here and there."

"I thought you said you didn't know anything about climbing."

Findo shrugged and considered. "I don't," he said. "Not the way you go on about it. I don't know anything about all these belays and crampons and stuff you lot talk about. I live in a city. We don't get many cliffs. I climb buildings, not rocks."

Mark looked slightly confused. "Buildings?"

Findo smiled and debated how to answer; Billy had pleaded with him not to say anything about how he lived.

"Well," said Findo. "There's some ruins of an old castle by the river and there's some other derelict warehouses and things about. I climb them. I always have. It's good fun."

Mark shook his head. "But no one's ever taught you how to climb?"

Findo looked slightly indignant. "No. I don't need anyone to teach me how to climb up a wall."

Mark smiled. "No, I don't reckon you do." He looked at Findo for a few moments. "But what about climbing up a cliff?"

"What cliff?"

Mark grinned. "You remember that place up Langdale we went the other week, where we saw those people going up with a load of ropes?"

"Yeah," said Findo slowly.

"How would you like to climb those cliffs?"

"You serious?"

Mark nodded. "Yeah. I'd have to teach you how to use ropes and all the gear first but I reckon you could do it. You learnt all that kayaking stuff in no time and you're a natural climber. A bit of rope technique and I reckon there'd be no keeping you on the ground."

33. Family ties

As November became December and the sheets of rain sweeping in off the Irish Sea turned into a perpetual downpour, the cottage in Eskdale began to feel smaller and smaller. Findo had contemplated moving back into the cottage to avoid the soakings he got crossing to the camper van. But every night, he decided a drenching was preferable.

The simple problem was that there were too many people in the cottage, which had four bedrooms but only one bathroom and a small kitchen and living area. Billy and Chloe were still sharing the spare room and Mark's girlfriend, Jennie, seemed to have moved in for good. And although none of the men would have mentioned it, the continued presence of the three women was starting to take its toll.

Evan had taken to withdrawing to the pub when not closeted in his room. His absence helped make extra space in the lounge of an evening but it was clear that Evan's willingness to share the house was fading fast. Barnaby's return from London had temporarily given a lift to the cottage's collective spirits but even his bounce had become insufficient to jolly the others along into a continued sense of bonhomie. And as well as adding his own presence to the numbers in the cottage, Barnaby would often invite a few mates round for an evening without considering where they were going to fit.

The situation was made worse by a cooling of affection between Chloe and Jennie. To begin with, Jennie had been delighted to meet Mark's sister and they got on famously. But over time, Chloe began to sense Jennie felt she had outstayed her welcome. The onset of the frost in their relationship had been gradual. Jennie had first begun to seek more of Mark's attention, diverting him away from his sister's company. Next, her occasional nights at the cottage turned into permanent occupation. Then the remarks started. To begin with it had been questions about Chloe and Billy's plans. But the word-salvos had started to get sharper – Jennie's latest had been to observe that there would be no room for the two visitors at Christmas. Now, Chloe's hackles had started to rise and it had reached the point where even quite innocent comments from either side were ruthlessly analysed for any hint of insult or point scoring.

Billy took great pains to keep out of the conflict and spent an increasing amount of time meditating in the barn and practising her yoga and various fighting moves. Sometimes she sparred with Chloe, who had become more aggressive than usual.

Chloe, mainly on a matter of principle, had declared that she was staying at the cottage until the New Year if Mark did not mind. Since she asked him in front of others, he could hardly object – the fact that Jennie was at the table at the time only adding to Chloe's satisfaction.

But by mid-December, Billy had had enough. She felt no strong desire to leave the Lake District; the now almost-constant rain and bitterly cold winds had hardly dampened her appreciation for the place. But Billy did not like emotional conflict. A simple physical fight for the challenge of the combat was one thing. Living in a house where petty conflicts were making everyone miserable seemed pointless; twisted relationships were why she had fled her home in the first place. She warned Findo about their departure first. Then, the next morning, she gave Chloe an ultimatum: leave together now or stay on alone to fight with Jennie.

The three of them left the next day. Findo was a little disappointed but, for his sister's sake, also thankful. The camper van took them south, towards the other half of England. There was less rain now although the countryside was still wet and dull. It was milder too, softer weather to match the landscape. For the most part they travelled in silence; Chloe was still trying to make up her mind whether to be angry or relieved at their departure, Findo had nothing to say and Billy was happy to travel in peace.

After leaving the M5, they swung round the south of Birmingham, picked up the M40 and cut across towards Oxford. They stopped at a service station near the old Peartree roundabout and settled around a plastic table for over-priced cups of tea. They were nearly ready to go when Findo stirred.

"I need to make a telephone call," he announced.

Billy looked at him in surprise. "Who to?"

Findo shrugged. "A friend. I won't be long."

He turned away and picked his way out of the cafeteria. At the entrance to the service station he found a bank of phones and dug in his pocket for some small change. He dialled the number quickly, punching in the familiar sequence of digits. The phone was answered on the third ring.

"Yes?" The voice was non-committal.

"John."

"Hey, Findo." There was a sudden increase in warmth from the other end of the line. "How's it going, lad? Where are you?"

"Down south."

John gave a sharp intake of breath. "Well I hope you're taking care then, they're a bit different down there."

"I know," said Findo. "It's a bit different everywhere."

"So what are you up to? That sister of yours still looking after you?"

"Yeah, she's looking after me."

"So, this just a social call then? Because, could I ring you back in a bit?"

"You watching *Star Trek*?"

"Of course. It's good one this, it's the one where . . ."

"John." Findo cut across quickly.

There was silence for a moment. "What's up?"

"Can I come back?"

"What's wrong?"

Findo leant his head against the telephone with the receiver clamped against his ear. He looked out at the service station's busy foyer and the bustle of people coming in and out: truckers, suits, families and casual travellers with no better place to be than a service station on a Wednesday evening.

"Everything. Nothing," said Findo. "I just want to come home."

John sighed. "Look, I don't know if that's a good idea. Let me talk to the boss. Is there a number I can call you back on?"

"Dunno," said Findo. "I can't see anything on this box."

"What about where you're staying."

"I'm in a service station. Oxford. We're going somewhere even further south than this. Billy's got this friend, Chloe. She wants me to go with her and stay with Chloe's family. They've got some farm or something. She wants me to stay there for Christmas. Lots of family and everything."

"Hmm, nice," said John. "Doesn't sound much like your sort of thing, Findo."

"No."

"Okay. You're on the way there now are you?"

"Yeah. That's the plan but I'm not sure I can face it. I'd rather take my chances back home."

"Yeah," said John slowly, "trouble is, you come back and you put other people at risk, not just yourself. But tell you what – see if you can get your sister to hold tight for a bit. I might be able to sort something. I know a couple of people around that part of the world. I can't promise anything but there's a good chance I can come up with something better than Christmas with the family."

Billy was reluctant to wait in Oxford for John's answer but eventually gave way. Findo did not tell her and Chloe the whole story; all he said was that the friend on the telephone had just told him that someone else needed to speak to him urgently. Billy tried to press for more details but without any luck. Findo claimed that he did not know any more but had promised to call back in a couple of hours.

"If you want to go on ahead, I'll wait," he told Billy.

She frowned. "How long are you going to wait for?"

Findo shrugged. "Maybe this evening. Could be tomorrow morning."

Billy looked cross. "Well, why don't we carry on? You can call this 'friend' from Chloe's family's place."

Findo shook his head stubbornly. "No. I said I would wait. They might need to see me so there's no point going further away."

Chloe saved the day for Findo. She had been listening to the exchange and held up a hand.

"Hold on," she said. "We don't have to get home tonight. I've got some friends in Oxford that I haven't seen for ages. I'm sure they wouldn't mind putting us up for a night. Let me give them a call. If it's that important to Findo, we can wait for a night."

Billy looked at Chloe in surprise. She stared suspiciously but Chloe's expression was angelic. A few minutes later the van was underway again but this time heading into Oxford. They found Chloe's friends in the leafy suburb of Headington. Theirs was a big, old house with large rooms full of stripped pine furniture and bright watercolour paintings. Liz Davie and her partner Gerry O'Connor welcomed the visitors, while a swarm of small children flocked around excitedly in case the newcomers had brought anything interesting with them. Liz was a typical English earth mother type: all ethnic prints, handmade jewellery and warm hugs for anyone who got in her path. Gerry was an Irish solicitor, hiding a sharp mind beneath easygoing banter and genial hospitality.

With the first introductions over, Findo did his usual trick of slipping into the background. He spoke enough not to seem surly but his words were brief and dull. He sat quietly, daunted by the range of the conversations going on around him and the amount of emotions on display. He let Billy and Chloe take centre stage; Chloe had been at school with Liz and, over several bottles of red wine, spent the evening telling the story of how she had met Billy and about their experiences and travels together.

Findo tried to slip out to find a phone later in the evening but was stopped in his tracks by Liz, who tried to offer him the one on the kitchen table right next to the yarn-swapping group. When he hesitated, Gerry stepped neatly in.

"You might prefer the one in my study, Findo. A bit quieter in there, it is. You'll be able to talk in peace and hear what you're saying rather than trying to compete with the racket in here."

Findo nodded gratefully and let Gerry lead him down the hall to a small book-lined room.

Gerry pointed to the telephone. "There you go. Take your time. You don't have to rush back if you'd prefer some sanctuary." He winked. "I come in here myself sometimes. It's hard to get a word in edgeways with Liz when she gets going and that Chloe is as bad. Put them together and the rest of us might as well just shut up and listen." Gerry backed out of the room, pulling the door shut. "Take your time, Findo. Make yourself at home."

Findo nodded his thanks and waited until he heard Gerry walk off down the corridor. He moved quietly to the study door, pulled it gently open and looked out. A couple of minutes later he was shutting the front door behind him and slipping off down the gravel drive in search of a public telephone box where he could feel happy that there was no chance of eavesdroppers.

He found a telephone near a petrol station about a quarter mile from the house where they were staying. John did not answer the first time that Findo rang so he went for a slow stroll around the block, looking at the houses around him, assessing their security and the degree of wealth on display. The survey brought a smile to Findo's face. There was a lot of potential in Oxford.

The second time he rang John answered on the third ring. "Yes?"

"It's Findo."

"Findo, good. Where are you?"

"Still in Oxford. We're staying with some friends of Chloe's. One's a solicitor."

"A solicitor?" John laughed. "You don't half pick them, Findo. Oh well, I suppose there's solicitors and solicitors. I've used a few in my time. They weren't all bad. Couple were quite creative."

"So, what's happening?" said Findo. "Can I come home?"

"Not sure about that, Findo."

"Oh."

"But hey, that's the bad news," said John. "There's good news as well. I did have a chat with Colin but things are still quite hot up here. Our local friends in blue are still working hard. They've got a few leads, enough to make them think they're getting somewhere, but they haven't got anything concrete. They have been trying to find out more about you though and putting feelers out in all sorts of places. You're worth a healthy prize these days."

John hesitated. "Look, I know you're a bit of a local hero in some eyes. The story that got around about the Muldoons' money made you more than a few friends. A lot of people were well impressed with the Custodian job too. But you'll find that even some of the ones who think you're alright will sell you for a price – and for some that price isn't very much. Colin and I both reckon we need memories to fade a bit more before you risk showing yourself on the streets again."

Findo listened quietly with a sinking heart. "So, what's the good news then?"

"Ah," said John, "well, I've got a few mates around the country in various lines of work. I've just been talking to one bloke I know from way back. I was with him out in Cyprus when we were in the regulars. He's into antiques now – got a couple of shops around Oxford. But he also does a lot of confidential business with private buyers. He's a good bloke. Not exactly orthodox but not too deeply involved with the local scene either. I've had a chat with him about you and he might be able to put a couple of jobs your way." John laughed. "Sort of consultancy work. Finding stuff for him."

Findo smiled into the phone. "Sounds good."

"Yeah," said John. "I reckon it should work out alright. He can probably fix you up with a place to stay too. Best thing is, you two meet up and see what you think; decide if you're happy to work together. Let me give you the name of a pub."

Findo set off into the centre of Oxford as soon as he had put the phone down. He reached the agreed rendezvous just after ten o'clock. The pub was tucked down a side street. It was busy but not heaving. Findo slipped in behind a couple that were already drunk and deep into a slurred argument about who had said what earlier in the evening.

Findo ignored the bar – back home he would get served without a question but John had warned him against asking for a drink. He was still not quite sixteen and looked younger. Attention was the last thing he wanted at this stage.

Findo walked through the bar, trying to look around while keeping his head down. He had only gone a few feet when an arm shot out and grabbed him by the collar. Findo started to twist away.

"You Gask?"

He looked round with surprise and relief. The man towering over him was at least six foot four and built as if he could stop tanks with his bare hands.

"Yeah," he said nervously.

"Good. Then let's go."

The deal was done over a table in a small café a few streets away. Unbeknown to Findo, the meeting was not much different from any other job interview: Findo on one side of the table, his prospective employer on the other firing questions. They briefly discussed his references, sounded each other out for character compatibility and weighed up respective individual qualities. After a quarter of an hour, a preliminary decision was made and Findo offered the terms of his contract.

Findo did not hesitate; the details had never been that important to him. He accepted and took the hand that Daniel Morris was proffering.

Morris drove Findo back to the house in Headington and dropped him off outside. He handed Findo a card with the details of an antiques shop in a place called Woodstock.

"Ring me there tomorrow when you've sorted yourself out. I'll come and pick you up."

Inside, Findo's return got a mixed reaction. The others were still seated around the dining table. As he walked towards the kitchen he could hear them talking volubly but his entrance created a sudden silence. Gerry arched an eyebrow and gave Findo a wry smile. Chloe looked curious, while Billy gave him an angry glance before pointedly turning away. Liz gaped at Findo for a moment then surged towards him in a wave of ethnic dress and red wine fumes.

"Findo! There you are. Billy was worried where you'd got too. We didn't realise you'd gone out." She wrapped an arm around his shoulder and guided him back to the fold. "Would you like something to drink? Something to eat?"

Findo shook his head.

"Did you have a quiet drink for me too?" said Gerry with a wink.

Findo smiled weakly. "I had something to think about," he said. "You were all talking. I didn't want to disturb you."

"Oh, don't you worry," said Liz brightly; pouring more wine into all the glasses she could reach. "You're back safe; that's all that matters. So what were you worried about? Girlfriend trouble?"

Findo shrugged. "Partly."

Liz shook her head. "Oh, relationships; they're the hardest things to work out, aren't they? I bet she was who you were talking to earlier. No wonder you took up Gerry's offer of a quiet place to talk. I should have realised."

"Liz." Gerry's tone was soft but cut through her babble with familiar skill. "Leave the boy alone. It's none of our business. I'm sure we don't know the half of it and the last thing Findo wants is group therapy."

Liz looked disappointed but nodded. Findo made his apologies a few minutes later and slipped away from the table on the excuse that he was tired and wanted to go to bed. Liz had already made up a bed for him in Gerry's study and showed him to it. She fussed around to see if he would like any glasses of water, books or extra pillows – hoping that what he really wanted was a sympathetic confidante to whom he could pour out his heart. Findo shook his head quietly and eventually she departed.

Findo lay there staring at the ceiling, which was faintly illuminated by a glow from the moon outside. He was just starting to drift off into a half-waking dream about Abby when Billy opened the door. She came in quietly and sat down in Gerry's desk chair.

"Hey, Findo."

"Hey, Billy."

Her voice was softer than earlier in the evening and he knew she already part-understood. "What's the story then, little brother?"

"I'm going to stay in Oxford. I've met this man who's going to give me some work. He's a friend of John's."

"What kind of work?"

Findo smiled to himself. "Getting things," he said.

"Stealing them."

"Yeah, probably."

"That's your life, is it?" Billy sounded sad.

"It's what I do," said Findo. "It's what I'm good at. I don't hurt people. I only take things."

Billy sighed. "It's all a bit of a joke to you, isn't it?"

Findo frowned. "What do you mean?"

"Stealing things, burgling places. You don't really do it for the money, do you?"

Findo shrugged as he lay on his back. "I guess not. No. You know how it is. You know how we started. We never had anything. I just took what we needed. That's all I ever did. We nicked food and other stuff. And people would ask me to get things for them because I was good at it. It's still the same really. I just get things for people, move them around a bit, that's all."

Billy reached out a foot and gave him a kick. "I came a long way to find you."

Findo rolled over onto his side. "And you did find me. I'm really glad you came. I missed you, Billy. I missed you for a long time. I

288

never forgot you and I always wondered if you'd come back."

"I did come back," said Billy hastily. "I didn't know it would take so long."

Findo shook his head. "I don't mind about the time," he said. "I don't hold that against you. I'm not cross it took so long." He reached up and took her hand in his. "You did come. That's all the matters. I don't care how long it took. That's not important."

"Then come with me," said Billy. "Don't stay here. You don't have to be a thief all your life."

Findo shook his head. "It's not about being a thief," he said. "You've got a life with Chloe. It's different. You want to be with her. You do stuff I know nothing about. That's okay. And you want to go and be with her family at Christmas. On a farm. That's alright. But you don't want me there. I wouldn't fit in."

Billy squeezed his hand. "You could do. You didn't like Eskdale to begin with."

Findo shook his head. "It's not the same, Billy. And anyway, that was fun for a bit but I couldn't have stayed there for long. It was good to do something new but those people, they're not the same as me. I didn't really fit in there. I liked the kayaking and the climbing but I wouldn't have wanted to stay there."

She sighed. "I know, but I don't want to lose you again."

"You won't," said Findo. "Just because we don't live in the same place doesn't mean you've lost me. We can still meet up, talk and stuff. I'll make sure you know where I am. I'll tell you before I go home, let you know where I'm going to be."

"You want to go back to the city?"

"Yeah," said Findo. "I do. And I will. It's not the same for me as it is for you. You decided to leave and you found a new life. But my life is in the city. I know it's dirty and violent and all that but it's still my home. I miss it. I don't want to be in Oxford but I reckon it's better than coming with you to Chloe's place. I don't want to go with you and pretend to be something that I'm not. I'm a thief, and a good one."

He looked up at Billy in the darkness. "I don't want to change the way I am. If I stay here I don't need to. But you can come up and see me. We can meet up, just the two of us." He grinned. "It's my birthday next month. I'll be sixteen. Come for that. You can have Christmas with Chloe. I'll only be in the way if I come and you know I won't fit in, not with all her family on a farm. Chloe won't want me there either. Leave me here. That way we can have our own lives, do the things that suit us, but we can still meet up and keep in touch. I can call you and you can write to me again. It's better this way."

34. Life among the dreaming spires

Findo had expected to be home in a few weeks, or months at worst. He took on the job and the accommodation provided by Daniel Morris assuming both were temporary. But he spent over four years working for Morris. During that time he never once went home and only travelled further than a hundred miles on odd occasions, mainly for trips to isolated properties in the West Country, the fens of East Anglia or the Welsh Marches.

Once he was settled in Oxford, Findo called John Biggs every few days to begin with to ask when he could go back to the city. Each rebuttal was a bitter disappointment and the only thing that made his exile more bearable was that he was able to be himself in a way that he had not been while at the cottage in the Lake District. Although far from home, he was on his own and had new territory to explore. And he was soon back doing what he did best – intruding and removing, entering and taking, burgling and stealing.

Daniel Morris had originally agreed to look after Findo only reluctantly. He had done it as a favour for a friend who, long ago but at a time not forgotten, had helped him out in his own time of need. But to the surprise of both parties the arrangement turned out to suit both employer and roving 'finder'.

The first thing Morris did was to find Findo a bolthole. It was a flat, which until then had only been used for storage, above one of his two completely legitimate shops. It was little more than a bedsit – one large room with a kitchen area and a tiny shower room – but offered all the comforts that Findo required. Morris told his staff that he was renting out the flat so that the presence of someone living overhead would act as an extra deterrent against burglars. He gave Findo a wad of cash to keep him going and for the first few days left him to his own devices.

Nearly a week later, Morris popped up to see Findo just after the shop below had shut for the day. He knocked briskly at the door to the flat. Once Findo had let him in, Morris got straight to business. With him, he had a picture from a magazine of a man at a desk. It was from a trade magazine about the food retailing business. The story was about the appointment of a new chief executive to head the foods division of one of the big supermarket chains. But Morris was not concerned about supermarkets or the fat cat with the new job. What interested him was that the picture had been taken at the man's

291

Oxfordshire home – and the small statuette of a bronze panther on a shelf behind the smiling appointee.

The panther in the magazine picture, which was missing its hind limbs and both front paws, was mounted on a small black plinth. Morris also had a photograph from a sale catalogue of a similar work, with a five-figure guide price next to it. It was described as an Achaemenid bronze from the eastern Mediterranean, dating from around the sixth century BC.

He also had several photographs of the outside of the man's house, taken a week earlier. More importantly, he had a tracing, taken from the local planning department, of a floor plan of the house that had been submitted as part of the application to build the property two years earlier.

"I don't care how you do it," he told Findo. "All I want is the bronze. Get it and you'll get a share of the price I sell it for."

Findo nodded. "Okay." He frowned. "What if there's other stuff, more statues?"

Morris shook his head. "Not interested. You take anything else that's up to you. But I won't have anything to do with it. All I want is this bronze. You can clear the house out if you want but you'll have to find another fence or get rid of any other stuff you take yourself."

Findo shook his head. "Nah. It's alright. I'll just get you your panther."

Morris gave a brief smile. "One thing, though."

"What?"

"You don't bring it back here. You don't ever bring anything that's nicked back here. This is a legitimate business and I don't want complications. You ever give the cops an excuse to poke their noses in and I won't help you at all. I'll break your legs and send you back to John Biggs in a box. Got it?"

Findo nodded. "Don't worry. I won't take chances. I won't get caught either."

Morris scowled. "Don't get overconfident, boy. Get too bloody cocky and you start getting sloppy. I was told you're a pro. I don't want any cocky amateurs giving me grief. That's no use to me."

Findo nodded. "I'm not cocky, I'm just careful. That's why I'm good." He grinned. "I've stolen more things than you've got in that shop downstairs and I've never even been questioned by the police."

Morris grunted. "We'll see about that. There's a first time for everyone – however good you reckon you are."

Findo shrugged. "So?" he asked.

"So, what?"

"What do you want me to do with the statue when I've got it?"

The first job went as smoothly as the next and the ones after that. Findo delivered the bronze three days later and the theft was not reported until two weeks after that – by which time the artwork had already left the country. The supermarket man had been away on an overseas trip for half the time since Findo's night visit and only finally called the police two days after noticing that the figurine was gone. He told them he had initially thought one of the cleaning staff must have moved it while they were dusting. He was as baffled as Thames Valley police by the odd business card lying where the antique had been.

Daniel Morris did not ask how the boy had managed to get the statue. But he was impressed that Findo had got into the house without leaving any traces and had managed the job with no fuss or bother. From then on – in a similar fashion to how he had been tested by Colin Speed – Findo began to find more tasks coming his way. Morris also began to trust him. He softened his brusque manner and started to discuss Findo's jobs in advance. For Morris appreciated art as well as selling it. He had a good general knowledge of his subject, plus an encyclopaedic knowledge of certain specialities. The dealer's enthusiasm was infectious; Findo did not really care about what he was stealing but would find himself listening with interest as Morris enthused happily about the next piece to be stolen.

Morris came from a different background to any of the men Findo had known back home. He was from a wealthy family and had gone to public school before attending the Royal Military Academy at Sandhurst and enlisting in the British Army as an officer. Now in his early sixties, Morris blended in well with the types who frequented his shops. His still-impressive physique added extra gravitas to the slightly off-hand but knowledgeable manner that helped persuade many customers to spend more money than might otherwise have been the case. Morris spoke with a deep but plummy tone and had habits that seemed bizarre to Findo, like drinking tea with lemon and reading oversized newspapers.

Morris had been a captain in the British Army when he met John Biggs, then a corporal in a different regiment. Morris, who was a few years younger, was already treading a dangerous path. He had got involved in a plot using British military flights to smuggle stolen works of Greek and Turkish art out of Cyprus. The military police discovered what was going on and prepared an operation to break the ring. John Biggs was not involved but got wind of what was happening and saw an opportunity to frustrate the red caps. Just as it was about to go horribly wrong for Morris, he produced a false but watertight alibi that allowed the young captain to protest innocence and avoid prosecution. John's action saved Morris from a possible prison sentence and certain dishonourable discharge – which would also have seen him cut off from a sizeable inheritance.

Morris was posted away from Cyprus soon after but the two men kept in touch over the years that followed. John had also introduced Morris to Colin Speed and, from time to time, the two men conducted mutually beneficial business deals.

The Oxfordshire antiques dealer had been surprised at being asked to look after Findo. The idea of having his own private burglar tickled Morris but was not something that he initially took seriously. Morris had occasionally contracted jobs in the past but was mainly involved in buying and selling as a middleman, not as the actual procurer of stolen items. He had only planned to give Findo somewhere to hole up, presuming it would be for just a couple of months. But the strength of John's verbal reference was too tempting to ignore. After a period of deliberating, Morris had to find a job on which to try Findo out.

The money made on the stolen bronze, and the ease with which Findo delivered, made Morris realise that John had not exaggerated about the boy's skills. So, he tried him out again, and again.

By the time six months had gone by Morris would have been loath to lose his secret employee. Findo was also settling into a quiet routine that suited his needs. He had never done many domestic burglaries before, mainly concentrating on commercial premises for Speed. And the kinds of houses that he was breaking into for Morris were different from anywhere Findo had ever known; they were too big, too luxurious, too divorced from the reality of what Findo viewed as normal, everyday life. Most were also full of things, too many for any one family to need or own. Taking a piece of furniture, a picture or some other odd item did not even register in Findo's consciousness as being wrong.

The jobs that Morris found provided challenges by which Findo could hone and demonstrate his skills. Findo also had the freedom to tackle each one as he saw fit. And although there was a certain satisfaction in impressing Morris, it was not really the fact that he was performing for an audience, albeit only of one, that mattered. What made the achievement of each task rewarding was the knowledge that they were all deadly serious. Morris did not send him off to break into country houses for the fun of the game. It was not a performance but a business and he was treated like a professional, and given jobs worthy of a professional's time.

To Findo, neither money nor the things it bought were important. What he had been steadily earning since becoming a career criminal was respect. It was a currency with a value impossible to quantify but the only reward he sought. The one thing Findo was given as a child had been a slim chance. Through his early years he sought safety in the form of freedom but underlying his actions as he moved into manhood was another motivation; every ounce of respect that he earned as a thief helped tip the balance of self-esteem back in his favour.

But what kept Findo in Oxford was not the pleasure of proving his worth, establishing himself in a new place or testing his skills against new targets. It was Abby.

After weeks of prevarication at Eskdale, Findo finally wrote to her just before Christmas. Billy had bullied him into making the effort – pointing out during one of their phone conversations that not taking the trouble to contact Abby at Christmas might be the final nail in his coffin. It still took Findo several goes to compose his thoughts and the result was not exactly a romantic sonnet.

Dear Abby,

I'm living in a place called Oxford now. I've got a new flat. It's above an antiques shop. It's quite nice but different from home. The flat's okay. It's got one big room and a kitchen and a shower. I've got my own entrance – I don't have to go through the shop when I go out.

I'm working for the man who runs the antiques shop. He's called Daniel Morris. John fixed it up for me. He used to be in the army with Daniel. They were in Cyprus together a long time ago.

I went to the Lake District when I left home. Billy knew some people there and we stayed with them in a little cottage. Actually I slept in Billy's van because there were too many people in the cottage. One of them, an Australian called Barnaby, taught me how to go kayaking. I learnt how to roll over in the water and go upside down. It was quite scary to begin with but I liked doing it. They also took me climbing and were all surprised how good I was. I told them about climbing up the castle and said I learnt doing things like that.

I'm sorry I didn't say goodbye properly before. I wanted to but Billy didn't let me get out of the van to talk to you.

You can write to me if you would like. I haven't got a phone but I can call you if you let me know when. I hope you and your mum have a really good Christmas.
  Findo

He sent the letter with one of the largest Christmas cards that he could find in the local shops. He had put his address on the letter and waited, hoping desperately for a reply.

Nothing came by the end of the year and at the beginning of January Findo was kept busy with his second job for Daniel Morris; this time asked to retrieve a set of three rare books from the library of a small stately home near Abingdon. The house was well protected with alarms and other security devices. But it was also open to the public one day a week and Findo was able to spend some time looking around, getting the feel for the place's defensive strengths and weaknesses.

He completed the job on the night before his sixteenth birthday. Using a combination of the skills developed in the city and the climbing techniques learnt in the Lake District, Findo scaled the outside of the three-storey building and got in by removing a small section of roof slates. Inside, he lowered himself by rope onto the first-floor landing and only had to disable one motion detector in order to gain access to the library and remove the books. Once more, Findo was able to get out without leaving any obvious traces and it was several days before the theft was noticed and the second of his calling cards found.

On the day of his birthday, Billy arrived. She stayed for three days and they spent the time exploring the Oxford sights, gawping at shops, wandering though mediaeval colleges and strolling through the covered market. They also went punting together, although Findo found the experience tame compared to kayaking. It was a good time for both of them and they parted happy and affectionate.

Abby's reply came nearly a week later. The letter was handwritten but only covered a single sheet of paper and its words doused Findo's smouldering hopes like a shower of iced water. Abby wrote:

  Findo
  Thank you for your letter – I was wondering if you were going to bother writing.
  I'm glad you've got a new job and a place to stay in Oxford. I've heard it's supposed to be very pretty. I expect you'll probably stay. I hope the new job is a proper one and nothing

illegal but somehow I'm not sure it will be, particularly if it was organised by one of those people you used to work for.

It's a shame you had to run away from the city but I suppose you had to if you didn't want the police to catch you. Maybe you think being on the run is romantic?

I expect this means you won't ever be able to come back. It's sad our friendship had to end like this. I was so frightened when I saw your name all over the paper. I could not believe what a stupid thing you had done.

I hope things work out for you in the future and that you don't get involved in anything really dangerous. I know you're not actually a bad person – please try to stay out of prison.

Abby

Findo read the letter through fives times the day it arrived. He went over the words slowly. He did not attempt to pick at possible meanings; he read it as it was written, taking it on face value.

Reluctantly, he concluded the answer was clear. Abby expected him to stay in Oxford and she viewed their friendship as over. Sadly, Findo crumpled the letter, placed it in the flat's fireplace and put a match to it. She obviously did not want him to write again. He would do what she wanted.

As a result, Findo stopped pestering John Biggs to know when he could return home. He still called occasionally but the intervals between calls got less frequent and Findo no longer asked about going back. They talked about other things instead. Findo spoke – at John's insistence in guarded terms – about some of the jobs he had been doing for Morris and the methods used to retrieve particular objects. John talked about the books he had been reading and the films he had watched.

John also posted a regular supply of sci-fi and fantasy novels and videos down to Findo. The books and films became a regular subject for late-night discussions.

John assumed from the dropping of the subject that Findo was happy in his new career as country house burglar. Findo never revealed otherwise; he had never told even John about Abby's existence. In truth, he enjoyed his Oxford career but never stopped missing the streets of home. The city where he had grown up was ugly; it was raw, cheap and a bitter place to be poor. But it also had an edge that Oxford came close to in only a few isolated enclaves like the estates of Blackbird Leys. Findo's hometown was a dangerous place for those who, without knowing the turf, sought to live life on the edge. But Findo did know the city; it was ingrained within him and he missed it. Life in Oxford was easy – too easy.

But he stuck it out for over four years, carrying out an average of a burglary every month for Daniel Morris. His cut was paid promptly, through an anonymous shell company, into a building society account as soon as the item was sold. Findo paid regular rent to the antiques dealer and to all appearances their relationship ended there.

During the time between his sixteenth and twentieth birthdays, Findo burgled houses across Oxfordshire, Berkshire, Gloucestershire, Warwickshire and Wiltshire, plus making a few forays further afield. In search of antiques and works of art, he entered suburban mansions, country retreats, historic halls and the occasional castle. Most of the time he was after single items: generally small, easily transportable and worth a good price to a buyer not interested in provenance.

From one collection he took a Greek marble head of a veiled goddess, dating from the Hellenistic period and insured for sixty-five thousand pounds. Tucked inside a desk in a townhouse in Bath, he located a sapphire ring-stone bearing a portrait of the fifth century Visigoth ruler King Alaric II. That item had been withdrawn from auction a year earlier when it failed to meet its reserve of forty-five thousand pounds. A rare Ming iron-red and green enamelled saucer, dating from the mid-sixteenth century, was recovered from a stately home on the edge of the Cotswolds. If Findo had not got there first, it would have been offered for sale by Christies a couple of months later and been expected to raise at least twenty-five thousand pounds – money that would have gone to help pay for essential roof repairs to the rambling Elizabethan manor house. Other items swapped for Findo's business cards included an Egyptian bronze and gilt wood ibis from the Ptolemaic period, valued at around thirty thousand pounds, and a diamond rivière necklace dating from around 1860. That was Findo's most valuable prize in the first year, clocking in at an anticipated (legal) sale value of somewhere between one hundred and a hundred-and-fifty thousand pounds.

For the first six months or so Findo made his way to his targets under his own steam, using public transport or his feet. But then Morris started to look at opportunities further afield – not wanting to make Findo too vulnerable by concentrating his activities within the area of a single police force. To get to some of the new locations Findo obviously needed transport. He knew, more-or-less, how to drive and had seen Mickey Dunn in action often enough that he would have had little trouble stealing most cars. But Morris did not want Findo taking extra risks by driving stolen cars.

298

He decided the best thing was to make Findo's travelling arrangements as legitimate as possible. Findo was still only sixteen at the time and had no paperwork of any kind to prove who he was. But with the network of contacts that Morris had that was not a problem. He procured a birth certificate in the name of Philip Gates, showing Findo as being over seventeen. Morris then taught the teenage thief to drive properly – rather than in the style of Mickey Dunn.

They also used the false identity to build up Findo's cover. A new savings account was opened in the name of Philip Gates and Morris changed the rental agreement on his flat. Findo Gask 'moved away' and the new, slightly older tenant took his place. The teenager stayed anonymous in the sense that he still declared no income and claimed no benefits but Philip Gates slowly became more of a real person, buying a television licence and even registering with a dentist after his wisdom teeth caused him some aches and pains.

A few months after Philip Gates came into existence, Findo had a full driving licence in his possession, taken under the name of his new alter ego. Using the money from his building society account he bought a good but nondescript Ford Fiesta, which Morris ensured was properly taxed, MOT-ed and insured. A friend of Morris also did some work on the interior panelling and back seats, creating several well-disguised voids complete with padding and webbing straps that made ideal storage containers for any goods that needed to be discretely hidden while in transit.

The car gave Findo a freedom he had never experienced before. He felt like the king of the world for the first few months. He drove everywhere, even a quarter mile down the road to buy a pint of milk. He spent hours slowly pottering through the countryside around Oxford, watching the world from behind his own windscreen. As his confidence grew his trips grew longer; one day he drove down to the New Forest to meet Billy and took her on a tour of the Dorset countryside around Corfe Castle.

The Fiesta was also invaluable for his professional exploits. Findo was able to use it to reach the locations Morris had given him, expanding his range of operations enormously. But he followed the advice given by Morris and was sensible about where he took the car. He never parked closer than a mile from the location of any burglary and preferred at least double that distance. He tried to leave the Fiesta in locations where the presence of an extra vehicle would draw no attention, like busy side streets and car parks. Occasionally, for some more rural jobs, he would have to leave the car alone in the countryside. Then Findo would make sure he parked a good distance from his intended target and would sometimes hike for several miles cross-country to get to where he needed to be.

Within a short time of becoming Philip Gates and getting his driving licence, Findo could not imagine life without a car. He had freedom to travel as well as freedom to live. The car was a tool but for a while it also became a way of life. It also helped Findo to shut himself off further from the world around. He had never been garrulous or gregarious and always felt safer alone than with strangers. Only a few people had ever broken through that reserve and none were in Oxford. And so, although still surrounded by people, Findo became more of a recluse than ever.

He felt safe enough with Morris but they had little in common and only spent time together when discussing jobs. Other than that, Findo had no compulsion to seek out company and lived his own strange and solitary life. Part of it was his upbringing. As a boy he had been taught – and learnt from first-hand experience – that everyone around him was potentially dangerous. The logical consequence of that had been to always avoid contact with anyone that he did not trust absolutely.

Findo also withdrew into himself because he was lonely, and too shy and lacking in social graces to know what to do about it. He missed his home and felt uncomfortable in Oxford. Its streets were unfamiliar, lined with strange buildings and filled with the wrong people. It was a big town but it was the wrong town. Even the weather was too soft and warm.

Loneliness had become a way of life for Findo but he also made no effort to find friendship because he was sad. He missed Abby. Although he had burnt her letter, she was often in his thoughts and he never forgot her. Sometimes he would lie awake at night, staring at the ceiling and thinking of her face. He remembered the day they had met and the time that he had painted her name across the side of the old gas register. He remembered the puppies and the look on her face when they stole the toy sports car from the MP's house. He remembered her but tried not to. As far as Findo was concerned, Abby had made it clear that she wanted nothing more to do with him. It never occurred to him that she might be prepared to change her mind – or even want to have it changed. He just accepted her loss and tried not to let it hurt too much.

On the days when Findo was not involved in a job for Morris, either carrying out or planning a burglary, he lived a simple life. He read a lot, mostly books sent by John, although he sometimes acquired his own. He watched videos and occasionally listened to music. He would study maps and check his equipment for hours on end. He walked the roads around the flat where he lived and the streets in the middle of Oxford. He also drove, sometimes spending whole days in his car. The Fiesta became an extension of Findo. It allowed him to travel in safe isolation. Sometimes he would park and walk, roaming woods, parks or the streets of a new town. But other times he just drove.

35. The ghetto Raffles

It was over two years before Findo's calling cards came to the public attention. Even then it took another six months before the connection was made, and then only by chance, between the country house burglar of middle England and the thief who once helped rob a security depot in a northern city.

Back home, the files were still open on Findo but he was no longer a priority. The investigation into the Custodian raid had eventually been shelved. Technically, the inquiry was continuing but it was months since any police officer had done any work on the case. A new wave of prostitution involving Eastern European women shipped in to work the city streets had been linked to a sudden rise in the amount of heroin on sale. Smack was now being peddled almost openly in some of the city's roughest neighbourhoods and there had been a corresponding rise in petty crime as new addicts sought to feed their desires. There had also been a rise in the number of violent crimes – muggings and sexual assaults – involving gangs of youths. Policing priorities were directed to meet the new demands and official interest into tracing the identity of Findo Gask declined swiftly, particularly as his name had not been heard – or seen – for a considerable time.

In the tower blocks of Tibbermore, among the dirty streets of Hobbes Town and East Park and in the ghetto estates like Meadowfields, however, his name was not forgotten. The name Findo had moved into common parlance. 'Doing a Findo' became a term for any audacious or clever act, particularly of theft. But the question of where Findo himself had got to was soon forgotten. John Biggs and Colin Speed told those who asked that Findo had gone away but never mentioned that they knew where. And in time, even the few who had known the boy thief relatively well gave up asking where he had gone. The only other person aware of his new whereabouts was Frances Reid and no one even knew to ask her.

But as interest in Findo's activities declined in his hometown, it was on the increase in the Thames Valley. His name first came to the attention of local CID officers when his card was found at the scene of the break-in at the home of the supermarket chief. Initially, the police were not sure what to make of it. But when the same card was found in a stately home near Abingdon where a set of rare books had been stolen, they knew that the card was exactly what it appeared to be.

Over the next year, Findo's calling cards were found at the scene of burglaries in Chipping Norton, Banbury, Thame, Wantage and other locations in villages and the countryside around Oxford. They were also found at burglaries in Marlborough and Stroud but Thames Valley Police did not investigate those incidents and the connection was not made until later.

After the first four or five cards turned up, Thames Valley CID got into the habit of checking crime scenes to see if Findo had put his name to the theft. The officers dealing with the thefts of arts and antiques puzzled long and hard over the meaning of words on the cards. The quotes on Findo's business cards seemed clear enough and so did the overall message; it was a boast, a claim to glory and a taunt. But the thing that confused them most was Findo's name. They read the quotes from Karl Marx and from Pierre-Joseph Proudhon, and traced their origin. Then they tried to work out who Findo Gask was. The name meant nothing to them, either as the name of a person or an organisation. Some tried to look for hidden meanings, analysing the letters for possible acronyms. They also tried anagrams – although the best they could come up with was 'if God sank', which hardly took their inquiry any further forward.

Other than his cards, Findo left few clues at the properties he burgled. Forensic experts found a few fibres, the occasional footprint and the odd hair that may or may not have belonged to Findo but that was it. The consensus was that the thefts were the work of one person but even that was not certain. There was also no real pattern to the burglaries. Findo generally took only single items of high value, normally worth at least five figures and sometimes more. But he targeted all manner of properties, from solitary country homes to terraced town houses. He mostly worked at night but not always, and his intrusions were so neatly done that they were often not discovered for some time, making it harder for the police to know exactly when he had broken in. He also ranged widely (particularly once he had his car), striking one time in the London commuter belt, the next up on the edge of the Cotswolds or down near Salisbury Plain.

It was clear to the police that the items were being stolen to order but they had no idea who was doing the ordering. They knew that the artefacts taken could have been identified in various ways. Some were in collections open to the public; others had been sold at auction to known collectors. They guessed that an insider in the trade, either a dealer or someone in the insurance business, was helping to pick out the targets but there was no obvious link. None of the items stolen by Findo had been recovered so there was no way of tracing the chain back.

The lack of evidence was partly down to Findo's skill; he had become a real adept at forcing an entry and leaving hardly any traces. He was well practised in disabling alarms – and sensible enough to know to retreat if he came across a system that was too complex for him to overcome. He also avoided using the same method for different burglaries. Each plan of attack was based on the weaknesses of the building that confronted him, not on any personal strengths or preferences.

The absence of any associated trail was down to Daniel Morris. He profited enormously from Findo's activities but was smart enough not to overuse his young finder's talents. Morris also only stole when he knew he had a buyer. Sometimes his customers came to him already knowing where a particular item was to be found and having heard of Morris' ability to procure wanted artefacts. Other times, Morris had to do the research himself and would scour old sale catalogues, country house magazines and other publications in search of particular works. He also had a couple of contacts working for insurers who would, for a fee, tell him the whereabouts of certain pieces. But like Findo, Morris varied his approach and used a number of different sources to track down what he wanted. That variation in approach, combined with the fact that he always had his buyers lined up and was not too greedy, managed to prevent any common thread emerging that could have given the police the break they wanted.

Findo never told Morris about the cards. Findo had not explained exactly what it was that had happened in the north to drive him into exile and Morris had not enquired, initially not being that interested.

When he started work again, Findo had taken his cards with him without thinking about it. Leaving them at the scenes of his exploits had become habit. Part of him knew it was foolish but he was also too stubborn to concede the point. He carried a small stash hidden inside a slit in the lining of a jacket sleeve; knowing better than to carry them loose in a pocket where they could be discovered if the police ever stopped him. Findo left one at the scene of every successful break-in – normally lying in the spot that had been occupied by the item now in his possession.

Findo was eighteen when the story of the cards and the quotes they carried first appeared in a magazine about the antiques trade. Under the headline 'Who Is Findo Gask?' the article reported on the strange story of the business cards turning up at the scenes of burglaries across the Thames Valley area. The story related how pictures, antiques, sculptures and other valuables worth nearly £1.5

million had been stolen over the past two years in a series of break-ins linked only by the discovery of the cards.

The story was quite short. It was a novelty item, a serious subject, nothing unusual apart from a particular quirk. Burglaries were not rare; what was unusual was for thieves to leave calling cards. The report said, accurately, that the police were baffled by the cards and had so far failed to solve any of the burglaries in question, thought to be the work of a single thief.

To begin with, the story made little impression. It appeared in the magazine, was read by a few thousand people and promptly forgotten.

Then, just over six months later, a journalist sitting in a doctor's waiting room spotted the story. Rosie Kelly was a reporter on the Gloucester Echo and had gone to see her GP about her asthma. While waiting for her appointment, Rosie flicked through a couple of copies of *House & Garden* but soon lost interest in articles about glossy lifestyles she could not afford. Most of the rest of the assortment of dog-eared periodicals had equally small appeal and she picked up the antiques magazine only to pass the time.

The first articles did nothing to relieve Rosie's boredom and she was about to cast the magazine aside when a headline on a news page caught her eye. Rosie frowned and started to read with new interest. She remembered the name Findo Gask well. She had come across it on her previous job on a local daily up north. If she remembered correctly, it had been the name of the chief suspect in an audacious robbery at a security firm which had netted the raiders more than half a million pounds.

Rosie considered the story; it was an odd twist but an unusual name – there was hardly likely to be more than one Findo Gask. Rosie smiled. Her asthma did not feel quite so bad now. She smelt a story, a good story.

When the story of Findo Gask next went public it was to a far wider audience. The story appeared in a national Sunday newspaper a few weeks after Rosie's visit to the GP – with her byline underneath that of one of the paper's regular journalists.

The article took up most of a page. There was a map of Britain that showed Findo's hometown and some of the stately homes that had experienced his visits. It had even included the location of the hamlet from which he took his name. There was a photograph of the supermarket executive in his panther-less study and a right honourable gentleman in a tweed suit outside a picturesque Georgian mansion that had lost two valuable sketches from its walls. There was a close up of Findo's card with the Marx quote – and the silhouette of a shadowy figure climbing a drainpipe. They even had a photograph of Clement Dallaway's stolen miniature Maserati, graffiti-ed with Findo's name and dumped in the ornamental fishpond in the city centre.

Again, the paper asked who Findo Gask could be. There was speculation about whether or not he had a gang behind him but, either way, the paper was confident that there was a single master-thief behind the crimes attributed to Findo.

The story spoke authoritatively about his life story, calling Findo 'The Raffles from the Ghetto'. It described how this thief from one of the country's grimmest northern cities had baffled police in his hometown with theft after theft, culminating in the raid he had 'masterminded' on the security firm. There were quotes from 'sources' in both the city's police force and underworld telling stories about the early years of Findo Gask's one-man crime wave. One story (untrue) told how he had emptied a jeweller's shop in the middle of the day after tying up the shop staff in a back room. Another story (true) related how he had used a storm drain to sneak into a police station's fenced compound and steal, from inside a police van, a collection of stolen car radios about to be used as evidence against another thief (Jimmy Ray).

There was an account of the robbery of the Custodian depot and how Findo Gask had then disappeared from his hometown, only to re-emerge as the person behind a string of country house burglaries in southern England. According to the newspaper, he was stealing priceless antiques from collections across the country and, yet again, the police had no idea who he was, where he came from or how to stop him.

John called the day after the article came out. It was evening when he rang. Findo had just come back from driving out to a village near Didcot, where he had been inspecting the layout of a large private school. Morris had found out the headmaster collected antique firearms and had a pair of rare flintlock pistols that would fetch around £20,000 each to the right buyer.

Findo was making himself a cup of tea when the phone rang.
"Hello?"
"What are you like?"
"John?"
"Findo, you're a nutter. What you going to do next, a bunk across the Channel and start over there?"

Findo frowned. "What're you on about?"

"You didn't see the story in the paper yesterday?"

"What story?"

John sighed. "No, I don't suppose you would have. Been leaving your business cards around again have you?"

Findo was silent for a moment.

"Yeah," said John, "exactly."

There was a long pause.

"Listen," said John, "you might not be able to get a copy of yesterday's paper. I'll stick a cutting in the post. Meantime, keep your head down. Give me a ring when you've seen what I'm talking about."

This time around it was easier for Findo to ride out the storm. John tore him off a strip but had to eventually concede that the newspaper story probably made little difference. Morris never even mentioned the article, although Findo had no way of knowing whether that was because he had not seen it, did not care or had forgotten who Philip Gates really was. Billy never saw the article and Findo never told her about it. On John's advice, after reading the cutting a few times he burnt his copy of the story.

For a few weeks after the article came out, Findo looked over his shoulder even more than usual. But it did not stop him leaving a card when he stole the flintlock pistols at the end of the week, or a month afterwards when he burgled a country house in East Devon. To all intents and purposes, Findo Gask was a ghost. He left his cards behind at the scenes of his thefts but no one ever saw him. He had no official identity – except as a name that appeared in police logs and inquiry files. In Oxford, he lived under a pseudonym. A few people, like the staff in the shop below his flat, knew him as Philip. The only people who could have identified him as Findo Gask and knew where he lived were Daniel Morris, John Biggs, Colin Speed, Frances Reid and Billy.

And so life went on. Another soft southern winter came and went, followed too soon by spring. No heavy hand descended on Findo's shoulder and he continued his solitary and lonely existence as before. He read books, watched films, wandered the streets and lanes of middle England, and burgled houses to collect items requested by Morris. But he never felt at home.

It had been raining heavily for about four days without a break. Findo was holed up in his flat watching television. Unusually for him, he was watching the news. The appalling weather of the last couple of months was still showing no signs of letting up. It had been one of the wettest winters on record and Britain was getting too waterlogged to cope.

Rivers were bursting their banks up and down the country. In Yorkshire, they were nervously watching water levels and desperately using lines of sandbags to raise the banks of watercourses swollen far beyond normal limits. In the Severn Valley and Devon, villages had already been evacuated and the footage on the lunchtime news showed an inflatable boat zooming up a high street normally packed with shoppers. Scenes filmed from a helicopter showed thousands of acres of farmland under water. At one point the camera crew circled above a flock of sheep trapped on a rapidly diminishing hillock of dry land, now over half a mile from the edge of a new lake covering much of Somerset.

Findo watched with mild curiosity. There was little else to do. He had celebrated his twentieth birthday a few weeks earlier. Billy had come up to visit, this time with Chloe, and they had gone to Bristol. The women had taken Findo to a restaurant. The food and drink had been good but afterwards they took him to a small club they knew. That had not been quite so successful. Although Findo liked the music – a kind of trip-hop mix of ambient sounds with funk and dance rhythms – and enjoyed the lightshow, he could not cope with being penned into an underground cellar with hundreds of other people. He had sneaked out after about forty minutes and escaped into the open air. It was nearly an hour before Billy and Chloe realised he was missing and, after they had found him, it had taken Findo the best part of another hour to convince them, quite truthfully, that he had not minded sitting outside alone on his birthday while they danced.

Following the club, they had gone on to all-night café for more food and drink. There, they met a pair of West Indian girls who invited them to a party. The night got more hectic from that point on. The party was in a big warehouse converted into a dozen luxury flats, each of which seemed to be taking part in the celebrations. There was a contrasting atmosphere in each flat, with different music, food, drink and drugs. Findo, Billy and Chloe ended up in the 'chill out' flat, where they had listened to weird soundscapes being created by an amateur

DJ with an eclectic collection of CDs and vinyl albums. Findo had also got more stoned than he had ever been before in his life after being fed a constant supply of joints rolled with hydroponically-grown Dutch skunk.

Sometime later he had wandered outside into a courtyard area for some fresh air. It was approaching dawn and the cold January sky was clear. Hemmed in by the buildings around him, Findo decided that he wanted to see the view. But rather than go back in and work his way through the still ongoing party, Findo decided to climb to the roof via the outside of the three-storey building.

Soon a small crowd had gathered in the courtyard and leant out of the windows as Findo used a ladder of drainpipes and ledges to work his way up to roof level. Shouts of encouragement and warning echoed around the enclosed area. Some of the more sober partygoers tried to persuade him to climb down or get into one of the windows. Others urged him on, partly in the hope of seeing him succeed, partly out of pure devilment. Billy stood white-faced on a balcony with Chloe's arm tight around her.

There had been a nasty moment when one of Findo's feet slipped on a wet section of angled down-pipe and he dangled for a few seconds by one hand. But he recovered himself and continued with dogged persistence, eventually pulling himself into a gully in the angle of the roof. From there it had been an easy scramble to the ridge and he had pulled a can of lager out to toast the cheering onlookers as he watched the sun come up, later sliding down to a welcoming roof-light and a scared and furious Billy.

 Since that trip, life in Oxford had been dull. Morris had run out of leads for the time being and there had been no jobs since before Christmas. Apart from trips to the video shop, supermarket and library, Findo had hardly ventured out since returning from Bristol. There had been little incentive; outside the rain never seemed to stop, while the flat was cosy and comfortable.

When the phone went, Findo jumped with surprise. He rarely got calls in the middle of the day. Grabbing the receiver quickly, he took a deep breath to calm his nerves before answering.

"Yeah?"

"Findo."

"Hey, John. What's up?"

"Trouble, mate."

"What's wrong?"

There was a sigh. "Bad problems. It's Colin," said John. "He's been nicked."

"What!"

"Yeah. Happened a few days back."

"A few days?" said Findo. "Why didn't you tell me? What's happened? How did they get him?"

"Hey," said John. "Just shut up and listen for a minute, okay?"

"Okay."

There was a short pause.

"He got busted by Customs and Excise," said John. "They'd got wind of some duty-free ciggies Colin had. They were in the back of one of his workshops at the garage. He doesn't normally store anything there but we'd had a consignment come in late and there was a problem with the normal place. So we stuck them in the garage for a couple of nights. But either someone squealed or they've been on to Colin for a while. I wasn't around but there was a whole mob of them came in. They must have been watching and waiting because Colin was late in that morning and they came in minutes after he'd arrived. Went through the place like they were the fucking SAS. Stripped everything, took away order books, supplies for the garage, everything."

He sighed. "Not a good day. But you know Colin, he's careful and he keeps a good brief. We thought we'd get him out on bail. We had the court hearing today and we thought it would be a formality."

"What happened?" asked Findo.

John grunted. "They brought in the heavy brigade. There were a lot of them in court. Mainly customs but a few police as well. I didn't recognise a couple of them; I think they might be Special Branch or something. They had extra charges ready too, not just to do with smuggling. They're trying to make out he's been money laundering and that he's behind all sorts of scams. They dropped a few big hints as well. I think they're trying to nail the local drugs trade on him."

"Oh. But that's not what he's into, is it?"

"Well, not really. He's been middleman in a few deals but he's not the big fish. There's a group with Polish connections that do most of the smack importing. Colin's . . ."

"John!" Findo cut across John's words. "You want to talk about this on the phone?"

John gave a quiet laugh. "Don't worry. I'm in a phone box near Dubmore. I'm going out of town for a couple of days."

"What's going to happen?"

"Well," said John, "he's on remand now so that means he's banged up. They've got him out at East Allonby. I'm closing up what I can of things but the trouble is, once they've got your number it can be hard work keeping in the clear. The longer they can keep Colin locked up, the easier it'll be for them to find something that'll get him put away for a long time. And the trouble is, if they look in the right place they'll find enough. We need to get him out. I've got a couple of ideas. You might be able to help me with them, that's why I wanted to talk."

They met two days later at another service station, this time off the A1 motorway just outside Durham. The journey there was one of the longest drives Findo had done and it had been raining all the way. He was nearly an hour late and pulled into the car park with relief. He parked the Fiesta outside the services and went to find the cafeteria.

John was at a window seat with an empty coffee pot in front of him and a novel in one hand. He looked up as Findo approached the table and frowned slightly before smiling. He stood up and held out a hand. As Findo took it to shake, John reached out with the other arm and gripped his shoulder.

"Bloody hell, lad, you've grown up."

Findo shrugged. "Yeah?"

John held him at arms' length. "Yeah, you have. Last time I saw you, you were still a scrawny kid. You still look scrawny but you've grown up." He ran a rough hand across Findo's cheek. "And what's this? Stubble?"

"Get off." Findo pulled away with an embarrassed smile.

John laughed. "No, seriously, it's good to see you again, lad. Bloody good." He looked across at the counter. "Sit down. I'll get some more coffee and some grub. You hungry? What do you fancy, burger and chips, fish and chips?"

Findo collapsed into one of the plastic bucket seats. "Whatever."

Once Findo had shovelled the last chips into his mouth and drained his coffee, he looked around, glancing at the other tables. "Where can we talk?"

"Not here," said John. "Let's go for a drive. Find somewhere quiet."

They went out and got into the Fiesta. Findo took them back to the motorway and rejoined the northbound carriageway. The traffic was heavy and the spray from the wet surface rose in a continuous curtain. Findo slotted in behind a line of trucks.

"So how are we going to get him out?"

John sighed. "I'm not exactly sure. Like I said to you, I've tied up a few loose ends. Most of the really important paperwork –

bankbooks, stuff like that – was in a safe in a place that we've got out of town. I managed to clear that out, left it for safekeeping in a place in Newcastle. Should be well out of the way there. But they've got quite a bit of evidence from the garage and a couple of Colin's other businesses. We always tried to keep things looking clean on the surface but I'm worried that if they dig too hard they'll get something. And once they've got a lever to work on, they'll keep on poking and probing. That's what I'm worried about, the books and stuff they've already got. If they're going to try and pin these money laundering charges on him they must think they've got something to go on already." John stretched his hands as if he was itching to get them around something. "So that's what we need to deal with, those books."

Findo frowned. "The books?"

"Yeah," said John. "Without them, they've got precious little to go on. They've got the cigarettes but that's nothing major. A good brief can come up with a story. They'll get confiscated and Colin will probably get a fine, suspended sentence maybe, but that's it. He's got a pretty good record, should be able to put a convincing case. Then, once he's out, that's it."

"That's it?"

"Yeah, time to call it a day," said John. "He's been careful, Colin has. He's got a good whack salted away. Plenty really. More than enough to cut and run. And there's no point staying now they've got his number. More sensible to cash in the pension plan and go and enjoy the sun somewhere. Trouble is, we've got to get him out first."

Findo shook his head. "So what's this about the books? How you going to deal with them? I thought you wanted to get Colin out?"

John laughed. "Findo, I'm not talking about a fucking jail-break. I wasn't planning on trying to get Colin out that way. That's not something you tackle lightly. Try and bust him out and you'll have every copper in the country on your case. What I want to do is deal with the evidence. If we can do something about that, they'll have a hard job putting together a case that'll stand up in court. If they lose the evidence, they'll have to drop the charges. That's how we're going to get Colin out the slammer."

"So how do we do that?"

John gave a dry laugh. "That's the six million dollar question. I know where the investigation is based. The customs boys are working out of an office next door to Alexander Cross. I figure we need to get in there. Then there's two options – remove the books or just put a match to them. The advantage of torching the place as well is that then they can't be certain we were after Colin's files, could be any aggrieved punter."

"How do we get in?"

John grinned. "Ah, that, Findo, is what I'm hoping you can tell me. I've had a good look at the place and I've got a few ideas. Problem is, the security is pretty tight, plus there's people around most hours of the day and night. I was hoping you would come and have a look at the place with me. See what you reckon."

Findo swallowed. "Go home? You mean I can come back?"

Findo arrived home the next day. It was strange driving into the city after more than four years away. As he drove along through Garvock Hill and turned off by the hospital to drop down through Chapel Bank, he felt excited but uneasy.

But as he drank in the familiar sights, he could not help feeling a sense of anticlimax. It felt like such a major event to be coming home but there was no one to notice. The city's absence had been an ache in his heart for years and returning should have been a momentous occasion. People he knew should have been lining the streets with bunting and balloons to cheer him on; instead there was just the everyday traffic of people going about their business, oblivious to the significance of the moment.

It was also obvious that the city itself had not been frozen in time while waiting for his return. Although Findo had been away for several years, subconsciously he had still expected the city to be the way he had left it. His memories of his home turf had never faded and, while he felt different, his images of the city were unchanged. But instead, there were new shop fronts in Trinity Parade and a roundabout at the top of Fort Hill that had not been there when he left. A couple of trees had gone from beside the road at the junction with Connor Terrace and the beginning section of Dubmore Road was completely different. Some rundown industrial units had been cleared to make way for a new housing development. The Dubmore Arms pub had been converted into a florists' shop and a mobile phone centre. The layout of the road had changed and a team of workmen were busy putting new traffic islands into the middle of the carriageway.

As he drove along, Findo felt slightly cheated; it seemed wrong that the city had moved on without him. He had thought the city was his but its life had continued without pause in his absence. He was just another ant in the hill, as insignificant as the others.

He left his car in a back street behind Corporation Road. His flat was still empty, although John had told him the offices on the floors below were now rented out. But Findo did not go in straight away.

Instead, he got his jacket out of the car and put it on. It was a lot colder here than in Oxford and he had forgotten quite how easily the wind here could slice through clothing. At least it was not raining. For a rare change, the clouds had even parted to expose ragged glimpses of the pale sky above.

Findo found a passageway back onto Corporation Road. There was a faint bounce in his step as he rounded the corner of the alley and came onto the pavement. It felt better to be on foot. Although he knew the roads like the back of his hand, it was as a pedestrian not a driver.

Looking back, Findo could see the bulk of the police headquarters rising up on the other side of the Alexandra Cross junction. The offices that John wanted him to look at were nearby. But first he had another mission to accomplish.

He settled into a steady pace, head half-lowered as he headed west along Corporation Road. He glanced sideways as he passed other pedestrians. Few people in the city had known him well and John said he looked different. But Findo was happy to stay anonymous. He wanted to get his bearings, get a feel for his home again before he was ready to talk to anyone. There was also the matter of Colin Speed's incarceration to sort out. If he was going to be involved in anything designed to help get his old boss out of prison, then the fewer people who knew that the now-famous Findo Gask had returned the better.

It did not take long to reach Newtown; the distances seemed slightly shorter than Findo remembered them. A couple of minutes later he was in Denmark Street. He approached Abby's house cautiously, not sure whether or not he was going to try knocking on the door.

But as he reached the front gate and stopped, the door opened. A middle-aged woman in a cheap nylon housecoat and pink slippers came out with a carrier bag of rubbish that she stuffed into an overflowing bin.

The woman saw Findo stood at the gate and frowned. "Yeah? What you want?"

Findo flushed. "I'm . . . sorry," he said. "I was just looking for someone."

The woman's eyes narrowed and she took a long drag on the cigarette hanging from one corner of her mouth. "Who?"

Findo shrugged awkwardly. "A friend," he said. "She used to live here."

The woman's grim expression relaxed slightly. "What was her name, then?"

"Abby."

She nodded. "Too late, love. They're not here any more. You should have come by a couple of years back."

Findo frowned. "They've left?"

The woman laughed with bitter humour. "Quick, aren't you?"

Findo scowled and was about to turn away when a thought struck him. "You don't know where they've gone do you?"

The woman smiled and Findo's heart rose for a moment.

"No." She took another puff on her cigarette. "No idea."

Findo left Denmark Street in a daze. Ever since he realised that he was going to be coming home, the thought of seeing Abby again had been lodged in the back of his mind. On the way into the city he had found himself looking for her on the city streets.

Part of him had warned against risking an encounter but by the time he got into the city centre he had known that he had to try. He had walked to Denmark Street with a mixture of excitement and fear tumbling round in his stomach. It had taken considerable will to force his legs to make the approach to her house without either turning around the opposite way – or running full-speed to her door.

Findo had not known whether Abby would close the door in his face or throw her arms around his neck. It had occurred to him that she would not be home but the idea that she might no longer live in Denmark Street had not even crossed his mind.

To begin with, he walked automatically, not thinking about where he was going. But as he made his way down St Patrick's Road and approached a familiar cut-through towards Dubmore Road, he realised where he was going.

As Findo had driven into the city earlier in the day he had only glanced at Frances Reid's house. His attention had been caught by the new housing development on the other side of the road and the workmen busy in the middle of the road between the rows of traffic cones.

Now, turning into the driveway to her small house, he noticed the state of the garden. The bushes and the privet hedge along the front were much more unkempt than he remembered them. Wet autumn leaves were rotting where they lay across the brick paths leading to either side of the house. Weeds had sprouted unchecked amongst the gravel of the main drive and there was an air of neglect to the whole garden that would never once have been permitted. For although a freethinker, Frances Reid had been a scrupulous gardener.

Findo frowned as he noted the changes but continued on his accustomed route around the side of the house. At the kitchen door he stopped and rapped three times on the glass, one slow beat and then two in quick succession.

There was silence for a while. Findo peered through the glass but could not see anyone in the kitchen or any sign of movement in the hall beyond. He was about to knock again when, faintly, he heard a voice from somewhere inside.

Findo tried the kitchen door but it was locked. Then he remembered the old hiding place and turned round. The old rowan tree stood next to the hedge. Reaching around the back of the trunk, he found the nail driven into the tree beneath the stump of a sawn-off branch. The key was on the nail.

Findo gave another triple knock as he opened the door. "Hello?"

"In here, Findo."

The voice came from the direction of the front room. It sounded weaker than Findo remembered.

He shut the door and made his way through the kitchen and down the hall, following the same route as he had many times before. The lounge door was closed and Findo opened it cautiously. Inside, the room looked as he remembered it but Frances Reid did not.

Findo frowned. Her face looked wrong. She was sat awkwardly and her hair was whiter than it had been. There was also a tremor in her age-spotted left hand that was new to Findo.

"Don't scowl at me, young man."

"Sorry," said Findo.

"I should think so," said Mrs Reid. "I'd have thought that you could at least smile if you're going to take the trouble to come and see me again after an absence of four years. And don't stand in the doorway. Come in and say hello properly."

Findo grinned sheepishly. "Okay."

As he stepped forwards, Mrs Reid levered herself up out of her chair. She did it awkwardly, twisting to the right and pushing up with one arm. Findo moved in to try and help but she jerked him away with her head.

"Off," she grunted. The old librarian held her left arm tucked across her body and as her legs straightened, her back seemed to bend so that she came to her feet with her spine doubled over. With obvious effort, she pulled herself upright and stood in front of Findo. She lifted her head to meet his eye and smiled as she realised how much further she had to look up now.

"There we are," said Mrs Reid. "Now we can say hello properly."

She put her right arm around Findo and pulled him into a bony embrace. Her dry lips brushed his cheek.

Findo let his hands rest on her elbows. "What have you done to your back?"

Mrs Reid smiled dryly. "I haven't done anything to my back, it's what my back has done to me."

"What do you mean?"

She chuckled. "It's called rheumatoid arthritis. I could give you some of the details but, to put it bluntly, the truth is that my back's packing up. I'm getting old and it's just about had enough and wants a rest."

Findo looked worried. "Packing up?"

He looked at her face, perturbed. Her smile seemed lopsided and there was an odd expression to one eye. Her left arm was still tucked across her chest as well.

Mrs Reid followed the movement of his eyes and smiled gently. "I had a stroke," she said. "That's why I look funny. The muscles down my left side don't quite dance to the same drummer as the rest of me any more."

Findo looked aghast. "A stroke? When? Why didn't you tell me?"

The librarian shook her head. "There wasn't much point, dear. You were a long way away and there wasn't much you could do to help. I couldn't see the point in burdening you with an old woman's aches and pains. I found it much more pleasant to write to you about more interesting things."

Findo shook his head. "But a stroke, that's like a heart attack isn't it? Why, how come you had a stroke?"

Mrs Reid laughed. She reached behind her with her good arm. "Come on, you can help me sit down again."

Findo darted around her left side. He took hold of her left arm gingerly as if not sure whether he should touch it. He rested his right arm solicitously around her shoulders and helped take her weight as she lowered herself back into the chair.

As Mrs Reid sank back down, Findo dropped into a crouch at her side. She reached across with her right hand and patted his hands. "Don't worry, Findo."

"But a stroke?" he said. "And your back?"

She smiled. "I'm getting old, Findo. I was seventy-six in September. This body of mine has seen a lot of action and it won't last forever. My back's on the way out, I've had one mild stroke and my

318

eyesight's not what it was. But don't worry; I may be on the last stretch but I've had a good run. I've no time for regrets."

Findo left about half an hour later. He would have stayed for longer but was given his marching orders.

"I need my sleep," said Mrs Reid. "I'm very glad that you came and if you would like to come back again tomorrow morning, or another day, I would be very pleased to see you. But right now, it's time for my afternoon sleep and I doubt if you would get much more sense out of me if you stayed."

He nodded reluctantly. He looked back as he left the room. Mrs Reid's eyes were already closing but her mouth opened slightly and he heard her soft-spoken farewell.

"I am glad you came, Findo. I missed your visits."

Turning back onto Dubmore Road, he began to walk in a brisk stride, leaving fears of age and infirmity behind him.

At least he knew what had happened to Abby. According to Mrs Reid, after leaving school, Abby had gone on to sixth form up at Garvock College. Then, the September before last, she had gone off to university in Edinburgh to study engineering. She would be there now, part-way through the spring term of her second year.

Abby's mother had moved from her old home nearly two years ago. Suzanne McGee had met a visiting archaeologist through her job at the city museum. There had been a brief and hurried courtship after which the newlyweds spent three months on a combined research trip and honeymoon in Central America – with Suzanne nominally employed as the academic's personal assistant. After returning to the city, Suzanne got her old job back and her new husband had taken a senior post in the council's archaeological unit. They now lived in a small village about ten miles north of the city.

Abby had written a couple of times to Mrs Reid since her mother's remarriage. Her most recent communication had been a card at Christmas. There was a return address that Mrs Reid had written into her notebook and Findo copied it carefully before he left.

Findo spent a total of fifteen hours over the following afternoon, night and morning reconnoitring the office building occupied by the Customs and Excise team that was investigating Colin Speed. It was a cold and wet experience but still enjoyable. The air had a taste that, if not pleasant, was familiar. The layout of the streets was imprinted into Findo's brain and as familiar to him as a favourite coat.

To begin with, he quickly explored the surroundings of the customs building, establishing its footprint and assessing all possible entrances and exits. The office block was new. It had not been there when Findo left the city and looked purpose-built. It stood immediately next to the police headquarters at Alexander Cross but was not linked to it. The front of the customs building opened onto the western end of Packhouse Street. A small service lane ran between the new building and a car showroom on its right, linking it with a narrow lane at the back of the block.

A walled compound enclosed the five-storey building. The brick walls were about twelve feet high and topped with strands of razor wire supported on metal brackets that angled out over the street. Surveillance cameras were mounted on each corner of the compound and on the building itself. The only openings in the wall were at the front, an entrance and exit to the car park inside. There were fire exits at either side of the building and a ramp leading down to an underground car park. Apart from that, there was a single entrance to the building itself and very little cover inside the compound.

Once he was satisfied that he had established the layout of the building, Findo spent most of the following night watching it from various vantage points, including the roof of the car showroom and a fire exit in an alley on the opposite side of Packhouse Street. He calculated how many people were inside through the night and whether it was ever left completely unoccupied. He tried to see if there were any weak spots in the fields of vision covered by the cameras. In the morning, he watched as the normal complement of office staff arrived for the day and noted where they parked and how many of them there were. Over the following couple of hours, he observed visitors coming and going, judging the type of people they were and the kind of clothes they wore as well as how they were checked by the security guard now stationed in a cubicle by the entrance into the walled compound.

It was nearly eleven-thirty when he returned to the flat to change out of his damp clothes. It had just started to rain again and he was dog-tired. He rang John quickly before stepping into the shower.

"We need to talk."

"You've had a look?"

"Yeah."

"Do you want to meet now?"

"Later. I need some food and a couple of hours' sleep first."

"Okay. I'll meet you at the Turk's Head at say . . . three?"

"Three's okay but come here. There's somewhere else I want to look at as well. Meet me round the back. We can go in my car. Bring some fishing gear."

There was a short pause. "Sure," said John. "I'll see you at three."

It was still pouring as Findo and John stood on the bridge over the Allonby. Beneath them, brown surging waters forced their swollen passage between the pillars of the old bridge. A small tree was jammed across the gap between two of the supports and its ragged, ripped branches were waving wildly as powerful currents tried to clear the obstacle from their path. Most of the banks of the river were completely submerged. There used to be a depth marker in the river not far from the bridge but there was no way of telling if it was still there; the water level was at least two feet above where it should have been.

Findo and John both wore long waterproofs. The Fiesta was parked just off the road on the south side of the bridge. In the back were a couple of fishing rods and some other equipment, all innocent.

"You sure about this?" said John. "The other place isn't a goer?"

Findo shook his head. "It's possible but I wouldn't want to try it. This is easier."

John was silent for a while.

"What do you think?" asked Findo.

"You're completely serious aren't you?"

"Yeah, of course. Why not?"

John stared at the view. "It's pretty radical, Findo."

"You don't reckon it would work?"

John turned his water-running face to Findo and grinned. "I didn't say that."

He stared again at the prison. It lay on the other side of a large ploughed field. Through the downpour, they could clearly see the main buildings and the huddle of workshops and other ancillary buildings on the other side of the perimeter fences.

John frowned. "It's not a bad idea," he said, "just . . . dramatic. I've never heard of getting someone out that way before."

Findo shrugged. "Just seems a good opportunity. We've got the perfect weather. It wouldn't work normally."

"And you seriously reckon that your part would work?"

Findo frowned. "I wouldn't suggest it otherwise." He gave a small smile. "It's the novelty factor," he said. "They'll never expect us to try anything like this. I'll be in and out before they know what's happening."

John gave him a considering look. "You're not just doing this for the hell of it are you?"

37. Bird release

It took another three days before John and Findo were ready. They met in a quiet pub in Chapel Bank for their final pre-mission conference.

When Findo walked in it was nearly three in the afternoon. As he tossed his sodden jacket onto a seat beside John, he noticed a large, familiar figure in the corner.

"Alright, Albie."

The big man stood up and grinned. He had gone completely bald in the four years since Findo had last seen him but the lack of hair did not make his presence any less intimidating.

Albie held out a muscled and tattooed arm. "Welcome back, mate. Phil isn't it?"

Findo smiled. "Yeah. Probably." He glanced at John. "Mickey not around these days?"

Out of the corner of his eyes, Findo saw Albie's brows furrow. John shook his head.

"Er, no," he said. "Didn't I tell you?"

"What?"

"It happened a week or so before Colin got busted. I guess I forgot with everything else that happened."

"What happened?"

John sighed. "I'm sorry, Findo, but he's dead. He was in a car on the motorway. Wasn't even nicked. He was doing a ton in the fast lane. Had a blow-out and lost it. The road was wet and he just flipped the motor. Died on the way to hospital. Ironic really, all those times he's got chased by the police and done all kind of crazy stunts, then he goes and kills himself in a stupid accident like that."

Findo sat down quietly. It was strange to think that Mickey Dunn was dead. They had never been close friends, probably in the main because of their difference in ages, but they had always got on well. Mickey had been one of the brightest lights on the street but he had been one of the few people Findo trusted. And although he had not tried seeing Mickey since coming back to the city, Findo had been expecting to meet up with him again before long. To discover that he was too late to ever see Mickey again took away a little of his enthusiasm for the job in hand. He had nothing against Albie but, when he and John had spoken about getting a driver for the job, Findo had just assumed it would be Mickey.

John stood up. "I'll get you a drink. What do you want?"

"Huh?" Findo looked blank for a moment. "Oh, just a Coke."

Findo and John huddled over the table looking at their list, trying to think if they had overlooked anything. Albie sat at the end of the table facing the rest of the pub. He had a pint in one hand and a smile on his face but no one else came too near.

"Okay," said Findo. "I can't think of anything. I've gone over all the equipment I want several times. It's all in the lock-up behind Jubilee Square with the van. You're happy that your stuff is set?"

John nodded. "Yeah. We went out yesterday. Took an Environment Agency van and some measuring posts and stuff – pretending we were checking the bridge. We can blow it whenever we want. I'll use a transmitter from the other side of the river. I can do it from those old sheds we saw."

"What if it doesn't go off?"

"It will," said John. "If the transmitter fails, I've got a backup switch down by the bridge."

Findo frowned. "Isn't that risky?"

John shook his head. "Don't worry, I've done worse – and that was with bullets going over my head. This'll work."

"Everything's organised inside?"

John nodded. "We've got a bloke inside who's got a mobile. He'll give us a call. If that fails or he can't get a signal, they've got a torch to flash from the window." He shook his head. "I'm more worried about you. It sounds simple enough the way you talk about it but it's still going to be pretty hairy. And once you're in there you're going to be on your own. We won't be able to help."

Findo smiled when he went outside; it was still raining and the forecast was for it to continue without break. He stared up into the sky and grinned. The more the water came, the easier it would be.

He drove back to the flat and dried off, then set his alarm clock and climbed into bed. He did not sleep much but dozed off and on for the next six hours, occasionally turning over to read his book when his mind was too active. It was just after ten in the evening when he turned the alarm off and got up. He dressed quickly but carefully and went into the kitchen for a quick bowl of cereal. Into his bag he slung a handful of chocolate bars and a couple of bananas, plus a couple of cans of Pepsi Max.

Fifteen minutes later he was in the Fiesta and driving across the city to East Park. He left the car in a side road and made his way on foot to a block of lock-up garages near the shopping precinct at Jubilee Square. He only passed one other pedestrian on the way and there were less cars about than usual. The roads were awash and there were deep puddles on the concrete apron in front of the garages.

Within twenty minutes of leaving the flat he was driving out of the garage. He left the up-and-over door open, an invitation to winos, druggies and tramps seeking somewhere out of the rain. He had taken care not to leave anything behind but, if the police did somehow trace the Astra van back to the garage, there would be little chance of them finding evidence once the lock-up had been open to local dossers and vandals – plus the elements – for a night.

He drove carefully, not so slow as to attract attention but only just above the speed limit. He headed west to begin with and turned onto Castle Drive. Traffic on the ring road was light and it did not take long before he was onto the motorway. Findo turned the blue Astra east and settled down to a steady sixty. Sheets of spray surrounded every vehicle on the road and even with the wiper blades on double speed it was hard to see more than a few yards ahead. Findo gripped the small van's steering wheel tightly in his gloved hands, driving nearly blind, working on the hope that he would at least be able to swing onto the hard shoulder if something in front braked suddenly.

It was with a feeling of relief that he saw the blue signs for the next junction and took the slip road up to the East Allonby junction. At the roundabout, Findo took the first exit, turning onto the A-road that bypassed the village to the north. There was hardly any traffic about here and Findo's stomach gave a lurch as he passed a police car parked in a lay-by. But the officer inside was busy pouring a drink from a flask and did not even look up as the Astra went by.

A few miles further on, Findo passed the turning for the B-road leading to the bridge over the Allonby where he had stood with John a few days earlier. He ignored it and continued on to the next junction, swinging right onto an unmarked service road leading to an electricity substation.

Where the concrete road reached the river it turned left to follow the bank. Findo's lights were already off as the Astra rolled to a halt on the bend. There was a thin strip of grassy ground between him and the swollen river, which was practically at the top of its banks, but no fence or other barrier.

The car gave a little jolt as its wheels touched the low kerb. Findo got out of the car and went round to the back. He opened the doors and pulled out the first bag of equipment. He changed quickly, stripping off in the rain and climbing into the black wetsuit, throwing the clothes he had been wearing into the van.

Once zipped into the wetsuit, he pulled on boots, a neoprene balaclava and a climber's harness, followed by a spraydeck. He put his own lifejacket and gloves down on the roadway, next to his tool belt, paddle and two other bags. Then he pulled the two kayaks from the back of the van and placed them with the other equipment.

Satisfied that he had everything ready, Findo got back into the car. He took a mobile phone from the glove box and dialled the number memorised earlier.

"Yes?"

"I'm ready to move."

"Okay. We've got the all clear from inside. I'll hit the button."

"Right."

Findo switched off the phone. A few seconds later, somewhere off to his right, he heard a dull thump like a car door slamming. Findo smiled.

He wound down both of the van's front windows and then started its engine again. Putting the vehicle into gear, he gingerly release the clutch and let the vehicle move until he felt it bump up over the kerb. As soon as the front wheels were up he jammed on both the foot brake and hand brake. The Astra slid a fraction but stopped.

Findo climbed out carefully and stood on the wet grass next to the van listening. All he could hear was the steady hiss of rain around him and the harder drumming of it hitting the vehicle's metal skin. There were no lights moving anywhere nearby. There was a faint orange glow in the sky coming from the direction of East Allonby but no other signs of life.

Cautiously, he reached into the van and took off the handbrake. He stepped away from the driver's door and moved round behind the vehicle. Bracing himself against the concrete roadway, he lent one shoulder against the van and pushed.

The Astra moved more easily than he expected and Findo almost lost his balance. The van rolled forwards across the narrow strip of wet grass and, by the time the rear wheels bounced up and over the kerb, the front bumper was already above the edge of the river.

Findo stepped back and gave the van a last push with one foot to keep it moving. The Astra seemed to pause for a moment at the top of the bank, as if drawing breath. Then it rolled on and slid quietly into the rapidly moving, dark depths. The swift current tugged the nose of the van sideways as soon as it entered the river. Through the darkness, just before the vehicle disappeared, Findo caught a last glimpse of the Astra rolling over as it succumbed to the summons of the swollen Allonby.

It only took a few minutes for Findo to load up. He put the tool belt around his waist, above the spray deck. He tucked his lifejacket and gloves into one kayak, along with his paddle and the lighter of the two equipment bags. He removed a head-torch from the second bag and put it on before stuffing the heavy-duty nylon carryall into the other canoe.

He lifted each kayak over the barbed wire fence dividing the roadway from the adjoining field then hopped over after them. He took each kayak in turn, carrying them along the inside edge of the hedge running between the field and the Allonby. After stumbling a few times, he turned his head-torch on to give himself a little light; he was shielded in part from the prison by an embankment and reasoned that the light would not show up far through the pouring rain anyway. The sodden ground was like a quagmire in places and, by the end of the first trip, Findo was splattered in mud to above his knees. He could also feel the water seeping into his boots and down the neck of his wetsuit.

On the other side of the field an embankment led up to the B-road and the bridge over the Allonby. At the bottom of the rough slope was another barbed wire fence and Findo carefully lifted each kayak over.

He had just followed them when he suddenly heard the swooshing hiss of a vehicle on the road above. Findo dropped into the wet grass, reaching up to turn off his head-torch as he buried his face in the bank. The vehicle slowed slightly as it moved onto the bridge but kept going. Findo lay still for a couple of minutes, listening to the sound of its passage merging back into the noise of the rain.

He rolled onto his back, tugged his balaclava back to uncover his ears and listened again. There was no sound of other vehicles or alarms. But over the splashing of the rain there was another noise. Somewhere close by, large volumes of water were gushing.

Findo rolled onto his front and scrambled quickly up the embankment. He glanced left and right and crossed the road then slid into a crouch on the other side and paused.

Off to his right, the lights of the prison shone weakly through the rain. Apart from that, he could see no other lights nearby or signs of anything out of the ordinary except for the sound of the torrent beneath him. Somewhere at the bottom of the slope water was pouring with great speed into the field that lay between the road and the prison.

Findo listened for a moment. John's explosives had clearly done the job. The charges planted the previous day had breached the raised bank along the edge of the field. Already strained by the weight of the swollen river on the other side, the explosion had easily punched a small hole through the barrier. The pressure of the water had done the rest. As it gushed through, the torrent had rapidly widened the opening and swept away a section of the bank over fifty yards long, allowing the waters of the Allonby to flood through. Already, tens of thousands of gallons of water had poured into the field. Blocked to the east by the solid embankment that took the road up towards the bridge, the flood had swept across the already-sodden field. Unchecked by the wire fences, the water had surged into the grounds of the prison, which stood inside a curve of the river. Already, the water around the buildings was nearly a foot deep – and rising fast.

It took nearly five minutes to get the kayaks up and over the embankment. The grass on the slope up to the road was saturated. Climbing unburdened was tricky enough; to make the ascent carrying or dragging a kayak and equipment felt close to impossible as Findo's feet repeatedly slipped and slid in the slick grass and soft mud.

But after several aborted attempts, Findo made it to the top with the first kayak. He took it quickly to the other side of the road and laid it ready. Then he returned for the other canoe and eventually laid it next to the other.

The next stage of the operation took nearly four minutes. First, Findo fitted the clamps to hold the two boats together, side-by-side. Next, he prepared his tools and rope, arranging them on the tool belt and around his lifejacket. Then he slid down the embankment to the edge of the flooded field and snipped the top two strands on the barbed wire fence – the bottom one already being well under the water. Finally, after climbing back up and getting into the right-hand kayak, Findo attached his spraydeck and grasped his paddle, ready to launch.

He took a last look around as he sat poised on the top of the embankment. It looked as though there were more lights on in the prison buildings now but it was hard to be certain through the curtains of heavy rain.

Then, holding his paddle in a brace position, Findo lent forward and flicked his hips. The two canoes lurched slightly and began to slide. As they moved, Findo bent quickly to the left, shifting his weight so more of it was over the second canoe.

The descent took barely seconds. There was a quick splash as the canoes hit the water and shot forward. The left-hand canoe lifted up again and Findo felt himself tipping. Instantly, he lent back to lower his centre of gravity and dug down hard with the flat of the paddle blade, pushing against the surface of the water to regain his balance.

The double craft rocked for a moment and then settled down into the fast-moving water. As it did so, the current took them and span them right, shooting them away from the road and into the middle of the field, towards the prison.

Findo used his paddle lightly. There was little need to use it for more than steering and balance. There was still so much water pouring over the field and through into the prison grounds that Findo was already travelling fast enough.

He was still several hundred yards away when the perimeter lights around the prison fences suddenly went out. Findo grinned and steered straight for the main buildings. It only took a few minutes to reach the first fence. It was still standing but the posts had bent under the strain of the torrent hitting them.

Findo span the kayaks so that his one was against the fence, pinned by the weight of the water. He reached down to his tool belt and unclipped the bolt-cutters that had been lying across his lap. He worked quickly, snipping through the links. He cut up for about two feet then sideways for about four, working the canoes backwards as he did so. Lastly, Findo made another downward cut.

Then, using the noses of the kayaks to push the flap down, he slid his two canoes into the gap and bent across the deck of his craft. The cut ends of the fence scraped his back and shoulders as he went through but nothing caught and a few seconds later he reached the inner perimeter fence. He repeated the process with the bolt-cutters and then he was inside, floating on the storm current towards the prison buildings, each one now surrounded by more than two feet of water.

Findo laughed as he steered left. He rode the current towards the first building and then paddled for its corner. The water was turbulent where it turned around the block and Findo's kayaks bucked and rolled as he fought his way through the eddies.

Once through the rough patch, he quickly passed the end of the building. On his right was another fence and beyond that the main exercise yard. On the far side of the yard was the main prison building – a grim Victorian jail with tiny windows and two wings that enclosed its entrance like muscular arms. But Findo was not interested in the main building or first accommodation block and headed on.

There was another patch of rough water on the corner of the second block but not as bad as the first. Then Findo was floating along in the lee of the accommodation wing, sheltered from the main flow of water, which was rising more gradually now.

He paddled along briskly, counting windows on the floor above him. The windows above him were nearly all dark. There had been a couple of emergency lights on somewhere inside the corners of the block and where Findo guessed what was a wardens' office overlooked the yard. There were also security lights beneath the eaves of the block but their glare hardly reached ground level – or what would have normally been ground level – through the pouring rain.

When Findo had counted five windows above him, he lifted his paddle and moved right against the side of the building. He turned his head torch on and ran his hand across the brickwork of the accommodation block, coasting on a gentle current.

He had gone about five yards when he found the string. It was hanging from the seventh window on the third floor. It ran taut into the water, held by whatever Speed and his cellmate had tied to the end.

Findo gave a firm but careful tug. A few seconds later, the string jerked up.

Findo gave one more pull on the cord and then cut it off at water level with his knife. Then he freed the coil of climbing rope that had been around his shoulders and lashed the two together.

He gave another two tugs on the string and then watched as it began to lift the climbing rope towards the broken window above. Once the end of the rope had disappeared inside, Findo gave the pair inside a few moments to secure it. Then he leant over into the cockpit of the second canoe and reached into the heavy equipment bag. He pulled out a small angle grinder, which he lashed carefully to a loop in the rope.

Findo gave the rope a couple of swift tugs and watched as the angle grinder began to rise through the rain, pulled towards the opening above. The casing of the heavy-duty battery pack scraped against the wall but the power tool stayed attached to the rope and soon disappeared from sight.

From twenty feet below, Findo had no trouble hearing the whine of the machine and then a deeper groan as it cut into the steel bars at the cell's small window. A few sparks flickered briefly in the night air before they were extinguished.

As he waited, floating on the dark waters below, Findo used his paddle to back the canoes a little way along the wall, so he was no longer directly beneath the cell window. He glanced around, as he bobbed lightly against the brickwork. The perimeter lights were still off and he could see no sign of trouble from either inside or outside the buildings.

It took less time than he had expected for Speed to be able to cut the bars. Findo heard a soft call from above and then watched as a head emerged from the window. Findo flashed his head-torch a couple of times and gave an answering whistle.

Speed's head disappeared back inside. A moment later the end of the climbing rope came snaking back down, this time without the angle grinder attached. Speed's legs followed, waggling in midair as he worked his body out. There was a brief pause as his shoulders came through and then Findo's ex-boss came sliding down the rope in what was essentially a controlled fall. He landed with a loud splash a few feet from the nose of the canoes.

Speed surfaced again quickly. "Fuck, that's cold!" He grinned at Findo. "Fancy seeing you here."

Findo smiled and handed Speed a lifejacket. "Get that on," he said. "It could be rough out there and some of the currents are fast. You get swept out towards the river, you might disappear for good."

"Aye, aye, captain." Speed tugged the lifejacket on as he stood with the water lapping round his midriff. "No trouble getting in then?"

"No," said Findo. "I said it would work."

Speed grabbed hold of the side of the empty canoe and went to climb in.

"Hold on," said Findo. "Not yet. Get this on. Step into it like it was a skirt and pull it up round your waist."

Speed took the proffered spraydeck. He looked at in puzzlement for a moment and then quickly did as he was told. While he was getting into the spraydeck, Findo took a small plastic bag from inside his lifejacket and pinned it to the climbing rope, which was still hanging from the cell window.

"Now," said Findo. "Don't climb in the side. Get up on the back and then slide your feet in first."

Speed grabbed hold of the rear of the second kayak and pulled himself up with his arms until he was sitting astride the empty canoe.

"That's it," said Findo. "Now swing your legs up, slide them in together and lower yourself down."

Speed followed instructions. It was an ungainly operation and the canoes rocked from side to side but he made it safely. As soon as Speed was in, Findo leant over and tugged his spraydeck into place, pulling the rim of the neoprene apron tight over the lip of the kayak's cockpit.

"Okay," he said. "Sit tight."

Findo pushed them away from the wall of the prison block and back into the open water. It was relatively calm to begin with but got choppier as they headed away from the shelter of the building. Findo paddled quickly, working mainly on one side but occasionally leaning over Speed to put in a few strokes on their left.

After about sixty yards they hit the inner fence.

"Now what?" said Speed.

"Stay still," said Findo. "I'll deal with it."

He cut through quickly. Seconds later they were at the outer fence and then out into another field. The water was slightly shallower but there was still a good current moving them forward.

Findo kept paddling, this time steering to the left.

Speed frowned. "Don't you want to go the other way?"

Findo shook his head. "No. The flood will probably be into East Allonby now. Even if they haven't realised that something's happened at the prison, there could still be police and fire brigade about. They see us floating about in canoes and they might want to ask some questions. It could look a bit odd; you don't normally get people canoeing round here in the middle of the night."

Speed laughed. "True. Where we going then?"

Findo did not answer for a moment. He used a deep forward sweep stroke to send the canoes out further to the left. "We're going round," he said. "Downstream."

Speed's eyes widened. "Oh shit," he said.

It took only a few more minutes to cross the field. They almost paddled into the raised riverbank before they spotted it.

Findo back-paddled as they drew close, looking for the best place to cross. Inside the field, the water level was only about six inches below the top of the bank. On the other side, the Allonby was practically lapping at the top of the barrier. The wide bank normally stood a good three feet above the ground inside and had not previously been breached for around fifty years. Now it was little more than a shallow bump on the surface of the spreading floodwaters.

"Do we get out?" said Speed.

Findo shook his head. "Probably not," he said.

He turned the kayaks left but, if anything, the bank was higher that way. He swept them back the other way, towards East Allonby. They could see the lights of the village about a quarter mile away. Most of the houses were on higher ground but some of the newer dwellings were built lower, on the edge of the floodplain, at the same level as the prison. By now their ground floors would be underwater.

"Look." Speed pointed through the rain. Among the orange glow of street lamps, blue lights were flashing.

"Don't worry," said Findo. "This is as close as we get."

He grunted as he dug the paddle into the water and turned them away from the bank and back out over the field. After a few yards, he turned again and began to paddle hard, straight for the bank.

"Lean back."

Speed did as he was told and the noses of the two kayaks lifted as they hit the edge of the almost-submerged bank. Findo continued to paddle for as long as he could and the canoes slid forward until the edge of the muddy barrier was directly beneath their seats.

"Flick with your hips," said Findo.

He lent forwards and then back, thrusting with his legs as he did so. Speed copied him on the second go and the canoes edged up over the wet grass. When they were on a bit further, Findo reached forwards with his paddle to help get some extra purchase. Soon they were both able to lean out to the sides and dig into the wet earth with their hands, pulling the canoes over the barrier.

"Okay, said Findo, "hold on."

With one last flip, the kayaks slid forward and they were out into the Allonby itself. The pull of the current caught them instantly and the boats span round as they were sucked free of the bank and out into midstream. Findo worked quickly with the paddle, moving them away from the river's edge and any hidden obstacles. He guided them out, not attempting to do anything but steer.

Minutes later they were passing underneath the motorway, the big double flyover giving a moment's break from the rain. Then they saw buildings and streetlights on their right, the grey suburbs of Clathy. Over on the right side of the river, were the watery lights of Garvock Hill, where the houses were bigger and spaced out in leafy closes.

The ride was fast but smooth. Small waves broke occasionally across their bow and eddies attempted to put the boats into a spin. But the double nature of their craft gave them extra stability and the rippling muscles of the swollen river carried them powerfully on. The river was flowing faster than anything Findo had paddled before but he knew that in the middle of the Allonby's course the deep water would be reasonably safe.

The experience was worse for Speed. He had never been in a canoe in daylight let alone in the dark and pouring rain. But he sat quiet and still, gripping the sides of his cockpit and trusting in Findo's knowledge and ability.

They passed beneath bridges, following the river's curves past

Chapel Bank and White Gate. They passed under the St Patrick's Road Bridge and turned south – on their left was the slope leading up to the remains of Fort Hawley and Garvock College. Next, the river turned north again, up towards Newmills. Speed got a fright as they rushed between the pillars of the railway bridge but then they were back into open water again and still upright, with Findo steering a confident course.

Next, the river began to bend back to the west and Findo steered them closer to the bank. There were a few houses and industrial buildings lit by street lamps but after that the banks were dark.

Then they saw a small red light on the right-hand bank. A few seconds later, they saw a green one.

Findo steered them hard towards the bank, the kayak sliding only a foot or so from the edge of the river. Tufts of wet grass and straggling brambles went past just an arm's length away. An old pipe sticking out of the bank came within an inch of snagging the canoe. Findo noted it with surprise. The pipe was normally about six feet above the river's high-tide mark.

Then there was a sudden gap in the bank and Findo dug in with the paddle as quick as he could. He twisted the kayaks hard right, trying to escape the pull of the Allonby's current and turn them into the calmer, shallower water.

But the river did not want to let them escape and kept pulling them downstream. They were only a couple of foot into the opening when the left-hand canoe bumped against the opposite side of the entrance. Despite Findo's work, they began to slide backward, being sucked out into the current again. The bare stalks of a scrubby sycamore sapling clattered against the canoe behind Speed.

"Grab hold!" shouted Findo. "Pull us in."

Speed did not need to be told twice. He grabbed at the first branches with his left hand, then twisted round and grabbed the main stem with his right. The sycamore's trunk was only about three inches in diameter but enough to hold them. Findo worked furiously with his paddle and between them they pulled the kayaks tight into the bank.

"Can you hold it?" yelled Findo.

Speed nodded. "Yeah. But I'm going to need both hands. I don't think I dare let go with one or we could be back out there."

"Okay," said Findo. "Hold tight."

He ripped back his spraydeck and pulled his knees and legs up out of the cockpit. Findo twisted his body across the two canoes and pointed his feet to the bank. Carefully, making sure he did not dislodge them, he slid towards the edge.

As soon as he was onto land, he turned and grabbed Speed's lifejacket.

"Okay," said Findo. "Pull up on that toggle above where your knees are. Rip the spraydeck back towards you." He wrapped one leg around the sycamore. "Right. That's it. Now keep hold of the tree and slide you legs out. Don't worry about the canoes, we don't need them any more."

Speed kicked the kayaks away from him as he came up out of his canoe and they shot into the darkness, lost from sight in an instant. Findo kept a tight hold on Speed's lifejacket and together they scrambled up the bank, heedless of branches and the brambles that tried to snag them. They were panting and staggering with relief as they pulled themselves up the last stretch and collapsed onto level ground.

38. In and out of exile

The escape was the last time Findo saw Colin Speed. A few moments after they reached safety, Albie Hooper emerged out of the gloom bearing a flashlight. He led them out of the downpour into the old steel factory were Findo had first met Abby. Inside, Albie handed them towels and dry clothes. All the wet gear, including Speed's prison clothing, the lifejackets and Findo's wetsuit and equipment, was stuffed into a heavy sack and thrown back into the Allonby.

Once they had changed, little time was wasted on farewells. Speed took Findo's hand and grasped it hard. "I owe you. You know that."

Findo nodded. Then he grinned. "That's alright. It was fun."

Albie chuckled and Speed slapped Findo on the shoulder.

"You're mad, you know," said Speed. "But I still owe you. You ever want anything, get in touch. Go through Phil at the bookies. You can keep the flat too; it's all legit, should be safe as long as you want it."

Findo nodded. "Thanks."

Albie jerked his head to the side. "We'd better go."

Speed nodded. "Yeah, I've survived the wet and wild ride from Disney hell. No point taking chances now. I might as well make sure it was worthwhile." He gathered Findo into a hug. "Take care of yourself, Findo."

Findo nodded. "I will."

Then they were gone, out into the darkness and rain. Albie led Speed to a car parked in a nearby side street. They were out of the city twenty minutes later and heading west towards a small airfield.

It was the end of Colin Speed's nine-year reign as the big fish in the city's underworld. He did not really mind. The perpetual temptation of just one more scheme had, until then, led him to keep putting off the day but Speed had always vowed to quit while he was ahead. There was enough money in the bank and the attention of HM Customs and Excise, plus a brief spell in confinement, was all the encouragement he needed; it was time to face up to retirement and burn his bridges – better than wasting his fortune gambling that lawyers could keep him from a lengthy jail sentence. Besides, the rain had been starting to get on his nerves. The idea of a sun-kissed beach and tropical waters seemed more attractive than ever.

Findo did not go back to the flat for several days. Instead he visited an old haunt, the castle. It was colder than he remembered it and the floor seemed harder; it was a while since he had lived the kind of primitive existence of his youth and the adjustment took a few nights.

But apart from the discomfort, the ruined tower was as he remembered it. There was a store of dry wood that Findo had moved in a couple of days earlier and the mediaeval fireplace drew as well as ever. He had a supply of food, bedding, a stove, books to read and a gas lantern.

Findo did not really need to hole up in the castle. His face had never been well known and four years of extra maturity had changed it enough that few would now recognise him in the street. The flat that Speed had provided him was safe enough and there were other people, like Albie or Mrs Reid, who could have given him shelter.

But that was not what Findo wanted. He was home again. He was also free. Speed had gone and John would be joining him in exile too, which was more unfortunate. But Findo did not mind. He was back and he had the city to himself again. He had no boss and, apart maybe from the police, no enemies after his scalp. It was almost like the days when he first roamed the city, alone, aloof and untouched.

But unknown to Findo, there were plenty of people who would have liked to get their hands on him. Initially, the breaching of the Allonby's banks near the prison had been treated as just the latest in a series of weather-related trials and tribulations for the city's emergency services. Fifteen houses were flooded and the residents of a number of other homes had been evacuated as the water spread across the fields and into the village of East Allonby. Work to hold back the flood and deal with its consequences had continued until well into the next morning.

During the night, the prison buildings had remained cut off by their new moat. The wardens were annoyed but not particularly worried. It was a nuisance when the flood knocked out power to the lights and alarms around the perimeter fences. On the other hand, it did not seem like a reason to worry unduly. The waist-deep and bitterly cold water swirling around the prison seemed an effective deterrent to escape.

It was not until the morning, when the wardens on the western accommodation block opened the door to find Speed's cellmate, a petty swindler called Themba Webster, alone that it began to dawn on them what had happened. The inevitable investigation, accusations and recriminations began straight away. Webster, despite telling the truth – or an economical version of it anyway – was hauled in front of the governor for questioning after warders initially refused to believe his story about Speed being spirited away by a man in a canoe. But Webster stuck to his story. He said Speed had been arranging, via mobile phones and messages, to escape for several days. The conman said Speed had boasted in the cell that he was going to vanish in the middle of the night but had not explained exactly how.

There was a pause in the official inquiry when the governor had left the room to speak to his secretary, who was already fielding the first calls from the press about the escape. One of the two warders present approached Webster with a smile and crouched down by his side.

"Listen, you black fuckwit," he said. "You'd better come up with better than this shit or I'm going to make your life hell."

Webster's eyes rolled up. He shook his head. "I'm tellin' the truth. Believe me, Mr Kelly."

"Believe you, Webster? You must be fucking joking." The warder stabbed a finger at Webster's face. Webster recoiled but the warder jabbed his finger hard at the ridge of cartilage between his nostrils and forced the convict's head back. "Listen. You tell us the truth or the rest of your stretch is going to be very uncomfortable, understand?"

Webster squinted down at the stubby forefinger grinding its broken nail into the end of his nose. "I hear you, man. That's why I'm tellin' the truth. Speed went out the window and down a rope into a canoe."

"So why didn't you warn us that something was going to happen?"

Webster blinked. "Coz if I had, he'd have hurt me more than you could, Mr Kelly, sir. Everyone knows he was a big man. If I'd grassed him up, he'd have known it was me. You might make my life hell, Mr Kelly, but, Mr Speed, he'd a killed me. For real."

The door to the room opened and the governor walked back in. "That's enough of that, Mr Kelly. It sounds like Webster might even have been telling the truth for once. We've recovered the angle grinder they used to cut the bars and the fences have been cut in two places. It might just have been possible to use a canoe to get in and out, although God knows how they got away again. I can hardly believe they used the river in conditions like last night."

He dropped a small plastic bag on the table. Inside it was a white business card.

"You can take Webster away for the time being. But put him somewhere safe and handy. The police will be here soon – assuming they can get up the drive past the floods and the TV cameras – they'll probably want to talk to him."

No evidence was found of the explosives used to blow the bank that had been keeping back the Allonby. Any traces had been swept away in the torrent that had scourged the fields and flooded through the prison and on to the neighbouring village.

Work to plug the breach continued throughout the next day. A joint council and Environment Agency team carried out the first inspection. They were joined later in the day by the fire service and members of the army. It kept raining for much of the morning, although not as heavily as it had during the night. The Allonby was also still as swollen as the day before, the watercourse struggling to drain the rain that seemed to have been falling without a break for weeks. The breach in the bank was now getting on for one hundred and twenty yards long and still getting bigger.

The repair team were surprised when the police turned up to try and see whether the flood could have been the result of sabotage but were soon able to persuade the officers that any investigation would have to wait. The inspector who looked down from the road at the lake of muddy water stretching from the bridge to East Allonby surveyed the scene without enthusiasm and headed back for his dry office.

After he had gone, one of the Environment Agency team turned to the army officer next to him. "What do you reckon? Could it have been sabotage?"

The lieutenant snorted. "See those fences over there?"

"Yeah."

"They've been cut. That's why those warders were out there earlier. Bit of a coincidence, eh?"

The Environment Agency man's eyebrows rose. "Bloody hell." He frowned. "How do you reckon they breached it then?"

The lieutenant shrugged. "Well, I doubt they'd have done it by hand unless they were suicidal. When that bank started to go, it would have gone fast. You'd have had a lot of water coming through a narrow space at speed. I should think a small shaped charge detonated remotely would do it nicely, wouldn't have needed much."

The Environment Agency man scowled. "Well, if it was done on purpose, I'd like to get hold of whoever was responsible. I don't care about the prison but have you seen the state of those houses over there? There's one old girl just come back from having a hip-op and now her bungalow's ruined." He sighed. "We're going to be cleaning this mess up for days. As if we didn't have enough on our plates."

The sun had just started to come out when Ross Kirkbride walked down to the conference room on the floor below. The chief superintendent frowned as he saw the watery glow coming in through the glass side of the stairwell; the sunlight had been away for so long that it seemed almost unnatural.

When he entered the room Kirkbride nodded greetings to them all before turning to the detective inspector. "So?"

Charlotte Brown smiled briefly. "Looks genuine. We've compared it with the old cards and forensics says it's the same."

"Same design?"

She shook her head. "Not just that. They reckon it's probably from the same print run. The ink's gone off a bit now; the card that was left hadn't been printed recently."

"So, what do you reckon, Snoopy? Same man or someone who likes a joke and decided to pick up where our original Findo Gask left off?"

Charlotte Brown pursed her lips thoughtfully. "Well, whether Findo Gask is one person or several, there's no reason why it couldn't be the same individual or group. I've been talking with Thames Valley, Avon and Somerset, and Wiltshire. The last job we know about was a private house near Swindon; they lost five paintings out of a collection of over thirty. Clean entry, through a ventilation shaft, alarm immobilised. Pictures had a combined insurance value of £1.6 million. Even despite the fact that they probably won't get more than a fraction of that, that's probably one of their best hauls yet."

She smiled. "But that break-in happened early December. Since then, none of the forces I spoke to know of any cases on their patches and they haven't heard reports of others in neighbouring forces either. So, there's no reason why Findo Gask couldn't have left the country house burglaries for a while." The DI gave her boss a quizzical look. "You still think it's a single person?"

Kirkbride nodded. "Oh, I'm sure of it. Our Findo Gask was born and bred in this city. I always wondered if he would come home one day. I didn't know he was linked with Colin Speed but it makes sense. I've got a feeling we've only been scratching the surface with Speed so far. Customs reckon those businesses of his were nearly all genuine but they acted as fronts for other activities too. Added to what Mayfield's been coming out with, I think we'd hooked a pretty big fish there – even if more by luck than judgement. And if he was one of this town's 'Mr Bigs', it's no surprise if Findo Gask worked for him."

He picked up a pen and began to doodle on a pad in front of him.

Brown picked up a cup of coffee and took a sip then pulled a face; it was almost stone cold. "You think what Dave was giving us was the truth?" she asked.

Kirkbride nodded. "At least some of it. He knew he was facing more than just a disciplinary offence. With what we were piecing together about him, he could easily have been looking at time inside – and we still don't know if we'd reached the bottom of the barrel with Mayfield. He'd been taking money for years and he knew this city inside out. I'm sure he figured that with Speed locked up it was safe – well, safer anyway – to give us some dirt in order to save his own skin."

"Do you think he knew Speed was going to be sprung?"

Kirkbride nodded. "I wouldn't be surprised. He'd started to come up with some quite damning evidence in the last few days. That could have been a dangerous course. Even if Mayfield kept himself out of jail, he would have been risking some nasty reprisals if he'd been the one responsible for putting Speed away."

"So where does Findo Gask come in?"

The chief superintendent shrugged. "Ah, that's the question. I've been thinking about the Custodian job. I was always a little confused about that one. We know that was a team effort but up until then Findo Gask always seemed to work alone – that was one of the few hallmarks he seemed to have."

"Paul suggested once that maybe someone else had planted the card."

Kirkbride shook his head. "No. Possible, but I don't think so. The other thing that distinguished the works of our Mr Gask was that he didn't do anything the easy way. He's done some unlikely things in his time and, apart from the fact that it wasn't a solo effort, the Custodian job fits the bill on that score. We know someone clung on underneath that truck; now that's quite a feat and for that reason I never went with Paul's theory. No, I think Findo Gask was part of that job. He may not have had anything to do with the guns and actually taking the money. I think he was the doorman; he got inside and he let the others in." The policeman began to shade in the truck that he'd scribbled on the paper. "Now I'm wondering if Colin Speed was behind that robbery."

"Speed?" Brown looked at him in surprise.

Kirkbride nodded. "Well, if he's half the man he seems to be turning out to be, it would fit. I'm not saying he was actually involved but he might have been the one doing the organisation. We know now that one of his mechanics had an interesting past; maybe he was the leader on the ground. And that could provide one link between Findo Gask and Speed."

"But why come back to spring Speed from jail? Was he worried Speed might identify him?"

Kirkbride shook his head. "I doubt it. I've got a feeling that Findo Gask did it because he could. His record here makes for impressive reading and we've never got any closer than a few fingerprints, a couple of hairs and a footprint or two. Since he left us, he's had detectives from forces across half of Southern England chasing their tails. Now he's gone and thumbed his nose at us by stealing a man we'd got locked up at Her Majesty's displeasure." Kirkbride started to draw wings on his doodled truck. "I doubt it was just a random act. He must have known Speed. Maybe he owed him a favour."

"And now he's back on your turf again."

Kirkbride smiled. "That's right. Maybe he's like me; he likes this place. Perhaps he wanted to come home again."

39. Old haunts and dirty habits

The need to walk the city streets again was what drew Findo out of his self-imposed confinement. He had spent three nights in the castle and only left a few times to top up his supplies. The theft of Colin Speed from East Allonby Prison had taken place in the early hours of Sunday morning. Findo packed up his camping gear and began to put it back into its plastic sacks as the sun was coming up on Wednesday.

Everything was cleared away and packed up, any rubbish jettisoned out of the window into the still-furious Allonby. Findo used an old newspaper to scoop up the ashes from his fire and scatter them to the winds.

As he was casting away the ball of grimy newspaper and brushing his hands, he paused to look out of the tower. The sky was clear and early sunlight was illuminating wreathes of mist that hung over the river and the wood on the opposite bank. There was a light sheen of frost on the stones around the window. The wet was being followed by cold; in place of the procession of water-laden lows sweeping in from the west, the city was about to get the first taste of the bitter February that was to come, howling its way down out of the north to layer ice across water.

Findo stowed his camping gear in a corner of the first tower. Dropped down between some of the scattered blocks, the black bin liners merged into the gloom. It was an extravagant precaution. He had never been aware of anyone else getting into the castle but caution had always been part of his life.

By the time he left, the city was starting to come to life. The morning rush hour had begun but there was still half an hour before most shops and businesses opened. Findo sat for a while on the wall above the ruined pumping station, watching traffic flowing around the roundabout and office workers and shop staff trudging wearily towards their places of daytime confinement. Findo was wearing an old fleece jacket with a hooded top inside. He sat with the hood over his head and hand stuffed into his pockets. Nobody spared him more than a glance; with his faded combat trousers and scuffed boots, he was as anonymous as the tarmac around him.

After ten minutes, Findo stretched and began to walk into the city centre. He went first to the Burger King in Albert Parade – the same one where Albie Hooper had bought his burgers eight years earlier, just before catching Findo and delivering him to Colin Speed.

With breakfast out of the way, Findo went back to the flat above the betting shop in Corporation Road. Before going in, he spent a few minutes walking past the front to check for any sign that the place was being watched, then did the same at the back. Only once he was satisfied that the coast was clear did he slip in and up the stairs. The door in the lobby was already open and there were people in the offices on the first floor. But Findo slipped quietly past their door and took the dogleg around and up to the flat.

Hiding in the castle, Findo missed the beginning of the media furore over the escape. To begin with the news had attracted little attention except from the city's press. The police and prison authorities had declined to say exactly how Speed got away and had managed to give the impression – without exactly lying – that he had escaped as a result of confusion caused by the unexpected breaching of the Allonby's banks. Official statements concentrated on allaying public fears on whether Speed was dangerous.

But then the story leaked out of how the escaped prisoner had escaped by canoe in the middle of the night. The information came from a van driver working at the prison who had overheard some warders talking on Monday. He spoke to a journalist from a local radio station. The next day the prison governor came onto the station's morning news programme – thinking he was going to be talking about the impact of the flood on the prison and reassuring listeners that all the fences had been repaired.

For the first minute, the interview seemed innocuous enough. But then the journalist sprung his question about the method of Speed's getaway. The governor was caught. He could not lie because he did not know how much the journalist knew. So he began to hesitate and flounder, anxious not to seem evasive but not wanting to give anything away. The interviewer scented blood and, with a leap of logic, took a stab in the dark and asked whether the breaching of the Allonby's bank had been a deliberate act to allow the escape. The governor did not admit anything immediately but the answer was clear from his response and the journalist realised that he had got the best scoop of his career.

After that, the story went national and was even picked up by some of the foreign press. It was on all the radio and television news bulletins by Tuesday lunchtime and the next day – as Findo left the castle – it was front page on most papers.

The link with Findo did not come out until later on Wednesday. Chief Superintendent Kirkbride, accompanied by a dour-looking

Detective Inspector Paul Sweet, held a joint conference with the prison governor. Also at their table were a senior manager from the Environment Agency and the city council's chief officer. For the chance of getting a new angle on the story, stringers for most of the national papers, journalists from several press agency and cameras from local BBC and independent television teams were there. The hacks wanted to be able to give their readers and viewers more juicy details about the unlikely nature of Colin Speed's escape from custody. But they got more than they expected.

Ross Kirkbride began the conference by asking for their patience, a request that did nothing to impress the cynics among the press. Then, to their surprise, instead of explaining about the prison-break, he began talking about an unnamed thief who had preyed on the city for around five years without ever being caught. The assembled reporters were confused and several tried to question the relevance of the story. But Kirkbride ignored their protests. Instead, he continued by relating how this same thief had left the city following an unsolved robbery on a security depot and started burgling country houses and similar properties in Southern England.

At this point, a few journalists put two and two together and began paying closer attention to Kirkbride's tale. He gained the attention of the rest when he quietly stated that his officers now believed that the same person was responsible for 'stealing' Colin Speed from East Allonby Prison.

A few moments of chaos followed as the accusation sank in and reporters started to shout questions. But Kirkbride reined them in again and this time none tried to interrupt. He named Findo and spoke some more about the crimes with which the police were linking him. With the prison governor nodding sagely by his side, the policeman outlined how Colin Speed had been spirited away. Then he called on the representatives from the Environment Agency and the council to give statements detailing the damage that the flood had done to homes in East Allonby and the likely cost – both in financial terms and human suffering.

Between them, Kirkbride and his colleagues spent the next ten minutes blackening Findo's name. Then they announced the reward being offered for information leading to his arrest.

Findo was oblivious to the press conference. At the time, he was in the shopping precinct at Jubilee Square. He was leaning against a fire escape – the same one that Mickey Dunn and his young gang had once used as their roost – watching two boys of about ten years old.

The pair, who looked half-Chinese, were in the middle of the square next to the old, still broken fountain. They had skateboards and were huddled together talking nervously.

For a while Findo could not work out what the boys were up to. He could tell they were plotting something but could not decide whether they were just trying to pluck up their courage or were waiting for something to happen.

He had been watching them for about five minutes when one boy, slightly taller than the other, jumped on his skateboard and glided towards one of the precinct corners. The boy looked out into the road beyond then went back to his mate and they resumed their furtive conference.

This happened twice more and Findo gave up leaning against the fire escape and sat down. Apart from keeping an eye on the boys he was also watching the other people coming and going in the precinct. It was quiet; it was not giro day and most East Park residents would be out of money by now. Findo did not really care. He was just happy to be home. He felt comfortable, easy with his environment. Sunk into his old fleece and with a hood over his head, he blended almost perfectly with the background – all he needed was a can of Special Brew by his side and a few biro tattoos on his hands to complete the picture.

Findo had been watching for nearly quarter of an hour when the boys finally went into action. The taller one had just made another check on the precinct's corner when he made a quick hand gesture to his friend. A minute later, a postman came into the square, walking blithely past the watching half-Chinese boy. As the postman continued on towards the first couple of shops, the boy jumped onto his skateboard and propelled himself forward, snatching at the postman's bag from behind as he went.

The idea might have worked if the boy had been fifty pounds heavier or on something a bit more secure than a skateboard. As it was, he got hold of the bag but his weight was too slight to do more than tug the strap off the postman's shoulder. Then he came to an abrupt halt. The skateboard kept going but its young rider landed flat on his back with a loud thud.

The boy tried to scramble up but was not quick enough. The postman turned quickly and his boot caught the young would-be mugger square in the thigh. It was a hard kick and Findo gave a little wince as he heard the crunch. The boy rolled over with a yelp and managed to get up on his second, scrabbling attempt. Another kick helped send him on his way. The smaller boy had already grabbed the loose skateboard and the two would-be robbers fled, the taller one limping badly. There were four other people, apart from Findo, in the square at the time but none attempted to intervene on either side. The postman grunted with satisfaction as he hoisted his bag back up onto his shoulder and continued on, passing the kiosk that the Turk had once owned, now run by two Pakistani men.

Over the next week, Findo visited many of his old haunts. The only one he avoided was the old factory where he had delivered Speed into Albie Hooper's hands. The Fiesta stayed where it was, parked in the lane behind Corporation Road. Findo walked the city's streets, getting their pattern back into his brain and their feel into his feet.

He continued staying at the flat but avoided going in and out more than once a day and never at the same time. He was quiet during the day, padding about bare foot and not turning on his television or tape player so that people in the offices below would not even realise he was there. At night, he kept the curtains drawn and the lights low.

Findo did not visit anyone, even Frances Reid. Although he was unaware there was now a price on his head, he was not stupid enough to think that the prison break would have gone unreported. And he could guess at the effect that leaving his card would have had on the local police. In many ways announcing his return was an illogical thing to do but it had also felt like a necessary one; Findo had to tell someone he was home. There were not many people left in the city that he really knew and few that he would trust. For the time being, it was safer to remain anonymous and satisfy his need for recognition by raising his profile in a way that did not involve lifting his hood and showing his face.

The news of Findo's return – and involvement in recent events – was all over the local press for several days. But there was a kind of ambivalence to the reporting. On the one hand, he was blamed for wrecking homes by recklessly flooding part of East Allonby. On the other hand, the reporting on the prison break showed a kind of sneaking respect. That escapade had shown the kind of audacity, cunning and bravery that could not be gainsaid.

The stories also tended to gloss over his past life in the city with the usual airbrush treatment employed for dealing with an inconvenient history; rather than a thief, he was portrayed as a lively larrikin, a boisterous jackanapes instead of a pilfering parasite. Even the robbery of the Custodian depot got light treatment. Again, more attention was given to the cleverness of the ruse employed and the facts that nobody had been hurt and the crime never solved, rather than the criminality of the incident.

In the coverage of his recent career, the illegality of Findo's actions in stealing antiques and artefacts from the homes of collectors across the south of the country was hardly mentioned. Instead, his thefts were listed more like sporting achievements as if the fact that they had been done to rich people living hundreds of miles away made them something laudable rather than reprehensible.

As a result of the press coverage, both nationally and locally, there were all kinds of sightings of him reported. Some were less plausible than others. According to one eyewitness, he had been seen in a black Jaguar cruising around the houses in affluent Garvock Hill, another report placed him on the Tibbermore estate handing out new ten-pound notes to local children.

Findo's presence in the city was also a subject of much debate in pubs, clubs and other watering holes. There were still some who remembered his link with the letterbox giveaway of a quarter of a million pounds – although some of those who had received the money had spent it long ago and barely even remembered it. Plenty would have liked to get their hands on the reward being offered for his capture but there were as many that would as soon have seen the city's football team relegated. Findo was becoming a folk hero, a man whose legend was already fast outgrowing the facts. The city's history had never offered much in the way of a claim to fame and it had few sons or daughters of which it could really be proud. Which was why, for a growing number of residents – even those outwardly law-abiding and respectable – Findo helped to fill an empty niche. For many, the notoriety he gave the city was better than the ignominy of inconsequence.

Findo had been back in the city for nearly six weeks before he bumped into any members of his family. He had been living a quiet life, content for the time being simply to be where he was. He had spent weeks exploring the city on foot and had recently begun to widen his range. Using the Fiesta, he had moved out of the city and was visiting villages and areas nearby that he had never seen during all the time that he lived there before.

He had plenty of money in the building society account Daniel Morris had opened for him – although he had still not received payment for the job done before Christmas. There was no need for Findo to steal anything and for a while he was wise enough not to risk the temptation – being back at home was more important for the time being.

It was a Wednesday afternoon at the end of March and Findo was driving down Fortress Hill when he suddenly thought he recognised a familiar figure among a knot of people crossing the road at some traffic lights near the hospital.

Findo pulled over at a bus stop a little lower down the hill. He watched in his window as a group of young men came closer. He could not be sure until they were nearly there. Then he saw the smile.

Findo leant over and wound down the passenger window. "Hey, Otis."

The figure in the middle turned his dreadlock-covered head. "Yay." He peered at the Fiesta, then came closer. "Who's that then?" He bent to look through the car window. "Christ!" Otis' eyes suddenly went wide and the same grin split his face again. "Man, I didn't think it was true."

"Hop in," said Findo. "Come for a drive."

Otis nodded then looked over his shoulder. His friends were standing nearby. "Look," he said. "I've got something on this afternoon. I can't just split at the minute. You around this evening?"

Findo nodded. "Sure."

"Good." Otis dug into a pocket and pulled out a pen. "Got something I can write on?"

Findo looked around the car, baffled for a minute. Then he held out his arm. "Here."

"Okay." Otis carefully scribbled some numbers onto Findo's arm. "Give me a call, right? Come round tonight. I've got my own place, it's completely cool."

Findo nodded.

Otis stood up but before he went, he bent down and squeezed Findo's arm. He added a soft farewell. "Good to see you, bro." Then Otis turned away to his friends. "Right, boys. Let's get to the game. That's a cousin of mine. Haven't seen him for ages."

Findo called from a payphone in the city centre that evening. He arranged to come round to the address that Otis gave him at about nine-thirty.

The flat was in a block in the White Gate area. It was a ten-storey building, put up sometime in the 1950s. There was little imagination to the design but it was better than some of the constructions on the Tibbermore estate. The stairwells were full of graffiti and most of the lights were broken but Findo did not see any needles lying about and only one drunk, lying in his own urine on a third-floor landing.

Otis' flat was on the seventh floor. Findo approached it via the stairwell at the far end of the building. He went up to the ninth floor and then followed two landings along until he was above the flat. The block was quiet and most of the ninth floor was in darkness, although whether that was because people were out, they were saving on electricity or the power had been cut off, Findo did not know.

It was still only about a quarter to nine when Findo went down and approached the door to Otis' flat. On the way, he passed two boys in their early teens. They were smoking a joint and using an air rifle to take pot shots at a street lamp below. One of the boys gave Findo a stare and blew an ostentatious cloud of smoke in his direction.

"Don't waste it," said Findo.

"Fuck off," said the boy.

Findo walked past.

"Where you going then?"

Findo ignored him.

"Oi, I'm talking to you."

Findo stepped past a pile of bin bags outside one flat, stopped at the next door and rapped on the panel of wired glass set into it. From the end of the landing, the two teenagers began to unleash a string of obscenities.

The door to the flat opened. Otis looked at Findo in surprise and then grinned. "Hey, man. I wasn't expecting you yet." He stood aside. "But come on in."

As Findo walked past, Otis leant out the door. "Hey, Marky?"

"What."

"Stop dissing my friends or you don't get no more ganja, okay?" Otis waved his arms dismissively as he showed Findo through. "They don't do nothing, just like mouthing off and acting hard."

They went down a short hallway. To the left was a door into a large room where a set of turntables was balanced between two stacks of plastic crates. There were records everywhere, mostly in sleeves but also cast across the carpet, a nearby sofa and a handy window ledge. There was a strong smell of grass in the air and a large, bright red lava lamp cast a warm wash of colour through the room.

There was another man behind the record decks. He was holding a pair of headphones clamped to one ear and cueing up the next disk. The music sounded like a mix of Herbie Hancock and hardcore dance.

"Sorry about this," said Otis. "We was still working on our set – DJ Lemon, sharp and sweet, coming to the bangingest clubs and underground boogie shacks you can find this side of euphoria."

Findo gave a blank look as his older half-brother completed a short song and dance routine. "What?"

Otis grinned. "Don't worry, man. Just part of the act. Total bollocks but sounds cool."

The tubby man behind the decks looked up and grinned as the next record began – a remixed version of an old Northern Soul hit.

"Alright, DJ Lemon," he said.

Otis grinned and picked up a fat joint that had been lying in a nearby ashtray. He gestured at Findo. "This is a cousin of mine," he said. "Was supposed to be coming round later but he must have heard how good we are."

Otis hesitated a moment. Findo laughed and stepped forward. "Name's Phil," he said. "Phil Gates."

The other man nodded. "Clint."

Introductions over, the DJ seemed to lose interest and went back to the records strewn about him.

"What's all this?" asked Findo.

"Rehearsal," said Otis. "We're doing a set at this club called Resist, off Packhouse Street. It's an old fire station, got converted into a club a few years back. Me and Clint have got a regular slot there now. We're just working out a few numbers, keeping it fresh, you know."

It was nearly midnight by the time Clint and Otis packed up. Findo was crashed out in an armchair. He was stoned and drifting off on the sounds being woven by the two DJs; after finishing the end of their club set, they had moved on to an impromptu chill-out session, mixing samples from whale song recordings and the *Gladiator* soundtrack with ambient sound doodles by the likes of William Orbit.

After Clint was gone, Otis stuck on Massive Attack's *Blue Lines* and sat down on an old kitchen chair opposite Findo. From beneath a pile of discarded discs, Otis dug out a silver-coloured tin and started to roll a joint.

Findo prised open one heavy eyelid. "Clint gone?"

Otis nodded. "Yeah. Him and some mates are off to an all-nighter down town."

Findo grunted and levered himself up out of his slumped position. "I'm starving, you got anything to eat?"

Otis grinned. "Sure, bro. Hold on a mo."

He put his half-made joint to one side and wandered out towards the kitchen, scratching his dreadlocks absently as he went.

Otis returned a couple of minutes later with his arms full. He had a couple of big bottles of Coke, a packet of chocolate biscuits, some crisps and a bag of satsumas.

"Here you go." He deposited the load on Findo's lap and sat back down to resume rolling his joint. The two half-brothers were silent for a few minutes as Findo demolished a bag of crisps, most of the biscuits and nearly a litre of coke. When he had finished, he belched loudly.

"Better?" asked Otis.

Findo smiled. "Yeah. Where does that weed of yours come from?"

Otis laughed. "Friend of mine's got a place near Dubmore – a converted chicken farm. Does it all proper: hydroponic tanks, UV lights, even one of those things keeps the humidity right. Pretty good, huh?"

Findo nodded and took the finished joint Otis was offering him. He took a gentle pull and sighed, then giggled. "I had all kind of things I wanted to talk to you about but I can't remember any of them."

It was nearly afternoon by the time they got up again. Findo had slept in the same armchair in which he had spent most of the evening. He only woke when Otis waved a cup of fresh coffee under his nose.

There was a tiny balcony outside the flat's lounge and they squeezed themselves and two chairs onto it. Despite coats they shivered but the chill air helped the coffee cut through the fog in their brains.

"So what are you doing these days?" said Findo.

Otis shrugged and laughed. "Nothing as interesting as you. Christ! My life's tame in comparison even if half what they say is true."

Findo shook his head. "No, come on. I want to know. I haven't seen you for years. You and Lou were the only ones in our family apart from Billy that were halfway sane. Tell me what's been happening. How did you get this place? What are you doing these days?"

"It's not that exciting."

"I don't care."

"Okay," said Otis. "Well, I think last time I saw you we were still out at Meadowfields. We were there for a few years, although we moved around the estate a couple of times. So, what happened to me? I got busted, that was the main thing, happened about a year after you disappeared."

"Busted?"

"Yeah. I was doing a bit of dealing – just weed mainly. I think they'd had their eye on me for a bit. I got picked up coming out of this place over Tibbermore. I used to get my supplies from this bloke there. He got it in through Port Annan docks. Anyway, I was just on my way home when these coppers suddenly appeared from nowhere, did a stop-and-search on me. Complete bummer – I had eight ounces of really nice block, good sticky black like you don't get too often."

Findo grinned. "So, did you tell them it was just for personal?"

Otis laughed. "I thought about it. Nah, they had me fair and square."

"What happened then?"

"Did six months in a young offenders'." Otis shook his head. "Not my idea of fun. There's some nasty bastards in there and some of them didn't like me. Young black bloke with a silly smile and stupid hair? I had my card marked from the start." He gave a shiver and the light in his eyes faded for a moment. "Nah. I wouldn't go back there again."

"So what did you do when you got out?"

"I was lucky," said Otis. "Had this good parole officer. I'd done this computer course while I was inside and quite liked it. Once I got out, Ronnie – that's the parole officer – he helped me get a temporary job at this DIY place. Got me enough cash that I was able to rent a place to stay. I started off in this bed-sit down Cowfield Heights. It was pretty grim but better than being in a homeless hostel. Anyway, I worked for this firm for a bit and they decided I was alright and made it permanent. After that, I went back and did this evening class to catch up on a few of the basics."

Otis shrugged. "I wasn't like you. She used to send me to school for the first couple of years, so I did reading and writing and all that before I dropped out." He grinned. "Still, wasn't much of an education record. I think I stopped going for good when I was about nine. We'd just done a bunk from Tibbermore and I don't think the truancy people knew where to find us – not that they came on Tibbermore much. Anyway, after I'd done this evening class, I got a place on a foundation course up at the college. Finished that and now I'm doing an IT course – proper student now I am, got a grant and everything."

Findo looked at him in surprise. "Computers?"

"Yeah," said Otis. "It's a laugh. It's really easy when you know how and there's some cool stuff out there – music, games, all kind of information. Whole world at your fingertips."

"What about the DJ thing?"

"Oh, that's just for fun really. Well, and it brings in some good money. I still do my old DIY job at weekends but the DJ-ing pays much better."

Findo shook his head slowly. "You got it sussed, haven't you?"

Otis shrugged then nodded. "Yeah," he said. "Reckon I have. I'm happy, man. My life's okay. I'm doing what I want and I'm my own man."

"So what about the others?"

Otis raised his eyebrows. "The others? What do you want, details or quick summary?"

"Quick will do."

"Okay, well, let's start at the top. The old woman's still around, hasn't got any better though. Gone downhill if that's possible. Last I heard she was over Hobbes Town somewhere. Still pulling tricks, though from what I hear she's not so choosy these days. She was hanging around with all these squaddies from the army camp for a couple of years but I think they got bored with her in the end; probably after they'd all had a go." He shook his head. There was a bitter hint in his tone, reproachful but resigned. "I don't know how she does it. She must be fifty now. She still manages to pull young blokes though. Last time I saw her was a year ago, in the Oak House. Had some grease monkey in tow, busy guzzling every drink he'd buy her." Otis scowled. "Anyway, I don't want to talk about her."

Findo shrugged. "I didn't think there'd be much to tell. What about the others?"

Otis flicked the dregs of his coffee out into mid-air. "Let's see. Natalie, I dunno where she's got to. Can't really remember when I saw her last. She's probably still on the game up in Aberdeen. That's if she hasn't got too fat to stand on street corners. Jimmy Ray, he's living out in Dubmore. Reckons he works in security these days."

"Security?"

Otis snorted. "Yeah, a laugh isn't it? Truth is, he's living in a caravan at this big scrapyard. He's got a pack of dogs supposed to guard the place. He claims they're Staffies but they're really pit bulls. They've got a square down there and Jimmy Ray trains the dogs and organises the fights. I've heard they get some big money changing hands. He invited me down once but it's not my thing, not watching two dogs chew each other's ears off – although the dogs are probably more civilised than the kind of people that go there."

Findo nodded. "What about Rob and Louise?"

Otis gave his brother a sideways look and paused before replying. "Rob's still Rob. You know what happened to his hands?"

Findo nodded.

"Well, he hasn't forgotten either," said Otis. "And he still blames you. I'd steer clear of Rob if I was you."

Findo smiled. "I wasn't planning on calling on him."

"Don't," said Otis. "You know there's a price on your head. Rob would probably turn you in for free. He was always a nasty piece of work and he hasn't got any sweeter. He's bitter about life in general and he hates you. He's living in some real scum-hole over on Clathy with some poor girl that he knocks around just for the hell of it. Just don't go there, okay?"

Findo nodded. "Don't worry."

"Now, I suppose you want to know about Lou?"

"Yeah."

"It's not a good story."

"What happened?"

Otis sighed. "After I got sent inside, she was stuck with just Rob and the old woman. Jimmy Ray had already disappeared. She was going through one of her bad patches, back on smack again. Anyway . . ."

Otis blinked a few times. "She'd been trying to get Lou on the game for a while. Lou had managed to avoid it one way or another. You know what she was like; she'd just drift around in her own little world trying not to get in anyone's way. She was still only seventeen at the time. Then one night the old woman invited a couple of blokes back. Once they'd finished with her, they had a go at Lou."

Findo's eyes narrowed. "What about Rob, didn't he help her?"

Otis spat. "I don't know, Fin, I don't know. I didn't know anything about it until just before I got out. Rob claims he was out at the time. But I heard another story. I heard that he was there and it was his idea."

"What!"

Otis held his hands up. "I don't know for sure. Lou doesn't know. She didn't see much. I think she just blanked it out."

"Where is she now?"

"Don't know, vanished just like Billy. Same story. It broke her, it really did. She ran off afterwards. She was hiding out in some squat out the other side of the motorway. Started doing smack as well. She wrote to me once just before I got out of prison. I went and saw her but she was in an awful mess. She vanished not long after that. Left a note saying she was going to London. I don't know what's happened to her now." He turned to Findo. "I'm just glad you're okay. You might not be exactly normal but at least you're human."

Findo nodded slowly. "What did you mean about Billy? When you said 'same old story'."

Otis looked down at his hands. "You didn't know?"

"No. What?"

"Something similar happened to her. I don't know how bad it was. But that's why she vanished."

Findo nodded. "It figures." He smiled at Otis. "But she's alright, you know."

"What, Billy? You've seen her?"

Findo nodded again and started to relate how Billy had whisked him out of the city after the raid on the Custodian depot. He told Otis about what Billy had done since leaving the city, her life now, the time they had spent in Eskdale and the reunions they had held there every summer since.

By the time spring arrived, Findo had settled back into life in the city. There were holes in his life but in most ways he felt happy. His only regret about coming back was that he had left it so long.

He saw Otis regularly – they spent more time together than ever before. It was a strange experience for both and, to begin with, they sounded each other out slowly. But confidence in their relationship soon grew and Findo was surprised at how much they had in common. Back when he was still living with the family, Findo had liked Otis but not really known him. Before Billy left, Findo had not spared any time for his other half-sisters and brothers. Then, by the time that his protector left, Otis had been spending as little time at home as Findo and their paths rarely crossed. Now, they explored each other's characters and sought comfort from being family.

Findo also visited Frances Reid regularly. He was saddened by the infirmity that had snared her in his absence but reassured by the fact that her mind was as sharp as ever. Their encounters were always affectionate but she also kept Findo on his toes. She had begun to question his morals, always pushing him to justify himself. Sometimes it was a hard job but for some reason Findo always came away from her home feeling as if he had achieved something.

Apart from the man running the betting shop beneath his flat, the only other person that Findo saw regularly was a girl who worked in one of the offices on the first floor. She often seemed to be out on some errand or other and they would meet from time to time on the stairs. She was in her late teens and quite pretty but seemed painfully shy – although she would always smile sweetly at Findo and say a mumbled hello. He had also caught her staring after him in the street on a couple of occasions.

A couple of times, Findo nearly plucked up the courage to ask her upstairs for a coffee but he never quite took the plunge. Although intrigued by the girl, thanks to Otis he was not desperate for female company. Findo had taken to staying at his brother's flat a couple of times a week and had been there on one occasion when Otis and Clint came back from a session at the club. The two DJs had brought a small group back with them, including several girls. After a few joints, Findo and one of the girls had slipped off to bed without even needing to discuss what they were going to do. The same thing – with a different girl – happened a couple of weeks later. Since then, Findo had taken to timing at least one of his visits to coincide with his brother's stints as a DJ.

The only other people he was in contact with were Billy, who he would speak to on the phone at least once a week, and Daniel Morris. Findo had called the antiques dealer about the same time as he met Otis again. Out in his car, exploring the rolling hill country up above Port Annan, Findo had spotted the chimneys of a rambling old house stuck up amongst some trees. The building looked stern and forbidding, an early Victorian monument to class distinctions.

Later the same day, Findo was walking through the house. He had only really broken in for the fun of it. After finding his way through the copse surrounding the mansion, he had slipped in through a side entrance. The door had been shut but it had only taken a minute to pick the lock with the tools from his roll. There was no one in the house and Findo strolled through it all, wandering in and out of rooms at will. The place smelt of old money – and the kind of shabbiness that sometimes hides true wealth.

The thing that caught Findo's eye was a large earthenware plate. It was tucked away on a windowsill in the corner of a big study on the first floor. Findo had gone to the window to look at the view – parkland sweeping down to a quiet curve of private fishing-river. But his attention was drawn to the pottery dish. It was an unusual work: an oval, slightly dished plate decorated with the raised figures of a snake and a lizard sat amongst a scattering of leaves and snail shells. The plate's mottled glaze was hazy with fine cracks but the colours were fresh and vibrant, as if all it needed was a good dust.

Findo frowned as he looked at it. It was remarkably similar to a piece that he had stolen for Morris from a private collection in Buckingham. That work had been by a sixteenth-century French potter called Bernard Palissy. Findo could not remember how much it had been worth but seemed to remember that he had received several thousand pounds for the job.

After a good look at the plate, Findo set off to investigate further. He prowled past bedrooms the size of his flat, bathrooms with industrial-looking Victorian plumbing and into what looked like it had once been a nursery. Dustsheets covered an old crib and a rocking horse half the size of the real thing that was kitted out with immaculate tack in red leather and silver chasing. Boxes of toys were stacked carelessly in one corner; out of one spilt a pirate's treasure of old costumes.

Back downstairs, Findo found a more modern study, complete

with PC, fax and all the other paraphernalia of the information age. He found what he was looking for in a drawer – a camera. It even contained a part-used film.

Findo took the camera upstairs and finished off the film by taking several pictures, from different angles, of the plate with the snake and lizard. He left after that, replacing the now empty camera in the downstairs office. The next day, after getting the film developed, he sent four photographs that he had taken off to Daniel Morris, along with his new telephone number.

The phone rang the next afternoon.

"It's Morris."

"You got the pictures then."

"Yes, I did. Very interesting too."

"What do you think?"

"It's not the original."

"Oh."

"No. That's in the Louvre. It's a good copy though. It's hard to tell from pictures but I'd guess it's nineteenth century. Probably by Avisseau. He was one of the main copyists of Palissy's work."

"Oh, well."

"Don't worry," said Morris. "It's still fairly valuable. Be worth a good few thousand at auction." He paused. "Leave it for the time being but if I come across someone who might be interested I'll let you know. On the other hand, if you're looking for work I'm sure I could find something interesting for you."

Findo shrugged. "I hadn't really thought about it. I just saw the plate and thought it looked like one you wanted once."

"Well," said Morris, "up to you. I take it you're not planning to come back to Oxford in a hurry."

"No."

"Really?" said Morris. "After what I read in the papers, I'd have thought you'd have been better off getting out of that place for a while. You must be public enemy number one up there."

"I'm staying," said Findo.

"Fair enough, that's your decision. But while you're around there, do you want some work? Give me a week or so and I can easily find a few jobs in your old neighbourhood."

"Okay."

And so, Findo went back to work for Daniel Morris. Following leads provided by the antiques dealer, he roamed widely during the spring months, covering great tracts of northern England and Scotland in pursuit of items sought by collectors who prized possession above scruples. His first target was a set of three early eighteenth-century Queen Anne silver-gilt casters, attributed to the artisan Philip Rollos and weighing in at a solid estimate of one hundred and sixty thousand pounds. They were stolen direct from an auction house in Manchester just eight days before they were due to go on sale.

Then there was a rare Tang dynasty piece, a glazed pottery model of a camel and rider dating from around the eighth century. The piece, recently valued by a firm of auctioneers at about ninety thousand pounds, was stolen from the Loch Lomond retreat of a reclusive American collector.

Following that theft, Strathclyde police initially concentrated on the firm of auctioneers, looking for the inside link. But they never found one – although the presence of their officers did prompt a junior member of staff to confess to his boss about a spot of creative accounting that had helped bolster his already reasonable salary. The reason the police never found any link with the theft of the Tang piece was that one did not exist; Morris had traced the item forwards from when the American had bought it at auction in 1973, tracking down his UK address after an exhaustive Internet search of dozens of newspaper archives and other databases.

For Findo, the work for Morris, although still only occasional, gave some structure to his life. Once given his target, Findo would set off to reconnoitre. Sometimes, he would travel hundreds of miles to the location Morris had given him, spend a few hours or days surveying the area and then go home. He would return, often weeks later, for the actual theft. His record time was forty minutes from getting out of his car to setting off for home, although most intrusions took at least twice that time. Then there would be the long trip south to deliver the goods.

In between burglaries, he continued to spend an increasing amount of time with Otis. Otherwise, the rest of his life was as quiet as ever; he read, wandered the city and outlying areas and watched films. But there was one hole in his life that would not go away, even on the rare occasions when he tried to ignore its existence.

The thought of Abby gnawed at him. It was worse being back in the city. Although while in Oxford he had never forgotten her, his existence had been different enough that he had been able to push her memories further away. Now, back in the town where they had grown up together, shared escapades and confidences, it was harder to ignore the ghost of her presence. It was hardest sometimes in the flat. Lying in his bed, Findo could almost feel her next to him. He could see her lying on his sofa listening to music. Sometimes he half-expected her to emerge from the kitchen with a drink for them both.

There were times when thoughts of Abby brought tears to his eyes and sank him into a black depression. But it was a misery he had no desire to escape. He could have found somewhere else to stay so he would not feel her image slipping into the flat to join him. But other times the thoughts of Abby made his heart swell and spirit feel glad. Findo was used to solitude; he was used to a hard life. Putting up with the dark days was a small price to pay; he preferred her ghost to her complete absence.

It was because of Abby that he fought shy of getting too close to the girls that he met through Otis and the nightclub. He was happy to share their company. He was happy to let them use him in the same way that he used them but he was also always ready to slip away the next day. He had half a dozen fleeting liaisons that way and most had been happy to let him go the next morning, his purpose served.

There was one young woman, however, who had been reluctant to let him go. A plump blonde called Julie, she had tried to persuade Findo to take her out. He had mumbled some insincere, non-committal answer at the time and left without waking Otis, still comatose in an armchair. But Julie had not given up and came back to the flat several times in a vain bid to turn the young man she knew as Phil into her regular and win a promise of his affection. When she turned up a second time Findo slept with her, led by his loins rather than heart or brain. The third time that she appeared Findo had pleaded a headache and kept his distance. The next few nights that Otis was DJ-ing Findo stayed away from the flat.

But when Julie turned up a fourth time, Findo realised just saying 'no' was not an option. Not expecting anything to come of it, Findo made a pass at another girl who had joined the after-hours party. But far from being rebuffed, Findo's advances were welcomed and a couple of minutes later he was on his way to Otis' bedroom, the girl on his arm oblivious to the killer glares being directed at her. It was a crude manoeuvre but it worked; Julie never came hunting Findo again.

But the young women that were prepared to trade their bodies in exchange for his were no more than a diversion. Each party enjoyed the temporary illusion of being cherished by a stranger but it was an animal coupling, a gratification, pleasurable for both but of no significance. Even in the act of entering another woman's body there were times when Findo was blocking out the reality of the face beneath him; he was thinking of the only girl that meant anything of substance to him.

Sometimes he talked about Abby to Frances Reid – often because it was easier than answering the old woman's probes about his own life but also because the old revolutionary was the only person with whom he could really discuss Abby.

Abby had never stopped writing to Mrs Reid and through that correspondence Findo learnt about her life in Edinburgh. To begin with, he got a potted history of what Abby had written over the past few months, highlights from past letters. Through those he heard about the flat she lived in and the girls she shared with, their loves, fears and concerns. Abby wrote about the course she was on but mainly from the angle of the people that she came into contact with, creating sharp and wicked word portraits of those around her. Findo heard about her job working in a local bookshop and the voluntary job helping at an RSPCA rescue centre. There was news of her mother and her thoughts on various world and local events of which Findo was mainly oblivious.

Most of the time Findo listened avidly and with a smile on his face. He could hear Abby's voice coming through the words, imagining the look on her face as she pushed her cascade of red curls back from her face and concentrated on her pen.

But there were also times when she mentioned boys she knew and had been out with. Then the smile would fade and an empty look would cross his eyes to accompany the hollowness in his innards. To begin with, there was no obvious favourite and Findo got no hint that Abby had a particular boyfriend. There was also, though not surprisingly, no mention of any physical relationship in the letters to Mrs Reid and Findo could only listen to what was not said and try to avoid imagining the worst.

When the Easter holidays approached, Findo hoped he would hear that Abby was coming home; in an older letter she had mentioned coming to visit Mrs Reid. But then she appeared to change her mind. A new letter came in which she spoke of staying in Edinburgh. She said she had coursework to do. The rescue centre also never stopped wanting help. And then there was the mention of Patrick. His name had cropped up a couple of times before. But this time it was repeated several times in the same letter. Findo heard that he and Abby had gone out a few times, that Patrick was also staying in Edinburgh and Abby had decided to remain too so that she could keep him company.

Findo was sitting on the floor as Mrs Reid read the letter. He listened in silence and felt something shrivelling inside him.

It crossed his mind to go to Edinburgh but he fought the urge down. He had never forgotten the letter that Abby had sent to him in Oxford. Although it had been over four years earlier, he still remembered it practically word for word. The message he had read in it still burned in his heart, a deep-down commandment that he had never thought to take at anything other than face value. As far as he was concerned, Abby had told him they were through. She had made it plain that she could no longer accept him and Findo had never thought to question or challenge that declaration.

But while Findo was learning about Abby from Mrs Reid, it never occurred to him that the old librarian might be writing to Abby about him. It also did not strike him that Abby might even be aware that her letters were now being read to Findo.

41. Heat and doubt

It was the summer of Findo Gask's twentieth year and a good one. High-pressure ridges seemed to have taken a liking to the north of England and southern Scotland, rarely moving out of an area that stretched from Morecambe Bay to the Firth of Tay. Consequently, the city basked in temperatures that set tar bubbling and sent flora and fauna into a frenzy of display and copulation – followed by a dreamy, heat-induced lassitude.

The balmy weather had come unusually early. Following the floods of late autumn and early winter – unprecedented in recent memory – an ice-laden northern wind had laid siege to the city for nearly a month. But by mid-March the Arctic airs had retreated to their own domain and from then on the weather had got steadily warmer. Bulbs erupted from the frost-free earth, the unfurling of new leaves was so hasty that their rustling could almost be heard and the first swallow had been spotted by late April – followed days later by flocks of the swooping aerial acrobats, eager after their long flights from Africa to snap up the insect bounty also brought on by the unseasonable warmth.

Findo spent days with Otis soaking up the unaccustomed heat. Occasionally they made it no further than the balcony of his brother's flat but more often they were to be found up on the roof of the block. Findo had picked the lock on the door onto the roof and replaced it with one of his own. Up there they had the place to themselves. Using an extension lead draped down the side of the building, they had power for Clint's mixing desk, space to lie out and no one to disturb them. There was also the chance of a cooling breeze, although more often they sweltered in a dead calm. By late May, as temperatures rose into the mid-twenties, they stripped down to shorts and let the sweat puddle around them as they lay out in the sun, baking until their senses were dulled by heat and glare.

As the days got longer and longer, the two brothers more or less moved up onto the roof. Clint, who lived with his family in a neighbouring block, joined them. They took up mattresses, deckchairs that Findo bought from a Homebase store on the Warner Drive estate and umbrellas that Clint and one of his friends stole from a pub out in Dubmore. The drains in each corner of the roof made convenient urinals and there was little need to go down to ground level except for supplies.

For a while, the biggest nuisance they faced was the need to traipse up and down several floors every time someone wanted a cold drink. Findo solved that problem, however, turning up one day with a brand new fridge-freezer sticking out of the back of his Fiesta. It took four of them several hours to manoeuvre the appliance up nine floors by the stairs and then onto the roof, where they rigged a piece of tarpaulin across the top just in case it did rain. At the time, exhausted by the unaccustomed exercise, Findo's new companions collapsed into their deckchairs and cursed the infernal machine. But later that day, with the fridge-freezer connected to the power supply and stocked with beers and soft drinks, opinions soon changed.

A carnival soundtrack accompanied the days of lazing. Clint had rigged up another tarpaulin over his decks and tended to spend much of the day hunched over them, mixing and sampling whatever sounds took his fancy. The Beach Boys and Lonnie Liston Smith joined Carlos Santana and Bob Marley, snatches of their songs drifting out across the rooftops along with Ibiza dance grooves, the sound of breaking surf and tropical bird song. Clint's eclectic tastes were further revealed when he dug deeper into his stock, displaying a fondness for early English folk rockers like Steeleye Span and Fairport Convention, as well as the music of Brazilian stars like Milton Nascimento and Gilberto Gil.

Sometimes Otis – the other half of DJ Lemon – joined Clint at the decks. Other times, Findo's half-brother was content to crash out, smoke his joints and drift away into a stoned reverie while his partner spun his musical web. But despite some mockery from Clint, Findo was surprised to notice that Otis did not completely laze away the summer. As well as getting stoned and dozing in the sun, Otis would also spend at least a couple of hours each day flicking through coursework, reading textbooks and magazines, and working on college projects. He also went to nearly all of his lectures and tutorials, only skiving off when it was so hot that he could not even be bothered to move.

Inevitably, news of the rooftop escape began to spread. To begin with it was just a few of the other younger occupants from the block of flats that came knocking at the door to the roof. They were joined by a few of DJ Lemon's friends from Resist. A couple of more energetic individuals hauled a large gas-powered barbeque up to the roof. One day a barrel of stolen lager – complete with line and tap – appeared.

The evening parties started to get wilder and bigger. Instead of mixing tunes for their own amusement, Clint and Otis began to find they had an eager audience, sometimes from mid-afternoon. The roof turned into a heaving dance floor from dusk to dawn and the pulsating sounds of DJ Lemon reached new parts of the city as the volume increased along with the tempo.

There were few complaints from within the block – most of the ninth floor was empty, the flats boarded up and derelict. But things came to a head on the night that Findo was coming up the stairwell from Otis' flat. Two men he vaguely recognised as living in a squat on the sixth floor barred his way.

"Five quid," said the larger one of the two.

"What?"

"Five quid if you want to go up. Otherwise, piss off."

Findo drew a deep breath. There was no one else around on the stairs. He could hear the music above him and the babbling cries of a party crowd.

"Look," he said. "That's my brother playing the music up there. This is our party."

The second man, a lanky punk in ripped leather, shrugged. "You on the guest list, are you?"

Findo closed his eyes. "What guest list? There isn't a guest list."

"Alright," said the first man. "Half price. Give us a couple of quid and we'll say no more."

Findo could feel his temper rising. He was unsure whether he wanted to bang his own head against the wall or those of the two blocking his way. Trouble was, it was two against one and neither of the self-appointed doormen looked as if they would bat an eyelid at kicking him all the way down the stairs – or at helping him to bash his head against the concrete block-work to their side.

"Look," said Findo slowly. "We've got two options because I haven't got any money on me anyway. Either you let me in for free or I go back down to my brother's flat."

The second man laughed. "Fuck off then."

Findo swallowed as he started to turn away. "Okay. But when I get down there, I'll turn the power off. Soon as I do that, the party's going to stop pretty quick. I'll also call my brother on his mobile and let him know why. Then you're going to have some pretty pissed-off customers who'll be wanting their money back. I can let them know what flat you're in too."

The punk glowered and began to start down the stairs towards Findo but his friend held him back.

"Alright," said the first man quickly. "Just go on up."

Findo nodded and walked past, ignoring the punk and trying not to hurry.

At the top of the stairs, a thought struck him and he turned round. "By the way. If you're charging people five quid a head for this, you'd

369

better be paying the DJs."

"What!" The punk snarled the word and Findo backed away a couple of steps.

"Listen," he said. "You're onto a good thing here. I'm not going to stop you charging. It's still only early. Last night there were probably over a hundred people up here – that's five hundred quid."

The punk stopped, his friend's hand gripped onto his leather jacket. "Keep going," said the first man.

"Well," said Findo, "they're the ones playing the music. That's why people are coming up here. If they pack up, that's it; your little scam's over. On the other hand, there's two of them so I reckon a fifty-fifty split's fair."

The punk did not look impressed but his friend gave a relaxed smile. "Alright, mate. It's a deal. See us at the end of the night and we split it."

Findo shook his head. He could hear more people coming up the stairs. It was tempting to give up and slip back into the relative security of the throng behind him but he was also angry, resentful at being taken for a ride.

"No."

"Then what?"

"How much have you got so far?"

"None of your fucking business," said the punk.

"Not that much," said the other man.

Findo shrugged as coolly as he could. "Look, be sensible. You can make a good bit of money tonight or you can get greedy and lose out. It's up to you. We'll get a hundred people up here easy. Give me two-fifty and they'll keep playing until at least three. You keep anything else afterwards. That's fair."

The first man looked uncertain. "How do we know you'll get as many people up here tonight?"

He glanced back over his shoulder as three women wearing short summer dresses and carrying bottles of spirits and mixers in their hands came into sight from below.

"You don't," said Findo. "If we only get eighty then you lose out. But if we get a hundred and twenty people then you're quids in, aren't you? You come out on top." Findo shrugged again. "Besides, think about it. There's no point falling out – we can do this more than one night. It doesn't have to be just tonight. It could be several nights of the week."

The first man nodded slowly. "Yeah," he said. "Alright." He turned to his friend. "Give him the dosh."

The punk looked at Findo sourly as he dug inside his jacket. He pulled out a wad of notes and counted it out. There was eighty pounds.

Beneath him, the first man turned to the young women who had just arrived. They looked surprised when he stopped them and a little annoyed but all looked resigned and began to dig into their handbags.

The punk handed Findo the bundle of notes. "That's it. We'll give you the rest later, when more people turn up."

Findo glanced over his head at the number of people already on the roof. "No way. I want two-fifty now and the party continues."

The punk shoved his tattooed face towards Findo. "I'm going to fucking stick you in a minute. You want a blade in the ribs?"

Findo stared back, looking as calm as he could. Gut instinct told him to back off but a colder, more calculating part of him was beginning to enjoy the confrontation. He also knew that if he backed down now he would never get another penny from the pair and, having taken an instant loathing to the punk, he was determined not to show any weakness.

"Not really," said Findo. "How do you fancy being used as a training aid for my brother's dogs?"

The punk looked uncertain. "What fucking dogs?"

Findo smiled. "Not this brother. Another one. He organises fights over Dubmore way. He's got three pit bulls that always need a bit of exercise." He leaned forwards and pushed his face until it was almost touching the punk's. "Don't forget, we know where you live and I've got a lot of friends in this city. Probably more than you and some of them a lot uglier. So stop pissing about and give me the rest of the cash."

The next morning, after almost everyone apart from a few who were incapable of moving had gone, Findo helped Otis and Clint clear their equipment from the roof. Several people had seen the council van cruising round the block at about five in the morning. The van had stopped briefly in a parking area up the road and a man had got out and taken some kind of readings with equipment from inside.

"But if they was council, why didn't they try and bust us last night?" one of Clint's friends, a Scouser by the name of Flea, had asked.

"Too much bother," said Otis.

"Yeah, but are they going to come back?" said Clint, thoughtfully touching the shirt pocket that held his half of their night's unexpected earnings.

Findo shrugged. "Probably."

Otis nodded. "They will if it keeps going like it has been."

"Nah," said Flea. "We ain't bothering no one."

Clint grinned and opened a can of Carlsberg. "Yeah, they probably appreciate some good sounds for a change."

Otis grinned. "Yeah, but . . ."

"Come on," said Flea. "If they was going to bust us, they'd have done it last night."

"Not necessarily," said Findo.

"Why not?"

"Because the bloke down there probably realised there were too many people up here. He couldn't have done anything on his own and if he'd called the police there might have been trouble. A riot on a rooftop wouldn't be too much fun. They'd have a lot of trouble getting everyone down without a nasty fight."

Flea grinned. "Sounds like a laugh."

Clint looked uncertain. "What do you reckon they'll do, then?"

"Wait until tonight," said Otis. "See if we get going again. Then come in mob-handed before things really get going and there's too many people up here."

"Probably seize your decks and all the rest of the stuff too," added Findo.

Clint looked horrified. "No way. I'm not letting no one get their hands on any of my gear." He looked around at his friends. "Right. Let's get packed up and out of here."

All traces of their occupation, apart from a litter of empty drink containers, cigarette butts and the roaches from spent joints, were gone by midday. Most of the gear went back down to Otis's flat. Findo also removed his lock from the door to the roof and put the original one back.

Although the rooftop parties were over by mid-June, the summer was only just getting going. For a while, Findo and Otis took to hanging out in the city's main park, whiling away the time watching the level of women's skirts rising to match the temperature. But the park was crowded and Otis and Clint got fed up with having to watch for prying eyes as they rolled their joints.

So, often accompanied by one or two other acquaintances from Resist, the trio took to piling into Findo's Fiesta and driving to the coast beyond Port Annan or into the hills north of the city. They got hold of several ice-boxes for drinks and Findo bought a big portable tape and CD player to keep Clint amused.

Otis and Findo also made one trip over to the Lake District to meet up with Billy. The reunion went even better than any of them had ever expected. Otis broke down in tears when he saw Billy again – his display of emotion even prompting a break in his half-sister's normally tough and unruffled poise. Chloe was there as well and Billy was even more pleased when she saw how Otis and her partner immediately clicked into an easy rapport. The two brothers stayed in Eskdale for five days – Findo happy to snatch a chance of indulging his liking for white water again in more usual circumstances – before heading back to the city so that Otis could get to an important tutorial for his college course.

Findo had plenty of time on his hands because he had recently pulled out of a job for Daniel Morris and turned down another one that the antiques dealer had offered. Findo had not explained anything to Morris but was having second thoughts about their relationship.

It was Mrs Reid that had made him question what he was doing. He had been round at her house one Thursday morning, keeping a promise to tidy up her front garden. He had to help the old librarian out into the garden and arrange her seat in the shade. Findo then set to work – under careful instruction – to get the unkempt foliage back into a semblance of shape and order.

They had also been discussing, after a fashion, the apparent decline of union movements across most of the Westernised world. Mrs Reid had been doing most of the talking, with Findo adding in the odd 'yes' or 'no' at what seemed appropriate points.

"These personal contracts they talk about are just another way to divide and rule," said Mrs Reid. "Managers encourage individual workers to think they can do better by negotiating their own private bargains. Anyone who believes that is a fool though. Individuals have no real strength; we have to bargain collectively otherwise there's no one to watch your back – or examine the small-print."

"Hmm," said Findo, tugging at a bramble reluctant to give up its purchase.

Mrs Reid gave a dry laugh. "We're all exploited, even you, but we should at least try and force employers not to take us for granted."

Findo grunted as he stumbled backwards, the roots of the briar having finally given up the struggle. "What do you mean I'm exploited?" he said absently.

"Of course you are."

He looked curiously at the old woman watching him hawk-like from the shade. "How?"

Mrs Reid shook her head. "If you're not even aware of the fact that's doubly disappointing."

Findo stood up and wiped at the sweat trickling down his forehead. "You mean because someone else gives me jobs to do?"

"No. Don't be silly." Mrs Reid's tone was sharp. "There's nothing wrong in principle with doing a job. We all need to earn our daily bread – even if your way is a little different from most."

"Well, what do you mean then?"

"Your wages."

"Wages? How do you mean?"

Mrs Reid shook her head. "I seem to remember that last time you got your name splashed across the papers, the reports highlighted the disappearances of certain valuable items."

A smile made the corners of Findo's mouth twitch. "What, not blamed on me?"

Mrs Reid looked severe. "Don't be frivolous."

"Sorry."

"Now, among the items listed as stolen was a rare Ming dish. Taken from an exhibition at a gallery in Oxford. Valued at fifty thousand pounds. Do you remember it?"

Findo considered. "Yeah, I think I know the one you mean, blue and white with some sort of inscription on it, Islamic I think it was supposed to be."

"And how much were you paid for that job?"

Findo shrugged. "Can't really remember."

"Roughly."

"A few thousand? Might have been two thousand. Good money, anyway."

"Good money?"

"Yeah."

Mrs Reid raised her eyebrows. "What about the Elizabethan silver gilt cup that you took from the castle in the Welsh Borders?"

Findo looked uncertain.

"The one with the tall stem and the cover. It would have looked more like the type that's used as a trophy – like footballers win – than the sort of cup that you drink your tea from."

"Oh, that one."

"Yes. That one. Any idea what it was worth?"

He shook his head. "No, don't think I remember."

"Any idea how much you were paid for it?"

Findo rubbed his brow again as he racked his brain for the details. "I'm not sure. I think it was quite a good one. Might have been five thousand."

"Really? What if I told you that it was worth up to a quarter of a million?"

Findo looked shocked. "That much?"

"Yes," said Mrs Reid. "So even if your friend who takes these objects off your hands only sold them for a fifth of their real value, he'd be making about ten times as much as you."

Findo shrugged uncomfortably. "Well, he comes up with the ideas and he knows where to sell them."

Mrs Reid looked at him silently for a moment. "And you really think that you're not exploited? So, tell me, what would happen to you if you were caught?"

Findo scowled. "Yeah, I'd probably end up in prison. But that's not the point; I don't just do it for the money. The money's not important. I don't really care how much things are worth."

Mrs Reid gave a slight nod. "Well I suppose that's one consolation. But your friend obviously cares how much they're worth." She waved a hand at him dismissively. "But if you're happy to take nearly all the risks for a fraction of the reward and let him get rich at your expense, that's fine. Just don't pretend you're not being exploited. It's no different because you're, shall we say, 'self-employed'. You need to at least recognise what's happening if someone is taking advantage of you – even if you're prepared to accept it because it happens to suit you."

Mrs Reid pointed to Findo's side. "Now. Stop slacking. Under that laurel, I can see some more brambles that need digging out."

42. Still Abby

It was the end of June when Findo heard Abby was coming back. She had finished her second year at university and was returning home the coming weekend to visit her mother. The news came at the end of a short letter to Frances Reid.

Findo nodded quietly as he heard the news. "Yeah?"

He was unaware that Mrs Reid had skipped the two paragraphs of postscript.

"Oh, what a shame."

"What's that?"

"She's planning to call on me on at eleven o'clock on Saturday morning. But I won't be here. I've got a check up at the hospital."

"Have you?"

"Oh yes." Mrs Reid nodded. "That's a shame. It'll be a wasted visit for her."

Findo frowned. "Can't you write and tell her you won't be here?"

Mrs Reid shook her head. "I'm not sure there's time, dear. She's off to visit some friends in Dunfermline first and then coming home from there on Friday. And she's leaving this evening."

"Oh well," said Findo.

"I suppose I could leave a note on the door," said Mrs Reid. "At least then she'll know why I'm not there to say hello. I wouldn't want her to worry."

Findo frowned. "You shouldn't do that. If someone else comes they might see it and realise you're not home. You might get burgled."

Mrs Reid sighed. "Well, we can't have that can we. But what else do I do? Maybe you could let her know for me?"

"Me?"

"Why not? You haven't seen each other for ages. Abby knows you've been visiting me. And I'm sure you'd like to say hello to her. That wouldn't be too much trouble, would it?"

Findo could feel the uncertainty in his racing heart. The idea of seeing Abby again was exquisite torture. He nodded his head slowly, never stopping to realise that he had just been stitched up by someone much more devious than himself.

On Saturday morning Findo was sitting in Mrs Reid's front garden from nine-thirty. He had not called to see her first but had watched from down the road until he saw a taxi come to pick up the old librarian.

Only after he had seen the car disappear over the Allonby Bridge had he made his way up Dubmore Road and taken up his position.

It was another scorching hot day but Findo was hardly aware of the heat. A couple of times he wondered if he should have brought a couple of joints to help calm his nerves but he did not want to seem too fuddled when Abby arrived. The chair that Mrs Reid had been sitting in on Wednesday was still in the garden and Findo spent most of his time perched on its edge, fidgeting and shifting, unable to keep calm.

Every five or ten minutes he would get up and walk around the garden, scuffing at weeds with his feet or pacing with his hands stuffed into his pockets. He tried to avoid going to the entrance to the drive, although he could not resist the temptation entirely. But each glance up Dubmore Road was quick and furtive; he did not want Abby to see him staring along the street as if he could not wait for her to arrive.

The wait was agony. He could not think clearly but he could not stop thinking. His stomach felt cramped and he wondered if he had eaten something bad the night before. He thought about going into Mrs Reid's house to use the toilet but did not want to miss Abby's arrival. If he was inside and could not get to the door in time she might think there was no one in and just go away.

Abby turned into the entrance to Mrs Reid's drive at two minutes past eleven. She was on foot and did not immediately see Findo, who was in the shade, momentarily petrified.

He watched her approach with an open mouth. She was everything he remembered and more. Her mass of red hair was longer than ever and tied loosely behind her head with a thin patterned scarf. She was wearing sandals, baggy blue trousers and a dark green singlet. On the front of the shirt, printed in large white letters, was the message: 'Don't Nuke The Whales'. Underneath, in smaller writing, it proclaimed: 'Afro-Celt Green Resistance'.

Abby was looking around as if expecting to spot something and Findo stood up just as her eyes turned in his direction. He did not say anything, unsure what words to use or whether they would come out right. She did not speak immediately either but turned across the gravel towards him.

Abby was still a few paces away when she spoke. "Hello, Findo."

The tone of her voice could have been interpreted as warm or cool depending on the optimism of the listener. It was reserved but not defensive or aggressive, possibly lukewarm or ambivalent – and certainly not surprised by his presence.

He was silent for a few seconds, trying to gather his thoughts – a harder process than he had imagined.

"Hi," he said finally, as Abby stopped in front of him. He continued to stare at her. The sun had turned the freckles on her face into an almost continuous dappled pattern. Her shoulders and arms were bronzed. He noticed that she still did not have her ears pierced.

She smiled with a slightly mocking expression – although at whose expense was an open question – and raised an eyebrow.

Findo smiled back tentatively. "You look really good."

The words seemed to tumble from his mouth almost of their own volition.

Abby grinned and laughed. "Straight to a woman's heart."

"What?"

"Never mind." She shook her head. "But thank you."

Abby looked him up and down. Findo was wearing a Spearhead T-shirt that Otis had given him and faded khaki trousers adorned with more pockets than even he had found uses for. On his feet was a pair of old blue baseball boots.

"I've seen worse," said Abby. "I must admit; you don't look like an arch-criminal."

Findo looked down for a moment. "Are you disappointed?"

Abby shook her head. "I don't know yet."

Findo nodded, uncertain how to proceed. "Mrs Reid's not here," he said. "She had to go to the hospital for a check-up. Just routine though, nothing to worry about, she said. She asked me if I could meet you. So you didn't think something had happened to her."

Abby smiled. "Thanks for coming, then." She paused. "I wondered if I might see you."

Findo shrugged, awkward, afraid and desperate to say the right thing. "I didn't know if you'd want to or not."

Abby frowned. "Why? Didn't you think I'd want to see you?"

Findo shook his head, miserable. "I thought you might not want to see me ever again."

Abby looked astounded and a little angry. "Why? What do you mean? Just because you haven't spoken to me for years doesn't mean I'd never want to see you again. I'm not like that."

Findo looked surprised at the heat in her voice. "I haven't spoken to you?"

"No."

"But you haven't spoken to me either."

Abby shook her head, eyes narrowing. "That's different. You were the one that went away. You never tried to write to me or call me. I didn't even know where you were. You never replied to the letter that I did send. I thought maybe you'd never got it. Or that you'd given up, that you couldn't be bothered to get in touch with me. I didn't know whether you'd found someone else or got yourself killed or locked up in prison or what."

Findo stared at her in astonishment, mesmerised by the tears that had suddenly started trickling down her flushed face. He shook his head and took her by the shoulders without thinking.

"But I got your letter," he said. "I thought you didn't want anything to do with me. That's what you said in your letter."

Abby blinked. "I did not!" Her voice was indignant and she shook his hands away from her shoulders.

"You did," said Findo. "That's what you said in your letter. I still remember it. You said 'it's sad that our friendship had to end like this'. That's what you wrote. I thought you didn't want to hear from me again. That's why I never wrote back. I wanted to but I thought I was doing what you wanted."

Abby looked aghast. "Oh, Findo! Even if that's what I wrote, I didn't mean it like that."

"I don't understand," he said.

Abby scowled. "That's clear enough." She shook her head. "Look, I wasn't even sixteen then. I was scared and really worried. I didn't know what was going to happen. You got hooked into that stupid, stupid robbery and I was frightened sick. I was angry at you. I didn't know whether you were going to end up in jail or whether the police would come after me because I was your friend. My mum was going absolutely ballistic, she was threatening to take me back to my grandparents and she must have been desperate because you know how much she hates them." Abby lent her forehead against his. "Oh, Findo, Findo, Findo. What will I ever do about you?"

They walked to begin with, strolling slowly. They wandered towards the bridge over the Allonby and stood watching the dark water sliding calmly by beneath them. On the Chapel Bank side a group of children were splashing in the edge of the river. They had rigged up a rope from a tree and were swinging over the water – daring each other to see how far out they could get.

"Looks like fun," said Abby.

"You want to go and join them?"

She shook her head. "Not at the moment."

The pavement was quite narrow over the bridge and the cars and lorries going by were too close for comfort to stand there for long.

"Where do you want to go?" said Findo.

Abby frowned. "I'm not sure."

"The old factory?"

"No. Not today. Somewhere neutral."

"Neutral?"

"Not too many memories," said Abby. "I want to talk to you, not just remember the past."

Findo considered. "Fort Hawley? That's just up the hill. It's normally quite quiet there too."

"Okay."

They set off in silence again. The leaves of the trees in Chapel Bank gave some welcome shade. Then they were heading up Fort Hill. They went past the crossing where Findo had spotted Otis. A little further up, a small path turned off right and disappeared through some sycamore trees. Findo and Abby followed it round, emerging onto the strip of open space that ran around the base of the fortifications that gave the hill its name.

After a few hundred yards they came to some benches. They were not as badly covered with graffiti as most park benches in the city and only one had been set on fire. There was a man walking an elderly Labrador some way off and a group of nurses from the hospital on the grass twenty yards away but other than that it was quiet.

They sat on the furthest bench. Below them they could see trees and the roof of a small church. Beyond, although hidden by the trees, was the Allonby. Further into the distance, on the other side of Newmills, they could see the open countryside to the south-west of the city.

"It's years since I've been here," said Abby. "I think we came here once, not long after you first found this place. I think that's probably the only time I've been here."

Findo nodded. "There's probably not many places where we haven't been."

Abby laughed. "Yeah. You gave me a good tour over the years. I hadn't really seen any of it until I met you. Just Denmark Street, my school and the old gas register. Is that still there?"

Findo nodded and pointed. "Yeah, it's over that way. See the railway line where it crosses the river? It's about a mile the other side of that."

"Oh, yes. I can just about make it out. Bit blurry. I'd probably need my glasses to see it properly."

"Glasses?"

Abby smiled. "I've been wearing them for a couple of years now."

Findo nodded. "Oh."

They sat in silence for several minutes. Findo kept glancing sideways at Abby, wanting to look at her but trying not to stare. He was still unsure how to start saying all the things he had thought that he wanted to say.

After a while, Abby laughed. "Stop it."

"What?"

"Looking at me like that?"

"Like what?"

She shook her head. "Oh, Findo. Where do we start?"

"Start what?"

"Talking."

"We are talking."

"No. Talking, talking."

"Oh. That kind of talking."

The silence returned for a while. Findo managed to stop glancing at Abby every few seconds but fidgeted continuously instead.

"Are you staying with your mum?" he asked eventually.

"For the moment."

"Then what?"

"I'm not sure," said Abby. "I can't stay there for too long. Mum and Stuart – that's her new husband – they're just totally wrapped up in each other. I quite like him but I don't want to share a house with them. It's too weird. And it's their home, not mine. They say they don't mind me staying there but I don't know. I just don't feel comfortable there."

"I've still got my flat," said Findo. "You could stay there."

His answer was instinctive and thoughtless. A brief, awkward silence followed.

"No." Abby shook her head. "Thanks but I don't think that would be the right thing."

"What are you going to do then?"

Abby paused. She looked away at the view. "I've got a friend who's getting a flat in the city, near Campfield. I'll probably stay there."

"A friend?" Cold despair gnawed at Findo. "A boyfriend?"

Abby nodded slowly. "Yes."

"A boyfriend?"

Abby frowned. "Yes. What did you expect? Did you think I was going to spend the rest of my life in a nunnery? I didn't know if I was going to ever see you again, Findo."

He turned his face away. He had not realised that he was crying until he suddenly felt the tears dripping off his chin.

"Findo?" Abby's voice was soft and sad. "Findo."

Her arms went around him and she drew him close, holding him against her.

"Oh, God. I'm sorry. I'm so sorry. I never wanted it to be like this either. I thought you'd left me for good." She rocked him in her arms. "For the first year I kept hoping you would come back. I used to read all the papers in case I'd see something about you. I don't even know what I was looking for, a crime report, a story to say you'd been caught. To begin with I used to dread turning on the local news. I kept wondering if there'd be something to say they'd caught the people who'd done the robbery and that I'd see you being carried away by the police. And I knew how much you'd hate it in jail. I thought they'd all pick on you and you'd come out in years and years and your life would have been ruined."

Abby was crying as well by the time Findo raised his head.

"But I was okay, I wrote to you."

Abby shook him as she hugged him.

"But that was ages afterwards. You went on the run in October or November. I didn't get your letter until the beginning of January." She pushed him away and made him look at her. "Findo. I had two months of misery expecting the worst. I thought that the fact I hadn't heard from you meant you were in real trouble, or that you didn't care, which was even worse."

Findo shook his head. "I wrote as soon as I had my own place to stay. And I didn't know what to say before then. I tried to say goodbye to you before I left but you wouldn't speak to me."

Abby gave a small smile. "Well? I was really angry with you. You were so stupid." She gave him a guilty look. "I think I was quite rude to your sister. Did she say anything?"

Findo shook his head. "I don't remember. But it doesn't matter. Anyway, then when I did write to you, you wrote back saying we weren't friends any more. You said our friendship was over. I didn't think you wanted anything more to do with me."

Abby sighed. "Oh, Findo."

She reached up and stroked his cheek. "I didn't mean it like that. I guess I was angry because you'd left me not knowing what had happened. I was furious with you for getting involved in that robbery in the first place and then you disappeared and that made it worse; I thought that because I'd refused to speak to you you'd gone and got yourself into worse trouble and that meant I'd never get to speak to you ever again. Then you suddenly wrote and it was a really stupid letter. You made it sound as if nothing much had happened – so I got really mad at you all over again."

She shook her head in exasperation. "But I didn't expect you to take my letter seriously. I thought you'd come back to find me. You were supposed to read between the lines, Findo. I thought that if you really loved me, you'd come and get me. I don't know – whisk me off to your hideout so I could go on the run with you."

Findo looked astonished. "Would you have?"

Abby grinned. "Probably – if you'd asked nicely."

Findo looked at her in amazement, trying to absorb the idea.

"But I never heard from you, Findo. I waited. I kept hoping that you would turn up and you never did. So eventually I thought that was it. I thought you'd disappeared for good. I thought maybe you'd run away to Brazil or wherever it is that robbers go. But then there was that story in the papers a couple of years ago, calling you the new Raffles of all things."

"You saw that?"

Abby nodded. "Oh yes. I'd just finished at college. Mrs Reid told me about it. My mum saw it too. Said all sort of things about you."

Findo frowned. "Why?"

Abby shook her head. "Because you scared her silly too. She used to worry stiff that you'd end up getting me in all sorts of trouble." She glanced down at their hands, which had somehow become entwined together. "And because she realised how much you'd hurt me. I'm her little girl, Findo. Still am. And she knew how miserable I was. She and Mrs Reid were the only people I could talk to about you, Findo. So she heard it all. I poured out my heart to her. So when we saw your name in the paper again it brought back bad memories. It gave us both a bad time. I thought it meant that you had just forgotten me, and she thought I'd get hurt again. Which I did." She added the last words softly.

Findo pulled her into his arms. "Oh, Abby. I am so sorry. It's all so stupid. I really thought you wanted me to leave you alone. I'd never have done it otherwise. But I never forgot you. I never did."

He leant forwards and kissed her gently. Her lips melted against his and long-buried passion poured into their embrace. But then Abby pulled away. She turned her head but Findo could see her shoulders moving and knew she was weeping.

"What is it?"

Abby shook her head. He put his arm across her bronzed shoulders, feeling the weight of her hair brush across his skin. It felt perfect.

"Abby. Come here."

She turned slowly towards him but moved a little further away down the bench. "No. It's not that simple, Findo. We can't just walk off into the sunset together. It doesn't work like that. Just because it was right in the past doesn't make it right now."

"It could be."

She sighed. "It could be. But we don't know and it's not the same." She clenched her fists. "Oh, this is a mess!"

"Why?"

Abby straightened up. "Because I've got a boyfriend, Findo. I didn't know what had happened to you and then last time I did hear about you I thought that you'd just forgotten about me. I didn't know you were going to come back. I didn't know it would be like this. I was miserable for years but in the end I had to try and forget. I had to get on with my life. I couldn't shut myself off from the world for years just in case you turned up one day. And now I've got a boyfriend. I care about him: he's a really nice person. And I can't just abandon him just because you've suddenly turned up and want me back."

She shook her head. "I don't know you any more, Findo. In a few months, it'll be five years since you disappeared. Our lives aren't the same. You don't know me any more. Maybe we could just pick up from where we left off but I don't know. And I can't just throw Patrick away in case you're still the right person. I can't do that to him. It's not fair and you can't make me."

43. Time of trial

It was nearly two weeks before Findo came up with his idea for winning Abby back again. In principle it was a good idea; there had been a day and an age when it might have worked.

He had been given plenty of time to think about it. Following the eruption of emotions caused by their reunion at Fort Hawley, Abby had fled, leaving Findo there on the bench, tormented and confused. But he had not been the only one suffering. The meeting – and parting – had been a painful experience for them both. In truth, Abby had been as loath to leave him as he was to let her go. Her flight, however, had been essential; she was scared – of the feelings his reappearance had brought back, of how easy it had been to kiss him. And desperately afraid of getting hurt once more.

Abby had come to Mrs Reid's house nervous, uncertain and determined not to show weakness. She had set up their meeting with conflicting emotions, balancing curiosity over seeing Findo and a determination to lay her demons to rest, against an underlying anger that had smouldered unchecked for years. And beneath that slow-burning rage was another ache, although one to which she would no longer admit; an absence that longed to be filled, a desire for completion that her life had lacked since Findo had gone.

But the outcome of their coming together again had been the discovery that her resentment and much of the pain caused had been based on mistaken assumptions. Her bitterness had also fled in the face of the revelation that Findo appeared to have suffered her loss just as much as she had pined for him.

The kiss that had briefly promised to sweep away the pain of the previous years had been a crucial turning point. Which was why Abby had hastily pulled back from the brink. Part of her could easily have let the moment sweep her away. But Abby's life was no longer that simple and the fears and doubts that held her in check were not to be vanquished that easily.

Abby had known the kiss was a symbol that, if prolonged, would have been difficult to later deny as being no more than an instinctive reaction. It was a crossroads that also marked the way onto a road from which it would be difficult to turn back. To go ahead was to commit to something largely unknown, led only by a companion who had previously been judged as less than perfect.

Therefore, before Abby could cope with resuming their friendship

– let alone anything else – she had quickly realised that she needed to come to terms with their past. She needed to reassess her judgement and claim for injuries on the new evidence that Findo had presented. It was an appeals process that could only be conducted by one person. Alone.

Re-opening the Pandora's box of her feelings for Findo was a dangerous process. They had grown up together and, through the middle years of their childhoods, been as close as could be. For Findo, Abby had started of as a surrogate for Billy, while Findo was the brother that Abby had never had. Later, as hormones began to unbalance previous assumptions, they had moved almost seamlessly into a more mature relationship – although whether that had been the result of a conscious and mutual adult attraction or the result of simple drift was uncertain.

And whether what emerged between them now was a renewed friendship or more, there were consequences to consider. Carrying on a relationship with a criminal wanted by half the police forces in the country was a much more serious matter than hanging out with a juvenile delinquent. Abby still wore the gold St Christopher that her mother had given her on top of Clathy Hill when she was nine-years-old. She was also well aware that Suzanne's reaction was unlikely to be positive if she ever learnt that Findo had re-emerged into Abby's life.

But most complicated and unpleasant of all was the question of Patrick Roberts. He had pursued Abby by gentle stealth for more than a year. He had been a loyal friend through most of their first year at university and only confessed his feelings at the end of their first summer term, just before Abby left for the holidays. His declaration had caught Abby by surprise; she had just had a brief but unsatisfactory relationship with an older student and when she poured out her problems on Patrick's shoulder had not realised that he might be biased by emotions other than simple friendship.

To begin with Abby had not been looking for another boyfriend and, as each went their separate ways over the holiday, had been able to postpone the issue until the start of her second year at university. On her return to Edinburgh, she had been half hoping that Patrick would have lost interest – although another part of her would have been deeply insulted. As it was, he had been circumspect but dogged in promoting his cause and in the end Abby had succumbed. At the time, she had avoided analysing her feelings, which in truth consisted of a slightly disturbing mixture of resignation, relief and affection fuelled in part by sympathy.

In many ways, Patrick was ideal. He was intelligent but not domineering. He was mild-mannered but idealistic. Physically he was gentle, perhaps a little timid. His academic ability was more highly developed than his common sense but he was less naive and more observant than many of his fellow students and lecturers gave him credit for. He had an ironic sense of humour and was not unattractive, even if not the kind of prime physical specimen that attracted glances in the street. He was also able to dissolve the sometimes-glacial reserve that Abby had developed as a balance for her otherwise fiery temper. He could absorb her furies when something provoked her wrath and was quite good at being able to know when to offer comfort and when to ignore.

Just as importantly, he had been consistent. He offered stability; he gave loyalty, was rarely demanding and was a known quantity, there when needed.

But still Abby was troubled. She had lived with the passion and trembling depth of her mother's love for her father. Suzanne had pined for years following Alan McGee's disappearance at sea and, although now remarried, had come to terms with her anguish rather than bury it. The ideals of romance had been part of Abby's life as well as something she read about in books and saw on the big and small screen. As a result of that exposure – and her own temperament – Abby had always lived with the assumption that she would one day find a soul mate to stir similar feelings in her.

For a while she had thought that she had found him. Findo had been infuriating, sometimes exasperating, unreliable and reluctant to show emotions. He was a bad risk when it came to stability and dangerous to know – in many ways. But she had never had any doubt over how much he had meant to her.

And then Findo had hurt her, badly. Once she had thought that she would never trust him, or any other boy, again. But to her confusion, Abby had just discovered that the damage caused by their parting had not, after all, been enough to destroy or reverse her feelings. In fact it had been the opposite. Almost from the moment that she saw him again, a churning in her stomach had revealed that he was far from being just a part of her history. After just over four-and-a-half years apart, the haunted look in his eyes as they met hers had acted like a depth charge into the wells of her bottled-up feelings and memories. And before she could go any further, she had to retreat and assess the damage, debate whether to shore up the defences and fight on, or let them drop and let the storm take her where it would.

She was also not a betrayer. Patrick Roberts had served her well and had laid himself bare to her. That was something that Abby could not simply ignore or forget.

And, although she had never made the kind of unqualified declaration that her new boyfriend wished for, Abby recognised that she had, nevertheless, made a commitment of sorts. Despite some reservations, she had agreed to share a flat with him for the summer. It was an experiment but one to which she had agreed. Circumstances may have been turned on their head but that was no excuse to rip her agreement to pieces and let it blow away in the wind along with the shreds of Patrick's hopes.

Apart from which, once the fire that Findo had awoken had burnt down, there was the question of whether the fuel needed to keep it fed might have dwindled away. Wild fire sometimes left nothing but cinders and a taste of ashes. Her feelings for Patrick were more of the order of a carefully controlled central heating system – less exciting but far more practical and requiring much less maintenance.

The situation was much more straightforward for Findo. He had endeavoured to bury his thoughts for Abby. Now that he realised that she had never meant to sever their tie – and having seen her again – he simply wanted her back.

Following their first meeting it had been a day before he heard from Abby again. Before she left, he had insisted on giving her his telephone number. She had called the next afternoon, supposedly to apologise for having left so abruptly the previous day. Since then they had spoken a number of times and met up four times. Abby had refused to come to the flat and been reluctant to arrange anything in the city, partly because she could not get it out of her head that Findo was wanted by the police for a long list of crimes but also because she did not want to be seen with another man by someone who might report the sighting to Patrick – already in their new flat and waiting for Abby to join him.

So far, Abby was still staying with her mother and new stepfather, using the excuse that she wanted to spend sometime with Suzanne and get to know Stuart a little better. The truth was that she had still not found a way or a moment to broach the subject of Findo's reappearance.

Patrick still knew nothing of the dark cloud looming on his personal horizon. He knew something of Abby's past and was subtle enough to have recognised there was more to the story than she had admitted. But through both fear of knowing and of reawakening old pains he had been content to wait for the story to either be forgotten or emerge in its own time.

Findo and Abby's second meeting had taken the form of a long walk in a forest park near Falloch Moor, a hilly region to the city's north-west. They met a third time at Mrs Reid's house, the presence of a chaperone making the situation easier for both of them. The fourth occasion took place eleven days after the original reunion. This time they took a long drive in an arc around the city, ending up in a county pub near Port Annan. Later, they sat for hours through twilight and into the night, watching slow waves breaking against the strand under a hunter's moon.

Their conversation was circumspect. They talked of the past but stuck to the childhood years of their friendship, not venturing into the territory of their teenage years. Abby spoke for a while about her new stepfather and the peculiarity of seeing her mother in love again after over a decade of solitude and sadness. Findo talked in loose terms about his life. He gave few details of the things that he had stolen or the properties that he had burgled but recounted his thoughts about the places where he had lived. He told Abby about Billy, the life that she had forged for herself against the odds. He spoke of his time in the Lake District and his introduction to kayaking and rock-climbing. He described rediscovering his youngest half-brother and how their rooftop parties had mushroomed into summer madness.

Abby listened quietly for the most time, soaking up not just Findo's words but also his presence and his mannerism; unknown to him, his appeal hearing was still ongoing and the jury had yet to retire.

Findo was wandering through the city centre on his own the next day, deep in thought, when a poster on a billboard halfway along Albert Parade caught his attention.

It was the simplicity of the design that struck him. On a deep, cerulean blue background glittered an enormous diamond. The image showed soft beams of light striking the gem from behind, causing flares of brilliance on its facets.

Findo spared it a quick glance and turned away. But he had only walked about twenty yards when he noticed the sign for a jewellers' shop a little way further down the shopping precinct. Somewhere in his brain the connection was made between the poster and a marketing slogan for the diamond industry.

Findo stopped. He paused for a moment and then turned back to take another look at the poster and see exactly what it was advertising.

His operation began about an hour later. He spent a little time in the park behind the city museum thinking about it first but it seemed almost inevitable – also necessary. He had no faith in whether patience would secure Abby again; he had to do something and the opportunity seemed to have been created for the purpose.

To begin with, as with any other theft, he prepared by scouting the ground, looking for weaknesses and openings. He studied walls, windows and rooflines. He looked for security cameras and alarms. He eyed up railings and spiked fences, main doors and service entrances. He surveyed neighbouring buildings and the position of trees, manholes and drainpipes. He analysed the placing of lamp posts and any other lighting that might hinder his freedom to move without being observed. His research involved walking the whole area, both immediate and in wider circuits, looking for avenues of approach, areas of opportunity and the options for escape.

It was a slow but thorough process. It had to be. Findo was never given to taking chances without having first evaluated the risks; that was why he had rarely been foiled and never been caught. The plan he had in mind, if it was to succeed, would mark a high point in his career to date. He was also determined it would work for another reason; this was not just for the challenge or for feeding another's greed – this was for him and for Abby. If his idea worked, he hoped to prove how much he loved her. It was a gesture that would say, in the words that he did not know how to use, how desperately he wanted to be hers again.

The first part of his reconnaissance took the rest of that afternoon and part of the evening. Findo took his time. He moved casually: just another pedestrian, another gawper on the pavement, another passer-by seeking shade on a street corner. He bought drinks and sandwiches from a take-away to eat in one position. Later he sat and read a book in another. He also bought a ticket for the city museum, so he could get another perspective from windows on the upper floors and look for alternative options.

It was approaching three in the morning when Findo made his first foray into the target territory. He was already inside the park behind the city museum, where he had spent four hours waiting. The moon was just starting to set and he reckoned he had the best part of two hours of darkness before dawn started to light up the city again.

Findo slid gently out from under the cover of a large rhododendron where he had been dozing. He checked the luminous dial on his wristwatch and began to flit forwards. He moved quickly across the open areas of grass, trying to stay underneath trees or close to the edges of shrub borders. But it would have taken good eyes to spot the movement as his black-garbed figure eased fast and soft across the park.

He paused at the edge of the last stretch of lawn and looked around. Nothing moved except a few ragged strips of cloud sailing high and slow across the starlit sky. Down at ground level there was little breeze; the leaves of the bushes around him barely stirred.

Something rustled in the undergrowth off to Findo's left and he froze, holding his breath. There was silence then the noise came again. An odd, snuffling grunting followed the second rustle. Findo breathed softly, holding still.

He smiled a few minutes later as he saw a small shape emerge from a bush and trot purposefully away across the lawn – a hedgehog on night patrol.

Findo turned his attention back to the museum. There was one security camera on a wall directly above him and another on a corner off to the right. Both cameras were currently angled away from Findo. He watched them for a moment and then sprinted forwards.

Seconds later he was underneath the shelter of a large holm oak. The tree stood alone on the edge of the lawn. Three yards beyond the oak was the wall dividing the park from the museum. The wall was built of rough stone but with few foot or handholds. It was about twelve feet high and topped with a metal railing with two rows of curved spikes that curved out towards the park.

Findo ignored the wall and pulled a length of thin climbing rope from a pouch inside his sleeveless jacket. There was a lead weight on one end and he twirled it a few times before lobbing the end of the rope upwards. He missed first time but on the second attempt got the weight over a branch about eight feet above his head.

Once the rope was safely over, Findo flicked the loop forwards so that it was nearly flush with the trunk. He passed the double length of rope round his shoulders and under both arms. Then, draping the loose end over his left arm, he took the hold of the two cords above him with both, gloved hands. Leaning back, he began to climb, using his feet to push against the oak's trunk and pulling himself up, hand over hand on the rope.

He was up in less than a minute and standing on a thick branch. He stowed his weighted rope away again and edged forward along the branch, carefully crossing the space between the tree and the wall. Findo took tiny steps, feeling his way with his feet. Smaller branches to either side helped him balance and there was just enough background light under the tree's canopy to roughly see the line of the branch supporting him.

When he was over the top of the wall, Findo dropped down and slid sideways off the branch. His feet found spaces between the metal spikes, now curving out away from him, and he lowered himself into a crouch.

Seconds later he was down, inside the museum's rear compound. Next to him were a couple of parked council vans. Findo crouched between them for nearly quarter of an hour. One of the security cameras was pointed in his direction.

It swivelled away after about three minutes but Findo did not move. He sat in the shelter of the vans and waited until the second camera turned towards him. Only when that one had swung away again did he move, darting towards the base of the museum building. Just beyond the parking area was a raised terrace. A small wing of the building projected out and in the corner Findo found a large metal drainpipe.

He began to climb, using the ornamental stonework around an adjacent window to find extra purchases for his feet. After ten feet it got even easier; a succession of minor pipes branched off the main drain like the fingers on a child's drawing of a tree.

Findo reached the building's third floor in less than four minutes. He shuffled sideways along a pipe until he was directly in front of a small sash window. He wedged himself into the stone recess around the window and dug into a pocket on the side of his jacket. From inside he pulled a cloth-wrapped bundle of small tools. Selecting one, he slid it between the window and the frame and worked it carefully around, checking for any sign of an alarm. He found nothing but had not expected to. Swapping the tool for a stiffer piece of metal, he forced the second tool between the two halves of the sash and slid it to one side until he found the catch.

Ten minutes later, Findo was back on the drainpipe and climbing higher. The window had led to a staff toilet. Beyond was a corridor leading into the main body of the building. He had got into the corridor without any problem but then come to a halt. Infrared movement sensors protected the passage ahead, and the offices to either side.

It might have been possible to disable the sensors or find gaps in their coverage but that would have taken time; it was quicker to move on and continue up.

Two floors up, Findo reached the parapet around the museum's main roof. He stepped over and dropped down to a seated position, giving his muscles a chance of a brief rest. He checked his watch. It had taken him just under forty minutes to get this far and he still had a comfortable margin for the rest of this reconnaissance.

From the edge of the museum roof, he used a gully to cross over the ridge and down to where the building ran around a central courtyard. It was easy enough going, the roof was covered with lead and the slope was gentle enough that there was little danger of slipping. It was also completely dry and protected by an ornamental parapet.

Findo followed the edge of the courtyard around. He was also in no danger of being spotted here. He could not be seen from the road and the only cameras were looking down and into the courtyard rather than at the roof.

The only barrier between the museum and the city's theatre and art gallery was a low wall. There was even a service ladder to help him over. Findo continued quickly on. Beyond him was the domed roof above the theatre's main auditorium. Findo was a quarter of the way around the dome's arc when he saw a small window set into the roof above him. Scrambling up took a few attempts because of the curve of the dome but a lightning strip gave Findo the necessary hold.

There was a latch on the window but it was loose and Findo was able to flick it open with one movement. The beam from his pencil torch showed him a large, completely circular attic room with walls that curved up into the ceiling to follow the shape of the dome. It was empty apart from dust, spiders and a few broken light fittings. There were several square hatches set into the floor, which Findo ignored for the time being. Otherwise the wooden boards were covered with old linoleum. The room looked abandoned. There was only one door, opposite the single window where Findo had entered.

Findo moved carefully across, listening for creaks from the floorboards and using his torch beam to check for obstacles. He made it without incident and opened the door carefully. A narrow wooden staircase led downwards.

He stepped through and began to descend, holding on to a rail on his left with one hand. The ceiling was low and he had to duck his head to one side. Hunched over and partly twisted to his left, he used his right hand to scan ahead with his torch beam.

He had gone down about a dozen steps when he suddenly realised there was something wrong. Findo stopped abruptly. He crouched slightly so that he could look ahead without bending his neck and shoulders to the side.

The surprise nearly made him drop his torch and his knees went slightly weak. Findo breathed out in a long sigh, thankful he had not being going down the stairs any more quickly. Three steps ahead of him, the staircase ended – in mid-air.

The only thing beyond the final step was a straight drop into darkness. Peering down through the final few feet of the passage, Findo could see why the room had been abandoned. Way below him his torch beam could just pick out the shapes of the theatre's front rows of seats. It was hard to tell exactly how far down it was but it must have been at least sixty feet.

There were no lights inside the theatre and after a quick look below Findo turned his attention towards his own level. He squatted lower on the step – gripping the handrail by his side even tighter – and lifted his torch beam to sweep it around.

In his crouched position, his head was just slightly lower than the theatre's stuccoed ceiling. To either side ornate plaster swags and swirls were set into deep-red geometric panels. A few patches of paint had flaked off and he could also see the ancient tobacco stains, spiders' webs and dust that had accumulated over the years. About ten feet ahead of him a kind of inverted wall projected down, marking the division between auditorium and stage. The hanging wall framed the stage, moulded grooves and flutings mimicking the patterns of a curtain.

Immediately in front of Findo was an opening in the hanging wall that lined up neatly with the bottom of the steps. On the other side of the opening was what looked like an old suspended walkway that had once linked the staircase from the attic room with the area above the stage.

Findo shone his torch through the gap. Beyond, he could see some of the bars and gantries used for hanging lighting rigs above the stage. He could also glimpse sections of other catwalks beneath the suspended walkway, as well as ropes and cables that hung in loops and swags above the aerial frames. Further back was the machinery that lifted sets, props – and sometimes actors – on and off the stage.

Findo looked slowly at it all and then began to smile as an idea dawned on him. He bit his lip and frowned. He would have to investigate further before he was sure if the concept was possible, let alone practical. And if it were feasible, it would probably be the trickiest manoeuvre of his life to date. But there was a certain insane charm to the idea – and, anyway, the whole purpose of the enterprise was to prove himself.

44. Stage diving

Five nights later Findo was in position. He had spent the whole of the previous day hidden in the abandoned room in the theatre's dome. Its original purpose had been for lowering a main chandelier and other, smaller lamps from the ceiling of the theatre in the days before electricity. But now, cut off from the rest of the building except via the roof, the circular room made an ideal hiding place. It had allowed Findo to get into place under cover of darkness and conceal himself well out of the way until the moment came.

Now, he lay on the old wooden walkway, suspended above the stage, listening to the muffled rustle, bustle and chatter of the audience arriving. He could also hear some quieter talk, clanking and rattles from more directly below him as theatre technicians made final preparations for the show.

He had found the way to get to the walkway when he returned to the theatre the night after his first foray onto its roof. Set into the roof above the actual stage were several skylights. These led to another large attic room, an old loft once used for set painters and prop builders to store their equipment. There was a door at the rear of the room but this was locked from the other side. The only sign that the loft had been used in recent time was a pile of coloured gels dumped near the door. But when Findo looked most were cracked or split and he guessed that the gels were all discards.

A hatch in the floor of the loft also gave access to a rickety ladder, riddled in places with woodworm, which led down to the suspended walkway. The first time that Findo ventured down the ladder he had inspected it and the walkway extremely carefully. Although in places the suspended planks ran just above the metal frames and catwalks of the modern lighting rig, they obviously had not been used for years – if not decades. A couple of boards were missing, the railings were loose and the whole construction wobbled lazily as Findo made his way along it. The thick dust and scattered mouse droppings on the walkway added further evidence that no one had been up there for a long time.

Now, he lay on his back on the boards in near darkness, waiting with the patience developed over years of putting himself into places where discovery was a constant danger. He was only about five feet below the ceiling of the stage and knew that if he stayed still and silent the chances of anyone realising he was there were miniscule.

Eventually, he heard the noise from the audience fade away and guessed that the house lights in the auditorium had gone down. A few moments later, he heard the whir of electric motors as the safety curtain – which had deadened the noise of the audience – was lifted. There was a short pause and then the orchestra struck up the introduction to the first, instrumental piece.

Findo rolled onto his front and started to creep forwards. He ignored the music – for him it was no more than cover. After about ten feet, he reached a point where the walkway crossed the main front gantry for the lighting rig. He looked quickly to either side but the catwalk between the batteries of lamps was empty. The lighting was all operated from a control desk at the far end of the auditorium; the only reason a technician would come up during the performance would be if there a problem with the lights.

Findo turned sideways and slipped feet first off the walkway. He landed cat-like and immediately dropped down on all fours. Around him were rows of lamps aimed down at the stage. Only a few were on so far but he could already feel the heat coming from them.

Satisfied with his position, Findo reached up and lifted two sandbags, which he had placed there earlier, down from the walkway. He placed them at his feet and then began to uncoil a long cord from around his waist. He clipped one end of the rope to a heavy strut that helped secure the lighting gantry to the roof of the building. The rest of the cord Findo played out in loose loops, positioning them so that they hung just over another beam, careful to ensure the rope was arranged without any snags or twists. Finally, he reached back up onto the walkway and lifted down a small bundle of nylon netting. He secured this to the gantry with more ready-attached clips and laid it just above a row of lights.

Then he settled down to wait and watch. He was now about forty feet above the centre of the stage.

The applause from the first piece of music – 'Venus' from Holst's *Planets Suite* – was still dying away when the soft purple background lighting above the empty stage faded away. The only illumination left in the theatre came from the signs above the emergency exits and the small spot lamps fixed to the orchestra's music stands.

The theatre was left in darkness for long enough for the audience to start trying to peer into the gloom and wonder if something had gone wrong. Then two spotlights lanced down from above the stage and the audience gave a collective gasp of admiration.

The stage was no longer empty. Transfixed by the two brilliant beams of the spotlights was one of the stars of the evening. The young French soprano Catherine Decazes, although only twenty-eight, already had a considerable international reputation. Bringing her to the city had been quite a coup for the organisers of tonight's one-off gala performance, during which she was appearing in a solo role, singing parts from a variety of well-known and less famous operatic works.

For the occasion Decazes had selected a simple but elegant blue gown – similar in colour to the poster Findo had spotted in Albert Parade six days previously. The way the dress clung emphasised the singer's figure and part of the reaction from the audience had been a response to how Decazes looked.

But there was another element to the intake of breath elicited by the appearance of Decazes. For nestled in her dark tresses, was the other principal star of the evening – the work known as the Widower's Tiara. Created by Alfred Cartier, the collection of diamonds poised on the soprano's head represented more wealth in a single item than almost any member of the audience would earn during their lifetime. Commissioned in late 1898, its price at the time had not been important. The Russian tsar, Nicholas II, had ordered the tiara as a gift for Princess Marie Louise de Bourbon. The princess had recently married Prince Ferdinand of Bulgaria and the present was intended as a symbol of recently improved relationships between the Russian empire and its vassal state. But then Marie Louise had died suddenly in January 1899 and the tiara was never delivered.

Now, it was to form the centrepiece of an international exhibition of jewellery being staged in the adjoining Garvock Gallery. The show was the biggest cultural event – certainly in terms of value – to come to the city in decades. As well as the unique Cartier tiara, the exhibition was also due to feature items by other famous jewellery houses such as Boucheron, Tiffany and Van Cleef and Arpels, alongside work by more contemporary artists. Tonight, a selection of high-paying guests and various influential invitees were getting a private preview of the exhibition before it opened – under conditions of strict security – to the general public.

The concert just getting underway had been arranged as part of the preview and, after the Widower's Tiara had been escorted through to the theatre by six burly guards, Decazes had been invited to model the work during her performance. The idea had been an inspired one. The exquisite collection of antique diamonds sparkled like white fire in the glare from the spotlights and the soprano, with her striking figure and shimmering gown, looked as if she had been born to wear tiaras.

For the first two pieces performed by Decazes, Findo stayed in position. By the end of the second aria he was starting to worry. The soprano had taken a few paces forwards just before she began to sing and was showing no sign of moving back again.

Then, at the end of her second song, the spotlights on Decazes faded away. The orchestra began to play the overture to Rossini's 'La Gaza Ladra' and the soprano moved back from the front of the stage, disappearing into the wings.

Findo frowned but a few minutes later Decazes was back in sight, waiting for her cue. It came as the orchestra moved on, flowing straight from the overture into the beginning one of the arias from the same work. Decazes stepped towards centre stage and this time she stopped further back, almost immediately below Findo.

He watched, mesmerised by the rise and fall of the young Frenchwoman's impressive chest as she started to sing the aria 'Di Piacer Mi Balza Il Cor' from the part of Ninetta. For nearly a minute, Findo joined the rest of the audience as he watched Decazes with fascination and some awe.

Then he switched his attention back to the purpose of his presence. It was time to act. If he delayed, she could move forward again and he might not get such another good view of his target. And waiting also meant more time to think about the risks of what he was about to do.

Reaching up, Findo gently lifted the free end of the cord coiled across the lighting gantry's support beam. He took the clip woven into the end of the cord and felt behind his neck. Working slowly and carefully, he found the loop on the back of the climbing harness that he wore beneath his sleeveless jacket. He held the loop up with his left hand and clipped the end of the cord on with the other. He tugged it several times to make sure that it was securely attached.

Then, taking care not to suddenly tug the coiled cord, Findo bent down. He picked up his roll of net and lifted it carefully over the lamps on the back edge of the gantry.

Below him, Decazes was in full, passionate voice, staring out to meet the loving gaze of the audience that the stage lights made it near impossible for her to see.

Findo watched for a moment and then flipped the net forward. It unrolled as it fell, dropping twelve feet to hang, gently swinging, in mid-air. Moving quickly and purposefully, he picked up the two waiting sandbags, taking the loops of cord attached to their tops in his left hand. With his right hand, he took hold of the support strut to which his rope was clipped. As soon as his gloved hands had a firm grip, he stepped off the gantry and onto the bar that held the row of lamps. Positioning his feet as precisely as he could, Findo took a last glance at the coils of cord resting to his side.

Then he looked down at the French soprano and jumped.

Findo hit the stage with a thud, landing with a crunch that knocked him sideways. Momentarily winded he found himself looking straight up the nose of the frozen soprano, her mouth open but silenced.

Behind them part of the orchestra was still attempting to play on, while others had already stopped mid-note, joining the audience in staring at the stage in mixed horror and bemusement, uncertain whether what they were viewing was a tragic accident or a bizarre stunt.

But the bungee cord was already pulling Findo up and he threw himself back into a crouch. Dropping the sandbags in his left hand, he reached out for Decazes' head as he sprang back into the air.

"Excuse me." He gasped the words at the same time as his hands seized the Widower's Tiara and lifted it off the singer's head, pulling a few clips from her hair at the same time.

The scream from the soprano was matched, although not in volume, by shrieks and shouts from the audience. There was also a loud cry and the thudding of heavy feet as two of the more quick-thinking security guards positioned around the stage's wings sprinted forward.

Findo took his right hand from the tiara as he hurtled back skywards and stretched it above him. He missed the first two squares of his net but grabbed and caught the third just as his upward momentum was fading away. Stuffing the tiara into the pouch on the front of his jacket, he snatched for a hold with his other hand, looping it through the net.

As soon as he had a grip with his hands, Findo brought his feet forwards. He swung back and forth several times but managed to get his left foot onto the net. That gave him the purchase he needed and he began to climb.

His head banged against the fitting for one of the stage lights and he jerked it away as the hot metal burnt through his hair and into his scalp. The shock nearly made him lose his grip and for a second his fingers fumbled at the cords of the net.

But he shook his head and reached over the lights. Grabbing hold of a mounting bar, he pulled himself up and onto the gantry's catwalk. He collected a couple more burns on the way but his clothing protected him from the worst of the heat and he was ready for the shock this time.

As soon as he had his balance, Findo reached behind his neck and unclipped the bungee cord fastened to his harness. Pausing just long enough to make sure the tiara was safely lodged in his front pouch, he reached up for the old wooden walkway and pulled himself up.

There were more shouts coming up from below now. Some were still incoherent but a couple of voices were giving more forceful commands. One end of the lighting gantry was also shaking slightly as one of the security guards began to climb.

Findo did not stop to see what was happening. Using some of the support struts for the gantry to help, he pulled himself up onto the walkway. It creaked loudly as he ran forward but he ignored the noise, aiming straight for the ladder to the old set-painters loft. There were a dozen steps to climb and Findo's feet only touched four of them.

He had to pause for a moment to fling open the hatch at the top of the staircase but then he was through. He ran straight for the nearest skylight and shoved it hard, lifting the entire frame from its surround. He jumped at the opening, pulling himself straight up and out. Emerging onto the lead roof, Findo rolled onto his side, sliding down until his feet hit the flat edge just inside the parapet.

It was still light outside but Findo wasted no time looking at the view or stopping to listen for pursuit. As soon as he was back on his feet, he started running. He went round the outside of the theatre's dome and down the service ladder to the roof of the city museum. From there, he crossed quickly to the parapet above the courtyard, followed that round and then went back up and over the ridge.

Above the corner where he had first climbed up the museum, Findo found the coiled rope that he had secured to the balustrade previously. He looped it through the figure-of-eight clip attached to his harness at the hip and stepped over onto the edge of the roof. Ignoring the pipe work and ledges that he had used previously, he leant back and abseiled straight down the face of the museum, dropping down into ten-foot swings.

From there it was a short dash across the car park to the final rope, which took him up over the museum's perimeter wall and into the city park. He was not worried about the security cameras any more; all they would show would be a running figure in black, nothing more than several thousand people inside the theatre had already witnessed.

Although it was still light, the park was empty and quiet; its gates were locked every evening at six and it contained nothing more threatening than the anxious noises of a group of pigeons disturbed from their roost.

Findo reached the other side of the park four minutes later. He used a handy tree to help himself over its spiked railings and dropped down onto the pavement. He was on a back street not far from the main railway station. One car had gone by while Findo was climbing the fence and he could see a couple walking on the other side of the road a couple of hundred yards away. They were heading towards Findo but seemed too intent on their own conversation to have noticed him.

Findo crossed the road at a quick jog and trotted into an alleyway between two small hotels. Twenty yards on, just before the other end of the alley, he turned through an open gateway. On the other side was a strip of concrete that ran down the side of a disused office building. At the back of the building was a small courtyard containing an old wheelie bin with a broken wheel.

Findo pushed the top open and reached inside. From beneath a couple of carrier bags of rubbish from his kitchen, he pulled a black bin bag. Taking the bag by its bottom, Findo tipped the out the contents.

A few minutes later he had changed. The black clothes and the climbing harness were inside the bin bag, while Findo was now wearing an old pair of red tracksuit bottom and a white T-shirt. Beside him was a battered sports bag containing a damp towel, trainers, shorts, a sweaty football shirt and underwear.

Findo threw the bin bag into the wheelie bin and picked up a small can from beside him. Flipping up the nozzle on the top, he squeezed hard, jetting the lighter fuel into the open top of the bin bag and over the other rubbish inside the bin.

Once he had finished, he took a last glance around. The courtyard was almost completely surrounded by walls and none of the surrounding buildings, apart from the empty office block, were high enough to see over. Findo took a quick breath to calm his nerves and pulled a box of matches from his pocket. He struck one and dropped it into the bin, paused for long enough to make sure the lighter fuel had caught and then turned away.

A few minutes later, he walked out of a side street and into Eastgate Road. He turned right and began to stroll south, heading towards Packhouse Street. Findo smiled as he swung the sports bag over one shoulder; he could almost sense the diamond tiara through the bag and its wrapping of dirty shirt.

Findo Gask was still only twenty. He was in his prime and thieving was his life. He had never been offered any alternative options and had taken the one that seemed logical; it was, after all, something that he was extremely good at.

Disregarding the question of parentage, Findo's life of illegitimacy had begun when he was only a few weeks old. (Although, to be fair, he had only been a sleeping partner in the housing swindle pulled off by his temporary mother.) He had first really shown his approach to the rules of property – plus a remarkable coolness of head for his tender years – at the age of six. From then on, with no shortage of tacit encouragement from his family, he had progressively honed his skills.

He had many ideal qualities for a thief. Physically, he was slight but wiry. He had sharp eyes and was good with his hands. He was supple, with feline agility and a predator's ability to stalk, crouch, sprint and freeze on the spot. His natural predilection for climbing and exploring – plus the need to escape the occasional hot pursuit – had helped provided the exercise needed to develop his muscles and hone his skills.

He also had the right mental attributes. Naturally quiet, he preferred not to draw attention to himself but could be cool under pressure – capable of brazenly facing a threat with confidence that far outweighed the strength of his real situation; he had a poker player's nerve and ability to bluff. Given a target for a break-in, he could think in three dimensions, visualising the layouts of buildings on several floors and their positions relative to each other. He could memorise floor plans and calculate the changing distances to different exits as he moved around. He also had a flair for lateral thinking and improvisation that gave him an extra edge when it came to finding solutions to both problems of ingress and egress, and in dealing with other, potentially hostile, situations.

Coupled with all these abilities was a certain mindset. Findo Gask had grown up with little help – parenting had come much harder to Bosnia than snaring men and producing children. His early education had been limited to Billy's tips on street survival. As a child, his food supply had been scarce and erratic, while other comforts were even more rare. Officialdom had never been informed of his existence and he had survived childhood without the aid of teachers, doctors, social workers or any other state-appointed worthies. He had learnt instead to take what he needed from those who had it – and to not get caught.

Other than in his relationship with Billy, family ties had counted for little when he was a child and friendship had been an alien concept until he met Abigail McGee. Until very recently, the only other people he would have regarded with any real affection were Frances Reid and John Biggs. He had liked Mickey Dunn, Colin Speed and his Australian kayak teacher, Barnaby. To a lesser extent, he respected Daniel Morris. Now, he could add Otis to that select list and a few other peripheral characters like Clint. But principally Findo was a loner, emotionally and physically.

As he grew up and saw more of the world, both in the city and outside, he had become a little more aware of the existence of the construct known as society. He was vaguely aware that he was a threat to it: not only because he stole but also because he did not conform. But he had never been invited to join and never had to face the choice of whether to meekly accept its terms and submit like so many others to the grinding drudgery of a menial wage-slave existence, the spiritual decay of mindless conformity or the bleak and pointless life of benefits dependency and no hope. He preferred anomie; choosing his own standards and judging his own behaviour seemed a far more intelligent decision than accepting apparently arbitrary and irrelevant rules created by a history and society to which he owed no allegiance.

On its own, the approach seemed quite rational. But the problem facing Findo now was one of a clash of cultures, a conflict of lifestyle choices. His and Abby's paths had begun to diverge even before they parted. Her attitudes to right and wrong – and what was proper or acceptable – had become as far divorced from his as the different paths their lives had taken. To regain her was going to be a difficult manoeuvre, to co-exist in their different spheres without compromise a tricky balancing act.

He met Abby again on the afternoon after the jewellery snatch. He had telephoned her mother's house earlier, gambling that no one else would be at home, too eager to wait for her to call him.

Abby had been surprised to hear his voice. Until then, she had always been the one to make contact and had suggested previously that it was probably not a good idea for him to ring Suzanne's number.

"Findo! Hello, what's up?" After an initial hesitation, her tone had been warm although slightly guarded.

"Can you meet me?"

"Meet you. Why?"

"I need to see you."

"Oh . . . I did have plans for this afternoon."

"It's important."

"What is it?"

"I can't tell you. I have to see you. It's really important. But it won't take long."

Abby sounded bemused. "Okay," she said. "When?"

"Now?"

"Where?"

"I can drive over?"

Abby was silent for a while. "No," she said. "I don't want anyone seeing us. It's quite a small village. It would only take someone to drop some comment to Mum and then she'd be asking who it was, and I don't want to lie." She sighed. "Look, there's a bus into the city in fifteen minutes. I've got to come in anyway. It takes about forty minutes. I'll meet you at the end of Albert Parade, opposite the cinema."

"Okay," said Findo. "I'll be there."

He was waiting when Abby's bus arrived at the stop. He waved and walked slowly over to greet her as she stepped down onto the pavement. He grinned and pulled her into an impromptu embrace.

Abby looked at him in surprise. "You look very happy with yourself."

He nodded. "I am."

She smiled wonderingly, pleased to see him but slightly nervous at the same time. "Why? What have you been up to?"

Findo gave a chuckle. "I'll show you in a minute." He grabbed her hand. "Come with me."

"Where?"

"You'll see."

He led her by the hand down the top end of Albert Parade, towing her past shoppers and other pedestrians. A little way down the road, he led them into a side road and then down several back streets. He was walking fast and Abby had to hurry to keep up with his pace.

After about ten minutes they came to a corner of the fence around the city park. As they went in through a gate, Abby could see the roof of the city museum over the trees and wondered briefly where her mother and Stuart were working, whether they could see down into the park.

But Findo did not take them much further. He led them along a path across an area of lawn and around some flowerbeds. They stopped at a bench overlooking one of the park's three duck ponds. There were a few other people around, mostly lying on the dry, sun-baked grass, but no one too close. Findo sat down and pulled Abby down next to him.

"I've got you a present," he said in response to her smile.

"A present?"

"Yeah. A present."

Findo had been carrying a small rucksack over one shoulder. He swung it up onto his lap and began to pull open the top.

"What sort of a present?"

He smiled. "The best sort."

Findo turned to Abby and looked her in the eyes. The smile on her face melted a little as she saw the intensity of his expression.

"Abby. I wanted to get you something special. I wanted to tell you how much you mean to me."

"Findo . . ."

He held up his hand. "No. Let me say this. You're the most important person in my life, Abby. I really care about you. When I lost you before it was awful. I really thought you didn't want anything to do with me. Now, I know that I got it wrong and I can't make that right again. But I don't want to ever lose you again. That's why I had to let you know how much you mean to me." He paused. "I love you, Abby. I always have."

He pulled open the top of the rucksack and held it towards her before she could respond. "Look."

Abby glanced down reluctantly then gave a little gasp of surprise. "What's this?" She reached into the bag and gently took hold of the tiara. She began to lift it out then stopped part-way and looked up. "Findo. What is this? Is this real?"

He smiled. "You haven't seen the news today, then?"

She shook her head, starting to look extremely worried. "No . . . What have you done, Findo? What is this? Where did you get it?"

Findo smiled, although some of his earlier confidence was fading and he was just starting to wonder whether this had really been such a good idea. "Have you heard about the big exhibition at the city gallery?"

Abby's eyes widened further. "Oh my God, Findo." Her voice cracked slightly and he could see her bottom lip trembling. "You haven't? Tell me you haven't?"

He nodded. "I did."

"Oh my God, oh my God." She stared at him incredulously and

then, to his surprise, reached out and threw her arms around him. "Oh my God. You did that for me?"

He nodded, his cheek pressed against hers. "Yes."

Abby began to cry but she was also laughing at the same time. "Oh my God, Findo. You're crazy. Is this what I think it is?"

He nodded and she suddenly pushed him away again. "But how? How did you get this?"

Findo shrugged. "It wasn't easy."

She stared at him in disbelief. "But why, Findo? What am I supposed to do with this? Why?"

He looked down at his hands. "I just wanted to show you how much I cared. I thought that if I did something really hard you'd know how much I loved you."

Abby thumped him on the chest. "Are you crazy! Haven't you learnt anything?" Her voice was furious and her eyes blazed. "You stupid, stupid idiot. Why do you think you have to do stupid things to impress me? I know you, Findo. I know what you're like. I know you care about me. You don't have to steal stupid, useless things like this. What am I going to do with this? I can't take this. It's no use to me or you. I doubt if you could even sell it if you wanted to. Why couldn't you have just got me a bunch of flowers or some chocolates like any other bloke?"

Findo lowered his head. "I don't want to be like any other bloke," he muttered.

Abby grabbed his shoulder and shook him in frustration. "But, Findo, I know you're not just anyone. That's the whole point. I've known you since we were both kids. We've done so many things together. You don't need to impress me – not with stuff like that."

He sniffed. "I just thought that it would show you how *much* I cared. I thought that if I did something really difficult it might make you stop and think." He stared up at Abby. "I don't want you with some other boyfriend. I don't want you living with them. I want you for me. I want us to be together - for good. That's why. I can't go on just seeing you once a week. We split up for four and a half years for no reason. Now that's over we should be together again. That's why I didn't want to be just like any other bloke." Findo shrugged and gave a weak smile. "It's all over the papers. They're calling me the 'King of Thieves' now. They reckon I'm untouchable."

Abby closed her eyes and gave a soft scream. "Oh, Findo. You just don't get it, do you? I don't want the King of Thieves, or even the Prince of Thieves. I just want someone normal – someone who can love me in a normal way. I don't want to have to live with a fugitive –

or cope with having you locked away. I just want to live an ordinary life and be happy. One day I want to get married. I might want to have children. I don't want any of this."

She pushed the rucksack back at him. There were tears streaming down her face again. "I'm really sorry, Findo, but I can't do this. I can't. Why don't you just take this and put it back where you got it."

Abby stood up and turned away, leaving Findo alone on a bench again.

"Sir! Hold on!"

Ross Kirkbride was on his way out of the building when he heard Charlotte Brown's voice coming down the stairs from behind him. He stopped and turned.

"Will it wait?" he asked. "It's the police authority meeting. I don't particularly want to be there but I think it'll be more painful in the long run if I don't appear in person and allow them their pound of flesh."

The DI grinned. "Oh, I think this is worth losing a couple of minutes."

She trotted down the flight of stairs.

The chief superintendent looked expectant. "Really? Don't tell me you've got some good news for me."

Brown grinned. "Could be the break we've been looking for."

"Really? You've found Findo Gask?"

"Not quite that good a break."

"That's a shame. I might have been able to convince the police authority I was still fit to command the division if you'd given me that."

The DI smiled sympathetically. "They really that bad?"

Kirkbride shrugged. "One or two aren't. The rest are worse." He held out one hand. "Anyway, that's my problem. Come on. Give. What have you got for me?"

"I think we've found his car."

"His car?"

"Yes." The DI nodded. "That job up near Loch Lomond in April, the report mentioned a sighting of a blue Ford Fiesta parked at the entrance to some Forestry Commission land. It was about two miles from the American's place around the time of the break-in."

Kirkbride shrugged. "So? Probably a hiker."

"Maybe," said Brown, "but maybe not. There is a track on the other side of the gate but all the ground for some distance on the other side was still flooded. The only way through would have been to wade. One of the local officers picked up the sighting from a woman who works in a hotel down the road. She remembered seeing the car because she knew there was no way through and thought it was odd to see a car parked there."

"Okay," said Kirkbride. "So we've got an unaccounted-for car."

The DI nodded. "I've had a couple of my team going through the reports we've got from the other forces. They've been ploughing through every log and note for the last week or so. And – surprise, surprise – we've found three other sightings of a blue Fiesta in the vicinity of Findo Gask's burglaries."

Kirkbride nodded slowly. "Interesting but hardly conclusive. Fiestas are not exactly uncommon and it's hardly your classic getaway vehicle – although maybe that's the clever bit."

Brown smiled. "Sure. Anyway, I've also been looking at the distribution of the break-ins over the past four years. They're pretty much confined to the Thames Valley area to begin with and then spread out."

Kirkbride glanced at his watch. "Come on."

"Okay. Well, I've been asking street units to look out for blue Fiestas and a patrol has just come across an interesting one. It's parked in a back lane just off Corporation Road. It's got a sticker from an Oxford garage and the tax disc was issued in Oxford. There was also a length of climbing rope in the passenger footwell."

Kirkbride nodded briskly. "Good. Who's the owner?"

"Registered to one Philip Gates. We're checking other records."

"Okay. Keep watching it. I'll keep this under my hat for the time being but I want an update on Mr Gates, his Fiesta and anything else you can give me as soon as I'm back."

The chief superintendent was about to leave the building when he turned. "Oh . . . and Snoopy – well done."

It was nearly four in the afternoon when Findo walked into the lobby of the Royal Northern Hotel. It was the third hotel in the city centre that he had tried and he was starting to doubt his luck. He glanced around nervously, unfamiliar with the environment, and walked to the marble reception desk. A clerk looked him up and down sceptically.

"Yes?"

"I've got a message for Miss De Cazes."

"Who?"

"Miss De Cazes, the singer. Isn't she here?"

The uniformed woman continued to look uncomprehending for a moment and then gave a slight sniff. "Do you mean Mademoiselle Decazes?"

"That's the one."

"And who are you?"

"Er . . . I'm from the theatre." Findo reached inside his jacket and pulled out an unmarked envelope. "I wanted to get this to her." He smiled. "They said it was urgent."

The desk clerk nodded slowly. "Yes. Well, I'll have someone send it up to her room. And what was your name?"

Findo shook his head. "Er . . . Phil. But she doesn't know me. I was just asked to deliver the note. But they said it was urgent, that's why I came straight over."

The woman frowned. "Don't they have telephones at the theatre?"

Findo shrugged. "Yeah, but I think they're not working or something. I don't really know. Someone from upstairs just came down and asked me to deliver the note as quickly as possible." He leant forward in a conspiratorial fashion. "I think it's about what happened last night."

The woman's pencilled eyebrows rose slightly. Findo nodded and turned quickly away. He walked briskly back to the revolving entrance door and was out before anyone could try and ask him questions.

It was nearly twenty minutes before the Frenchwoman appeared. Findo had been starting to wonder if she would show. When she did enter the park, he did not recognise her immediately. The blue gown of the previous night had been swapped for a pair of black jeans and a white T-shirt, while her long hair was pulled into a simple ponytail. The glamour was gone but she still looked elegant, if nervous, glancing from side to side and over her shoulder as she walked out onto the lawn.

Findo watched from behind his sunglasses. He stayed sitting, leaning back against the tree with a Coke can by his side.

He waited until Decazes reached the lake at the centre of the park and had stood next to the willow tree. The only other people to have entered after her were a young woman with a pram and an older man with a stick who was hobbling across the grass.

Findo stood up, brushed himself down and picked up his small rucksack and the Coke can. He set off at a tangent, walking towards the far end of the lake, not straight towards the singer.

He strolled slowly across the grass, not looking at Decazes but taking a few casual glances around as he went. The woman with the pram was crouched down; it looked as if she was talking to her child. Two schoolgirls had just come into the park and were walking along clutching brightly coloured folders adorned with the faces of some boy band or other. The man with the stick was still hobbling slowly across the lawn towards the other end of the lake.

Findo raised his empty Coke can to his mouth and tipped it up as if draining the last drops. He smacked his lips and crushed the aluminium can in one hand, then looked around for a bin.

The nearest one was a couple of yards from Decazes and Findo changed tack to take himself past it. As he drew close, the Frenchwoman was standing still, seemingly watching some ducks on the water. She glanced quickly at Findo as he dropped his empty can into the bin, apparently dismissing him.

Findo stepped closer. "Hello."

Decazes gave him another look and frowned. "You?" she said.

Findo nodded. "I'm sorry."

She stared hard at him.

"I'm sorry," he repeated.

The young soprano looked confused. "Sorry? But why? Why steal this thing from me and now give back?"

Findo shrugged. "It was for someone," he said. "But she didn't want it. She wouldn't take it. She told me to give it back." He held out the rucksack. "I hope I didn't frighten you."

She smiled slightly. "No one has done this to my performance before." Then Decazes glanced around. "You take this for someone you love, yes?"

Findo nodded.

"Okay but now you must go," she said in a quick, quiet voice. "The police they are here. You must leave. Fast."

Findo took one last look at her face and then turned round. The young woman had abandoned her pram in the middle of the path and was walking briskly towards them. The man with the stick was not hobbling any more either and was closing in from behind Findo.

He grinned at the Frenchwoman as he turned and started to run. "Thank you."

Findo sprinted. He started to run around the side of the lake but had only gone a short distance when he saw two men jogging around the lake towards him. He swerved quickly left and doubled back the way he had come. The young woman was coming towards him fast from his left and for a few seconds it was a close race as to whether she would intercept him.

But Findo was too quick. He bolted across the lawn, crossing the path from the entrance where he had come into the park. His route took him past the abandoned pushchair and he glanced at it as he went past; it was empty.

He ran straight towards a clump of rhododendrons. A few yards before them, he dived to the ground and rolled forwards. A couple of branches scratched his back but then he was through the edge of the outer canopy. Jumping and twisting, he worked his way through the dark branches inside. Behind him he could hear shouts and someone starting to push through in pursuit. But then he was out of the leaves on the other side and back into the open.

Ahead was another, smaller area of grass. Beyond were some gravel terraces leading to an ornamental bridge over the small stream that fed the park's ponds and lake. A couple of people looked at Findo in brief surprise as he emerged from the rhododendrons but did not seem that interested in him.

He trotted swiftly down through the terraces and crossed the bridge. On the other side was a path leading up through some flowerbeds and into a wooded area. Findo followed the path for about twenty yards, running round a woman walking two dogs, and then struck off to his right into the trees. He pushed through a couple of shrubs and wove around several tree trunks until he reached the base of a large yew tree growing next to a brick wall.

It was dark underneath the yew and most of the lower limbs were bare. Findo grabbed hold of one branch and began to climb. A few minutes later he was able to step out onto the flat roof of a block of garages that butted onto the park. The yew's branches spread out over a good third of the roof and Findo made no attempt to leave their cover. Instead, he lowered himself flat and stretched out on the asphalt surface, lying on his back. He kept himself still, listening for any noises from the park. But none came and after a while he relaxed, letting his pulse and breathing steady and calm.

Findo stayed with Otis for the next four nights. After the chase in the park he spent the rest of the afternoon and the first part of the evening hiding on the garage roof. The park would have been closed by the time he finally stirred but he did not try and go back through it, suspicious that the police might still be searching its grounds or watching its exits.

Instead, he moved cautiously out from his cover in the yew tree and climbed down a drainpipe into the garage block below. The area was parking for a block of flats and there had been nobody around.

From there, getting to Otis' flat on foot had been straightforward, although Findo had found himself constantly looking over his shoulder for any signs he was being followed. Otis had not been surprised to see him.

"Yay, bro. I was wondering if you were going to turn up." He gave a slight bow as Findo came in.

"You know you are one mad mother but . . ." Otis touched a finger to his forehead. ". . . respect, man. That was one wild stunt you pulled off." He grinned. "It's just a real bummer that no one knows I'm living with a genuine celebrity. They think you're just this guy called Phil. If they knew who you really was they'd be round after your autograph."

Findo did not go out again for the next three days. He gave Otis his building society card and instructions to draw out some cash and bring back plenty of food, some drink and a packet of writing paper. He spent most of his first day in hiding trying to compose a letter to Abby, trying to think where he had gone wrong previously and avoid the same pitfalls again.

Creating the letter was a painful process. Several attempts almost made it only to be aborted at the last moment. When Otis returned from college, where he had been sitting his end-of-year exams, Findo was pacing the flat's main room, surrounded by a litter of screwed up paper.

Otis watched his brother for a while with a wry smile on his face. He cooked them a stir-fry to eat, then sat down to roll a joint. Findo started trying to write his letter again, copying snatches of phrase from earlier attempts, frowning as he looked for the elusive form of words to persuade Abby why she needed him in her life.

After nearly an hour of quietly watching and getting stoned, Otis could stand it no more. "Look, man. What's the problem?"

"This letter! That's the problem."

Otis exhaled a long stream of smoke. He waved the joint at Findo. "Want some?"

"No. I'm trying to concentrate."

"Maybe that's your problem."

"Huh? What do you mean?"

"You're mad about her, yeah?"

"Yeah. You know that. I've told you."

"Sure. Well how about you stop trying to explain yourself? Just tell her how much you love her. Don't try to justify what you've done, just admit you screwed up and tell her you need her help. Tell her she's the most wonderful person in the world. She's the only hope you've got. You need her to set you on the straight and narrow. You need her to turn you into the nice guy that you could be if only she would lower herself to help you. You want her to feel the lurve that's in you . . ."

"Yeah! Okay, okay. I get the idea. You reckon it would work?"

Otis grinned. "No idea, bro. But whatever you're trying to write there isn't working for you. She's a woman and, from what you've told me, she's probably equally crazy about you. Don't try to complicate things. Just give it to her straight to the heart."

Findo sent his letter first class the next morning, getting Otis to drop it in the collecting boxes at the city's main post office before going to college.

In the end, Findo went for the short and sweet option. He did not know what else to do.

Dear Abby,

I don't really know how to say the things I want to say but the main thing is that I want to tell you how much I love you.

I'm sorry about the other day. I know it was crazy – I don't know what I thought you would do with the jewellery. But I did it because I didn't know what else to do. I really, really wanted to show you how much I love you and I couldn't think what to do. Then I saw a poster for the exhibition and it seemed like a sign. Maybe I am a bit crazy but only because I'm crazy about you.

I don't know what to do now – I need your help.

When we met at Mrs Reid's house it was a real shock. You never mentioned me in your letters – she used to read them all to me and I really thought you'd probably forgotten about me –

or just didn't want to know about me. I was amazed when I found out that I'd got your letter all wrong – anyway you know that.

It was wonderful to see you again. You're really beautiful now. The days that we went out together were brilliant. You were still the same Abby – the same one I've always loved. That's why I went a bit crazy – I was desperate to make you believe how much you meant to me.

I've got to see you again. I'll do anything you want. I just want to be able to love you like I was meant to.

Love
Findo xxxxx

The day that he sent the letter, Findo went back up to the roof of the tower block. It was the first time he had been there since the final party and it was back to its normal, bird-spattered condition. There was a new lock on the door that the council had put on two days after Otis and Clint had held their final session. It took less than a minute for Findo to pick the new lock and change it again for his own.

He stayed indoors the next day, waiting to see if the phone would ring. He had scribbled the number at the flat as a postscript. But no calls came and he sank into a bitter depression, alternating between hope that his letter had gone astray and despair that he had burnt his bridges with Abby forever.

By the end of his third day at the flat, Findo was in a filthy mood. Otis had gone to Resist for his Tuesday night residency at the club. Left alone, having spurned his brother's attempts to coax him out, he paced the flat, stared out of the window, glared at the telephone, sat and stewed. By the time it got to eleven, Findo knew that Abby was not going to call that day and started on the biggest bender of his life.

Findo never normally drank much – the night in the Turk's Head with Mickey had left a lasting wariness for alcohol. But now he felt like catching up. First he went to the fridge. There were six cans of Carlsberg Export inside and he emptied those first, throwing the empties out of the flat window. The next thing he found was a half-full plastic bottle of White Lightning that one of Clint's friends had left behind. The cider was pleasantly flat after the gassy lager and the first half-pint went down easily. After that, Findo began to feel a little queasy but he persevered and drank himself through the nausea.

Once the cider was gone, Findo collapsed into an armchair for a while as he tried to roll a joint. But his fingers had lost their normal dexterity and he gave up after a few minutes. Then he remembered the bottle of vodka that Otis kept in the freezer compartment.

It was nearly four in the morning when Otis got home from the club and found Findo sat on the kitchen floor in a puddle of cold water next to the open fridge-freezer. He still had the vodka bottle in one hand but about a third of its contents were gone. Findo's mouth was wide open and he was snoring gently.

Between them, Otis and Clint bundled him into the shower fully dressed and turned the water on. Once they had made sure that Findo was awake, Otis bullied him into stripping off his wet clothes and took him to the kitchen, where he forced a couple of pints of water down his brother's unwilling throat.

It was nearly midday before Findo stirred again. When he finally emerged from his sleeping bag, he was a grey shade, a wraith moving with the speed of a tortoise and the coordination of a puppet with half of its strings broken. He stared vacantly into space and only mumbled when spoken to. Otis gave him sugar-thick strong coffee for breakfast, followed by two paracetamol and more water to drink. By six in the evening, Findo was able to face forcing some toast down. At just after seven he went back to bed. He did not stir again until nine on Thursday morning.

There had still been no call from Abby on Thursday – or a return letter. Findo paced the flat for a couple of hours debating what to do. Eventually he rang Billy.

She listened patiently as Findo poured out his troubles. Her answer was simple. "Go and find her."

"Really?"

"Of course. You've written and you've given her time to think. The longer you leave it now, the harder it will be. Go and find her. Just tell her in your own words what you think about her. Be honest. Plead if you have to but don't grovel – she won't respect you for that. Make her give you an answer."

"What if she says no?"

Billy sighed. "Well, you won't be happy but at least you'll have tried and you'll know one way or the other. You'll be miserable if she rejects you but not knowing is just as bad. I mean, listen to you. You're a complete mess at the moment. That's not going to get any better until you know one way or the other."

"Okay."

There was a pause. "And, Findo?"

"What?"

"Good luck. I really hope you can sort this out. And if you do..."

"Yes?"

"Don't let her go again."

Findo rang Abby's mother's number next. He was thrown for a moment when Suzanne answered the phone.

"Er, is Abby there?"

"No, I'm afraid not. Who's calling?" Suzanne's voice was cautious.

"Er . . . my name's Phil. I'm a friend from Edinburgh."

The tone on the other end of the phone got warmer. "I'm afraid she's out, Phil. I haven't seen her today. She went over to her boyfriend's place this morning. I'm not sure when she's coming back."

Findo closed his eyes in pain. "Er . . . is she on the phone there?"

Suzanne hesitated and he heard her rummaging through some paper. "No. I don't think it's been connected yet," she said. "But Patrick's got a mobile. Do you want his number?"

Findo hesitated. "Um, that's okay. You got the address? I'll send her a note; it's probably easier."

"Sure, hold on. Okay. Have you got a pen and paper ready?"

"Yes," said Findo. He stared into space as she read out the address, memorising the flat number.

Findo walked from the flat in White Gate. His route took him up to Packhouse Street and then up Eastgate Road. It took him nearly an hour.

The address Suzanne had given him was in an old industrial area where the original brick-built warehouses and factories – empty and crumbling for decades – were being converted into new housing. Most of the buildings in Cotton Lane were still being renovated and building materials surrounded several of them.

At the end of the lane were two former mill buildings. The left-hand one was still covered in scaffolding.

Findo walked slowly up to the right-hand building. The main door was propped open and the corridor inside was littered with decorator's tools and equipment: pots of paint, ladders, brushes and piles of sheets and rags. There was no sign of the workmen and Findo guessed they had downed tools for lunch.

He paused at the door. There was a speaker grille set into the wall beside the entrance and a row of buttons. But none had numbers and there were no names up yet either.

Findo hesitated. It was tempting to turn around and walk away; he knew he could have rationalised the decision somehow. On the other hand, Abby was probably inside – with her boyfriend. And Findo knew that if he did not confront her now, he might never summon up the courage again.

Talking a deep breath, Findo walked into Lydon House and set off in search of flat three and the woman that he loved.

The doors to the first two flats were unmarked but Findo guess that the numbering would start on the ground floor and work up. Ten yards further down the corridor was another pair of doors, both closed and also without numbers.

Findo was wondering which to choose when he heard the sound of music coming from the door on the left. It sounded like Pink Floyd. He swallowed and knocked on the door.

A stranger answered it. He looked flustered and none too pleased to see a visitor. "Yes?"

Findo tried to stare past him. "I'm looking for Abby."

"Yeah? Well who are you?"

"Findo?" Abby's voice came from inside. It sounded faint and uncertain.

"Abby!" Findo tried to push past but the young man facing him was not going to let him in without a struggle.

"Hey! You can't just come . . . Get out!"

"Findo?"

As the door was pushed wider, Findo could see into the room. It was quite large but fairly spartan. There was a futon in the middle of the floor and a bookcase against one wall. A stereo sat on a rug in one corner with a scattering of CDs around it. There were other rugs on the floor and a few posters on the wall. Clothes spilt out of a suitcase in another corner of the room. An empty wine bottle and a stack of empty takeaway cartons stood on a tray.

There was a large window opposite the door but a heavy blanket had been hung from a pole and was blocking out most of the light. There were several candles burning in the room, mostly in pots around the edge of the walls. One large candle sat in a dish in front of the futon.

Abby had been sitting on a beanbag against the wall. She was rising to her feet as Findo barged in. "What are you doing here?"

"Look, get out of my bloody flat!"

"How did you find me?"

"Hey, I'm warning you."

Findo leant round Patrick's flailing arms. "Abby, I just want to talk to you."

"Well you can't, you bastard! You've upset her enough already. You're just a bloody criminal. Clear off before I call the police. Go on. Get out of here – now!"

420

Findo gave Patrick an angry glare. "Look, shut up! I'm not talking to you."

Patrick stepped back a foot or two but he looked almost at boiling point. He glanced over his shoulder at Abby.

Findo moved round him and walked towards Abby, who had stopped where she stood and was staring at him in confusion. Findo held out his arms and tried to take her hands but she stepped back. "No."

"Abby, please. I just want to talk. I have to talk to you."

Findo saw Patrick coming out of the corner of his eye. As the other man swung for him, Findo jerked his head back and the fist sailed by just in front of his chin.

"Stop it!"

Findo was already lifting his fists but he stepped back in response to Abby's shout. Patrick did not stop. He surged forwards, fists waving, eyes blazing and hurled himself at Findo.

But his feet caught on the edge of the rug in front of the futon and instead of throwing himself on top of Findo, Patrick toppled over mid-charge and crashed to the floor, knocking over the big candle and cracking the dish it was in.

Findo started to draw back one of his feet but halted as he saw the look on Abby's face. He backed off instead and watched as Abby crouched by Patrick's side and tried to help him up. But he pushed her away angrily. Humiliated and furious, he scrambled to his feet.

Patrick looked ready to go for Findo again but Abby quickly moved between them – herself taken aback by the degree of passion shown by her normally placid boyfriend.

"Patrick. Just stop. Okay?"

"Tell him to get out then! Or call the police. That's the best idea!" Patrick's voice was bitter and he would not look at Findo or Abby.

"No." Abby shook her head. "Look, I know you must hate this. But you can't solve it with violence. Or calling the police."

"Just tell him to go then."

Abby sighed. "No. He's right. We need to speak. I owe him that at the very least. If it doesn't happen now, it'll be another time. It won't go away. Let me talk to him. Please?"

Patrick sighed and nodded reluctantly.

Abby hesitated. "In private?"

Patrick's head jerked up again. "No! I'm not leaving you with him."

"Patrick." Abby's voice was harder this time. "You're going to have to. We've got things we need to say to each other and they're between the two of us. No one else. You're going to have to let us talk." She sighed. "Go up to Jo's flat. She's in. Wait for me up there. I'll come and find you."

Once Patrick had reluctantly left, Abby turned away from Findo. She walked to the other side of the room and stared at the hanging blanket as if wondering whether to open it and let some light into the room. When she turned, Findo could see the fresh tears on her face although she had stopped crying.

Abby stared hard at him. Neither spoke for a long time; Findo because he had no idea what to say, Abby because she did not want to voice the decision that she felt she had to make.

Eventually she looked down and took a deep breath. "Findo, we have to say goodbye."

He made a small, shocked sound like a wounded animal. "Why?"

Abby closed her eyes and exhaled slowly. "Because it will never work between us."

"But I love you, Abby. I'll do whatever . . ."

She held up a hand. "And I love you, Findo. I really do. I love you with all my heart." She came across the room and took his hands in hers. "But it's not that simple. Your life is too different from mine. I can't live with always being frightened about whether you're going to get caught. I can't live being on the run or being in hiding. I would be scared all the time, scared for you, scared for me."

Abby squeezed his hands and looked deep into his eyes. "You see, if we were to be together we'd have to do it properly. I don't want half measures in my life. I want someone who will always be there – not someone who might have to suddenly disappear because the police are after them or they've been locked up."

Findo shook his head. "But they've never caught me. And I can stop. If that's what you want I'll become like you. I'll go to college or get a job or something."

Abby smiled softly. "I know. I believe you. I'm sure you'd try. But you've done so many things already. What if they don't stop looking for you? The police have got long memories. There are some big rewards on offer for you." She shrugged. "Or what if you suddenly change your mind in a few years' time? What if you get bored with having to get up every morning and go to work? It might be hard giving it all up – the freedom, the excitement."

Findo shook his head. "That doesn't matter. I'd rather have you."

Abby reached up and stroked his cheek with one hand. "Oh, Findo. Why couldn't you have been ordinary? Why couldn't you have been more like . . ."

"Patrick?"

She frowned. "That's not what I meant."

Findo shrugged. "But I'm not," he said. "That's the point. I'm me. I do things other people are too scared to do."

"Too scared?"

He nodded. "Sure. I just do the kind of things that most people are too scared to do. People don't want to do boring jobs or just sit on their backsides all day. But they do. And it's because they're too scared to take a chance. There are plenty of people out there would love to rob a bank and run off with the money. They wouldn't feel guilty, that's not why they don't do it. It's because they're scared of getting caught."

Abby shook her head. "People aren't all like that."

"Yes they are," said Findo. "Maybe not everyone but most are. I bet if you took fifty quid and left it lying in the street next to a piece of paper with your name and address on it, you'd never see it again. I reckon if you did it a hundred times you'd be lucky if more than one or two people brought it back."

Abby looked unconvinced but said nothing.

"People are scared," said Findo. "They don't obey the rules because they're good but because they're taught to do as they're told. They're told that if they break the rules they'll be punished. That's why most people don't take what they want – because they're cowards. That's why I'm different. I don't hurt anyone, I just take what I want." He smiled. "It's not even that hard normally. It's just that most people are too scared to try. That's why they admire people who get away with it."

"Admire them?" said Abby.

"Yeah, admire them," said Findo. "You've seen the papers and all that. They don't hate me. They go on about what an incredible thief I am. They take the piss out of the police because they can't catch me. I'm famous – not because I'm bad but because I'm so good. I do the things that other people don't dare – and I get away with it."

Abby was silent for a while. They were still standing, loosely holding hands, when Patrick appeared in the door. He looked smug, although his smile drooped a little when he saw Findo's hand in Abby's.

"You still here?"

Findo ignored him but Abby frowned at Patrick over her shoulder. "We haven't finished yet, Patrick."

"Oh, well." He shrugged and they heard him walk back out into the corridor and start up the stairs. "Never mind," he called, "I expect it'll be a couple of minutes before the police get here."

Abby's jaw dropped and Findo closed his eyes in dismay.

"Oh." Abby pulled him to her and held him tight. "You see – this is what I'm scared of Findo. I love you but I can't live with this." Her voice choked briefly. "You'd better go. Please. Don't get caught for my sake. You're too precious." She turned away hurriedly and stormed out into the hallway. "Patrick!"

Her voice was controlled but Findo could tell that the anger she normally tried to keep in check was not far beneath the surface. There was a faint answer from upstairs but Findo did not hear what it was.

Abby stuck her flushed face back round the door. "Go on," she urged. "Get out of here. I'll deal with him. I'll make him say it was a wind-up or something."

Findo nodded. "Okay."

Abby gave a last, weak smile. Findo heard her running up the stairs shouting Patrick's name.

"Fuck!"

The large candle that Patrick had fallen on was lying in front of Findo and he turned on his heel and booted it as hard as he could at the CD player. There was a satisfying crunch and the music stopped. Findo turned away and loped towards the door. He never noticed the small oil lamp on top of the CD player topple over and fall on its side. The lid of the lamp was only fitted loosely and the oil inside poured out in a pool around the base of the bookcase. There was a quiet 'whumpf' as the flame caught and sent tongues of fire across the floor and up the spines of the lower books.

Findo left through the front door, pausing to look around before he stepped out. It was still quiet and there were no sounds of any cars or sirens.

He walked to the end of Cotton Lane and stood for a moment, deciding which way to go. To his right was a short stretch of road that led round to the Castle Drive ring road. To his left was an unmade track that ran into another section of the old industrial estate. There was a wall along the left and a strip of rough ground to the right. A few hundred yards along the road doubled back to run round parallel with Cotton Lane. A footpath led off from the corner; Findo remembered that it went down to a stream that came in towards the city across some overgrown fields.

He turned slowly and began to plod wearily up the track. He could not be bothered to run; his spirits felt drained and for the moment he no longer cared.

There was an old car abandoned beside the track just where the footpath started. Findo climbed onto its bonnet and slumped back against the cracked windscreen, staring into space. In his head were vague, unformed thoughts of a dream world where he ran back into the house and led Abby away, whisking her out of the country and off to some undefined exile where they lived together in peace and love.

He had been there nearly ten minutes – hardly remembering to even listen out for possible police cars – when he became aware of shouts and screams from back the way that he had come.

Findo sat up quickly. For a moment he wondered if it was the pursuit coming after him. Then he saw the smoke billowing up from the direction of Lydon House.

He leapt from the car and began to run straight back to Cotton Lane. When he rounded the corner he saw a group of men in the road outside Lydon House, gesticulating and shouting. One was speaking urgently into a mobile phone.

Findo ran up behind them. He stared in through the open front door in horror. The hall was a mass of flame and smoke was pouring out into the street. The decorator's sheets and pots were blazing fiercely. As he watched, the lid exploded off one paint tin and went spinning into the air.

Findo grabbed the arm of the man standing next to him. "Are they out?"

"What?"

"The people inside. Are they out?"

The man looked terrified. "People! What people?"

Findo turned to another, older man with a grizzled head of stubble. "Has anyone come out?"

This one was slightly calmer. He shook his head. "I don't know, mate. I haven't seen anyone. How many's in there?"

Findo swallowed. "I'm not sure. At least three."

"Oh Christ! Hey! Mike!" The older man turned to the one on the phone. "Sounds like there's at least three in there. Tell them that. Tell them to get here quick! It's going up like matchwood."

Findo grabbed hold of the man's arm. "What about the fire exit?"

"What?"

"The fire exit. Where is it?"

The man's face fell. "Oh fuck."

"What?"

"Oh shit."

"What?" screamed Findo.

The man shook his head. "Some bloke on a digger smacked into it last week. They took it down to fix it."

There was a sound of breaking glass from above and the group all looked up.

Lydon House was five-storey. Framed in a window on the top floor was a young woman. She was cradling a young child and screaming. Thin wisps of smoke drifted out from around her as the woman smashed at the glass.

"Help," she shouted. "Please. We're trapped."

Findo backed away from the group of decorators, who all tried to shout back at the terrified woman, trying to offer comfort and encouragement. He stared up at the building. The ground floor was already completely ablaze. Some of the windows had shattered in the heat and steady plumes of smoke were pouring out and drifting up the side of the building. He could also see a flickering from inside windows on the first floor and there was a grey haze behind the glass on both the second and third floors.

Findo looked to the side. The unfinished building next to Lydon House was a mirror image of its neighbour. There was about a space of about twenty-five feet between the two old mills. But the scaffolding around the left-hand building narrowed that gap by about six feet.

Findo took off at a run; it was clear there was nothing that he could do at ground level.

There was no door at the entrance to the other old mill building, just a wire mesh screen that was propped open. Inside, the building was little more than a shell. It had been stripped out and the conversion into flats was still at an early stage, with walls unplastered and loose wiring hanging from ceilings.

But the stairs were solid enough and Findo began to climb, taking them two or three at a time. By the time he reached the top floor his heart was hammering and his lungs burning but he did not pause.

There were no dividing walls on this floor yet, just the original pillars holding up the ceiling. Dust motes hung in the air and there was a pile of buckets to one side of the stairs, next to a stack of plasterboard and timber for creating partition walls.

Findo sprinted across the open floor. The window openings were empty and he stepped straight out onto the scaffolding. He looked around rapidly, reviewing the situation. He was almost directly opposite one of the windows in Lydon House. The window was closed and he could see no sign of flames inside but there was a steady flow of smoke pouring up between the buildings. He could also feel waves of heat rolling up from below.

Findo crouched down and tugged at the nearest scaffolding board. It only rested on the framework of bars and Findo dragged the plank out. It was heavy but at least that meant it was also quite strong. Working as quickly as he could, oblivious of the splinters driven into his bare fingers by his haste, he pulled the end of the plank back into the unfinished building, then slid it back out as far as it would go and still balance. When he stopped, the loose board lay at right angles across the scaffolding and jutted out like a gangplank.

It reached about eight feet into the gap between the two buildings. Not far enough.

Findo thought fast. He grabbed another board from the scaffolding and dragged it so it sandwiched the projecting plank, helping to hold it in position. He pushed the gangplank out about another three feet. Now, about four feet rested across the scaffolding, with another three sticking back into the mill building.

He darted back into the room and looked around but could not see what he wanted. Back on the scaffolding, he ran round towards the front of the building, dodging around the holes that he had left in the boarding. At the front of the old mill was a banner advertising the firm of builders doing the renovations. It was tied to the scaffolding with long lengths of heavy nylon cord.

Findo pulled his knife out and slashed the banner away. Taking two lengths of cord, he raced back to his gangplank and lashed the boards holding it in place to the bars of the scaffolding. Now, it might wobble but it would not go anywhere easily.

As soon as the plank was secured, he darted left to where a long ladder came up through the scaffolding. He had to drop a couple of levels to cut one lot of ties but then he had it free and was able to start heaving it up.

The builder's ladder was heavy and it was a struggle to lift it to the top but with a combination of brute effort and adrenaline-fuelled fear he was able to do it. The moment it was up, Findo dragged the ladder round and into the building as he had done with his gangplank.

He paused for a moment, weighing up the gap in front of him and preyed that he could get the ladder far enough. There was no time to think about what would happen if it were not and it was too late to try and think of another plan. The fire brigade should be there soon but Abby was inside and every second counted. He could not wait and hope; he had to act.

Lifting the ladder as if it was a lance, Findo stepped back out onto the scaffolding. One end of the ladder pointed up to the sky, the other stuck back through the empty window of the unfinished building.

Then he ran forwards.

Findo took only two paces along the gangplank before he stopped. He pushed back hard with his legs, letting the ladder slide through his hands as its momentum carried it on. As it thrust out into the gap between the buildings, Findo let the far end of the ladder drop. At the same time, he grabbed at the side rails and shoved it forwards as hard and straight as he could.

Findo felt his balance going as he pushed the ladder and he threw himself down, kicking his legs in opposite directions. His thighs rasped down either side of his gangplank he pitched forwards, concentrating on using his legs to save himself while keeping hold of the ladder with his hands.

As he fell, he twisted to his left and nearly dropped. But he managed to lock his legs around the plank. At the same time he heard the smash of glass as the ladder landed in the window opposite. Then his end slammed down and Findo felt himself drop alarmingly then bounce up again as the board reverberated from the combined impact.

For a couple of seconds Findo's legs started to slip but he clenched his muscles tighter and pulled himself and the ladder closer to the gangplank. The board sagged and bounced again but then steadied.

Findo slowly opened his eyes. He was clinging onto the plank sideways but it was only vibrating gently now and the ladder appeared to be balanced safely. Findo took a slow breath then coughed as he tasted a mouthful of the smoke billowing past him. He tugged the ladder more securely onto the middle of the gangplank and then wormed his way back to safety.

Once his feet found the bars of the scaffolding again, Findo pulled himself upright and scrambled back onto the end of his makeshift aerial bridge. A good foot of the ladder had crashed through the top floor window of Lydon House and was lodged neatly across the sill. At Findo's end, the ladder rested squarely along the gangplank, almost reaching the whole way to the scaffolding.

He looked sideways down towards the road but he could hardly make it out through the smoke. Findo drew a deep breath.

"Hey!" he bellowed. "Up here! Up here!"

He thought he might have heard some kind of answer but did not wait to be sure. Findo glanced down briefly at the smoke-filled chasm that divided the two buildings; it was probably best that he could not see ground level. He paused for a moment, took another deep breath and walked out over the abyss.

The balancing act itself was not too bad; Findo had done harder stunts in his time. The ladder bent and sagged a little as Findo reached the middle but it was solid and stayed firm enough. What made the crossing hard were the intense heat and choking, disorientating clouds of smoke rising up around him.

But then he was grabbing at the frame of the broken window and sliding through, hardly noticing the shard of glass that slashed into his upper arm. The room inside was a kitchen but it was empty and bare. Findo jumped down into the room, stumbling as he briefly lost his footing.

The living room beyond was also empty – the flat clearly unoccupied. There was also very little smoke inside it but a strong smell of burning. Findo darted towards the door. He grabbed at the latch, tugging it open as he pulled at the door.

A wall of smoke and heat met him. It poured towards him, thick clouds of choking, acrid fumes trying to push past, while a torrent of air seemed to flow the other way, sucked into the building by the greed of the flames below.

Findo shoved the door back again, choking. He glanced around frantically then hastily pulled his T-shirt over his head. He rammed it to his nose and mouth and flung open the door again. Ducking low, he stepped through. The landing area beyond was almost completely invisible. Findo could faintly see the outline of a banister rail in front of him and the carpet on the floor but that was about it. There was also a flicking glow from somewhere not too far below.

Findo jerked his head from side to side, trying to think. The woman at the window had been at the front of the building.

Findo turned right. He had stumbled a few yards through the smoke when he nearly crashed into a child's pushchair parked on the landing. Grabbing at the wall for balance, he began to cough as his hand came away from his face and he took in a lungful of hot smoke.

Findo threw the pushchair away from the wall and heard a crash as it fell down a flight of stairs. Behind him, the open door to the empty flat was acting like a chimney, clearing some of the worst of the smoke from the stairwell and landing – but also letting more oxygen through to the fire.

Eyes streaming, Findo suddenly found himself in front of two doors. He paused for a moment and then flung himself at the right-hand one. He hammered at it, then stepped back and kicked. His foot thudded into the woodwork just below the lock and the door shook in its frame.

Findo stepped back, coughing and reeling. But before he could attack the door again it opened. A young woman clutching a frightened child stood in the door. She looked bewildered and terrified.

"We can't get out," she said.

Findo pushed past her and into the flat. He slammed the door behind him and leant against the wall, dragging in lungfuls of relatively clean air.

"You can," he said. "There's a way."

Findo's eyes darted around the room. It had more furnishing than the flat below and for a moment he did not spot Abby. She was slumped on the floor near the window, her eyes closed but her chest moving.

Findo turned back to the woman. "Get wet cloths," he said. "I'll get you out of here."

The woman clutched her small child tighter. It looked like a little girl of about two.

"There's no way out." Her voice was trembling. The girl's eyes were wide and she was sucking one thumb furiously as she clung to her mother.

"Yes, there is!" Findo snapped the words at her. "I've got a ladder. We don't have time to talk. Get some cloths."

He pushed past the woman and into the kitchen. There were tea towels on a rack next to the cooker. He snatched two and stuffed them under the tap along with his T-shirt.

As soon as they were wet, he snatched them from the sink and turned back to the woman, who was stood staring at him. Findo grabbed her arm.

"Look," he said, "I'll get you out of here – you and your baby. But there's no time." He roughly tied his dripping T-shirt around his face. "Come on." He handed the woman one of the tea towels. "Give me the baby."

"No." The woman backed away, clutching the child tightly. Its eyes widened and it started to cry.

Findo hesitated a moment. Then his arm snaked out and he slapped the woman across the face. He reached for the girl and pulled her roughly away from the mother.

"If you don't do as you're told, you won't get out of here at all and neither will your baby. Now, come on!"

The woman hesitated for a moment then nodded mutely.

"Follow me and be quick," said Findo. "Keep hold of my arm."

Back on the landing, he bent low, holding the child with one arm and pressing a wet tea towel against her face with the other. He ignored the girl's struggles and pinned her to his body.

The mother's fingers were digging hard into the flesh of his right upper arm, desperate not to lose either Findo or her child. He practically towed her out onto the landing and into the empty flat. The lounge and kitchen were full of smoke now and Findo had to steer them almost blind.

As soon as they were in the kitchen, he pushed the door shut behind them, stopping the flow of smoke. He frowned and hesitated, painfully conscious that Abby was still lying in the room behind them. He wanted to leave the woman to get herself and her child to safety on their own so that he could go back for Abby. But he was not sure whether the woman would make it across the ladder, not if she had to hold on to the little girl.

"Hold her."

Findo reluctantly gave the child back to her mother. Pulling his T-shirt from his face, he wrapped it around his right fist and punched at the fragments of broken glass still sticking out of the window frame.

As soon as the worst was cleared, he jumped onto the kitchen unit and ducked through the window opening. He pulled himself upright and stood with one foot on the ladder and another on the sill.

"Now. Give her to me. Quick!"

Slowly, painfully slowly, the woman lifted the child. Findo cursed her in his mind, seeing Abby collapsed in the other flat. But he took the girl, almost snatching her and turned to the ladder. As he did so, the mother's eyes widened, seeing where the ladder led, having previously assumed that it would have been leant against the side of the building, not balanced precariously across a five-storey high gulf between two buildings.

Findo looked down over the crying child's head. "Stay there," he said. "Don't try to come across while I'm on the ladder. Don't do anything until I tell you."

He turned and started to walk out.

He had only gone a few feet before he regretted not having put his wet T-shirt back around his face. There was still a steady flow of smoke pouring up around him. Findo coughed and buried his face against the child's hair. He blinked to try and clear the tears from his eyes and felt cautiously in front with each foot as he made his way painstakingly onwards.

He was about halfway across when a gust of wind suddenly shifted the smoke from around him and he was suddenly able to taste clean air and see where he was going. Seconds later he also he heard a sudden burst of shouting from below.

Findo speeded up as he approached the end of the ladder. He stumbled onto the gangplank and onto the scaffolding. Coughing and spluttering, he staggered through into the open floor of the building beyond. He lowered the child in his arms to the floor and laid her down. There was more shouting now; it sounded as though it was coming from somewhere in the building below. Findo ignored it and pulled himself back up through to the scaffolding.

He was about to start on his return journey when he saw the ladder wobble. Looking up, he realised with dismay that the child's mother had already started to follow him. She had crawled out onto the ladder and, continuing on her hands and knees, was already a few feet from the side of the building.

Findo swore; he had wanted her to wait until he had got back into the building and gone to get Abby. He opened his mouth to shout at the woman but then closed it. He could not risk startling her; if she fell, she might take the ladder with her and then he might not be able to get back again.

He watched the woman crawl a few more feet, then freeze. She started to shake and Findo saw the ladder shift on the gangplank. He darted forward and sat astride it, using his weight to pin it to the board. The woman looked up and saw him.

"Come on!" said Findo. He swallowed and forced himself to moderate his tone. "It's okay," he said.

The woman moved forwards again but very, very tentatively. Below, off to one side, Findo saw a cloud of glass explode away from a window on the second floor. A burning length of timber fell through the window and he saw tongues of flame lick up the outside of the brickwork, hungry for more to eat.

Findo gripped the ladder harder. "Come on," he repeated. He swallowed and coughed. "Your little girl's here. She's safe."

The woman looked up and seemed to find her courage again. She was lying nearly flat on the ladder but she lifted herself just enough to continue her slow crawl forwards.

Behind him, Findo heard feet thudding across the floor.

A voice shouted. "Up here."

A second set of feet and then another followed the first. "Look! There's a kid."

Findo heard and felt the men arrive behind him.

"Christ!" said one. "Can she make it?"

The woman was now halfway across. Findo edged out to meet her, still sitting astride the gangplank. He reached with his arms, urging the woman to him. She bit her lip and reached forwards again and again. Findo leant towards her, stretching as far as he could. The fingers of one of her hands touched his and then he had hold of her wrist.

Findo seized hold and dragged the woman forwards. She screamed as she slid along the ladder and her legs thrashed in panic. But by then he had hold of her other arm and hands were reaching round from behind him to take her.

"Careful, mate," said the man behind him. "Don't lose her."

Findo jumped up. "There's another in there."

As he spoke the sound of sirens came from just down the road. Findo stepped back onto the ladder.

The man tried to take hold of his arm. "You can't go back in there! You're crazy. Look, the fire brigade are coming."

Findo shook himself free. "There's no time," he said.

Oblivious to the smoke and heat, he made it back to the kitchen window again. Bending down, he grabbed the base of the frame and vaulted through. Again he cut himself, a sharp stub of glass ramming into his palm. But he never even noticed the pain.

His T-shirt was lying on the floor where he had dropped it, along with the woman's tea towel. He picked both up and retied his shirt around his face before opening the kitchen door.

He could hardly see anything on his way back to the woman's flat.

The smoke was thicker than ever and he kept his eyes shut most of the way. Out on the landing it was also noticeably hotter and Findo could clearly hear the crackling and snaps of exploding wood resin from below.

Abby was still sagged by the window. There was thick smoke in the woman's flat now and Abby's face was grey. Findo crouched by her side. "Abby!" Her eyelids flickered. "Can you hear me?"

Findo took the tea towel in his hands and pulled it quickly around her face, tugging a flap of damp fabric down over Abby's mouth.

Her eyes opened fractionally. "Findo?" Her voice was weak.

"Yeah. I'm going to get you out of here." He took her hands and put a foot in front of hers to brace himself. "Try and stand up."

He pulled but she barely moved.

"Shit!" Findo crouched down in front of Abby. He took hold of her arms and pulled them over his shoulders, dragging the upper half of her body across his. Then he stood up, hoisting her limp body across him.

As he went out onto the landing, Findo could see a steady orange glow in the stairwell. The flames looked as though they had already got a good hold on the third storey and were starting on their invasion of the one immediately below.

In the kitchen, Findo kicked the door shut behind him and rolled Abby off his shoulders onto the worktop. There was water in the taps at the sink and he took a handful of water and splashed it across her face. Her eyes opened again and her jaw moved as though she was trying to speak.

Findo smiled at her through a mask of soot and sweat. "It's okay. I'm going to get you out of here."

Abby's head moved slowly from side to side and she mouthed something. Findo pulled the flap of tea towel from across her mouth.

"What is it?"

"Patrick."

"What?" Findo's heart sank. He had completely forgotten about Patrick's presence. "Where is he?"

"Down." Abby's voice was a croak. "We tried to . . . find a way out. Too much smoke. He fell. On the stairs. I couldn't move . . ."

"Okay." Findo nodded. He squeezed Abby's arm. "I'll get him." He glanced out of the window. The group of men were still on the other side of the ladder; they were pointing at him and shouting something. "But I've got to get you out of here first."

Abby twisted her head and looked out through the smashed window. "That way?" Her voice sounded fractionally stronger although still ragged.

"Yes."

With obvious effort Abby managed to twist herself onto her side. She began to slide towards the window.

"Find Patrick."

"Abby . . ."

She gave him a firm look. "Findo. Find him." Abby reached up to the end of the ladder and started to heave herself onto it. "For me."

Findo was in anguish. But he nodded. "Okay."

It was louder and hotter than ever on the landing. Sparks and embers flew up through the air and the noise from below was starting to turn into a steady roar.

Findo pulled his wet shirt closer to his face, trying to suck air through the damp cloth. He ducked down and fumbled for the banisters on the other side of the landing. His fingers found the handrail but then he jerked them away as the metal burnt his skin.

He moved on in a crouch, trying to ignore the glow coming from below. It did not take him long to find the top of the stairs and he started to descend, forcing himself to ignore the blast of heat that was drying the tears from his eyes as fast as the heat produced them. He could not see much and concentrated on his finding the steps.

Part way down the first flight of stairs, Findo came across the pushchair that he had thrown aside earlier. He stepped around it carefully, conscious there could be someone below. A few feet further was a landing midway between the floors but it was empty. Findo continued on, gasping, sweat coursing down his face and body.

His will almost failed when, midway down the second flight, he caught sight of the floor below. Flames were already eating away at a doorway opposite the bottom of the steps and he could see spirals of smoke pouring up from the landing's wooden floor. He faltered, but forced himself on.

Then, just as he was contemplating stepping down off the last stair, Findo became aware of a shape beside him. It was Patrick, lying face down on the stairs, his body against the wall. There was a trickle of blood coming from his head and Findo noticed that his shirt was either smoking or steaming.

Findo did not wait to see if he could rouse him or to check for any sign of life. Squatting next to Patrick, he grabbed his arms and pulled one over each shoulder. It was a struggle to stand up; Patrick was a little taller than Findo and he no longer had the strength to pull him all the way up onto his back.

Climbing back to the first landing was torment. Every breath was agony and Findo felt as if his skin was crisping in the heat. His head was starting to spin and he was steering their route by memory as much as by vision. Patrick's feet and ankles were banging against each step as Findo part-carried, part-dragged him upwards. He was also struggling to keep hold of Patrick's arms, which kept threatening to slip from Findo's sweat-slick grip.

But they made it to the landing and Findo paused for a moment's rest. He leant back, balancing Patrick almost vertical, and then crouched and yanked the other man right up onto his shoulders.

Findo went to start off again but a paroxysm of coughing halted him, the convulsion making his chest heave and creating shooting lights that swam in front of his vision. The attack seemed to last for minutes and Findo struggled to regain control. Then there was a loud crash from somewhere below and a sudden gush of sparks shot up through the gap between the two flights of stairs.

Findo closed his eyes and grabbed tighter onto Patrick's arms. He lifted one foot onto the next step and then the other to join it. He paused then repeated the process — and again, and again. Each plodding step was a titanic struggle but eventually they reached the top and Findo was staggering along the landing, only just keeping his burden on his shoulders.

In the kitchen, he almost collapsed from exhaustion. There was also no sign of Abby and Findo felt his spirit fading, fearing the worst. It was tempting to give up. He wanted to lie down, to rest and sleep. But he had a promise to keep.

Coughing through a throat that felt like bloody sandpaper, he leant back against Patrick, holding him upright against the kitchen cupboards. Reaching out slowly, Findo turned the tap at the sink again. But this time no water came out, just a hissing trickle of steam.

Findo twisted round slowly, using all his might to hold Patrick propped up. He turned the unconscious student around so that his upper half slumped onto the worktop, then bent down and grabbed his legs, heaving them up to join his trunk. Climbing up and through the window seemed to take nearly all of Findo's effort. He was on his knees, crouched on the ladder as if at prayer, as he reached back in and grabbed Patrick's shoulders, slowly tugging his limp body along the last bit of the kitchen counter and pulling his limp head and upper torso onto the end of the ladder.

It seemed to take an eternity and Findo knew his strength was failing. But slowly, inch-by-inch, Patrick's body slid up and onto the ladder. Findo edged back a couple of rungs and heaved. With apparent reluctance, Patrick's body bumped along behind him. Findo shuffled back and pulled again. But he could sense darkness closing in around his eyes and there was a roaring in his ears that was threatening to pull him under. Once more, Findo backed along the ladder and once more Patrick's body slid after him.

Then nothing.

48. Days of reckoning

The hospital room was quiet. Outside, the corridor was busy – the usual flow of doctors, nurses and NHS staff about their missions of life, death and administration.

Several faces appeared at the window in the door but the room itself was hushed. The figure in the bed did not stir; the only things to break the silence were the slight movement of bed covers over the man's chest, a faint hiss from the oxygen mask and the mechanical clicks and bleeps from the monitors and other equipment stationed around the patient.

During the night that followed, nurses entered the room at intervals to check on the patient. As the hours passed, a drip was changed, another shot of antibiotics delivered and the level of painkillers slowly reduced. Just after midnight and around dawn, two doctors made visits, looking at breathing, checking monitors and skimming notes before moving on.

The next day brought rain for the first time in weeks. Streams of water ran down the outside of the hospital windows, washing away a thick layer of accumulated dust. The leaves on the trees dotted around the grounds began to look green again. The air smelt clean.

The rain would have helped at Lydon House the previous day. But by the time it arrived, the flames were already out. One fire engine was still at the scene. Some of the crew were damping down hot spots among the ruins. Two investigators worked their way carefully through the shell of the building, analysing the way the blaze had behaved, how the flames had spread and tracing them to their source.

The rain began slowly, fat drops thumping down like liquid pebbles that hissed among the ashes, adding to the haze of pale smoke and steam that still enveloped the building. The firefighters turned their faces to the sky at its arrival. The water falling from the sky was cool. After a night of skin-cracking heat, its impact was welcome.

Soon, the drops merged into a downpour and they retreated to the shelter of their vehicle. A copy of the previous day's paper was passed around and the men laughed at some of the quotes attributed to their station officer, knowing he would never have used the words printed. But they were silent when they looked at the stark image of the man falling from the ladder between the buildings, wondering what had happened to him.

Along with a break in the weather, the new day brought more faces at the door to the hospital room and more activity around the man's bedside. Medical staff checked dressings and readings on monitors. A drip was changed and the first steps were taken to reduce the patient's level of sedation.

Other visitors got to within varying distances of the bedside. Some had been at the hospital throughout the night; some were making their first visit. There was a young, dark-skinned man with dreadlocks who stood and stared from beyond the glass. Then, just before lunch, an elderly woman entered the room. Accompanied by a nurse, she stood and watched the unconscious figure for nearly a quarter of an hour.

One new visitor was a stocky man in a rumpled suit. He did not enter the room but spent several hours pacing the corridor, frequently breaking off to talk into a mobile phone.

Mid-afternoon, a pair of visitors came to look. A bearded man in an ugly sweater supported a woman of about forty. The woman looked haggard and her eyes were puffy. She spent several minutes looking silently at the figure in the bed and then turned away, back to the ward where she had spent the night.

Two young men came next. One was in a suit; the other carried a bulky bag over one shoulder. But they only got a brief glimpse into the room before the stocky man arrived at their sides. There was a brief, heated conversation but before long the pair of newcomers turned and left the building. The older man watched them go and then made a short phone call. A few minutes later, a uniformed policeman came and took up a post at the entrance to the ward.

It was nearly five in the afternoon before the man in the hospital bed started to stir. A nurse had just come into the room when his eyelids began to flicker. There was a short stream of visitors after that. A doctor was summoned and arrived ten minutes later to check on the patient. Once he had gone, several more nurses were in and out of the room seeing to various needs.

Despite the flurry of activity, the man in the rumpled suit still had to wait another three hours before the ward sister, with some reluctance, eventually let him in to see her patient. Once he finally had the all clear, the man knocked on the door and entered.

The figure on the bed gave him a vague, drugged stare. The older man picked up a chart hanging from the end of the hospital bed and looked at it idly.

"Philip Gates is it? How are you feeling?"

There was a faint shrug in response. "Like death." The rasped answer was muffled by the oxygen mask.

"Hmm. Hardly surprising under the circumstances. Still, they tell me you're not in any danger."

The younger man frowned. "You . . . doctor?"

"Hardly." His visitor gave a wry smile. "You could say I'm an admirer. Someone who's been looking forward to meeting you."

There was silence from the bed. The older man smiled again and pulled up a visitor's chair. "Although I must say I never expected to meet in quite these circumstances."

The man on the bed kept his head facing at the ceiling but his eyes flicked sideways. "Who . . ."

"Kirkbride. Ross Kirkbride. I would offer to shake your hand but . . ." He gestured at the cast around the other's right arm and the drips and monitors surrounding the bed.

The head turned slowly to face him. "Kirk . . . bride?"

"That's right – although I wouldn't expect it to mean much to you. It would depend on how carefully you read the newspapers. I'm not a celebrity. Not like you."

". . . celebrity?"

Kirkbride nodded. "Oh certainly. You're a celebrity okay. There's plenty of journalists would like to meet you. You're a hero. You risked your own life to save four people – including a lovely little toddler and a rather photogenic young woman. You entered a burning building twice to save others." Kirkbride shrugged. "You'll probably get a medal. Probably deserve one too. Which is part of my problem."

"Problem?"

"That's right. I think things are all a bit more complicated than they appear."

There was a pause.

"Why?"

The man on the chair sighed. "There's the question. Well, on the one hand we've got something fairly straightforward: a young man lying in hospital, suffering from some broken bones plus various burns, cuts and smoke inhalation. He carried out a pretty death-defying feat to rescue four others from an unpleasant end. At considerable personal risk – and not necessarily just of personal injury."

Kirkbride shrugged and unfolded his paper. "You probably weren't aware of it at the time but the second time that you climbed out of the building, just before you collapsed and fell four floors, there was a photographer from the local paper in the street below." He held up the front page. "Not bad, eh? Quite a dramatic picture; passer-by pulls fire victim to safety in amazing mid-air rescue before near-fatal fall."

Kirkbride grinned. "They've loved it. And not just the press. We've had flowers left at the hospital for you, people ringing up the local radio station. And they're not even the friends or family of the ones you rescued. Like I say, you're a hero." The policeman sighed. "Which is why my name would be absolute mud if I went and arrested you."

There was a long silence in the room. Kirkbride stared thoughtfully at his fingernails; the man in the bed stared at the ceiling. Eventually there was a hoarse, cautious question from the bed.

"Arrest me?"

Kirkbride smiled. "Well, that is part of my job. I am a policeman after all."

A hacking cough came from the figure in the bed. It took a while for him to regain his breath.

"But . . . why?"

Kirkbride was about to answer but a fresh explosion of coughs interrupted him. He stepped toward the bed looking uncertain, watching the other man's chest heaving in uncontrollable spasms. The door to the room opened and the ward sister walked briskly in.

"Okay, officer, that's enough."

"Enough?" Kirkbride looked frustrated. "I've hardly begun."

The nurse ignored him and bustled around the bedside.

"Later," she said. She gave Kirkbride a brief frown. "Visiting time is over for today. He's not going anywhere but you are." The nurse flicked a hand at him. "Out, out, out. You can come back tomorrow. That's it for today."

It was starting to go dark again when the young student nurse walked across the car park and into the alley that cut through towards the back of the college. She had not gone far before the big man stepped out of the alley and fell in beside her.

"Alright, Shelley?"

She looked up once and nodded. "I'd better not get in trouble over this."

The big man shook his head. "Don't worry about that."

The nurse shrugged. "Well . . . anyway, he's in H23 on floor two. There's a policeman at the entrance to the ward."

The big man nodded. "That's alright." He patted the nurse on the shoulder. "Here, take this."

He handed her a small bundle of notes.

"What's this?"

442

"For your trouble," he said. "Treat yourself."

Shelley grinned. "I wasn't expecting to get paid."

The big man grinned. "Makes it even better then, doesn't it? Anyway, fair's fair. You helped us, we say thank you."

The uniformed policeman standing at the entrance to the ward was bored. It was nearly midnight and he had been stuck staring at a pair of hospital doors for hours. Now, apart from the occasional nurse and shuffling patient, there was not even anyone to watch.

When the big man in the white coat came down the corridor, the officer watched his progress. The man's head was shaved bald and he had the build of a heavyweight boxer. He was pushing a trolley laden with cleaning gear.

As he came closer, the policeman realised there was something slightly odd about the way the big man held himself. His head was canted over to one side and he walked with a slight shuffle as if one side of his body did not work as well as the other.

When he was still a few yards away, the newcomer's face split into a wide grin. "Hello," he said. "Are you a policeman?" Before the officer could reply, the man let go of his trolley and held out a giant paw. "My name's David. I'm a cleaner. Are you really a policeman?"

The officer took the proffered hand cautiously. "That's right."

"Lovely." The big man pumped his hand up and down. And up and down. "My name's David."

The policeman tried hard to pull his hand back as the big man continued to grin broadly at him.

"I've never seen a policeman here before."

"Well . . . I don't normally work here."

"There's a policeman that lives in my road. His name's Paul."

"That's nice . . . well, I'm Mike."

"Hello, Mike."

"Hello, David."

With a sudden jerk, the policeman pulled his hand back. "Where are you going, David?"

"Cleaning. I'm going cleaning." The big man took hold of his trolley. "I've got to go through here."

He backed through the doors into ward H23, the policeman helping to hold the doors open. The big man was just disappearing through the doors when Kirkbride came out the other way. The divisional commander glanced over his shoulder.

"Who's he?"

The police constable grinned. "His name's David. He's a cleaner."

The younger officer touched one finger to the side of his head. "A bit . . . soft."

"Ah." Kirkbride nodded. "Well, I've got to go. But I want to know if anything happens. Don't let them move him to another ward or anything. Tell whoever takes over from you that I'll be back in the morning as soon after the morning briefing as I can."

The nurses' station was quiet and the big man slipped softly into the darkened room. The breathing from the bed sounded much less ragged than the previous night and the saline tube had been removed now.

Moving gently, he slipped over to the bedside and carefully shook the left shoulder of the man lying under the covers. There was a brief pause.

"Albie?"

The big man chuckled. "Certainly is." He crouched down beside the bed. "It's good to see you, lad."

"How did you get in?"

Albie shrugged. "My usual wit and charm."

Findo's eyes widened.

"Hey!" Albie laughed softly. "Not that sort of charm. Not in a hospital. What sort of thug do you take me for?"

"What are you doing here?"

"Well, I ain't brought flowers." The big man shrugged. "Seeing about getting you out of here, what do you think?"

"Really?"

Albie grinned. "Well, I caught you once. Now it's time for me to set you free." He stood up and walked to the window. "Can you walk out of here?"

Findo nodded and started to sit up. "Sure."

"Hey!" Albie pushed him back down. "Not now. You're staying there for now."

The curtains behind the bed were closed and the big man pulled them open a couple of inches. He peered out and then nodded. From inside his white coat he pulled a can of spray paint. Leaning through the open window behind the head of Findo's bed, Albie sprayed the parapet outside liberally.

"Right," he said. "Whatever you do, don't shut the curtains. I'll be back in about five, six hours."

Findo looked worried. "What do I do until then?"

Albie grinned. "Nothing. Get some sleep, keep quiet but don't let the nurses close the curtains."

Findo was still wide awake at five in the morning. Twenty minutes later, however, his brain finally gave up and his eyelids slid shut. He did not stir until Albie hissed his name for the third time.

"Uh!" Findo looked around in confusion but the room was empty.

"Findo?"

"Yeah. Where are you?"

"Outside."

Findo ripped the covers aside and stood up uncertainly. He tugged back the curtains and stared groggily: Albie was standing outside his window.

"What?"

"Stand back." Albie slapped a large sheet of glued paper across the window and gave it a sharp punch. The glass shattered. Albie pulled the paper away and dropped it. With a gloved hand he then swept the opening, smacking away shards of glass.

"Here, lean out."

Still confused, Findo leant through the new opening. Albie plucked him out with both hands, lifting Findo into the cherry picker's small compartment. With a hiss of hydraulics, the long arm dropped quickly down two floors towards ground level. At the bottom, Albie helped Findo down off the truck. It was an electricity company's vehicle, used for repairs to overhead power supplies.

Albie grinned. "Good job you weren't on the next floor. I don't think that thing would have reached any higher." He patted Findo on the shoulder. "Now, I think it's time we checked you out of this hospital."

49. Last words

Kirkbride was staring out at the city's skyline. In less than two months he would be retiring. He had no idea what he would do. He was still musing when there was a knock on the door ten minutes later. Charlotte Brown's head followed it.

"You busy, boss?"

Kirkbride gave a short laugh. "Depends."

"On what?"

"On whether you think contemplating the meaning of our lives is a worthwhile activity."

The DI pursed her lips. "Ah. One of those moments."

Kirkbride nodded. "Yes."

"Sorry for disturbing you, then."

He shrugged. "I was a long way from any meaningful conclusions. What can I do for you?"

The DI gave a wry smile. "Got something in the post might interest you. I think it's meant for you."

She walked across the room and handed Kirkbride a postcard. He glanced briefly at the picture of a beach and turned it over. The card was addressed to: The Man In Charge, Police Headquarters, Alexander Cross. The stamp was from Thailand. The only message was two quotes:

> *Who dares wins* – Anonymous
> *You can't win them all* – ?

Kirkbride looked at the card in disbelief. "It's not . . ."

"Take a look at the picture."

He turned the card over. As Kirkbride looked more closely, he realised that it was actually a photograph stuck over a postcard. The picture was a typical Thai beach scene – tall coconut palms drooping over white sands, plugs of jungle-covered rocks rearing towards a pure blue sky and gentle waves lapping at the beach. A few holidaymakers lay sprawled in the shade. Kirkbride could not see any of them clearly. But in the foreground of the picture, scrawled boldly across the sand, was a name he knew well.

We hope you enjoyed reading this book;

Please do feel free to get in touch and let us know your comments.
reviews@discoveredauthors.co.uk

Undiscovered Authors is a national writing competition searching out literary talent.

www.undiscoveredauthors.co.uk

This new initiative from Discovered Authors aims to help exciting, original works by talented authors get the bookshelf space and readership they deserve.

Please turn the page to find out more about our Undiscovered Authors winning titles to be published in 2006 and to learn more about our other authors and browse our online bookshelves please visit:

www.discoveredauthors.co.uk

Discovered Authors
50 Albemarle Street
Mayfair, London
W1S 4BD

Other Undiscovered Authors competition winning titles published in 2006 include:

Sentinel by Tony O'Reilly
Winner of the Undiscovered Authors 2005 National prize for Ireland.
After a viral artificial intelligence is accidentally created, a chain of events begin to unfold which promise to bring chaos to society. Spanning the Middle East, France, Spain and Ireland, Sentinel follows the journey of three strangers as they join together in a last desperate attempt to fight the seemingly unstoppable life force... but the final confrontation leads to a truth more terrifying and far-reaching than they could ever have thought possible.

Struggling Free by Margaret Penfold
Regional winner for Undiscovered Authors 2005
When conflicts and contradictions in Palestine during the British Mandate lead to the deaths of a Syrian property owner and a British police inspector, three women watch the events unfold.
Struggling Free follows Patsy, Dalia and Suzanna- three young women from very different backgrounds- as they unite through their trials of love, murder and war.
Margaret Penfold, spent her formative years in Palestine, and her experiences as a child inspired her to write a fictional account of the struggle she witnessed.

Laughing Star by Jo Nisbet
National winner of Non-Fiction for Undiscovered Authors 2005
Laughing Star is an autobiographical account of a mother's personal journey dealing with children who suffer from Attention Deficit Hyperactive Disorder (ADHD). When fourteen year old Emily becomes so out of control, sending her to Brat Camp becomes her mother's last and only resort.
Jo Nisbet, a counselling Psychologist, began to write Laughing Star as a means of catharsis to download her experiences after a challenging and confusing time.

All Discovered Authors titles are available to buy at
www.amazon.co.uk and all good bookshops.